FROM THE ASHES BOOK #2

Pretty Little Psycho

R.E. BOND

Cover Designer: Vicious Desires Design

Cover model: Darcie Hamilton

Photographer: Michelle Lancaster

To that one ex-girlfriend in high school who made me realize
it's okay for girls to kiss girls.
Even though we were toxic as fuck.

Spotify Playlist Link

https://open.spotify.com/playlist/
2ak5IBnBKCwLJSHMtqLM1U?si=7506fd325b164546

Content warning.

For all content concerns, please go to:
https://www.rebondbooks.com/content-warnings

80
100
120
140
160
180
200
220
km/h
240
260

Prologue

Riley

"Fuck, fuck, fuck!" I had no idea what this chick's name was, that information was long gone as I fucked her harder with my fingers, her climax close. Sweat coated my brow as I worked her until her pussy started to clench, a groan leaving me.

"Come on, babe. Give it to me." Her nails raked down my back, making me hiss at the sting. They dug in deeper as she screamed, her pussy clamping around my fingers like a vice while I kept up the fast pace until she was trying to push my hand away, making me chuckle. "I'm nowhere near done with you."

She moaned as if in pain, her overstimulated body twitching when I finally let her recover before she reached out to grope my breast, tweaking my nipple with a sleepy smile. "Stay with me tonight."

I raised an eyebrow, laying over her and sucking my fingers into my mouth, cleaning her juices from them before releasing them with a pop. "You know that's not going to happen. I told you I couldn't stick around."

I didn't fucking *want* to stick around once we were

finished. One-night stands were supposed to be for sex, not cute shit then fucking brunch. This wasn't a date.

I'd fucked my bad mood out of my system, and pain filled my chest as I remembered my whole reason for burying myself in pussy in the first place.

I'd started a fight with my best friend, Luna Hendricks, while at the racetrack my family owned. She'd been ditching me a lot lately to spend time with her piece of shit boyfriend, Stanley. I hated him.

I'd been in a foul mood, so when Luna had joined me at the track, I'd snapped, telling her to fuck off unless she was there to fuck me. I was such a bitch, and I really needed to get control of myself. Luna was straight, and there was no way she saw me as more than a friend.

I hated myself for the hurt I'd put in her eyes now that I'd calmed down.

No matter how many times I denied my feelings for her, my whole family saw right through my bullshit, always teasing me for how much I loved her. She laughed it off, not seeing the truth that had been right in front of her since forever.

Guilt hit me in the chest as I pulled myself away from *what's-her-name*, grabbing my bra and T-shirt to get dressed.

"Where are you going? I thought you weren't done?" she pouted, and I rolled my eyes the moment I turned away to snatch my panties off the floor.

"Sorry, I just remembered something I have to do."

"It's the middle of the night," she deadpanned. "Just tell me you want to bail, I'm a big girl. No need to lie to save my feelings."

I glanced at her, her naked, sweaty body sprawled out on the bed as her hair fanned the pillows, silently begging me to get back in bed. She was pretty, but she wasn't Luna.

I hoisted my sweats up my legs and tied the string to stop them from falling down, answering her bluntly. "Fine. I want to bail. I'm in a mood."

I wasn't apologizing for that either. It was a waste of words that would only be lies. I didn't give a shit about her feelings since this was only a casual hookup to begin with.

"I noticed," she said dryly, pushing her damp hair from her face. "I didn't even get to give you any orgasms."

I chuckled, snatching my oversized hoodie and pulling it on before sitting on the bed to shove my feet into my shoes. "Trust me, I get a kick out of being the giver."

"Thanks for the orgasms then," she mumbled, clearly not impressed with my abrupt exit. "I'll see you around."

"Probably not," I shrugged as I got to my feet and snatched my keys, phone, and wallet from the bedside table, leaving the room and making my way down to the kitchen. I smirked when the front door opened and one of the guys from school walked in with some of his friends, all of them pausing when they noticed me.

I didn't hang around people for the sake of it, so they knew me being here only meant one thing.

"Whoever's sister that was should be proud. She took it like a champ," I taunted, licking the tips of my fingers. "She's tasty too."

"Sister? I don't have a fucking sister," the first guy growled, his eyes darting over my shoulder as my hookup walked in, her eyes going wide.

"I thought you were coming home on Monday?" she squeaked as his face turned thunderous.

"That much is obvious since you've been fucking Riley Donovan!"

I scoffed, moving past them to let myself out before speaking over my shoulder. "Wrong. I fucked *her*. Big difference. You need to up your game if she's turning to me to get off. She was begging me for it."

I didn't stick around to hear their argument. If she had a boyfriend, the blame purely fell on her, not me. Did I care that I'd probably just been part of ruining their relationship?

Nope. She was an adult, and I hadn't forced her to take me home.

Unlocking my 2021 Corvette Stingray Z51, the bright graffiti paint job shining in the moonlight, I opened the door and climbed in, relaxing into the seat as I started the engine and it rumbled to life. I pulled my hood over my blonde hair before glancing at my phone, but Luna hadn't messaged me once, not that I could blame her.

I pulled up my tracking app, most of us had it to find each other in case of an emergency, and I scowled as Luna's location pinged at Stanley's house. Of course she'd run to him after I'd been a bitch.

I smacked my palms against the steering wheel before putting the car in gear and driving towards home, not bothering to go to her. I'd deal with our tiff later.

For now, I just wanted to go home and fall into bed.

100
120
140
160
180
200
220
km/h
240
260

Chapter One

Riley

Two Weeks Later

"I don't know how you guys enjoy this," Luna mumbled from beside me as we watched my older sister, Beckett, beat someone to a pulp in the fighting cage. She was a member of the Bloody Psychos' street crew, following in our parents' footsteps alongside our adopted brother, Maddox, who just so happened to be her fucking boyfriend.

She was also dating Jett Emerson, our other brother's best friend.

Not that Ryder seemed to mind losing his bestie to his twin sister.

We had a younger sister, Marla, but she tended to avoid us mostly. She was in her final year of high school, and she was really smart.

Our family wasn't exactly seen as normal. The fact that we had one mom and nine dads kind of proved that.

Diesel, Skeeter, Slash, Caden, and Tyler were all members of the Psychos crew, while Hunter and Marco ran the Devils. Lukas and Jensen helped out with bar work sometimes between the crews' establishments, but they were more than happy to leave the crew stuff alone.

The Psychos had the shed where they ran regular cage fights, the Devils owned Devil's Dungeon, which was a nightclub with adult entertainment, and two of the Psychos owned Harley's Bar, which was the main bar in town.

They served good meals too, so it was really popular.

Luna's uncles, Alex and Harley, owned it, but they sometimes needed help when it got busy and their wife, Jade, wasn't able to help, or their son, Landon, was at school with us.

I glanced at Luna, her brown and green eyes darting away from the action with a cringe as Beckett broke the other girl's nose, sending blood spraying across the cage. I'd grown up around the violence, so had Luna, but her parents ran the Reapers of Chaos crew which rarely organized fights, they were more about pussy and adult entertainment. They owned the biggest strip club in town, which was down at the Docks. Wet Dreams was impressive, I couldn't lie.

My family hosted fights multiple times a week here at their crew's main hangout. We called it the shed, nothing fancy. It was massive, and being the main base for the Psychos' crew meant it was busy daily.

A massive bar lined one wall, the fighting cage opposite it for easy viewing, then there was the main office at the back by the bathroom. There were other rooms where dodgy drug business was done, and I knew for a fact many people had been tortured and killed in another.

I didn't ask questions though since I wasn't a member, and I didn't want to be. I only knew what I'd heard over the dinner table at home.

"Why do you come if it makes you queasy?" I asked, my

lips kicking up into a smirk as I loosely held the handle of my trusty baseball bat, absently tapping it against the toe of my shoe. I never left the house without it, it was my baby. If it wasn't in my hands, it was always in my car. "If it's just an excuse to get away from Stanley, we could've found something else to do."

Irritation flashed across her pretty face, but she refused to look at me. "I wanted to hang out with you. It has nothing to do with Stan."

"We could've hung out at my place and watched those terrible romance movies you like," I pointed out, rolling my eyes when she gave me a silent shrug. She was infuriating sometimes, but I liked how soft and gentle she was. She was nothing like me, and that was a breath of fresh air.

Beckett won her fight, not that anyone was surprised, so I grabbed Luna's arm and tugged her towards the bar. "Come on, we don't have to watch the others. I only care about Beck and Maddox's stuff." She didn't pull away from me, allowing me to drag her across the shed and towards the bar where one of my dads was serving beer to people. I waited for him to finish before I leaned against the bar with a smile. "What's a girl gotta do to get a beer around here?"

Diesel's hazel eyes narrowed with annoyance until he realized it was me, his entire face softening as he pushed his light brown hair from his forehead to see me better. "I didn't know you were coming tonight. Hey, Luna." She gave him a small wave, stepping closer to me as someone bumped into her. I snarled at them to fuck off, finding immense pleasure in watching them drunkenly scamper away. My sister might have been the fighter, but everyone knew I'd beat someone into mincemeat with my bat if I wanted to. "Can you not scare away our customers?" he added dryly, grabbing two glasses to pour us each a beer.

"It's a school night too. Don't you have homework or something you should be doing?"

I snorted, raising an eyebrow as I leaned against the bar with my elbows. "Ashburn Valley University has the worst education system around. The curriculum is hardly even classified as a community college standard. So, no, I don't have homework."

"We did offer for you to go elsewhere if you're so passionate about your education," he replied sarcastically, handing me our beers. "I also know Hendricks wouldn't like Luna here this late. Things get rowdy, you know how it is."

"We just wanted to watch Beckett's fight and have a beer. We'll head home soon," I grumbled, flicking my gaze to Luna as she stiffened beside me. I turned around to find Penny walking towards us. She was one of our dancers from Devil's Dungeon, and her pussy was obsessed with me. I raked my gaze over her, and despite her being off shift, she was wearing a leather skirt with her ass poking out the bottom, a halter crop top with her hard nipples very obviously pushing against the soft white material, and her black, strappy, *fuck-me* heels.

She tossed her platinum blonde hair over her shoulders as she smirked at me, her voice sultry. "Hey, babe. Can I help you?" I smirked as I leaned back on the bar, wrapping an arm around her waist to pull her against me, my bat still gripped in my other hand. She fisted the front of my hoodie and crushed her lips to mine without a word, rubbing herself against me like a cat in heat.

I had no issue fucking a girl more than once if they kept it casual, and Penny liked her freedom. She came to me when she wanted to fuck, and left me alone any other time, sometimes going months without speaking to me.

"Riley," Diesel warned. "What have I told you about screwing our employees?"

I groaned, pulling back from Penny to peer over my shoulder at him, my arm brushing against Luna, the only sign that she was still there. "You don't give Ry the same pep talk. He fucks literally *all* of our employees. Maddox did too until Beckett tied him down."

He snorted, giving me a dirty look. "I reminded those boys regularly to keep their dicks in their pants, so don't pull that sexist shit with me."

Penny draped herself against my back as I turned around to face him, her voice husky. "C'mon, Diesel. It's not like I'm working right now."

"You don't usually give a shit if you're on the clock or not anyway," he grunted. "If you're going to climb all over each other, take it elsewhere. I don't want to see it."

"Because you're homophobic?" she asked with a giggle, and I swore he was going to hose her down with beer for being a bitch.

"No, because she's my daughter. I don't care who she spends her time with as long as she's happy," he snapped, giving me a look that wasn't hard to decipher. He didn't like me fucking her in the slightest.

I sighed, turning in Penny's arms to push her back a step. "Sorry, babe. Dad's spoken. Besides, I'm spending time with Luna tonight, so I can't sneak off to play with you."

Penny ran her finger down my chest between my breasts, her eyes flickering with heat. "She'll be fine. She's left anyway."

I frowned, turning to find Luna gone. I swatted Penny's finger away, giving her a filthy glare. "You didn't think to mention it when she took off?"

"I thought it was nice of her to give us some time alone,"

she said with a shrug before gasping when I gave her a shove, sick of her hands on me. "Hey! What's your problem?"

"Not interested," I grunted out, stalking across the room in search of Luna. I knew she'd be around here somewhere since she'd gotten a ride with me and she was staying at mine for the night.

I found her outside, a cigarette hanging from her lips. Luna didn't smoke a lot, she was mainly a mood smoker, so I knew she was annoyed.

"Hey. Why'd you leave?" I asked as I approached her, annoyance flashing across her face as she looked over at me.

"I don't care who you sleep with, Riley, but I don't want to watch you pawing over people all night. If I wanted to hang out with someone who was too busy trying to get laid, I'd hang out with my sister," she huffed, tensing as I stepped in front of her and dropped my hands to her slender waist. She was skinny, and she'd always hated how flat her body was.

All I could think about was how her perfect, small tits would fit in my hands, and how hot she'd look as I made her fall apart from under me.

Having an hourglass figure or big tits and an ass didn't mean shit to me.

"Let's go. I'm not ditching you for pussy. I know how annoying it is when you bail on me for Stanley," I promised, her eyes narrowing as she blew smoke in my face.

"You're being a bitch again."

"I won't apologize for it either. He doesn't deserve you," I muttered, tickling her under the chin with a grin. "I'll let you pick the movie though."

Her eyes lit up a fraction, and I had to bite back a groan at my mistake. She had an obsession with romantic comedies that I didn't share. I personally sucked at sitting still for long periods of time, so I didn't make a habit of watching TV unless I was with Luna.

"I'll hold you to that," she teased, amusement in her eyes at my obvious misery, but I was too focused on trying not to kiss her to hear her properly. She wasn't a virgin, but she was shy. Her plump lips would feel so good on mine, and I struggled not to test my theory about it.

If I somehow convinced her to kiss me, it would ruin our friendship.

She was straight, and she'd made it clear a long time ago that she wasn't into me. If I told her I was in love with her, it would make things awkward as fuck between us.

I took a step back, tugging my hood over my head so I could hide in it. "Let's go then before I change my mind."

She rolled her eyes but followed me to my Corvette, climbing in and helping herself to my music like she always did. *"Dirty Mind"* by Flo Rida spilled from the speakers, and I glanced at her as she got comfortable and tapped her fingers against her leg to the beat. The annoyance was gone from her face, and her shoulders had relaxed.

I'd made the right choice in deciding to leave.

She had no idea how perfect she was. Not a single fucking clue.

I backed out of my parking spot, heading towards home, a comfortable silence between us. It was one thing I loved about Luna. She didn't feel the need to talk all the time, being satisfied just by my presence. She didn't shut up around Stanley though, acting like he'd leave the moment her mouth stopped moving.

I parked in the garage that was bigger than the average family home, leading Luna inside through the internal access and almost running straight into my brother, Ryder, who had his tongue down some skank's throat and her fingers in his shaggy, black hair as they stumbled up the hallway.

"Really, Ry?" I growled, making him chuckle. He didn't pay me any more attention though as he continued dragging his evening date up to his room, slamming the door behind them. I rolled my eyes, taking Luna's wrist and tugging her through to the kitchen. "He has no taste."

She snorted, pulling back from my hold to walk beside me. "Didn't you sleep with her?"

I frowned, staring up the empty hallway for a moment as if it would jog my memory before shrugging. "I don't know. Probably. In my defense, I was probably drunk." I quickly made a bowl of microwave popcorn before leading her up to my room and turning on the TV to use as a light.

We climbed under the blankets, getting comfortable as Luna picked a movie, then we settled in for the night.

As usual, Luna was out like a light shortly after turning it on.

How come girls liked to pick a movie they knew you hated, then fall asleep ten minutes into it?

Keeping the movie running, I placed the popcorn on the bedside table so I could tuck Luna in properly. I had no idea how long I stared at her sleeping face before falling asleep myself.

I rolled my eyes as Ryder stumbled into the kitchen the next morning, his date nowhere in sight. They rarely stayed, but I always asked where they were to piss him off.

"Where's your pretty friend?"

He ran a hand through his hair, causing it to stick up at all angles. "Where she's supposed to be. Back at her place. It's not like you let them stay either," he said flatly, giving me a pointed look.

"I don't make a habit of bringing them here. I prefer to fuck them at their place so I can bail without a problem," I said with a dismissive wave of my hand, irritation sweeping through me as his eyes roamed over Luna beside me for a second before he turned his attention to the fridge, grabbing an energy drink.

He always joked about fucking Luna, but I knew he wouldn't. He'd tried once before, and I'd almost broken his leg with my bat after she'd left. Stanley was a shitty boyfriend sure, but I couldn't cope with Ryder touching her. No way in hell.

From what I'd heard, he was into some fucked up shit.

Luna gave him a smile though, always finding my brother sweet despite his bad boy reputation. "Morning, Ry."

He plastered his playboy smile on his face before leaning against the kitchen counter as he took a sip of his drink. "Morning, Luney. You still got a boyfriend? Maybe you're looking for a new one? I think I'd be an excellent upgrade." Luna laughed, but I raised an eyebrow at Ryder, giving him the only warning I would. Luckily, he took the hint and rolled his eyes. "I'm heading to school early to catch up with Jett. I'll see you two later."

"Don't count on it," I grinned as I grabbed my coffee, but then scowled as he walked past and kissed the top of my head.

"Love you too, Sis."

Believe it or not, but I loved the asshole too.

Once he'd left, Luna turned to me, a bright smile on her

face. "Landon's coming to the track tonight. How about you?"

"You don't have plans with the ball and chain?" I asked dryly, her face falling slightly. I bit back a sigh, knowing I was being rude again. I didn't want to lose our friendship over a dude. "Sorry, I'm tired. I was thinking of going to the track, but I doubt I'll race. I want to get drunk."

My rude comment was thankfully forgotten as she laughed. "You always want to get drunk."

"I get bored easily," I shrugged, draining the rest of my coffee before rinsing the cup in the sink.

"Apparently," she muttered under her breath, and I struggled not to roll my eyes at her. She hated the revolving door of women I had. Not because she was jealous, but because she didn't understand why people slept with anyone they weren't in love with. Sex and love were two separate situations for me, one I frequently enjoyed, the other I avoided.

I'd loved Luna for as long as I could remember, and all that had given me was anger issues and heartache as I watched her love someone else.

"Do we need to stop by your place on the way to school? If we do, we'd better leave right now," I stated, glancing at the clock on the wall. "We have less than an hour."

"Yeah, I need to grab my finance textbook." She sighed as she got to her feet, rinsing her mug too. "You can just drop me off. I'll drive my car."

That was her way of telling me she had plans with Stanley at some point throughout the day without starting a fight.

I should have supported her relationship, I wanted her happy, but there was just something about him that I didn't like, my feelings for her aside.

"Fine," I answered tightly, making sure I didn't bite her head off about it. I couldn't expect them not to hang out, they were dating after all, I just hated it.

We drove in silence to her place, which wasn't that far away, and her father was waiting for us as I pulled into the driveway. He knew the sound of my car coming from a mile away.

I rolled my window down, leaning on the frame with a smile. "Morning, Archer."

"Cut the shit, Riley." He pinned me with an unamused glance before running his gaze over Luna as she stepped out but continued to speak to me. "I told you I don't like Luna at the shed on fight nights."

"It was just to watch Beckett's fight. We didn't stick around," I said innocently, his eyes narrowing on me.

"I know, Harley told me when you two left. Luna, I want you home tonight," he said sternly as he turned to her, embarrassment taking over her face.

"Seriously? I'm twenty," she said flatly, a grin taking over his face.

"Twenty or forty, doesn't make a lick of difference to me. You're under my roof, and your mother wants a family evening. She gets what she wants."

"Since when?" I smirked. "Last I heard, Lexi's usually the one doing as she's told. Given into that daddy kink yet?"

"Shut your mouth and get to school before I call your *daddy*," he grumbled, making my smirk widen.

"Usually, I'm the one that gets called daddy. Right, Luna?"

Her face flushed red at what I was hinting at, but Archer glared at me. "Watch it. I allow you two to hang out so much because you're friends, but don't think for a second

I won't change the rules if it becomes more than that. Ask Stanley how much fun my rules are."

"I love your rules. I think you give that boy too much leeway," I tsked, ignoring the dirty look from Luna as Archer laughed lightly.

"He's not that bad."

"He fucks your daughter, you know?" I stated as the corner of my mouth quirked up, and Luna let out a sound of horror.

"Riley!"

"What? I'm just reminding him," I shrugged, knowing she'd be pissed at me for that. Archer knew what she got up to, but he hated the thought of his baby girl being touched by anyone.

He'd grounded her for months when he found out she'd lost her virginity.

He took a deep breath, making sure not to shoot me right here in the driveway. "I appreciate your concern, Riley. Might I remind you that you're not exactly the virgin Mary."

"Me? Oh, I'm aware. I didn't get these skills from YouTube tutorials," I laughed, amusement flickering in his eyes despite the grumpy look on his face.

"Get to school. Both of you."

I gave Luna a little wave, chuckling to myself as she flipped me off and stalked inside.

She'd be fine by the time we got to school.

Luna

I was still in a mood by the time I arrived at school, and Riley rolled her eyes as I walked right past her. She didn't chase me, she never did. She knew I'd always go crawling back to her once I'd stopped being angry, then we'd act as if nothing happened.

"Riley again?" Beckett asked as she fell into step beside me, Maddox and Jett nowhere in sight. I wasn't that close with Beckett, but she always told me to give Riley shit for being a bitch.

She was the reason I'd left the track a couple of weeks ago after fighting with Riley and jumped into bed with Stanley. She knew it would get under Riley's skin, and I had to admit, I'd enjoyed it.

"She reminded my dad this morning about the fact I have sex. She basically yelled it across our front yard," I replied dryly, gripping my textbooks tighter against my chest. "And she keeps giving me shit about Stan."

"She's protective of you. It can be a gift and a curse at the same time," she replied with a hum. "Want me to tell her to back off?"

"It's fine," I sighed. "It's my fault for letting her get away with it."

"Hey, fuck that. It's her fault," Beckett growled, giving me a stern look. "She's the one being a bitch. She can't keep talking shit about your man and not expect you to get upset about it."

"Either way, I'll deal with it." I didn't bother saying I'd see her later as we parted ways. She lived at Jett's house with him and Maddox, so we didn't make a habit of stumbling into each other.

I got to my lecture class early, so I ran my eyes over some notes while waiting for the professor to arrive. Education was important to me, which was another thing Riley and I didn't have in common.

We honestly shouldn't have worked statistically as

friends, because we were complete opposites. I was quiet, I rarely cursed, and I preferred a night at home instead of going out.

Riley, on the other hand, was ridiculously social and despite preferring to observe a situation than dive into the chaos like Beckett, that didn't mean she was quiet.

I'd witnessed her lose her shit plenty of times, but it took a lot to make her snap.

She was also extremely crude and very confident with her sex life and body.

Riley never showed up before our class was over, and I couldn't find her at lunchtime either.

I headed out to the parking lot to look for her car, finding it gone. That wasn't unusual, she bailed all the time on classes.

Everyone knew she'd pass regardless. No one wanted to fail one of Rory Donovan's kids, and I was pretty sure Rory paid a lot of money every year to ensure it didn't happen.

I wandered to the cafeteria, giving up on my search for her, and sat beside Landon. "Hey."

He glanced up from his sandwich, giving me a warm smile. "Hey. Where's Riley?"

"Beats me," I replied with a one-armed shrug. "I won't be at the track tonight. Dad's making me stay home."

"Are you and Riley fighting again?" he asked lightly, not falling for my change of subject. His blue eyes burned into me, and I grumbled as I told him about my morning. He was a really good friend of both mine and Riley's, and he always helped us get over our petty arguments.

His eyes gleamed with humor once I'd finished explaining everything, and I lightly smacked the back of my hand against his arm with annoyance. "It's not funny."

"She's just jealous. You know she likes you," he grinned,

my stomach twisting at his words. I was well aware of Riley's feelings for me. She'd drunkenly told me on multiple occasions, and I was pretty sure she didn't remember. I liked her a lot, but I wasn't into girls.

Part of me wished I could love her, because I knew she'd look after me and keep me safe, but I couldn't force my feelings.

"Am I supposed to end our friendship then? Because I can't do that, but it's obviously becoming too much for her," I scowled, raking my fingers through my brown hair.

"Just talk to her about it. Tell her you're aware of her feelings," he suggested without hesitation, grabbing my wrist to stop me from my nervous habit. "You two are usually good at being honest with each other, so why can't you discuss this?"

"It's an awkward conversation that will end with us arguing. I can't handle a big fight with her, and I don't want to hurt her by shutting her down so hard."

"You're hurting her more by giving her hope that she has a chance," he pointed out, making me snort.

"I've never once given her the impression that she has a chance with me. I have a boyfriend, for starters."

"He's a dick, and you know it. I don't know why you put up with him," he scoffed, embarrassment filling me. Stanley was sweet, but he had his problems. Keeping his dick in his pants was one of them, and his lack of life goals was another.

He'd dropped out of college in our first year, and he'd been happily living off whatever his parents would send him each month.

We'd been on and off a lot over the last year or two, and luckily most of his straying had been on the down-low.

If Riley knew the half of it, she would've beaten him to death by now.

I was terrified of starting over and being alone, so I clung to him in hope that he'd get it out of his system. Guys were supposed to mess around at this age, right?

Landon and I lapsed into silence for the rest of lunch, and he knew he'd overstepped when he simply gave me a small smile before heading to his afternoon class without saying goodbye.

I was supposed to head to the library to study with a few other girls, but I found myself walking to my car and heading home. I drove through town on the way, rolling my eyes when I spotted the graffitied Corvette parked out front of Harley's Bar.

Of course, she'd left school and gone straight to the bar to get laid.

I wasn't going to hang around and watch women paw over her. It made me uncomfortable.

I kept driving until I got home, grateful to find the house empty. Not even my sister, Tempest, was home, so I had a hot bath before calling Stanley, deciding if Riley was going to sulk and get laid, then so was I.

80
100
120
140
160
180
200
220
km/h
240
260

"Can you keep your pussy prowling away from my business?" Hunter grumbled as I smacked Penny's butt on her way past me in Devil's Dungeon later that night, making her giggle. I turned to face my father, who was standing behind the bar with his arms crossed against his chest. His face was void of emotion, but his tone told me he'd had a long day.

I grinned, lifting my bat to drop it over my shoulder casually. "I'm not prowling, I already got laid on the way here."

"I don't need to know," he groaned, running a hand through his black hair, making parts of it stick up. "Are you here to work the bar? Or are you just going to bother the employees?"

"Neither. I'm bored, and Harley kicked me out of his bar. The cops were sniffing around," I shrugged, earning a look of disapproval.

"You need to stop hanging out there. You could get him shut down. You're underaged."

"I drink here all the time. What's the difference?" I

scowled, leaning against the bar. "I've been completely wasted here."

"Yeah, but what cop's actually going to drag you out of here? They don't come in here anymore since your mother threatened to sue them for harassment." He chuckled, finding amusement in the memory. Pretty sure it was one of his favorites.

We had the local cops on our payroll these days, but sometimes their higher-ups would crack down on them. We always got a heads up from BG since he ran the Ashburn Valley Police Department. He'd been in our pocket forever. I had no idea what his real name was, but BG was short for beer guts. He was in his fifties, unfit, and he was too scared of my family to ever say no to something dodgy.

"I just stopped by to steal some vodka," I answered sweetly, his face turning serious.

"Are you heading to the track? Don't drink if you're driving. You know Skeet will burn your car to scrap if he catches you, and he'll rip the town apart if you crash. You know he's been touchy since Lloyd died."

That snatched the grin off my face real fast.

Lloyd was eleven years older than me. Like Maddox, Mom had adopted him, Mikey, and my sister, Angel, after saving them from the skin trade when they were kids. Angel had only been a baby, Mikey had been two, and Lloyd had been eight.

Lloyd had been a huge turning point for Mom, and they'd probably been closer than what she and I were, but he'd been killed in a car accident at the track three years ago. It had been a deliberate attack on my family by the Hell's Demons' crew, who was being led by a vengeful son of one of the original members. The Reapers of Chaos crew had been the ones to massacre them originally, but the son's problem wasn't with the Reapers.

It had been with Mom, all because she'd taken his play toy from him. He'd had a favorite kid he liked to abuse, which also turned out to be his nephew.

That was how Maddox had ended up with us when he'd been four years old, and he'd been glued to Beckett ever since. I should've seen their love story coming a mile away, but we'd all been blindsided a couple of months ago by their relationship.

The Demons were now gone, all of them dead thanks to my family with the help of a few other crews, but that didn't take the pain away. I hadn't been as close to Lloyd as Beckett or Mikey, but that accident would haunt me forever.

I could still hear his screams as he'd burned to death in his car, right there in front of my eyes while Ryder had held me back.

"Riley?" Hunter murmured, giving my shoulder a gentle squeeze to draw my attention, and luckily I didn't swing my bat at his face in response. I hadn't realized I'd zoned out, or that he'd walked around the bar to stand beside me. "Are you okay?"

"I'm fine," I said quickly, pushing thoughts of the accident away and plastering my usual smirk on my face. "Now. Where's the vodka?"

He sighed and reached over the bar to grab a bottle for me, keeping it firmly in his grasp until I met his dark brown gaze, his voice low with warning. "I mean it. If you're drinking this at the track, call me and I'll pick you up. Do *not* fucking drive."

"I promise," I nodded, taking the bottle in my spare hand once he let it go, and giving Penny a wink across the room as I left, one of the Devils opening the door for me. I didn't know his name, I didn't bother learning them unless they were at the house regularly.

I drove straight to the track, parking beside Beckett's purple RTR Mustang. I rolled my eyes when I climbed out and noticed Zane Evans' black Super Snake Shelby beside it. He was technically our cousin, his father, Rage, being the leader of the Shadow Kings crew.

Zane had never spent much time in Ashburn Valley, usually too busy back home in Stoneleigh, running around doing Kings' business for his father.

He probably kicked puppies or burned down orphanages just for fun in his spare time.

He was the Devil.

Somehow, the asshole had wormed his way into being besties with Beckett, so he stopped by all the fucking time now, much to everyone's annoyance.

He was leaning against his car, deep in conversation with Beckett while Maddox and Jett glared at him. The air was full of tension, just like it always was when he was around. No one liked Zane hanging around at all apart from my sister, and it probably wouldn't have been so bad if he stopped trying to fuck her.

We knew Skeeter was Beckett and Ryder's bio dad, there was no mistaking the resemblance, but it was still weird to think that Zane was our cousin and shamelessly tried to get in her pants.

I grabbed my bat and the bottle from the passenger seat and joined them, leaning against Beckett's car to give Zane the side-eye as I uncapped the vodka, resting my bat beside me. "Evening. What brings you to town?"

"What? I can't just drop by to hang out without a reason?" he scoffed, his muscles bunching as he crossed his arms tightly, and I was surprised his black T-shirt didn't rip from his fucking biceps. "Believe it or not, I needed to see Beckett about something important."

"More vigilante justice? You guys need capes to match your side dish of saintliness," I deadpanned, glancing at Beckett from under my hood. "You need better friends if you're that lonely."

"I take it you're not racing since you have a bottle in your hand?" she replied bluntly instead, but it wasn't a question, it was an order. She'd caught me driving drunk once before, not long after I'd gotten my license, and she'd slashed my tires. My sister was reckless, but there was usually reason and calculation behind it.

Cars weren't toys, and just like our parents, she'd been hounding me about being a safe driver ever since we'd lost Lloyd. I couldn't blame her, but everyone acted like he'd done something stupid to cause his crash. That wasn't the case.

"Nope. Landon's coming, so he'll probably drive me home," I said tightly, not wanting a lecture. "Are you racing?"

"Yeah. Reid's coming to race and wanted a challenge."

"You know, considering you don't refer to them as friends, you sure do spend a lot of time with them," I teased, taking a swig of the vodka, the burn sliding down my throat and warming my insides.

Reid Barron lived in Hawthorne Heights, the next town over, and he and his friends regularly came to the track to race. We'd never had much to do with them until a recent situation where Zane had kidnapped their friend, Zavier Lopez, giving him to Beckett to do what she wanted.

His brother had been the one who'd killed Lloyd, and Zane thought it was useful having him. It turned out Zavier wanted nothing to do with the Demons or his father, and he'd been running from them most of his life too.

We were all really surprised when Beckett became good friends with him and let him go home to the Heights, which was how Beckett met Reid and the others. She'd driven Zavier there herself so she could question Reid on an incident he'd been involved with at the track.

Beckett hated us calling them her friends, because she was so shut off from most people that she wasn't used to having people around her that weren't family. Whatever they'd done, they were weakening the walls she'd erected. I was kind of impressed they'd managed to get as close as they had.

I personally couldn't stand Zavier. He was cocky, and it was obvious he wanted to bang Beckett's brain out.

Well, I guess I was lying about not knowing them well, but I couldn't tell Beckett or my family that I'd met Reid and Logan first. That would open up the question of where I knew them from, and I couldn't tell anyone that.

"They're hardly my friends." Beckett's nose crinkled with distaste, but there was no heat behind her tone. She knew she was full of shit.

Maddox rolled his dark blue eyes, used to the argument, and he moved beside me to gently jab his elbow into my ribs. "How are you? Where's your girlfriend?"

"Don't piss me off then cry when I beat you to a pulp with my bat," I snarked, pinning him with a frosty look as he snatched my vodka and had a long drink, handing it back with a grin.

"You're so touchy. So, where is she?"

He was lucky I didn't grab a fistful of his messy, dark brown mop of hair and yank his face down to meet my kneecap. He knew he was pissing me off.

"If you're referring to Luna, Archer told her she had to be home tonight. Lexi wanted to have a family dinner thing. She's not always glued to me, you know?"

"Of course not. She spends so much time with her boyfriend," he taunted, trying to get a rise out of me. He was going to get more than he bargained for if he continued to be a dick.

His jaw tightened as someone slapped the back of his head, and Ryder walked around to join us with a smirk. "Now, now. Don't bully Riley or she'll beat you to death."

"Says the guy who tries to fuck Luna all the time," Maddox sneered, rubbing his head. "You tease her more than any of us, asshole."

"Yeah, but she currently has a bat on one side of her, and a glass bottle in her hand. Pick your battles, bro," he snorted, frowning as he looked across the track. The track was pretty fancy for this side of town, but we'd thrown a lot of money at it to make it a safe place for kids to race. A lot of padded safety barriers surrounded the main track, the dirt replaced by a fresh blacktop, and everyone who raced had to put their names down and sign a bunch of shit for legal reasons. A lot of kids from out of town probably used fake names, but we tried to do as much as possible to ensure everyone was safe and understood track rules.

The only real rule we had was you weren't allowed to deliberately cause someone to crash, you had to win by skill. I personally liked breaking rules, but since my family were the ones in charge, it would look bad if I did.

I only played dirty if I had a street race, but I couldn't tell my family that.

For starters, they'd kill me if they knew I raced illegally on public roads where anything could happen. It gave me a thrill that the track could never give me.

An engine rumbled close by, and Reid's 1995 matte black Dodge Challenger parked beside Zane's Shelby, both doors opening as Reid and his best friend, Logan Donahue, climbed out, Logan pulling the seat forward to let Raven Pierce and Zavier out of the back.

I ran my eyes over Raven, not giving a shit if she caught me checking her out. If she didn't want me looking at her, she shouldn't look so fuckable. I'd never push my attraction on her hard though, only little comments to let her know my door was always open for her if she chose.

She ran her fingers through her bright blue hair, her chipped, black nail polish catching my attention as I inspected her hands. Her nails were filed short, making me wonder if she kept them short on purpose so she could fuck herself, or if it was because she bit them out of nervousness.

"Just ask her instead of standing there gawking," Logan cackled, my eyes drifting to his. He was the jokester of their group, and he was also the biggest whore out of all of them.

I raised an eyebrow, giving him a bored expression. "Ask her what?"

"For a fuck. You're waving a *fuck me* flag at her," he said with a wink. "I'll put in a good word for you if you let me watch."

"You're a pig," I replied as I turned my eyes back to Raven to see her glaring at us. "Besides, I know I have no chance with her. I can't bullshit my way into her bed. She's too smart for that."

"You've got that right. I don't like pussy either," Raven snorted. "But I'm flattered that the infamous Riley Donovan wants to get me in bed."

"I wouldn't be flattered if I were you," Jett piped up like the asshole he was. "It's not like she has a high standard. She'll fuck anything."

"Says the reformed manwhore," I threw back. "You have no room to judge me, Emerson."

"I wasn't judging you. I was simply pointing out a fact," he grinned. "Yo, Logan. You need to get yourself some wheels so we can race."

"I could beat you on foot," Logan laughed, the two of them bantering as I rolled my eyes and pulled my phone from my pocket. Those two were as bad as each other, and it was no surprise that they got along so well.

I flicked through messages, smirking as I discovered a nude. I didn't recognize her face, but I remembered her tits. How could I forget those piercings?

"I didn't know you were fucking Sherry."

I glanced up, finding Logan peering down at my phone, amusement in his tone as he continued. "She's tight. Well, she was before I got my dick in her. I ruined that pussy for life."

Raven scoffed with disgust, but I couldn't help the taunting smirk that took over my face. "You must have a pin dick then since she nearly snapped my finger with her pussy when she came. She said I was the best fuck she's ever had too."

"It's a shame you're into girls. I bet you've got a filthy mouth in the bedroom," he groaned out, his hands dropping to my waist as I grabbed the front of his shirt and tugged him against me to speak softly in his ear.

"You think you could rock my world, Donahue?"

His fingers flexed against my skin as they confidently slipped under my hoodie, a chuckle leaving him. "I know I could. Maybe you just haven't found the right guy yet."

"I'm not attracted to guys," I murmured, suddenly slamming my knee up into his junk, making him hunch over in pain. "And for your information, if I was straight and you ever got me into bed, you'd be on your knees while I pegged you. There's a reason they call me daddy, and it's a good thing I'm gay because no man could handle me. I'm doing you all a favor if you ask me."

"You're not very nice," he wheezed, cupping his balls as everyone else snickered at him. I got a kick out of guys thinking they could turn me straight. It really made my week when I got to put them back in their place.

"I never claimed to be nice, fuckface. Get away from me before you scare all the girls away," I said dryly, swigging my vodka and giving Raven a slow once-over as she stared at me with annoyance as if trying to size me up for hurting her friend. "He's right though. I'd fuck you. You know where I am if you want to have some orgasms that aren't from your own hand."

"Fuck off, Riley," she bit out sharply as I walked off, leaving the others chuckling behind me while they teased Logan for falling for my bullshit so easily.

Landon jogged towards me, dropping an arm around my shoulders with a smirk. "What did pretty boy do? I saw you knee him in the family jewels."

"He's just a pig. Are you racing or strolling around looking for pussy?" I joked, knowing for a fact he wasn't looking for company. I was the only person he'd told about his sexuality, and he was as gay as me.

No one would have suspected it either because there were stories floating around about the shit he'd been up to with girls, but all of them were lies. I'd only found out because he'd had a bad experience with a guy one night and had called me to go and save him.

That was why I always drove myself to places when getting laid.

He let out a huff, giving me the side-eye as I innocently

peered up at him. "You're lucky I like you. You're a bitch, you know?"

"Noted," I chuckled. "So, are you racing?"

"Yeah, fuck it. Are you going to race me?"

"I can if you want to get your ass kicked," I taunted, hip checking him as I walked ahead in search of Rick, the guy who had the clipboard. He was good at running the track's paperwork, so we let him do it. He wasn't one of us, but he took it seriously which was all we gave a fuck about.

Once we'd put our names down, we trekked back to our cars, Landon going one way and I went the other. I tossed my vodka at Beckett as I approached, unlocking my car. "Don't drink it all. I'm racing Landon."

I almost stumbled as she jerked my door out of my grip to glare at me, her fiery, green eyes burning into me with violence. "You're not racing. You've been drinking."

"I've hardly had any. You've drank more than that and raced before," I hissed, snatching the door from her grip. "Back off, Beck."

"Whatever. I'm not going to sit here and watch you fucking die too," she spat, guilt nipping at my insides as she stormed off. Maddox groaned, jogging after her to make sure she didn't stab anyone who got in her way while Zane glared at me.

"The fuck's wrong with you?"

"Me? She can throw a hissy fit if she wants, but she's not my keeper," I bit out, his lips lifting in a sneer.

"Too bad, because you fucking need one. If you crash, you'd better pray it kills you or I will."

"Aw, is that how you ask all the girls out?" I deadpanned. "No wonder you don't get laid."

"Don't push me. I have no problem breaking your nose," he threatened flatly as he leaned back against his car to act casual, but his fingers and biceps flexed by his sides as if he were about to lay me out right here on the grass. I really wished he'd try, because I was ready to swing my bat at someone.

Mine and Landon's race was announced, so I had no choice but to back down from Zane and slide into my Corvette, putting the window down as I started the engine and placed my bat on the floor of the passenger seat. Zane continued to glare at me as I drove off, and I heard him tell Jett I was an idiot.

He couldn't talk, he'd driven while completely wasted before, he just hated that I'd upset Beckett. He didn't actually give a fuck if I died.

I pulled up beside Landon's 2015 deep blue Corvette Stingray, his eyebrows dipping with worry as he leaned his elbow on his open window. "You good?"

"Yeah. Just shit with Beckett," I replied, waving him off. He knew if I wanted to talk about it I'd just come out and say it, so he gave me a nod when I didn't continue, turning his attention out the windshield.

Landon, Luna, and I had all been obsessed with Corvette's from a young age, and it was no surprise that we all ended up with one. I'd upgraded mine the previous year and given my white 2019 model to Luna, much to her father's dismay.

He didn't like her having a car with that much power, not that she'd ever risk driving dangerously. We were very different people.

I also had a blue 2020 MK4 Supra, but I mainly used that on the streets.

"Sick Like That" by Will Sparks & Luciana thumped from my speakers, and I turned it up to get me in the zone. Both Beckett and I raced better with music, and I

treated it like a superstition. Every time I raced without it, I lost.

I glanced at the crowd by the fence, feeling bad when I noticed Beckett gripping the railing tightly in her hands, Maddox and Jett beside her. I knew she wouldn't leave, wanting to make sure I was safe, but it would be torture for her until I crossed the finish line.

We held the same trauma, but had two very different coping mechanisms.

Beckett was terrified of accidents and dirty tactics, and she always won her races with pure skill, where I enjoyed the adrenaline rush that fear brought me. I loved the danger, and there were multiple times I probably should've died behind the wheel, all of them while racing in the illegal street races.

I didn't understand how Beckett could drive so damn fast if she was scared of crashes, but to each their own. I wasn't going to question it.

I noticed Reid and his friends leaning on the fence close by, his eyes on me. He and Logan enjoyed street racing too, and we'd stumbled across each other plenty of times since we were part of the same racing circuit. I had no idea why they'd kept my secret from Beckett, but I was glad they did. I didn't know how long it would last though since they were becoming pretty loyal to her. Zavier and Raven had no clue about the races though, which was a good thing, and probably the only reason the guys hadn't mentioned anything to Beckett.

I knew Zavier would definitely rat me out for my participation in it since he was so far up my sister's ass.

I gave Reid a mock salute, his lips lifting into a sly smirk as his dark blond hair fell over his eyes. The last time we'd raced it had been in Hawthorne Heights, and he'd beaten me by a fraction of a second. He was really good behind the wheel, and like me, he preferred racing on the street than the track. He wasn't a fan of rules.

Landon revved his engine, getting antsy as he waited for the flag to drop, and the moment it did, I slammed my car into gear and floored it, my wheels burning rubber as I shot off.

Landon kept pace, not having an issue getting too close. He knew I wasn't worried about crashing and I enjoyed the danger. Beckett would beat his ass if he didn't back off though.

I downshifted as we came to the bend, slowing and following the curve of the track before slamming my foot down on the gas, my back tires kicking out and jerking my car sideways. I corrected it, knowing I'd gotten a little close to Landon, but he drove up beside me and flipped me off, a big grin on his face.

We were neck and neck the entire lap, and by the time we crossed the finish line, Landon had fallen back the smallest amount, making me the winner. I frowned when his car slammed to a stop in my rearview mirror as I slowed, and I climbed out just in time to witness him bail from the car, smacking his body like a maniac.

"Spider!" he practically screamed, running around like an idiot. It was something he had in common with my brother. Ryder was also deathly scared of those eight-legged bastards.

I rolled my eyes and walked towards Landon, grabbing the back of his hoodie to stop him running in circles, and I reached around to unzip the front to pull it off his arms. He had no problem bailing out of the way and leaving me with the beast, and I snorted when I found the tiny thing inside the sleeve.

"Really? This little guy is what had you dancing around like you were trying to summon rain?"

"He's huge!" he argued, glaring at his hoodie as if it was its fault, his eyes widening as I turned the sleeve inside-out and placed my hand against the fabric where the spider was sitting, waiting for it to walk onto me before tossing the hoodie back at him.

"There you go. Daddy's got you," I deadpanned, his eyes narrowing.

"I'm never calling you daddy."

"No? You should since you seem to be such a little bitch," I chuckled, walking towards the grass to let the spider run free. "You bottom, don't you?"

No one was close enough to hear us, but he still cursed at me for it, getting back in his car and slamming the door.

He was a little bit sensitive about being in the closet, even when he knew I was joking. There was nothing less masculine about being a bottom, it all came down to personal preference, which had nothing to do with me.

I walked back to my car, not surprised when I glanced at the fence to find Beckett and the guys gone. She'd act like she'd left and hadn't stuck around to watch, and I'd pretend that was the case. It was a fun game we played when she was mad at me.

I climbed into my car and drove back to my usual parking place on the grass, not surprised that everyone else had gone. It was usually how nights like this went.

My bottle of vodka was empty and lying on the ground, Beckett's way of telling me to go and fuck myself.

"It's unlike you to be lonely."

I turned around, finding Angel behind me.

"I pissed everyone off," I shrugged, leaning back against my car. "Why are you here? Not working tonight?"

"Day off," she answered, twirling her freshly dyed, caramel and blonde toned hair around her finger. "Are you going to hang around here or go somewhere else?"

Landon pulled up beside us, giving me a wince. "My dads need help at the bar, so I have to bail."

"That's okay. I'll run riot with Angel," I joked. "Tell them I said hey."

"Will do. Thanks for the race," he grinned, giving us a wave before driving towards the gate, his taillights vanishing into the night.

"So," Angel said slowly. "You want to get drunk with your favorite big sister?"

"Sold," I replied as I playfully swatted her arm. "Let me just grab something and we'll go."

"You mean *someone*?" she said dryly. She knew I didn't like taking girls back to my house, but she'd always let me take hookups back to hers for the night. It was usually where we partied anyway.

"That depends. Are we drinking at your place or mine?"

"Mine."

"Then yes, I'll be back with some pussy in a minute," I grinned, knowing she would've had some guy lined up herself. She had a healthy sex life like I did, which was probably why she'd moved out.

My eyes scanned the field until they landed on a pretty brunette. I knew she was a senior from Crestford Academy, but I couldn't remember her name.

I made my way towards her, one of her friends noticing me and tensing before I got there. She mumbled something under her breath, the brunette turning around to eye me suspiciously.

I couldn't blame them, I probably looked ready to rob them with my big, baggy hoodie over my face.

I pushed it off my head, relief filling her face as she relaxed her muscles. "Riley, right?"

"Yeah. I noticed you and remembered you from somewhere. You go to Crestford Academy, don't you?" I smiled, stopping in front of her. "I'd remember your pretty face anywhere."

Her cheeks heated and interest flickered in her gaze. "I'm Georgia."

I didn't give a shit what her name was. I'd never see her again after tonight.

"Well, Georgia, did you have plans once you left here? I'm leaving and thought you might want to come and keep me company?" I offered, biting back a rude comment as her friend gave me a disgusted once-over.

"Georgia, this is Ryder Donovan's sister. You know, that asshole we hate."

I wasn't surprised by their attitude. Ryder had made a name for himself and was notorious for breaking hearts.

"Don't be mean," Georgia hissed, giving me an apologetic look.

"She's just as bad as he is," she growled, turning to give me a dirty look. "You only want to fuck her then toss her aside. I've heard all about you."

I shrugged, crossing my arms. "That's why I didn't ask her to marry me. I don't make bullshit promises. I'm offering a night of fun, nothing more. Your friend is more than welcome to turn me down."

Georgia seemed nervous, but most girls I hit on were. Eighty percent of the time, they were straight girls who wanted the girl-on-girl college experience, and they'd never been with a chick before.

That was fine by me, because it meant they knew it was just fun and didn't intend on sticking around, and it also meant they were eager to take whatever I'd give them. If I felt like letting them go down on me, I could teach them how I liked it too, but that was rare.

"So?" I asked after giving Georgia a moment to think. "How about it? I'll be gentle, I promise."

I gave her a playful wink, her friends looking horrified as she finally gave me a nod.

"Yeah, okay. I'll see you guys later."

"Georgia!" her friend snapped, but she waved her off.

"C'mon. We were only going to head to the bar and try to get laid anyway."

"Yeah, with guys!"

I chuckled, reaching out to pull Georgia towards me, my fingers tightening around hers. "Yeah, but while you guys are having mediocre sex in an unwashed bed with a half-drunk dude that can't keep his dick up long enough to get you off, your friend here will be six orgasms deep on silk sheets, not able to stop the trembling in her legs."

"Georgia, we're supposed to stick together for safety reasons," another friend warned. I appreciated the statement, I hated it when girls got too drunk to look after themselves then wandered off alone. These girls seemed to genuinely care about their friend, so I figured I'd calm them down and be nice.

"I'll make sure she texts you when we get there, and again when I take her home. Expect it to be late though. I intend on having her for a few hours."

"Hours?" one squeaked, earning a fake look of confusion in return. Her response hadn't surprised me in the slightest.

"Well, yeah? Wait, you don't get hours of orgasms? Girl,

you really need to get laid by a woman. Men are such a disappointment," I tsked, turning my attention back to Georgia. "You ready to go then, babe?"

Her face flushed at me calling her babe, her hand tightening in mine as she said goodbye to her friends and followed me back to my Corvette. Angel gave me an amused glance as we approached, but she didn't mention it when she said she'd meet us at her place before walking off to her car.

I took my bat out of the car and put it in the trunk so Georgia had more leg room, then I climbed behind the wheel and started the engine, following Angel towards the gate so we could get this party started.

100
120
140
160
180
200
220
km/h
240
260

Chapter Three

Luna

"Stop pouting," Dad chuckled as I let out a sigh. We'd been sitting at the dining table having dinner, but I couldn't help but be annoyed that I wasn't at the track with Landon and Riley. No one else's parents seemed to make them stay home, and I felt like a child.

Tempest had picked at her dinner for five minutes before excusing herself, apparently not wanting to spend time with us when she could've been locked in her room instead. She was the life of the party outside these walls, but she was pretty quiet at home when it was just us.

We used to be close as kids, but it was as if we were strangers now. Something had changed with her in high school, and she just stopped confiding in me. I'd heard rumors from kids at school, most claiming she was on drugs. I wanted to defend her, but I honestly didn't know the truth.

I glanced at Dad, my voice soft. "Why do we have so many rules? No one else does. It's embarrassing. I'm twenty, and Tempest is twenty-one. She's legally allowed to sit at the bar and get drunk."

He rested his elbows on the table, eyeing me with understanding. He wasn't an unfair parent, but he was firm sometimes. Mom was lenient, but I didn't bother looking over at her for help. She'd always back Dad's rules.

"I'd prefer you to be embarrassed than in trouble. I don't do it to be a dick, I do it to keep you safe. You've been spending a lot of time at the shed lately on fight nights, which is one place I've asked you not to go, and I think it's good for us to spend family time together."

"We just watch Beckett's fights then leave," I mumbled, his brow creasing with confusion.

"You hate violence, so why do you go? To keep Riley happy? If she's a real friend, she won't expect that from you."

"I like Beckett. Riley doesn't push me, she's always happy to do something else if I don't want to go," I assured him. "But she shouldn't have to miss out on Beckett or Maddox's fights because of me. I like the shed. You know I'm safe there."

"Honey," he sighed, holding my gaze. "You heard what happened with the Demons. Danger can hide in plain sight, and I worry about something happening to both you girls. I hate that you're around the crews, but I also know I can't keep you from them."

"You don't like me spending much time with Stan either. He's not part of the crews," I pointed out, a frown taking over his face.

"It won't hurt that boy to work for it. If you're available every time he calls, he doesn't have to make an effort. Make him earn your love." All it did was make him jump into bed with other people, but I couldn't say that or Dad would blow his brains out.

"We've been dating for a couple of years," I argued. "What if I decide to move in with him? Are you going to stop me? I'm old enough to get married and start a family if I want to."

He paled. "Please don't do that to me yet. I can't handle it. You're my baby girl, so the thought of you being grown up enough to get married and have babies freaks me the fuck out."

"I know, but you can't avoid it forever. I'm not ready for that yet either, but that's not the point. I should be able to spend time with Stan or Riley whenever I want. You freaked when Landon asked me to hang out the other week too. I'm an adult," I said for what felt like the millionth time. "What's wrong with Riley and Landon?"

Mom hid a grin as Dad scowled. "I love those kids, but Riley's trouble, and Landon's a smooth-talking fucker. I don't want you falling for his charm."

"Riley's not trouble, and I'm not into Landon," I squeaked out. "He's my cousin."

"Hey, he's only blood-related if he's Alex's biological kid. He's too much like Harley for my liking. And have you *met* Riley?" he asked as a muscle in his jaw twitched. "She went to prison not long after her nineteenth birthday for assault, and she's a smart-mouthed little shit."

"It wasn't like she beat the shit out of them," I said, defending her.

Mom gave me the side-eye as she stood to clear the empty plates, adding her own thoughts to the conversation. "She smashed some guy's car to pieces, then broke a cop's nose and stole his patrol car when he showed up to escort her off the property."

"The guy called her a dyke!"

"She deliberately slept with his sister to make a point. She's got to expect backlash, despite it being disgusting," she said carefully, making me frown.

"Did people used to say stuff like that to you? You used to sleep with girls, right?"

Dad blew out a breath and got to his feet, kissing the top of my head before glancing at Mom.

"I'll leave that conversation for you two ladies. I'm going to check in with Wet Dreams, so I'll be home in about an hour unless something happens."

Chances were high their strip club was running perfectly, and he was just looking for an excuse to escape. My dad sucked at coping with girl talk.

"Be safe," Mom called out as he headed to the door, and I couldn't help but smile as he gave her a wink. Most people would find the mushy stuff between their parents gross, but I thought it was sweet that, after all these years, they still loved each other like they had when they were younger.

They'd grown up on the wrong side of town and been together ever since so they were always pretty close.

I wanted what they had, but I wasn't sure I'd found that kind of love with Stanley. I didn't know how to be enough for him, but he was enough for me. I'd had one or two boyfriends before, but he was definitely the only one I'd felt real love for, none of that puppy love stuff.

"Why all the questions?" Mom asked once we were alone, curiosity in her blue eyes. "Are you noticing women sexually?"

I scrunched up my nose, shaking my head. "No. I'm straight. I just don't understand why people are mean to others who aren't. How does it affect anyone else?"

Pride filled her eyes as she sat beside me, a smile on her

face. "I don't know, sweetie. People are assholes sometimes. Some don't understand it, others simply don't want to understand."

"But it's not hard to understand. It's just love," I said with confusion. "How's girls kissing girls any different from girls kissing guys?"

"It's not, but people are arrogant," she said as she studied me. "I'm proud of you, you know that? I know kids treated Riley a little differently when they caught onto the fact she liked girls, but you stuck by her. I'm glad you two have such a strong friendship."

"She never hid the fact she liked girls, so I don't see why people started acting differently towards her. It's not like she changed as a person. She's still the same Riley she was as a kid," I answered as my eyebrows drew together in thought. "What the hell does sleeping with girls have anything to do with it? Nothing else changed."

"Like I said, people are simply assholes. Does she have a girlfriend yet?"

I laughed, not being able to help it. "You think she's ever going to settle down? You know she likes playing the field. I think she'll just sleep around until she dies."

"You'd be surprised what she'd do for the right person. One day, someone will come along and she'll fall stupidly in love with them. People never thought I'd settle down either, but here I am, married to my first love with two beautiful kids," she chuckled. "I never thought I'd end up with your father. Our past is messy and toxic, but we grew up eventually."

"I'll always want what you guys have," I said, my cheeks flushing. "I love that you two are still so romantic and go on dates."

She got to her feet as her mouth curved into a soft smile

before leaning down to drop a kiss on my cheek. "It hasn't been easy, but it was worth the uphill battle. I hope you're loved this hard too, honey. You deserve nothing less. Since your father's left and we both know he'll be more than an hour, how about we watch a movie? I'll make some popcorn," she offered, waiting for me to nod before continuing. "Go ahead and pick a movie. I'll be in soon."

I loved spending time with my mom, but I couldn't help but wonder what Riley was doing while I was stuck at home. I felt like I never spent time with her anymore, and I hated that.

Riley

I woke up alone as always, Georgia's perfume hitting my nose as I buried my face in the pillow. I'd spent more of the night fucking her than I had drinking, so I'd driven her home close to two in the morning, before heading back to Angel's to get a decent sleep. Marla had texted me an hour before that, bitching about Ryder having a girl over, and they were keeping the house awake.

That was nothing new.

I rolled onto my back, reaching for my phone to check my notifications. There was a missed call and a message from Landon, calling me a hussy and hoping my silence was because I'd finally suffocated between a pair of thighs. We always liked to taunt each other, so I sent him the middle finger emoji to let him know I was alive.

I scrolled through Facebook for a while before climbing out of bed, making my way into the kitchen and rolling my eyes as I found Angel sitting on the counter in nothing but a shirt, her evening date fucking her with his hand over her mouth.

"Ew. Gross. It's too early to deal with this shit," I grunted as I walked to the fridge and pulled it open to grab some juice. It wasn't the first time I'd witnessed Angel getting laid, and it wouldn't be the last. I didn't give a shit, as long as the guys she fucked left me alone.

I found a glass, pouring a drink and checking my phone again as it buzzed with a text, Luna's name popping up on the screen. I sipped my drink and walked into the living room as I opened it, choking when a picture of her in her panties and her arm across her naked tits filled the screen. That was going in the spank bank for sure.

I had no idea why she'd sent it, but I wasn't going to complain.

I started texting a response, unsure what to say. Did I compliment her sweetly, or say something dirty back?

Before I could figure it out, she called me, my heart thumping in my chest. I felt like a damn virgin all over again when it came to her.

I hit answer, lifting the phone to my ear and hoping Angel didn't start screaming or something from the other room. "Morning, Lou. I was—"

"Don't open my message!" she squealed, cutting me off. "Oh my god. I didn't mean to send it to you!"

I should've known it wasn't for me, but that didn't make it hurt any less.

I suddenly scowled, anger burning through me. "Who the fuck was it meant for?"

"You saw it?!"

"It's a bit hard not to notice when there's a nude flashing on my phone," I snapped as anger poured through me, almost dropping my drink. "Why are you sending nudes to someone?"

She was quiet for a second before sighing heavily, and I could almost see her biting her lip. "It was obviously for Stan. I don't send things like that to just anybody, Riley."

"You don't send shit like that to anyone *ever*!" I hissed, practically burning a hole in the carpet as I paced. "The hell were you sending it to him for? Did he tell you to? I swear to God, I'm going to—"

"No! I wanted to spice things up a little! It was to surprise him!" she insisted, her voice cracking. "You weren't supposed to see it, I'm sorry."

"Why do you need to spice things up? You've only been together for a couple of years. If it's not still spicy, that seems to be a *him* problem. You're hot as fuck, Lou. If you need to make him pant over you by sending shit like that, there's something wrong with him," I bit out, not caring if she knew I thought she was hot. "It's okay to work for your relationship, but if only one of you are putting the work in, you're wasting your time. What's *he* doing to spice things up?"

"Fuck you," she choked out as a sob left her, hanging up without another word.

"Fuck," I growled, smacking the side of my head with frustration as I forcefully threw my phone onto the couch cushions, putting my face in my hands. I hated how sensitive she could be sometimes, because I always made her cry without meaning to.

I hated myself when I made her cry, and she must have been really upset if she'd cursed at me. She never cursed.

I got to my feet and grabbed my phone, heading up to the room I'd slept in, snatching my hoodie and shoving it over my head before grabbing my car keys. I forced my feet into my sneakers and jammed my phone into my pocket, stomping back through the house towards the front door.

"Hey, what's wrong?" Angel asked as she stepped in front of me, thankfully fully dressed and with my bat in her outstretched hand. I heard the shower running, so that explained where her company had vanished to.

"I upset Luna, so I've got to go and fix it," I said as I set my mouth into a hard line, taking the bat as amusement filled her eyes.

"What did you do now?"

"I technically didn't do anything wrong, I just told her the truth, but now she's crying. You know what she's like," I sighed and rubbed a hand over my face. "Trust my unfiltered mouth to end up with the most sensitive best friend on the planet."

"Was it about Stan again?"

"Don't start on me this early or I *will* punch you in the face," I scowled at her, knowing she was going to give me shit. "Move, I need to go."

She stepped aside, letting me pass as sadness clouded her face. "You're breaking your own heart, and you know it."

"Better mine than hers," I replied under my breath on an exhale before shutting the door behind me and heading to my car to slide into the driver's seat.

It didn't take me long to get to Luna's, and I didn't bother knocking as I let myself in. Neither of us knocked when we visited each other since we'd spent most of our childhoods at one house or the other. Her house felt like home, just like mine did.

"Morning," Lexi said slowly, seeing the obvious frustration on my face. "Something wrong?"

"You could say that. Where's Luna?" I asked, trying to

be polite but finding it difficult. I wanted to barge into Luna's room and shake her, but Lexi wouldn't appreciate that, and Luna would just cry more.

"In her room. Head on up," she said with a frown, her eyes following me as I took the stairs two at a time. I shoved Luna's bedroom door open, startling her from her spot on the edge of the bed. She was in one of Stanley's shirts and the panties I'd seen in the photo, and I had to force myself not to yank the shirt off her body and burn it.

"What the hell, Riley?" she demanded, her eyes red from crying. "I don't want you here."

I instantly forced my anger aside, blowing out a breath as I shut the door and moved towards her. I silently sat beside her and wrapped my arms around her before laying us down so that she was facing me. She stiffened, but thankfully let me hold her without fighting me off.

"I'm sorry."

She relaxed when she realized I wasn't here to argue, dropping an arm across my stomach to cuddle against me. "I know you don't like him, but I hate it when you're mean about it," she murmured. "I don't expect you guys to be best friends, I don't even force you two to spend time together, but it hurts me when you talk shit about him."

My expression softened, and I lifted my hand to toy with her silky, dark brown hair. "I know, but I won't let anyone treat you wrong. You shouldn't have to send him photos of you naked to catch his attention. Your name popping up on his phone should be enough. I feel like you're always the one chasing him, Lou."

She was quiet for a moment before tilting her face up to give me a curious glance. "Have you ever felt like that before? Just seeing someone's name made your heart race?"

I wasn't about to tell her it was her name that set me on

fire, so I chuckled instead. "Me? The queen of pussy? No. I'm not dating though, whereas you guys are. Every little thing that reminds him of you should put a stupid smile on his face and make his dick hard."

She frowned, and I couldn't help but run my fingers across the crease on her forehead. "Stop it, you'll get wrinkles. Did you end up sending the picture to the right person?" I added dryly, making her groan as her cheeks turned a dark shade of crimson.

"I'm really sorry. I'm mortified."

"Don't worry about it. You can send me nudes whenever you want. I've got a hot bestie, so I might as well get to see the goods," I said as I batted my lashes, amusement filling her eyes despite her face remaining red.

"I bet you have hundreds of photos in your spank bank. You don't need mine."

"You're wrong if you think any of them are hotter than you," I answered softly without bothering to lie, tucking her hair behind her ear. "At least you have a personality too. Most girls I've slept with are fake as fuck and I can't wait to get away from them once we're done. I never want to get away from you."

"You're so full of shit," she said with a giggle. "You get heaps of girls."

"If they were that good, why do I toss them aside so easily? If I had any interest in them, there's no way in hell I'd let them get away from me," I said lightly, looking away from her to stare at the ceiling. "Don't ever feel like you have to throw yourself at someone to make them choose you. It's a two-way street, sure, but if he wanted to, he would. It's as simple as that. Spicing things up isn't a fancy word for trying to get someone's attention. It's a way for two people to make things fun when they're both feeling the distance. I don't know what's going on with you and Stan, and I don't want to fight about it, but if you're the one trying to spice things up because you don't feel like he notices you above every other girl, then the only outcome for that is a broken heart."

"I love him, Riley," she whispered, my heart hurting for her at her unspoken words. She was trying too hard to keep his attention, which meant she'd already lost him. I knew she'd keep fighting for him until her heart couldn't take it anymore too.

"It's okay to love him, but don't let him consume you so much that you forget to love yourself too," I answered, dropping my other arm around her to hold her more tightly.

I had no idea how long we laid there for, but it would never feel like enough.

80
100
120
140
160
180
200
220
km/h
240
260

Chapter Four

Riley

I spent the day with Luna, watching those terrible movies she loved so much and eating popcorn. By the time I went home, switched cars, and drove my Supra into Hawthorne Heights, it was almost ten at night.

I turned into the abandoned parking lot that used to belong to the old school that had been burned down years ago, shutting my engine off as I parked beside Reid's matte black Challenger. I reached over and grabbed my baseball bat before opening my door and climbing out to lift my chin in greeting to Reid who was sitting in the driver's seat with his window down as he puffed on a cigarette.

"Evening, Barron."

"Donovan."

"Where's your boyfriend?" I questioned, knowing Logan always came with him. I was surprised they left Raven home for so long, in all honesty. Zavier could hold his own if it came down to it, but they all had attachment issues.

I could see childhood trauma bleeding off them in

waves, and I would almost bet money on it being the reason they were all so close.

He rolled his eyes, jerking his chin in the direction of the bushes across the parking lot.

"Railing some chick over there."

As if on cue, a moan echoed around us, making me snort.

"I hope he gets ants up his ass. Doesn't he have any class?" I crinkled my nose, leaning back against my car and observing the empty space around us. The others weren't here yet, and no one else would risk hanging around this place so late.

The crime rate here was ridiculously high.

"As if you've never shoved your fingers up some chick's pussy while in public," he scoffed, giving me an amused glance, the smoke from his cigarette swirling into the night sky. "I doubt you have an issue with putting on a show."

"An audience doesn't faze me, no," I shrugged, placing the tip of my bat on the ground and twirling the handle in my grip, the scraping sound loud in the quiet air. "Where are the others? Turbo texted me and told me to be here by ten, but I guess I'm the only one who got that message."

"Turbo and Slick should be here soon. Blake's coming too. She had something to do on the way though, so she'll probably be late."

"No offense to Blake, but I'm not waiting all night for her. I've got shit to do," I retorted, and he raised an eyebrow, tossing his cigarette butt out the window.

"The fuck do you have to do this late? It's not like you've got anyone lying awake in bed waiting for you to get home."

"Bite me, asshole. I want to stop by Harley's Bar on the way home and see Landon," I scowled but was quickly relieved when the sound of rumbling engines slowed close by and pulled into the parking lot.

Turbo's black 1994 MK4 Supra came into view, the headlights almost blinding me in the process. Mine was nicer, but I respected him for the effort he'd put into his. It was a pile of crap when he'd first brought it to these races a few years earlier, purchasing it as a wreck, but now it was flashy as fuck with a shit ton of time and money under the hood.

The bodywork didn't look half bad either.

I didn't bother to ask him where he got the money because he'd either lie or I'd get sucked into whatever illegal crap he was involved in. I knew he was a huge player in the underground, and he had more than just illegal street races happening as his business.

I had enough of that shit from most of my family being involved with the street crews, so I never bothered asking him for details. I'd never heard his real name used in conversation at home, which was a relief.

Ander Lavaro was someone my parents definitely wouldn't allow me to associate with. He was the enemy if he was involved in dealing drugs or weapons, which was why the less I knew, the better.

To me and the rest of the racers, he was just Turbo, the car fanatic.

Slick pulled in behind him in his black 1984 Mustang, both of them switching their cars off and climbing out. Slick leered at me like he always did, but Turbo gave me a nod. I had zero respect for Slick, he was a piece of shit, and I'd heard a rumor that he'd knocked some chick up and beat her when she refused an abortion.

I didn't even know what his real name was. He wasn't worth my time. He hated me, but he wanted to fuck me because he saw me as a challenge. No girl would willingly get in his bed, I was sure of it. I had no idea why Turbo associated with him outside of these races, because he wasn't too bad of a guy.

"Where's Blake?" Turbo asked, his attention on me as if I held all the answers. I rolled my eyes, placing my bat behind my neck and holding each end with my hands.

"Reid said she's coming, but she'll be late."

"She'll be coming when I shove my dick up her cunt," Slick snickered.

"You probably wouldn't know how to make a woman come even if she directed you," I laughed lightly, running my eyes over him with disgust. "And I doubt anyone would willingly take their panties off for you to find out."

"Watch it, whore," he spat. "Or I'll shove that bat of yours right up your filthy cunt."

"If you think you could pry it out of my hands to begin with, you're delusional. I'd beat you to a pulp with it before you got the chance. Don't try me, fuckface," I warned, tightening my grip around it and preparing to swing as he took a step in my direction, but Logan materialized in front of me, his muscles bunched as he stared Slick down.

"You think you can lay a finger on a woman and get away with it, asshole?" he growled, clenching his fists by his sides. "Try and throw hands at me instead and see what happens."

Slick sneered at him, but Turbo rolled his eyes and stepped between them before it could escalate any further. I'd seen Logan throw fists before, and he was just like all the other Heights born kids. Scrappy as fuck.

"We're not here for that. Get in your cars and let's get this race started. I have business to attend to when I leave here so I don't need your childish pissing contest."

Logan didn't move a muscle until Slick backed off and stalked to his car, and once he was away from us, Logan turned around and gave me a smirk.

"Can't take you anywhere without you causing a scene, can we?"

"You didn't take me anywhere. Where'd your girl go? It was bad enough that your *romantic* date was in the bushes, but then you bailed on her too?" I chuckled, relaxing once Slick was shut inside his car away from us.

"She had things to do. She took off, not me," he shrugged, not fazed that she was now wandering around in the dark alone. She must have been local with good self-defense skills, or he would've taken her home.

He was a playboy, but he wasn't a complete asshole.

"You were that bad she ran away? Damn. Next time give her my number so the poor bitch can at least get off," I teased as I placed my bat by my side, laughter leaving me as he gave me a gentle shove.

"Fuck off, Donovan. You should be nicer to me. From what I've heard, your sister wouldn't like to know you're an adrenaline junkie with a death wish."

I stopped laughing, my face becoming a void of emotion as my voice turned cold. "Are you threatening to out me to my family, Donahue?" I pushed him backwards, his back hitting the hood of Reid's Challenger as I pressed my bat against his throat with a hand on each end to apply pressure. "Don't fuck with me. You think Beckett's the only person who can ruin your life? Think again."

He cringed, his back probably burning from the awkward angle. "I'm only playing with you."

I pressed the bat down harder, standing between his legs and keeping him pinned in place.

"Why haven't you already told her? You hardly know

me. You two are closer than you and I," I hissed, pushing the bat down harder and making him gasp for air. "I don't trust you, and I don't like you holding something over my head like this."

Reid leaned out the window, giving me a bored expression. "Can you not dent my fucking car?"

"You should be more worried about your buddy," I deadpanned without looking over at him.

"My car's innocent in all of this. That fucker, on the other hand, isn't. Beat him up elsewhere. I have a race to get to if you don't mind," he threw back, fake offense taking over Logan's face as I pulled the bat away, his voice raspy as he choked.

"Hey! We're basically brothers, dude! Where's your loyalty!"

"If you wave a red flag at a bull, don't come crying to me when you get trampled," he huffed. "Now, are you gonna get the fuck in the car, or are you staying here?"

I leaned back without leaving Logan's personal space, my nose scrunching with disgust as I noticed Logan's erection against my groin. "Control your fucking cock before I rip it off. Are you seriously horny right now? You're disgusting."

I stepped away from him, a cheeky smile tugging at his lips. "C'mon, you're hot and you were rubbing against it. What do you expect?"

"I'm gay."

"Yeah, well I'm fucking not. You can't blame me," he grumbled, standing up straight to step around the car to climb in. I probably caught chlamydia from being that close to him. He was a walking STD for sure.

"The breeze brushes against his dick and he gets hard.

Don't feel too special," Reid chuckled and started his engine. "Looks like Blake's here just in time."

I lifted my gaze to see Blake's 1970 orange Pontiac Firebird pull in, a scowl on her face as she wound the window down. "Sorry. I was dealing with the cops. They shouldn't bother us tonight."

"What did you do?" I grinned, shoving my bat through my open window before walking over to her. "It's unlikely they'd bother us anyway. You know they're too lazy for paperwork."

"Oh, nothing really. The station's burning to the ground as we speak though," she shrugged casually. "So they're a little occupied."

"You burned the station down? Blake, they never bother us," I snickered while her face remained serious.

"Two of the pigs sexually assaulted my little sister when they had her removed from Dad's care this week. She's in an emergency foster home until they place her somewhere more permanent. I found the address and went to check on her, and she said the cops touched her. I burned that shithole down for her, not for us," she hissed, her knuckles turning white on the steering wheel. "She's nine, Riley. Those dirty fucking cunts touched a nine-year-old girl."

I'd heard so many stories about similar situations happening, but they rarely involved the cops. Ashburn Valley cops wouldn't dare, but I didn't have much to do with the cops here in Hawthorne Heights. I'd grown up sharing my home with abused kids since my parents were on a mission to end the skin trade and had been saving kids for years, so I'd seen some horrible cases.

To say I was furious about Blake's sister would be an understatement, and I knew I had to help in some way.

"Wait for me after the race. I want more information.

I'll get Mom to look into it and get your sister placed somewhere safe," I said firmly, her gaze becoming guarded as she studied me. I knew she didn't want to believe me, kids from the Heights knew people would always let them down, but she wanted to trust me for her sister's sake.

"Really? Why would you do that? They won't let me take her in because I don't have a stable home for her, and as much as I hate that, I can't look after myself half the time. She wouldn't be safe with me." She didn't hide the agony in her tone, and I gave her a small smile.

"Everyone knows Mom's place is a safe haven for foster kids, and we always have random kids walking in off the street when they need somewhere to go. If your sister's not safe, then we'll make sure we get her out of there, okay? I want details on the cops if you can get it too. If you need somewhere to go, you're always welcome to come and stay with us."

"I'm twenty-two, not exactly a defenseless kid," she said dryly, but hope flickered across her face.

I knew she'd had it rough growing up with an abusive father, but I didn't know much else about her. She seemed nice enough though, despite her tough exterior.

"So? Even if you just need a bed for the night, let me know. It's what we do," I answered, tapping the roof of her car as I stepped back. "Let's race, then we'll talk."

"Thanks," she said tightly as Turbo called out where we were meeting to start the race. I knew it would hurt Blake's pride to ask for help, so I didn't take offense to her tone. She had no reason to trust me, especially since not even her family had her back.

Just because we raced, didn't mean we knew each other well. We were only friends when it came to cars.

I climbed into my car, following the others as they drove towards the main road, Turbo leading the way.

He had connections, and they were responsible for planning our routes. We all received a digital map on a small tablet before each race, and the only thing we knew before that was the starting point. The devices were untraceable, and it meant we could turn our phones off so we couldn't get tracked by family or the cops.

They secured to the dash and showed us where everyone on the map was while we raced too. It was smart, and as much as I didn't trust Turbo, he seemed to know his shit about street racing.

Once we arrived at a dead-end street, he waved his tablet at us, silently instructing us to get ready. I put mine on its holder, loading the map so I could see where we were going. I didn't like the idea that half the race was in Rawson Grove since my family had connections there, but at least it wasn't Ashburn Valley. Turbo promised we'd never race there for the simple fact he knew my family would come down on him like a motherfucker.

We didn't allow shit like this in our town, especially after Lloyd's death.

The timer flashed on my tablet and I got myself ready, looking ahead as my fingers twitched on my gear shift. I could hear Logan trash talking out the window to me, but I ignored him and focused, refusing to lose to these fuckers.

To be honest, the only person I refused to lose against was Slick. The others I respected as racers and could admit they were damn good.

Slick raced dirty though, and he'd caused so many accidents in his time that I was surprised Turbo hadn't banned him. I liked taking risks, but he was just stupid.

I guess since there were no rules, he technically wasn't

doing anything wrong. The rest of us just preferred to win by skill or it didn't feel like winning. There had been a lot of deaths at these races over the years, but that didn't stop us.

I cranked my music to drown out the other cars, and the moment the timer reached zero, I slammed my car into gear and floored it, tearing through the gears as I nosed ahead of everyone. I chuckled as I glanced in the rearview mirror to see Slick cursing as he stalled his Mustang, and we left him in the dust.

I switched through the gears with ease as we dodged the few cars on the road, adrenaline spiking as I shot through an intersection without slowing down. I knew it was reckless, I was putting my life in danger as well as other peoples, but nothing made me feel alive like this.

It had become an addiction, one that grew after losing my brother.

I didn't want to die, but the thought of cheating death made my heart race and my skin tingle. I couldn't explain the exact feeling it gave me, and every time I had a close call and swore I'd stop, I came crawling right back.

Fate had made me his bitch.

Blake cut in front of me, her engine roaring as she fought to stay ahead. Reid was right on my ass, but he didn't try to overtake me. He didn't take as many risks as me, and the road was too narrow for all of us.

The map signaled to turn left, and I yanked on the wheel, the sound of screeching tires filling the air as we all followed the route provided. We all knew this road was going to suck before we even arrived. It was narrow and had multiple cars parked along the sidewalk, turning it into more of a single lane.

Blake glanced at me as we approached the parked cars, determination on her face as terror and excitement raced through me. It became a game of chicken, our cars careening forward even though we knew both of us wouldn't fit side by side.

At the last minute, Blake slammed on the brakes to avoid us colliding, and the fear that was tearing through me turned into a victorious laugh, my Supra speeding ahead as if we hadn't almost died.

I stayed in the lead until the end of the street, where we turned onto the back road to Rawson Grove. Turbo was catching up to me fast, and Reid took his opportunity to cut around me, almost losing control as his tires slipped off the sealed road and onto the gravel.

He straightened it, his car screeching as he floored it and barreled ahead, my heart practically beating in my damn throat as he narrowly missed clipping my car. At this speed, I wouldn't just spin out from being clipped, I'd definitely flip and die. I should've slowed down, but my adrenaline rush was coursing through me, stopping common sense from ruining the fun.

We sped through the narrow backroads, flying onto the main street and heading towards suburbia.

"Ready to Die" by TheUnder blasted from my speakers, the irony making me laugh. I wasn't delusional, I knew this shit would eventually kill me, but the devil on my shoulder kept telling me it wasn't going to be today.

Blake and Turbo were neck and neck behind me, Slick's car stuck behind them as he probably cursed up a storm. If I had to brake, we'd all be fucked.

Reid turned right sharply, his car fishtailing as he regained control, and I knew he was going to win. I was okay with that.

We shot into the next street, our tablets flashing as we reached the end to state Reid had won. He slowed, smirking at me as I pulled up beside him and leaned out to fist bump him.

"I'll get you next time, Barron," I chuckled. "Nice driving. I thought you were screwed when you hit the gravel."

"Me too," he laughed, motioning to Logan who was looking slightly green beside him. "This fucker almost threw up all over my dash."

"I did not," Logan said as he drew in a long breath, lighting a cigarette with shaky hands. "There were just a few close calls, that's all."

"Whatever helps you sleep at night," I snorted, glancing behind me as Blake parked close and climbed out. "I'll catch you guys next time. I have plans with Blake."

Logan groaned, leaning over Reid and ignoring his scowl. "Can I stick around and watch?"

"What do you think, Blake? Should we let Logan watch us get it on?" I called out the window as Blake rounded my car and leaned against the side to join the conversation.

She sighed, glancing at me with amusement. She loved toying with Logan.

"Does he have to? My pussy will dry up if he's there."

"I'll keep it wet for you," I smirked, giving her a wink.

She laughed lightly, looking over at Logan who was almost falling out the window to get closer. "Sorry, Logan. We'll have to film it for you."

"For real?" he exclaimed with excitement, and Reid growled, shoving him back into the passenger seat.

"They're fucking with you, idiot. Get off me."

I snickered, switching my engine off and climbing out. "You make it so damn easy too."

He sulked, not saying goodbye, and Reid gave us a wave as he moved his car beside Turbo's to talk money. We'd all put a chunk of money into Turbo's hand the previous week to cover our next few races, and the winner took home a nice cut of it each time.

It was probably why I didn't mind when Reid won. He needed the money, unlike me, and he used it for necessities, not drugs or dumb shit like most kids from the Heights. He lived at Raven's house with Zavier and Logan, so I knew the money would pay for bills and food for them all.

Blake and I smoked while we talked about her sister, and by the time I headed home, I'd promised to discuss it with Mom in the morning when I woke up.

I didn't make it to the bar to see Landon as I was too tired.

The moment my head hit the pillow, I was out like a light.

80
100
120
140
160
180
200
220
240
260
km/h

Chapter Five

Riley

"I'm so fucking tired," I grumbled as I sat at the table in the kitchen the next morning. I'd only had a few hours of sleep and felt like shit. It was the worst thing about the races, my sleep suffered because it was always a late night.

Mom glanced over her shoulder to assess me, her long, black hair tied in a braid, telling me she was on her way to spar at the shed.

"Maybe if you stopped coming home at three in the morning, you'd sleep better. Where were you? Angel said you weren't with her, and since you turned your phone off, you obviously didn't want to be found."

"You said you'd stop asking where we were when we turned eighteen," I pointed out, accepting a coffee from her as she joined me, sitting opposite me at the table. "I got home safely, so that's all that matters."

"You wouldn't happen to know how Hawthorne Heights' Police Station caught fire last night, would you?" she asked dryly, eyeing me over the rim of her cup.

"Why would I know anything about that?" I asked with

a sly smile, sipping the steaming hot liquid. "The Heights isn't my playground."

"Why'd you burn it down?" she asked sharply, her fingers tight on her mug. "If one of those fuckers did something to you—"

I shook my head, realizing she thought I'd been hurt by the cops and had retaliated.

"I didn't do it, but I know who did. I actually want to speak to you about it." I put my coffee down in front of me, giving her my full attention so she knew how serious I was. "Some of the Hawthorne Heights cops touched a nine-year-old girl who'd just been removed from her father's care."

Fury filled her eyes and her jaw clenched as she spoke through her teeth. "Where is she now?"

"She's in emergency foster care. Her sister, Blake, can't take her in because she doesn't have a stable home for her, so I said I'd see if we—" I didn't even get to finish my sentence before she downed the rest of her coffee and got to her feet.

"I'll have her here by fucking dinner tomorrow, and she can stay here until we find her somewhere permanent. Does Blake need somewhere to stay? Is she a friend of yours?"

"We've met a few times and she seems nice. I told her she's welcome if she needs, but you know what street kids are like," I shrugged. "Her pride already took a hit by accepting my help for her sister's sake, so she wasn't going to budge on my offer for her to have help too. I did say she was welcome whenever she wanted though."

"I have no idea how I got so lucky with you kids. I thought for sure I'd fuck you all up." Her face softened and she pulled me in for a hug as I stood. "And whatever you're doing that's so secretive, please be careful. I've lost enough already, I can't lose you too. Promise me you're safe."

Guilt filled me, but I gave her a wide smile. "I promise. You're the best mom ever, you know?"

"Thanks, baby," she mumbled, holding me tighter and pressing her cheek on top of my head. She hadn't been the same since Lloyd died, and I hated that she held some kind of self-blame. Nothing could've saved him that night. Not when his car had exploded right in front of me.

I was grateful that Mom hadn't been there to witness it, because it had fucked us kids up enough as it was, but it would've completely destroyed Mom.

"I'm glad you saved him and the others," I said softly, her body tensing. "At least he got to know what real love felt like."

"It's too early for this sappy shit," she scowled as she pulled back, her eyes glassy. "Don't you have school or something?"

"It's Sunday," I deadpanned. "I've got a bunch of information written down on my phone about Blake's sister if you want it. All her personal details and—"

"Text it to me. I'll go and pull some strings with BG," she confirmed, tucking my hair behind my ear. "Tell your friend to be here for dinner tomorrow so she can spend some time with her sister."

"She's not my friend."

"What is it with you kids being scared to call people your friends? You're as bad as Beckett," she tsked, grabbing her keys. "I'll let you know when I have it sorted."

"You don't like meeting new people either," I said in a playful tone. "But thanks, Mom. I love you."

She gave me a warm smile, her shoulders relaxing from my reassurance. The others didn't notice her insecurities about being a parent like I did.

"I love you too, you cheeky shit. Stay out of trouble."

"Never!" I called after her, making her laugh as she walked out the door.

I texted her all the information she'd need to get Blake's sister, Kate, then I headed upstairs to the bathroom and had a quick shower, needing to wake myself up more. The coffee wasn't doing anything for my energy levels.

By the time I wandered back down to the living room in a loose T-shirt and my favorite track pants, Ryder and Jett were there yelling at some shooting game, and Marla stormed past me with a comment about not being able to study with all the racket. She had a bag in her hand, so I figured she was heading to the library.

She spent a lot of time there.

"Can't you do this shit at Jett's place?" I demanded, crossing my arms. "Where's Beckett?"

Jett glanced at me, giving me a wink. "Your brother and sister wanted some alone time to fuck all over the house. So I offered to give them space for the day."

"Ugh, don't call them that. It's weird," I said as I faked a gag, not wanting the mental image of my two siblings banging each other. "You're okay with them playing slap and tickle without you? Can't you get your dick up anymore?"

"We can talk about my dick if you really want, but then I'll think about your sister and get a boner. You've been warned," he teased. "But I had alone time with her last week, so it's fair."

"When do you get alone time with Maddox then?" I taunted, but Ryder groaned, already sick of our bickering.

"Can you two shut the fuck up? I can't focus when you're talking."

"Fine. I'm going to meet up with someone, but I'll be back later," I huffed, Ryder letting out a laugh.

"You mean Luna? She's your only friend."

"No. I never said they were a friend."

"Are they hot?" he asked, suddenly losing interest in his game as he looked up at me, the corner of his lips curving into a slow smirk. "Can you put in a good word for me?"

"I'd never lie to my acquaintances," I grinned. "Besides, some of the people I know would eat you alive, and not in a good way."

"I've never had any complaints, thank you," he snorted before glaring at me as I quirked an eyebrow.

"That's because their complaints end up in my messages while they're trying to fuck me instead so they actually get off."

"Serves you right if you tongue fuck some chick after she's been in my bed," he scowled, making me gag again at the thought.

"You're gross and I'm never speaking to you again."

"Love you too," he replied as he blew me a kiss, turning back to his game and letting me leave in peace.

I texted Blake and told her to meet me at Harley's Bar for lunch, then I started my Corvette and headed to the gas station for gas and cigarettes, making sure my bat was on the floor of the passenger seat.

The bar was quiet, but that wasn't unusual for a Sunday. Most people were still hungover from the night before, and anyone wanting food usually went to the diner at the other end of town.

The best burgers were definitely at the bar though.

Harley gave me a blank look as I walked towards him, his voice dry. "You have to stop hanging around here. You're going to get me in trouble."

"I'm not here to get drunk, and Mom won't let them hurt you," I said as I fluttered my lashes innocently, leaning against the bar with my elbows. "Can I have two of your burgers and fries, and two cokes?"

"You having lunch with Luna?"

"No. I'm meeting someone else," I scoffed, my nose scrunching with irritation as my muscles tensed. "Why does everyone think I only hang out with Luna?"

"Usually, you do. Got a hot date?" he smirked, writing down my order. "She must be a really special woman if you like her enough to take her on a date."

I rolled my eyes, not surprised by his comment. "It's *not* a date. I have important things to discuss with someone I know. But yeah, she's hot," I added at the end with a small smile. I'd fuck the hell out of Blake if I knew she'd be into it.

He chuckled and told me to sit wherever I wanted while he put my order in, and by the time he was bringing the food over, Blake arrived. I gave her a quick once-over, loving how her tight jeans hugged her body. Her shirt was basically a damn bra, not leaving much to the imagination, and she had brown, strappy sandals on that showed off her purple-painted toenails.

She frowned when she saw the food, but she slid into the booth opposite me without argument. "Hey."

Harley gave me a look, silently telling me he thought I was full of shit about it not being a date, but he thankfully left us alone without teasing me.

"Hey. You're coming to mine for dinner tomorrow," I stated cheerfully before popping two fries into my mouth with a grin. "Mom's orders."

"Excuse me?" she demanded, her back straightening as her expression became guarded. I could tell she was going to argue so I got to the point to avoid it.

"She's organizing to get Kate by tomorrow. If there's

nowhere safe for her, she'll stay with us until something's available. You're welcome."

Her jaw dropped as she stared at me, disbelief in her tone. "She just agreed to take her in?"

"Of course she did. It's what we do."

"Thank you so much," she replied, surprising me as she basically threw herself across the table to hug me. I patted her back, smacking a kiss on her cheek dramatically.

"Any time. So make sure you come around for dinner. Mom's expecting you there to make Kate feel comfortable."

"To think people say you're mean," she joked, sitting back in her seat with a massive smile on her face.

"I *am* mean. I'm only nice to people who deserve it," I said seriously despite my lips lifting into a smile as I motioned to her food. "Now eat that before I get mad."

"I'll pay for it," she insisted, but I shook my head.

"Don't be stupid. I asked you here and ordered it, so I'll pay. Besides, I like throwing money around. I get off on it," I winked, a light laugh leaving her as she completely relaxed and started eating her fries.

"I'm not into girls, Donovan. So you're wasting your money on me if this is your attempt to lure me into your panties."

"Not even if I order dessert?" I joked, faking disappointment when she rolled her eyes. "That's a shame. I was looking forward to you sitting on my face."

"I say this respectfully, but you're a whore," she smirked, shoving a bite of burger into her mouth, humoring my flirting.

I changed the subject to cars, and her face lit up as she told me about everything she'd been doing to hers. I knew my way around my car, I could pull the engine apart and put it back together again with my eyes closed, but Blake had built her Pontiac herself, much like the others had.

From the way she was talking, I knew it was going to be a while before we left, which was fine by me. I liked Blake, so maybe Mom was right and I needed to make friends.

Luna

Riley wasn't answering her damn phone, so I tracked her down myself. She'd turned her phone off all night so I couldn't see her location, but it was back on now. She'd been doing that a lot over the past year or two, but she never told me why.

I walked into Harley's Bar, surprised to find her having lunch with someone. I'd seen the girl once or twice before, but I didn't know Riley was friends with her. They were laughing about something, and I wondered if I was crashing a date when Riley reached out and tugged on the girl's long, black wavy hair that was tied up in a ponytail.

I walked towards them, the other girl noticing me first and saying something quietly to Riley, who glanced over her shoulder at me. She smirked, moving over automatically to make room for me. "Hey. What are you doing here?"

"I was looking for you. If I'm interrupting something, I can—"

"Blake, this is my bestie, Luna. Luna, this is Blake. She lives in the Heights," she said, cutting me off and pushing her plate towards me, silently offering me to help myself. I grabbed a fry as they went back to talking, and jealousy filled me as they laughed together as if they'd been best friends forever. Most girls were just a conquest for Riley, but she actually seemed to be friends with this chick.

She never made other friends outside of me and Landon.

I frowned when Blake mentioned something about racing and Riley swiftly changed the subject because I'd never seen Blake at the track.

They talked about car engines for ages until Blake finally got to her feet and stretched.

"I'll see you tomorrow at six then."

"Sounds good. It's a date," Riley replied with a playful wink, making Blake chuckle on her way out. Riley turned to me, tilting her head with confusion as she assessed me.

"What's wrong?"

"Nothing." I was a terrible liar.

"I think you forget I have a direct line to your emotions." She dropped an arm around my shoulders, her tone gentle. "Talk to me. Something's bothering you."

"I didn't mean to interrupt your date," I blurted out and her eyes widened.

"You thought I was on a date? We're just friends, Lou. Well, acquaintances. I'm not even banging her," she explained, a sigh leaving me.

"That's worse. You're *my* friend. What do you need her for?" I mentally cursed myself when I realized I'd said it out loud as Riley's lips kicked up into a devilish smirk.

"Are you jealous?"

"No," I gritted out as I slid from the booth and walked towards the door to escape her. She hooked her arm around my neck again and tugged me against her side with a chuckle as we walked, not allowing me to run from her.

"You totally are. It's okay, I only have one best friend, and that's you. I promise no one will take your place."

"I'm not jealous," I mumbled, my face heating. "I'm

sorry for showing up unannounced. I should've asked if you were busy."

"You can crash my party anytime. You come before anyone," she said seriously as we reached her car. "You want to come over for dinner tomorrow? Blake's coming over to see her sister. Mom's temporarily getting custody of her because she's in an unsafe environment."

"Wait, that's why you're hanging around Blake? You're helping her sister?" I asked, feeling like an idiot. "How do you know her?"

She shrugged, dropping her arm from me to lean back against her Corvette. "We've met a few times and I heard her sister was in trouble. I asked Mom to help them."

"She said you two have been racing? I've never seen her at the track."

"What's with the millions of questions?" she snapped, cringing when she realized she was being a bitch. "Sorry. I didn't get a lot of sleep last night."

She was hiding something from me, and I didn't like it. We'd been seeing less and less of each other lately too, so I was probably being extra sensitive.

"It's fine. Can I stay over tonight? Or did you have plans?"

"If I had plans, I'd cancel them for you," she said without hesitation, relaxing me. I knew she'd always put me first, but it was selfish of me to expect it. I had a boyfriend, so if she wanted to date or have other friends, I shouldn't have had a problem with that.

"I'll follow you to your place if you want to head there now?" I offered, pulling my keys from my pocket.

"Sounds like a plan."

I shrieked as she swatted my butt sharply the moment I turned to walk towards my car, and I flipped her the middle finger without stopping, feeling her eyes burning into me. I knew she was checking me out thinking I didn't know. She'd always had a harmless crush on me, and part of me loved that someone as quiet and plain as me could gain her interest, but the other part of me worried about what it meant for our friendship.

I always sensed when her eyes were on me, but how long until she made a move? How was I supposed to handle that without upsetting her?

I followed her back to her house, parking outside while she parked inside the garage, then we walked up the steps together and headed inside.

"Heads up!"

I jerked my face in the direction of the voice in the kitchen, my eyes widening as Riley's hand shot out and caught the flying can of beer before it could hit me. Her jaw clenched and she held her hand out for a second as she glared at her brother, Mikey, who was leaning against the fridge. "You could've broken her fucking nose, asshole."

He tossed the second one more carefully, giving me an apologetic look. "Sorry, Luna. I didn't see you there until I threw it."

"You could learn to pass things to people the normal way," I said as I raised an eyebrow, taking a beer from Riley. He chuckled, leaning against the wall and taking a mouthful of his own drink.

"You've got to stop hanging around Riley. You never used to talk back."

"I'm going to teach her to throw hands next," Riley grunted, her mood simmering slightly. "Is Mom home yet?"

"Nope."

"Why are you even here? You know you don't live here, right? Did your wife finally throw you out?" she teased, amusement filling his golden eyes. He was insanely sweet to his wife, Poppy, but he was also a lethal weapon. I'd seen him fight in the cage before and do target practice.

I wasn't surprised he'd made it into the Psychos crew so easily.

"Poppy would never leave me, I'm too handsome. I've been hanging out with Ry and Jett. We're watching a movie if you want to join us."

"Yeah, we were just going to hang around the house until dinnertime," Riley answered, taking my wrist and tugging me along behind her. Mikey smirked, and I knew what he was thinking.

Everyone knew how badly Riley wanted me, and I was really worried her affections towards me would turn our friendship sour, even if she never made a move. Everything I did made me wonder if I was sending her the wrong signals, and eventually, she'd either try to take it further, or she'd start avoiding me.

Either way, I couldn't lose her.

She pulled me down onto the couch beside her, dropping her arm around my shoulders like she always did. I tensed, earning a frown from her as I leaned away a little. Maybe it was my fault she was into me since I'd always let her cuddle me. I didn't see other people doing that with their best friends.

Mikey and Ryder shared a silent conversation, apparently noticing it too, but no one said anything.

Riley sighed softly and sat up properly, but she didn't relax. If she'd had her hoodie on, I knew she would've been hiding under the hood by now.

Twenty minutes later, I gave in and leaned into her, her muscles loosening instantly as she wrapped an arm behind my back. Her fingers traced patterns on my spine, and I closed my eyes for a moment, enjoying the soft massage. I was a sucker for back tickles.

I forced myself not to jerk away as she slipped her hand up the back of my shirt, continuing the patterns directly onto my skin. She hadn't done that before.

It felt nice, but I kept fighting myself about it. I didn't want her to get the wrong idea.

Things were definitely easier before she'd drunkenly blurted out her feelings for me. Ignorance was bliss.

I sat there for ten more minutes before excusing myself to use the bathroom, needing a moment to myself. I heard Mikey warning her not to push me the second I left the room, telling me everyone else was thinking the same thing as me.

Riley was definitely starting to push the boundaries of our friendship, and that terrified me.

I didn't want to fight with her, but even if I liked girls, I wouldn't do anything behind Stanley's back.

I loved him, and I was trying to keep us together, not tear us apart.

I paced in the bathroom for a minute, finally getting a grip on myself and heading back to the living room. I had to be honest with her, and if she cared about me, she'd understand I didn't see her as more than a friend.

If she tried making a move, I'd politely call her out on it.

Luckily for me, Mikey's warning must have sunk in, because she didn't try to touch me for the rest of the movie. For some weird reason, I didn't like the distance between us even though it was exactly what I'd wanted.

80
100
120
140
160
180
200
220
km/h
240
260

Chapter Six

Riley

I'd mentally scolded myself for not being able to stop my hands from wandering under Luna's shirt. I hadn't even noticed I'd done it until she'd bailed from the room and Mikey told me off for pushing her and making her uncomfortable.

It was early the next morning, and despite the pep talk I'd given myself already, I found myself spooning her, my arm wrapped around her middle as she slept peacefully beside me in bed, just like she always did when she stayed over. I buried my face between her shoulder blades, my lips skimming her soft skin.

How was I supposed to keep my hands off of her when she kept wearing skimpy shorts and tiny tank tops to bed? This was torture, but I had to respect her boundaries.

I let out a sigh, forcing myself to roll away from her before she could wake up to find me practically humping her leg.

I laid there for a while just staring at the ceiling before tensing as Luna rolled over and snuggled into me, throwing her leg over mine. Her tiny shorts didn't cover the heat radiating from her pussy that was pressed against my thigh, and I had to bite the inside of my cheek to stop myself from moaning.

She blinked up at me as she woke up properly, her cheeks turning pink as she realized how close we were.

"Um, morning," she said awkwardly, blinking at me as if to make sure she was awake.

"Morning. We need to get up if we don't want to be late for our morning lecture," I replied brightly, not drawing attention to her snuggling. I didn't want her to feel embarrassed about it.

She nodded, pulling back and climbing out of bed as if her ass was on fire. She quickly snatched her clothes from the drawer she had here and darted from the room to get ready for the day.

I scrubbed my hands over my face before doing the same, quickly changing into my track pants, a shirt, and grabbing my hoodie and sneakers from the pile I'd left them in on the floor last night.

I brushed my hair and pulled my hood over my head once I was done, and by the time I had everything I'd need for the day and my bat in my grip, Luna wandered back in. She didn't meet my eye as she put her shoes on and followed me down to the kitchen. I decided to let her freak out in silence. Anything I said would make it worse anyway.

Particularly the part where I liked her heated core against me and wanted to pull her shorts to the side to shove my fingers inside her.

We ate breakfast silently too, and Mom gave us a frown from across the table as she sipped her coffee. "What's going on with you two? You're acting weird."

Luna tensed, making Mom's suspicions worse, but I shrugged. "Nothing. I'm just tired as fuck."

She hummed, telling me she didn't believe me, but she wasn't going to pry. "Remember to be home for dinner. Kate will be here and your friend would probably feel more comfortable coming to see her if you're home too."

"I planned on it," I grumbled, getting to my feet. "Come on, Lou. Let's get going before we're late."

"Thank you for letting me stay, Rory," Luna smiled sweetly at Mom, making her roll her eyes.

"I don't know how Hendricks ended up with such a polite kid. You know you're welcome anytime. Whether Riley's here or not."

"I know," she replied, thanking her again before following me outside to her car.

I went to get in the passenger seat, but she cringed. "I'm going to stop by Stan's this morning."

"Why? Need to erase the gay off you after sleeping next to me all night?" I asked sharply, her face falling. I wasn't usually so sensitive about it, but lately, it was getting hard to keep my emotions to myself.

I wanted to control the words coming from my mouth, but I couldn't stop them.

"It's not like that," she said as her forehead creased and she bit her lip nervously.

"Whatever. I'll see you later when you don't feel so dirty." Avoiding her gaze, I took off towards the garage, fishing my keys from my pocket. I climbed into my Corvette and put the window down so I could have a cigarette, leaving the engine off so I could have a moment of silence to calm down. I knew she wasn't into me and that it freaked her out when we got too close, but the longer I kept my feelings to myself, the more frustrated I was getting.

She'd never return my feelings.

I rested my elbow on the open window, leaning my

cheek against my fist as I smoked, trying to calm my mood. I wanted to tell her how much she meant to me, but I knew she'd probably run for the fucking hills, and losing her would kill me.

"Do you want to talk about it?"

I took a drag of my cigarette, not bothering to look up at the sound of Diesel's voice.

"Not particularly."

"I have a job to do in Stoneleigh. You want to skip your lectures today and come with me?" he offered, making me frown. I finally met his gaze, not hiding my confusion.

"What job? And Mom will kill me if I don't go. I need to be home for dinner too."

He grinned, his voice low. "She can't kill you if she doesn't know, and you'll be home for dinner. I need to see Rage about something. So, how about it? You want to spend the day with your old man?"

I couldn't stop the small smile that tugged at my lips. "You're hardly old, Dad."

"No? You're older than your mother was when I met her. So you make me feel *really* old," he teased, taking my keys from me. "And I'm going gray, so I can't deny it anymore. Jump in the Escalade."

"Why are we taking that?" I asked, raising an eyebrow, but he gave me a serious look as he opened the door for me.

"Because it's got bulletproof windows."

"But it's Rage's territory. Why would anyone risk shooting at us there?"

He sighed, locking my car as I climbed out with my bat, and followed me across the massive garage to unlock the black Escalade. "A lot of people don't like that Rage has both a crew and an MC for starters. Some of their rivals might target us. The MC Chapter up north have had some problems lately, which is why the Kings' crew has joined forces with them. We also like to be careful just in case the Kings decide to turn on us. Can't be too careful in this life, you know that."

I knew to keep a gun within reaching distance when on the road as a precaution, and all of our cars had one stashed. Most of my parents had multiples in their cars in case war broke out. I'd had to take shots at people once or twice in my whole life, so I knew to always be prepared for the unexpected.

I thought the bulletproof glass was a bit much though, especially since I knew for a fact the Escalade had no less than three guns hidden inside it.

We pulled out of the garage, and I checked my phone as a text came through as we hit the road.

> Mom: Tell D I'll castrate him if you're late for dinner. Love you both.

I chuckled, quickly telling her we'd be home on time before I glanced at Dad to relay her message, making him cringe. "She's terrifying when she wants to be. I don't know if she's plotting revenge on me or not for taking you away from your education."

"You should've known she'd see me leave with you," I replied, turning my attention back out the window. "Why did you want me to come with you?"

"You looked like you needed it," he answered simply, heading towards Rawson Grove which was the quickest way to Stoneleigh. "I know you said you don't want to talk about it, but I figured maybe you'd like to get away from her for the day."

"Mom?" I asked with confusion as I glanced at him.

"Luna," he corrected. "I'm not prying into your personal

life, but I know you're struggling to keep your feelings to yourself lately."

"I don't like her like that," I argued, but he knew I was full of shit.

"Take today to just breathe, okay? Hang out with Phoenix or something."

"Oh, her daddy would *love* that," I grunted, knowing Rage hated any of us near his precious daughter. He was worried Beckett would get her into trouble, and he was worried I'd get her naked.

I'd never cross that line, not when she could possibly be my cousin by blood. Rage should've been more worried about those who watched over her. She was always checking out the Kings MC members half the time when he wasn't paying attention, and a few of them had humored it for a while.

Jaxon, a member of the crew, usually kept them away from her though. He was working his way up the ranks with ease from what I'd heard, and he was doing everything to prove his loyalty to Rage.

"I swear I had a full tank of gas," Diesel grumbled as we neared Stoneleigh almost an hour later, and he flipped on his turning signal to turn off at the gas station. He hadn't, but I didn't correct him.

He jumped out to fill up, my eyes catching on a familiar black Supra at one of the other pumps. I was going to ignore him, but just as I went to look away, Turbo glanced up and met my gaze. He smirked, tilting his chin at me to motion me over, so I cursed under my breath and climbed out, leaving my bat in the car and walking over to lean against his Supra.

"Turbo," I greeted, biting back a groan when tires squealed and Slick's Mustang pulled up behind us. He climbed out and gave me a filthy look, apparently not wanting to undress me with his eyes for once.

"What the fuck are you doing here?" Slick scowled before continuing his shit. "Sniffing around Turbo's cock won't do you any good."

I laughed, turning to Turbo and giving him a wink. "Oh, I'm not too sure about that. I bet he could fuck the gay out of me. Right, handsome?"

Turbo snorted, eyeing my father discreetly across the gas station while speaking to me in a low voice. "I highly doubt that. You like pussy more than most men I know."

"I'd probably scare you anyway. What are you guys doing?" I asked, glancing back at Slick who was now right beside me. "Sexually assaulted anyone today?"

"Not yet, but it's on the cards," he sneered, looking me up and down slowly. "You act tough, but you'd be screaming on my cock in seconds if I got those panties off."

I noticed Dad's back muscles tense, and I knew he'd give me a few minutes to deal with my own shit before he intervened. Slick was lucky it wasn't Skeeter or Slash, or he'd already have a bullet in him.

"You know those girls scream because they're trying to get away from you, right?" I said dryly and gave him my back to dismiss him, clenching my fists when he wrapped an arm around my chest to haul me back, his hot breath fanning across my cheek as he chuckled.

"I'm aware. The way you keep taunting me tells me you must like the idea of that. Are you playing hard to get?"

"Hey, don't touch her," Turbo warned, narrowing his eyes as he finished pumping his own gas. "You know the rules. Not her or Blake."

I scoffed, giving him a dirty look. "We're the *exceptions*? He shouldn't be allowed to touch anyone without their permission. Fuck you, asshole. I thought you were better than that."

"He's not allowed to fuck with anyone, but you girls are one of us," he threw back, his eyes flicking over my shoulder towards my dad who was probably on his way over to put a bullet in Slick's kneecap for touching me.

Slick's hand trailed down my stomach, but before I could snap at him to fuck off, I heard the click of a gun behind us.

"Let her go and fuck off before I make your skull look like Swiss cheese."

I frowned, not recognizing the voice.

Slick let go, and I turned to find two guys behind us, one with a dark brown buzz cut who had a gun aimed at the side of Slick's head, and the other had dirty blond hair that fell over his sharp gaze. The blond guy gave me a once-over while the other stepped closer and tapped the barrel of his gun against Slick's head. "I said fuck off. Are you deaf?"

Slick glared at me as if this were my fault, but Turbo cleared his throat, stopping anything he wanted to spew at me. "Slick. Go. We don't need the heat, dude." Slick cursed at me and spat at my feet before stalking back to his car and slamming the door, taking off with a screech of tires. Turbo scrubbed a hand over his face, looking tired all of a sudden. "He's getting worse."

"Then stop letting him get away with it," I hissed, punching his shoulder, not that he even flinched. "You would've stabbed him two years ago for the shit you roll your eyes at now. If you don't rein him in, I'm siccing my sister on him. He's a menace."

"Riley, right?" the blond guy asked, making me stiffen. I hated it when people knew who I was when I had no idea who they were.

"That depends on who's asking," I said flatly, making him smirk.

"Yeah, you're Donovan's sister alright."

I relaxed, glancing at his friend. "You two know Beckett?"

Buzz cut finally put his gun away, meeting my gaze with a singular nod. "We're associates, yes."

"And you are?"

"None of your business," he snorted, but the blond guy was grinning like an idiot, throwing off golden retriever vibes hard.

"Don't be an asshole to her. I'm Cruz, this is Stone."

"The Night Thieves?"

I didn't know the exact details, but they'd helped my family save Jett when the Hell's Demons' crew had kidnapped him recently, and the Night Thieves had held some prisoners for the crews to torture to death too. That meant they were trustworthy.

"Your sister talks too much," Stone said coldly, glancing at Turbo. "My invitation to fuck off was also for you. Keep your predator friend out of Rawson Grove. You feel me?"

Dad was standing behind them now, his eyes burning into Turbo curiously. He was going to have a million questions about him and Slick that I couldn't give him answers to. He couldn't find out about the street racing, and if I said they were from the track, he'd ask Beckett about them.

Turbo nodded, glancing at me. "Tomorrow night. Usual spot and time. Bring Reid."

Fuck, Dad definitely heard that.

"I'll swing by if I have time," I replied lazily, his eyes narrowing as he started walking towards the driver's side door.

"Make fucking time, Donovan." Then he got inside and

slammed the door, leaving a lot more quietly than Slick had, but I heard him burning rubber once he got out onto the main road.

Stone was death-glaring me, but Cruz struck up a conversation as if we were besties.

"You're not going to set someone on fire at our place like your sister did, are you? We still can't get the smell out."

"Cruz, shut up," Stone snapped, having the decency to face Dad and hold his hand out to shake. "Diesel."

Dad shook it, but his eyes were on me. "Stone. I wasn't aware my daughter was going to bring trouble with us."

"I don't think it's possible for your kids to roll through town without causing a problem. Have you had any issues lately with street racers?" Stone asked, but his attention was back on me, waiting for my reaction. I didn't give him one, but by the way he was eyeing me, he knew I was involved.

Dad frowned, crossing his arms and swinging his gaze to the guys. "Street racers don't last long in Ashburn. We've got the track, and that seems to keep the kids occupied. You guys have a problem with them here?"

I pulled my attention away from them, finding Cruz smirking at me knowingly. He spoke to Stone without looking away from me. "I'm going to grab a coke. You want anything?"

"Hurry up," Stone warned, and I cleared my throat when Cruz raised an eyebrow at me.

"Uh, I'm thirsty too. I'll grab us a drink, Dad." He gave me a strange look, glancing between me and Cruz, but he nodded and let me go. I scowled as Cruz chuckled once we were inside, and I considered punching him. "What's your deal? What's funny?"

"We have the entire town under surveillance. You don't think we see everything that happens here or notice your

Corvette and Supra are usually one of the cars screaming around in the middle of the night? Your sister hasn't said anything about you racing here," he replied lightly, snatching three cokes and handing me two.

"Beckett can't find out, asshole," I said as my eyes bored into him. "She has her habits and I have mine."

"Give me one reason why we shouldn't tell her," he smirked, walking towards the register and motioning to all three drinks before waving his card at the employee.

"What loyalty do you have to her?" I continued, refusing to let him destroy the one thing I loved doing.

"She's scary."

"You don't think I am too? I'll beat your skull in with my baseball bat in seconds and leave you here for the crows," I spat as the employee's eyes widened with horror.

Cruz grinned, finding me hilarious. "Stop making jokes like that. You'll scare people."

"That's the idea. My bat's in the Escalade if you really want to test me," I snarked, grabbing his wrist and tugging him towards the door. "Keep your mouth shut about what I get up to, you got that?"

"Chill," he laughed, pulling my hood off to pat my head. "Don't cross us and we won't say shit. Your family drama doesn't affect us."

"Bite me, jackass."

"Word of advice? Get new friends. Those guys are assholes," he sighed, giving me a fake look of pity. "If you need to have some girl talk, you can always come and hang out with me. Beckett will vouch for me. I'm a really good listener and I love a good gossip session."

Diesel barked at me to hurry up so we could leave, and once we were shut in the Escalade where the Night Thieves couldn't hear us, he turned to me with narrowed eyes.

"What the fuck, Riley?"

"What?" I shrugged, strapping myself in. "I didn't do anything."

"If you're having problems with a guy harassing you—"

"I'm not having any fucking problems," I said sharply as I cut him off. "I'm friends with one of them, and the asshole is *his* friend. Turbo won't let him touch me."

"*Turbo* watched his friend manhandle you and hardly did shit. It took Stone fucking Barrett to step in. How do you even know Turbo? He's not in our crowd."

"*I'm* not in our crowd," I answered dryly, glaring out the window to see Cruz and Stone walking away, both of them glancing back at us every so often, probably wondering why we hadn't left yet. "I have my own friends, Dad."

"Yeah, well, Ander *'Turbo'* Lavaro isn't good company to keep," he growled, making me tense. I didn't like that he knew exactly who he was because that meant he knew what he got up to in his spare time.

"I stay out of his private business and he stays out of mine. We respect that," I said calmly as I peered over at him, my stomach twisting as he started the engine and shook his head.

"If I get one whiff of that fucker dragging you into his bullshit, I'm putting him down."

"He won't let me near his drugs or whatever the fuck he's running, I swear," I replied as he drove out onto the main road, luckily not looking at me to see me cringe as he answered.

"I'm talking about his fucking underground car races, not his wannabe mafia bullshit. Big money for big stakes. I could write you a book on the list of people who have been seriously injured or killed while participating in his races. I know you like fast cars, you spend more time at the track than Beckett or the guys, but don't let him tempt you, okay? It's not worth it."

If only he knew just how far I'd go to feel that rush.

"Oh, brilliant. You brought my favorite niece with you," Rage deadpanned as we walked into the Kings' crew house. I'd put my hood back on in the car, but I pulled it off now, giving him a bright smile, knowing he'd act like he hated it, when in reality, he was a big ol' softie for me.

"Hey, Angry Man. Did you miss me?"

"Never, you little shit," he grunted, his bulky, tattooed arms crossed tightly. "Did you come here just to piss me off? Or did your mother finally decide she's had enough of you and I get to bury you in the yard somewhere?"

Diesel grumbled about him being an asshole, but I laughed, annoying Rage as I threw my arms around his neck and kissed his cheek. "Love you too."

"Get the fuck off me," he snarled, shoving me so gently that it did nothing. "Go play at the bar. Plenty of tits over there for you to be occupied with for the remainder of your visit."

"Aw, you do love me," I cooed, not missing the small smile he tried to keep to himself as I walked off to the bar, not surprised to find Sniper behind it. He'd always run the bar at the MC Clubhouse, and that didn't change when he became the president of the MC.

Rage was one hundred percent in charge, but he'd needed someone to run the MC while he was with the crew.

Sniper visited regularly though so I had no idea who was in charge when he was here.

I sat on a barstool, giving him a smile. "Hey."

He glanced over, his eyes softening when he saw me, the creases around his eyes looking worse. I swore he'd aged ten years since I'd seen him a few months ago.

"What are you doing here? It's unlike you to visit."

"Diesel offered for me to come with him. How are you?"

"I'm surviving."

"I'm sorry," I murmured, hating that his entire life had been flipped upside down by the loss of his traitorous boyfriend. "Want to get drunk with me?"

"I've been managing perfectly fine with that task on my own," he replied lightly, but he walked around the bar and sat beside me, reaching for two glasses and a bottle of whiskey. He poured us both a glass each and sat in silence for a while until he spoke. "You got girl drama? You're not usually the type to mope and drink in the morning."

"We always fall for the ones who will just hurt us, don't we?" I mumbled, staring at my glass. "I'm starting to think it's a gay person thing."

He chuckled, but it sounded forced. "Sounds about right. I've sworn off relationships for the rest of my life."

"I'll drink to that," I snorted, lifting my glass to salute him before taking a large mouthful, the burning liquid sliding down my throat and helping me to temporarily numb my problems.

He had more things to be miserable about since the man he'd loved his entire life had turned out to be the backstabbing snake, Kristoff Lopez, so in comparison to him, I had nothing to complain about.

It wasn't every day a rival crew successfully sent in a

spy, but the Demons had Kristoff posing as Jonny for over twenty years.

I hated that bastard, not only for living a second life behind Sniper's back and betraying him, but also for what he'd done to Maddox as a kid. His own goddamn *nephew*.

I couldn't believe my brother shared blood with that piece of shit.

We drank until Diesel and Rage joined us, Diesel letting out a sigh. "You're drunk."

"Little bit," I grinned, leaning against the bar, my eyes catching on a woman as she walked through the door. "Quick, Dad. Move. You're going to cramp my style."

He rolled his eyes, turning his attention to Sniper. "You got her drunk? It's not even noon."

"She got *me* drunk, asshole," he threw back, getting to his feet. "I need to restock the bar. See you next time." Then he stumbled off without another word.

Rage grumbled about him being a useless prick, but I knew it was said with love. Rage didn't make time for anyone outside his family, but he respected Sniper. Especially after siding with the Kings over his own boyfriend who he'd been dating since he was a teenager. That spoke volumes for his loyalty.

"We need to get going," Diesel said firmly, not happy about me being drunk. "If you throw up on the drive home, I'll be pissed."

"Bye, Angry Man!" I practically shouted as I stood to head outside, waving dramatically and ignoring his cursing. He didn't really hate it, he just didn't want his men to know that.

Within two seconds of us being on the road, I passed out, dreaming about trailing my tongue all over Luna's hot little body as her fingers yanked on my hair while I made her scream my name.

Luna

Riley never showed up to our lecture, and she ignored my text when I asked her where she was. Landon didn't have any classes until the afternoon, so I drove to Stanley's.

I parked beside his car, climbing out and sighing as I heard the loud music. He'd been partying a lot, and it was annoying the hell out of me. He was hard to get a hold of, and it meant we never got time alone anymore since he always had people over.

I didn't like social gatherings, which was why I'd hardly seen him lately. At least I'd been able to spend some time with Riley.

There were only two other cars here, neither of which I recognized.

I headed inside, scrunching my nose as the strong smell of cigarettes and weed hit me. He never allowed smoking inside before.

"Are you lost?"

I looked beside me to find some girl, her face coated in makeup and a drink in her hand. She was dressed as if this was a cocktail party, a stunning dress hugging her body with high, strappy heels on her feet.

"No. Where's Stan?" I asked, but she grabbed my arm tightly, digging her nails in.

"Look, bitch. This isn't some walk-in party. It's invite only."

"I'm his girlfriend," I replied with a tight smile, amusement filling her eyes.

"Yeah, right."

I had no idea why she didn't believe me, but I was saved from explaining myself further as Stanley stumbled over, a grin on his face. "There's my girl! I didn't know you were coming!"

The girl looked horrified, but I ignored her and tucked myself under his arm, giving him a kiss.

"I was going to see if you wanted to watch a movie with me, but it seems you're having a party."

"Grab a drink and join us. The others are in the living room," he answered, gently pushing me in the direction of the kitchen. He muttered something to the girl, but he quickly followed to make me a drink before leading me to the others.

He tugged me down onto his lap once he was seated on the couch, nuzzling into my neck. "I missed you."

My chest warmed, and I took a sip of my ridiculously strong drink before replying. "I missed you too."

"Stay with me tonight?" he asked, biting my earlobe. "Find a way to convince your dad to let you."

"I have dinner plans, but I can try to come back for a few hours afterwards," I offered, making him frown.

"What dinner plans?"

"Rory's having some family dinner for a new kid she's helping," I shrugged, a scoff leaving him.

"So Riley invited you?"

"Well, yeah."

I had no idea why they hated each other so much, but it was getting ridiculous.

"You're just a challenge for her to conquer, babe. I bet if you let her fuck you, you'd never see her again," he grunted, his arm tightening around me protectively. "Just stay here. You have to stop jumping when she tells you to. Where is she right now?" My face heated with embarrassment, making him roll his eyes. "See? You don't know where she is, but she expects you to be available whenever she wants. You let her walk all over you and I hate it."

"She's my best friend," I said awkwardly, but he just shook his head as if he was disappointed with me. I always tried hard to please him, but it never seemed like enough.

"No. She's using you. She's been chasing your pussy forever. Bail on dinner and show her she's not in charge of you."

I thought the music was too loud for anyone else to hear us, but his friends all seemed to be waiting for my response. If I fought him on it, he'd look like an idiot in front of them and he'd be upset with me, but if I agreed, I'd piss Riley off.

"I guess I could stay here instead," I said slowly as I finally nodded, relaxing as he smiled.

"That's my girl. Come on, drink more. You've got to catch up."

I tried hard not to throw up as I downed my drink, and by the time I'd finished my second, Stanley was getting handsy. It wasn't unusual, we had a pretty active sex life, but I always felt awkward when he was so public with it.

The girl from earlier was glaring at me as she sat on another guy's lap on the other couch, her lip lifting into a sneer as I brushed Stanley's wandering hand from my breast. "Stop being such a prude. He's your boyfriend, isn't he?"

The guy she was sitting on snickered, running his gaze over me. "I bet she's a virgin."

"Don't be a dick," Stanley scolded, throwing an empty beer can at him. "She's been on my dick for years. Your ugly mug is probably making her uncomfortable."

"She doesn't even have tits. Is she legal?"

I looked away from him, knowing my face was bright red. I honestly didn't have boobs, my body was flat all over and I hated it, but the guy didn't have to point it out for everyone to notice.

"I love her tits, fuck you," Stanley laughed, leaning back on the couch and pulling me with him, my back flush with his chest as his hands cupped my breasts. "They're the perfect size."

"Stop it," I said as discomfort washed through me, swatting at his hands. "We don't need to talk about my boobs."

"Why not? They're nice." His lips trailed down my neck, his voice dropping. "Your shirt's just hiding them, that's all."

The girl muttered about him being full of shit as she climbed from the guy's lap and left the room, one of the other girls chasing after her. I heard the door slam, telling me they'd left.

"Show him," Stanley breathed out beside my ear, making me tense. "Show Raymond those perky tits."

"W–what?" I stammered, my stomach twisting as he gently squeezed them through my shirt.

"C'mon. Give him a peek at the goods. Don't let him talk down to you like that," he demanded, sliding his hands down my stomach to grab the bottom of my shirt. "You're hot, babe. Don't be shy."

"No," I said firmly, wriggling on his lap to try and get up. "I don't care if he doesn't like my tits. I'm not here to impress him."

"Live a little. I'm not asking you to fuck him or anything," he grinned, kissing my cheek. "Unless you want to experience a threesome, then I'd allow him to get between those pretty thighs of yours."

My heart was hammering in my chest, and fear tore

through me as he pushed my hands out of the way to pull my shirt up. "Stanley!"

"They're just tits, Luna. Relax," he scoffed, having no issue restraining me so he could flash my boobs to his friends, some of them snickering at me. Tears burned my eyes as the cool air hit my nipples, and Raymond gave me a smirk.

"They're not bad for small tits."

"They're just the right size," Stanley argued, reaching up to tweak one of my nipples painfully before cupping one in his palm. "They're sensitive too. Right, babe?"

"You're being an ass," I forced out, trying to fix my shirt but he held firm as his friend got to his feet and walked towards us. I shrunk back against Stanley as Raymond peered down at me, tilting his head.

"I guess they're cute."

"Seriously, dude. Big tits are overrated. Cop a feel. These are way better," Stanley insisted, and it took me a second to understand what he said. I jerked as his friend didn't hesitate to reach out and palm my breast, a tear finally falling and my throat went tight.

Stanley had never acted like this before, and he never let his friends disrespect me. Would he let them go further without my permission?

"You're pretty when you cry," Raymond murmured, a sick smile spreading across his lips as he held my gaze, leaning down to take my nipple between his teeth. He bit down firmly, making me squeal from the sharp pain.

"Don't touch me!" I snapped, but it came out as a sob, amusing him.

"Relax. I'm not going to fuck you right now."

That didn't make me feel any better. He had rocks in his head if he thought I'd ever let him sleep with me.

Stanley fixed my shirt with a snort, finding my reaction dramatic. "We're just playing, babe. There's no need to get upset about it."

He placed me on the couch beside him to grab us more drinks, and I hated how Raymond kept eyeing me silently from his seat. The others had moved on with their conversations, but not him. He just kept staring at me like a creep.

I took small sips of my drink once Stanley handed it back, but he kept chucking them down my throat like water, replacing them the moment they were empty. Luckily, they were all drinking just as much too, so once they'd passed out, I stumbled towards the door and headed to my car, locking myself inside it.

I was way too drunk to drive, but I had to get out of here. Tears fell uncontrollably as I started the engine and backed out of the driveway, and I could hardly see as I drove slowly along the road.

I had to pull myself together before anyone saw me or they'd ask questions, and I didn't want to come across as a crybaby. It's not like they'd raped me or anything. I'd seen Stanley's friends share girlfriends before, so maybe that girl had been right and I was just being a prude.

I had no idea where I was going, but I somehow got to Riley's house in one piece, turning the engine off to give myself five minutes of peace.

I wasn't ready to go inside yet.

80
100
120
140
160
180
200
220
km/h
240
260

Chapter Seven

Riley

I was pissed that Luna had ignored my texts and calls all evening. If she was that upset with me about that morning, she could've just told me she wasn't coming.

Blake and Kate were laughing at the other end of the table while Beckett and Maddox were ganging up on Jett to make him take shots, and Mom's eyes were firmly glued to me across the table. She knew I was mad, but she didn't bother asking me what was wrong.

She knew I'd been waiting for Luna.

Ryder walked in with a frown on his face, dropping his car keys on the counter.

"You're late," Mikey observed with a grin. "You're basically begging Mom to let you do the dishes."

He ignored him, turning to me. "What's up with Luna?"

"What do you mean?" I snorted. "She's being a bitch again. Where did you see her? She's supposed to be here but she's ignoring me."

"Uhhh," he dragged out slowly, giving me a weird look. "She's asleep in her car out front."

"What?" I demanded, shoving my chair back. "She's here?"

"Yeah. I knocked on the window, but she must be in a deep sleep," he shrugged, and I didn't hang around longer to find out more. I headed straight into the cool night air, walking towards her car and peering inside, finding her asleep with her face turned away from the window.

I knocked loudly for ages until she stirred, her eyes finally meeting mine with confusion. They were glassy, and my suspicions were confirmed when she opened the door and the smell of booze hit me.

"You fucking drove here drunk?" I hissed, snatching her keys and eyeing her with annoyance. "You didn't even put a seat belt on?"

"I can't go home this drunk," she slurred, trying to get out but almost landing on her face. "I wanted to come stay with you."

I sighed, slipping an arm around her waist to hold her up so I could shut the door and lock her car. "You should've called me."

I was probably way over the legal limit myself, but I would've made someone take me to her. Luna hated it when I'd driven drunk in the past, so I never expected her to do it.

I practically had to carry her inside, her feet dragging as I helped her up the steps. Everyone glanced up as we walked in, and I was relieved when Ryder got to his feet to help.

"I've got her," he offered, and as much as I wanted to argue, it would be a lot easier for him to take her. He hooked an arm under her legs and back, lifting her against his chest to carry her up to my room, and I gave Mom a pleading look on my way past.

"Don't tell Archer or Lexi."

"Honey, she's so drunk she can't even stand up on her own," she sighed, frustration in her gaze. "She shouldn't have been anywhere near the driver's seat."

"I know. I'll talk to her about it. Please, don't—"

"Riley," she bit out, surprising me. Mom rarely got mad at me. "If you were doing something reckless like that and her parents knew about it, I'd expect them to inform me. I'm not going to keep this from them. I'm sorry."

Archer would flip his shit and he'd definitely take her car away. Being safe on the road was the one rule we all had, so they had no problem taking them away from us for reckless behavior.

I didn't bother arguing, turning around and heading up to my room to find Ryder tucking Luna under the covers.

"She's out cold. Why the hell did she get that drunk?" he murmured, standing back to stare at her. "Is Mom going to rat her out?"

"Yep. Archer's probably going to show up soon and drag her home," I grumbled, looking up at him. "Thanks for putting her in bed."

"It's okay. I'm glad she got here in one piece," he answered, kissing the top of my head. "I'll make sure Blake's set up in her own room. It's a bit cramped in here."

"Thanks, Ry," I smiled, waiting for him to leave the room before I locked the door and turned to face Luna. She was snoring softly, her brown hair tangled and her shirt twisted.

I grabbed a shirt and some sweats to get changed into, figuring she was in a deep enough sleep for me to just change in the room. I slid my hoodie over my head, stripped down to my panties, and quickly pulled my sweats and shirt on, then I switched off the light and climbed into bed behind her.

She surprisingly shuffled back against me as I dropped an arm around her middle, and I placed a quick kiss on her shoulder as I got comfortable.

"Sweet dreams, Lou."

I woke to the sound of someone trying to unlock my door. I glanced at my phone to see it wasn't even seven in the morning yet, and since no one called out to me, I knew it wasn't my family.

I silently climbed out of bed, grabbing my bat from the floor before creeping towards the door, gripping it firmly in my hands as I swung it back, ready to swing at the intruder. I reached out to flip the lock, yanking the door open, and swinging the bat hard.

Archer's hand snapped out and grabbed it before it could connect with his head, annoyance in his gaze. "Don't you check before swinging?"

"No. Those few seconds could result in me or Luna getting hurt instead of a predator," I hissed, my heartbeat hammering as I tried to calm down. "What the fuck are you doing trying to break into my room?"

"She's lucky I didn't come over here last night and drag her ass home. She's grounded for fucking life," he threw back, looking over my shoulder and seeming surprised to see her sleeping peacefully in my bed. "Why's she in your bed? I swear to God, if you—"

"I'm not going to corrupt your daughter and magically make her gay," I deadpanned, leaning against the door frame and placing my bat beside me. "She always sleeps in my bed. I have control, unlike that dumbass boyfriend of hers."

I had no idea if he was pushy with her, but I got those vibes from him, so I was rolling with it.

"That *dumbass* boyfriend called me last night, freaking out that she'd gone missing. He said they'd been drinking and he'd passed out, but when he woke up she'd vanished. Did she mention why she left?" he asked, making me snort.

"You really believe him? Luna wouldn't drive in that state without a damn good reason. He only called you to cover his own ass. I bet he did something."

He rubbed his temples, glancing back at her sleeping form. "You need to let it go, Riley."

"Let what go?" I demanded, motioning to her. "Look at her. She was so fucking drunk last night that Ryder found her asleep in her car out front. He had to carry her up here because she couldn't stand up. She doesn't just go for drunken drives to clear her head. She had to be running from him."

He pinned me with a firm look, but his voice was low. "I mean, you need to let their relationship go. I know you like her more than a friend, but you can't just make him out to be the bad guy to break them up. I don't like him that much either, but he doesn't hurt her and she's happy with him."

"You honestly think that's my problem? I'm jealous?" I growled, but he observed her, not bothering to fight with me about it.

"It doesn't matter. I wasn't kidding when I said she was grounded for life. You'll see her at school or my place, and that's it."

"She's an adult!"

"Then she should fucking act like it!" he suddenly

shouted as he spun around to face me, losing his patience. "She's lucky she didn't kill herself or anyone else last night!"

Luna stirred, a groan leaving her. "Why are you yelling? I'm trying to sleep."

He stomped towards her, flinging the blanket back and grabbing her arm. "Get up."

"Why?" she complained, scowling as he jerked her upright. "What the hell, Dad? If I throw up on you, that's your own fault."

He was seething, but I could see the fear radiating out of him. He was terrified of the thought that he could've lost her last night. He was overreacting, but I shouldn't have been surprised.

Luna was his baby girl, his good kid, and he wasn't used to her acting out.

"You're grounded. All privileges revoked. You go to school, you come home. That's it," he spat. "Say goodbye to Riley and make sure you thank Rory for letting you stay when we leave."

She was suddenly wide awake, her eyes raking over me with confusion. "Riley? I—"

"You don't remember? I'm not surprised," he snapped, his face twisting with disappointment. "You got so drunk you could hardly walk, then you drove here. Stanley panicked when he woke up to find you gone last night."

Her eyes widened for a moment before she slammed a hand over her mouth. She looked freaked out, which I didn't understand until she gagged.

"Uh, Arch? She's going to be sick."

He let her go and she stumbled to the bathroom that was connected to my room, not bothering to close the door as she dropped to her knees and threw up in the toilet loudly. I followed, moving behind her to pull her hair back as she threw up again.

"I've never seen you this bad, Lou. Why'd you drink that much before coming here?"

She didn't reply, too busy bringing all the alcohol up, so I stood there in silence until she was done.

Once she flushed, she turned to me with a wince. "Sorry. I don't really remember what happened last night. I just got too drunk and I think I caused a scene in front of Stan's friends. He probably thinks I'm a total bitch."

"You got in a fight?" I frowned, but I didn't have time to figure it out because Archer walked in and glared at her.

"We're going. You can have a pity party at home."

"I'll have to get Riley to run my car home," she mumbled, but he shook his head.

"That's not necessary."

I didn't like the tone he was using.

A loud bang echoed through the house, and my heart hammered at the familiar sound. Images flashed through my head of Lloyd's accident, his Dodge Viper bursting into flames and exploding.

I left them in the bathroom, running through the house and almost colliding with Beckett who had pure panic on her face. She knew that sound well too.

We headed out front to find Luna's car parked further away from the house, the bright flames engulfing it as Skeeter stood off to the side with a gas can at his feet.

"What the fuck, Dad?" Beckett snapped, losing her cool completely. Her voice cracked, the terror weakening as anger took over. She'd been taken back to Lloyd's death too, but she held a different trauma response to me. She was terrified of accidents, while I chased the devil with flames licking at my heels. As much as the explosion had dragged me back to the past, it had pulled Beckett into a freak-out, thinking someone else had died.

"What the hell?" Luna gasped as she joined us, turning to Archer. "What—"

"This is what happens when children can't respect their toys," he said sternly, my jaw dropping.

Everyone else started wandering outside to see what was going on, Blake's eyes almost popping out of her head when she realized what had happened. Kate looked upset, so she ushered her back inside, knowing she didn't need to witness what was happening. I liked Blake, she minded her own fucking business.

"You set her car on fire as punishment?" I asked Archer in disbelief, and Diesel moved beside me with a sigh.

"You know the rules. Children don't get adult things."

"But he blew it up!"

He looked down at me, his stare blank but I could hear the underlying meaning behind his words. "Yes. If any of you disrespect your cars, this is what happens. You know this. If you're reckless, you lose things. You kids all need to learn that having a car is a privilege, not a right."

Luna stayed silent, watching her Corvette burn, and when Archer grabbed her bicep and tugged her towards his car as he scolded her all over again, she didn't argue.

Beckett had vanished, needing a minute to calm down, and I turned around to find Mom behind me, her eyes already on me.

"I don't know why he thought that was a good punishment. I'll just give her my Supra."

She shrugged and hooked her thumbs into the pockets of her jeans, her eyes drifting towards the burning car. "That's fine, but if she's reckless in that, Archer has permission to do as he pleases with it."

"You'd let him trash my fucking car?" I demanded, her eyes narrowing as she turned to me.

"Yes, because if you're going to try and find a loophole to his punishment, then you can suffer too. He took her car away for a reason, Riley. Don't fuck with his parenting."

"We're twenty!"

"You might be an adult, but you're still our kids, honey." She rubbed her temples, emotion in her voice. "We know the damage cars can cause."

"Don't drag us into your bullshit about Lloyd," I hissed, hurt filling her eyes that were a mirror image of mine. "He didn't die from being reckless. He died because your lifestyle got him killed."

"Riley," Skeeter warned, but I ignored him and stormed inside, heading up to my room to get dressed. I needed to go for a drive and clear my head before meeting up with Turbo later, and no offense to Blake, but I wasn't hanging around the house to make her feel comfortable.

Luna

"I can't fucking believe you," Dad growled as he drove me home, raking his fingers through his scruffy beard. "What the hell made you drive to Riley's while that drunk?"

"I don't remember," I lied, not wanting to tell him the truth. "It was stupid, I'm sorry."

"You bet your ass it was stupid. I mean it. You're at home unless you're at school. If you want to spend time with Stanley or Riley, they come to you, and only when I say so."

"Yes, Dad," I mumbled, staring out the window.

We didn't talk for the rest of the drive, and Mom gave

me a disappointed look as we walked inside. "Call Stan and let him know you're alright. We told him you were at Riley's, but he's still worried."

I nodded, wandering to my room and shutting the door, closing my eyes as my emotions rose to the surface again. I couldn't believe Stanley would treat me like that, and part of me wondered if it had been a terrible dream instead.

I pulled my phone from my pocket, finding it almost dead, so I plugged it in before calling him. It rang twice before he answered, his voice frantic. "Babe? Are you alright?"

"I'm fine."

"I'm so sorry. I was way too drunk last night, I shouldn't have spoken to you like I did," he blurted out, making me frown. I hadn't expected him to apologize.

"Really? You're sorry?" I asked, a deep breath leaving him.

"Yeah, I am. I have no excuse for my behavior other than I was too drunk, and that's a terrible excuse. Can you forgive me? Please? I swear—"

"It's okay," I said quietly, relaxing at knowing he didn't mean to take it that far. "I don't like your friends. I've never met them before and—"

"I won't let them speak to you like that again, alright?" he promised. "How much trouble are you in?"

"I'm grounded for life and Dad got Skeeter to set my car on fire, so I'd say I'm in deep shit," I sighed, scrubbing a hand over my face. "If you want to see me, you have to come here. I'm not allowed anywhere except school."

"He burned your car? Jesus. He knows you're twenty, right? Why don't you just move out? He can't stop you."

"I can't afford to move out," I said and hung my head in

shame as if he could see me. "I only have money because I'm here. If I left, I'd need a job or something."

"Just walk out and tell him you're staying at mine tonight. He can't force you to stay home."

"You think I should argue with him?" I questioned, unsure if I liked the idea. "I don't want to be a bitch to him. He's just worried about me."

"He needs to treat you as an adult. Show him he can't push you around anymore. Stay with me for a few days at least," he suggested, hope blooming in my chest as he continued. "We can have movie nights and dinner."

"A few days? Are you sure?"

"Positive. He'll calm down by then and everything will be back to normal."

"I'll talk to Mom and Dad then call you back," I finally decided, nerves mixing with excitement. "You'll have to come and get me since I don't have a car anymore," I added with a cringe, a loud snort leaving him.

"Yeah, I figured. Just let me know when you're ready. I love you."

"I love you too," I replied before hanging up, taking a deep breath before leaving my room and wandering down to the living room. This wasn't going to end well.

Mom was arguing with my sister about her vanishing acts lately, but Dad's eyes were already on me. This was going to hurt him, but Stanley was right. I was an adult.

"Stan's asked me to stay with him for a while, so I'm going," I said firmly, hoping I sounded confident, and his eyes widened.

"What?"

"He said he'll come and pick me up when I'm ready," I added, as if that cleared up his question, and I could tell he was struggling not to yell at me. I never talked back, so he was probably freaking out about how to handle the situation.

He finally sighed, scrubbing his face with his hands. "I grounded you so you decide to move out? I didn't ground you for the fun of it, Luna. I need to show you that your actions have consequences. I'm trying to keep you safe."

"I'm twenty. No one else gets grounded at this age," I replied and wrinkled my nose. "And I'm not moving out. I just think we should have some space for a few days."

"And a lot of those kids without discipline end up in prison or dead."

"Rory doesn't ground her kids. Neither does Aunt Charlie or Jade," I whined.

"I know, and most of them will end up in prison or dead, just like I said. I love those kids, but Beckett and Riley have already had one stint behind bars, Ryder's going to get called out by some drunk girl for rape eventually with the way he's going, Jade doesn't have to worry about Landon because he stays out of trouble, and Charlie still has rules for her kids. Phoenix is more guarded than you thanks to Rage, so stop complaining."

"Ryder's not a fucking rapist!" Tempest snapped, joining the argument with furious, sky-blue eyes. "He doesn't need to force himself on anyone, they throw themselves at him."

"I don't mean he's a rapist, I just mean he fucks around with these drunk girls, and one day, one of them will regret their drunken decision and cry rape. Especially because he's got money. Do you know how nice a payout would be to someone who cries rape on a rich kid? Ryder would be thrown in prison and Rory would pay ridiculous amounts of money to keep details quiet and to shut the person up. She wouldn't like her son's life ruined over bullshit like that, and it would destroy her being able to foster children. No one would let vulnerable kids live under the same roof as someone on the sex offenders list. Since when do you give a shit about him? Stay away from him, he's bad news and you're better than that."

She smiled sweetly, flipping her blonde hair over her shoulder. "Are you going to tell me women can't sleep around for their own pleasure like men can? Mom used to strip and get on her back in Wet Dreams, so don't give me that bullshit."

"Tempest!"

"What? I don't mean it in a bitchy way," she huffed. "I just wanted to make a point that you can't aim that shit at me after having a different opinion for Mom. She wasn't even legal when she worked for you."

"Where did you hear that?" he hissed, but Mom rolled her eyes.

"As much as I'd love to discuss this, our problem right now isn't Ryder Donovan's sex life with Tempest. Luna's leaving, remember?"

"No, she's not," Dad scoffed, turning to me again. "If this is a way to get out of being grounded, we can talk about it. What's next? Are you going to move out with him for real?"

"Dad," I sighed, looking down at my feet. "It's time I grew up. I should learn to stand on my own feet, right? Maybe I should talk to Stan about us getting a house together. I'm not a kid anymore. If that means you don't want to pay for college anymore, I—"

"Punishing you by taking away your education will never be something I do. I'm glad one of you kids take your futures seriously," he grumbled, giving Tempest the side-eye before looking back at me. "I thought you said you weren't ready to move out?"

"I'm not, but it's something Stan and I should talk about. For now, I'm just going to stay with him for a little while." I was proud of how strong I sounded, even though I felt awful on the inside from the look in Dad's eyes. He was hurt.

He was silent for a moment before nodding, defeat on his face. "I can't make you stay, but you come right back here if you need to, okay? Even if that's in two hours' time. As long as you're safe."

"You'll leave Stan alone?" I asked, needing to know he wouldn't threaten him or rough him up, but he gave me a sly smile.

"I didn't say that."

"Dad!"

"I'm joking. For legal reasons anyway," he said lightly with a one-armed shrug. "I'll make you a deal. I'll keep putting money in your account to pitch in with groceries if you check in with me or your mother so we know you're alright. I don't like the idea of you depending on Stanley. That gives him power, and my baby girl's the one in charge. Got it?"

I hadn't expected that, and I threw myself at him, hugging him tightly.

"Thank you."

Tempest snorted, not impressed with what was happening. "So, you'll pay her money to do whatever she wants but you won't help me? That's bullshit."

"Luna's studying, she's planning her future, and she has goals. You hardly made it through high school and you refused college, and now you want to have everything handed to you on a silver platter so you don't have to lift a finger. I won't help you ruin your life. If you want me to keep paying for your shit since you also refuse to get a job, you can live here," he said flatly. "I've given you options and you throw an excuse at me for every single one."

"Rory bought Jett a house and Beckett and Maddox live with him!"

"I'm not Rory Donovan!" he snapped, frustration seeping out of him. "I don't have millions of dollars lining my pockets. Yes, Rory bought that house, but she has houses for a lot of troubled kids that struggle. When kids age out of the foster system, where do they go? Either the streets or Rory's doorstep. Do you know how many kids have lived in that big-ass mansion? Hundreds. Every week she's helping someone new, and it's not because they're entitled kids who refuse to lift a finger, it's because they're helpless, abused, or living on the streets. You have a perfectly good home, loving parents, and full access to everything you need. Those kids have nothing, Tempest. You can't compare your situation to theirs."

"Maybe I should go and cry on her doorstep then," she threw back before stomping towards the front door. Dad rolled his eyes, crossing his arms.

"Go for it. She'll give you the same speech I just did. She's not a halfway house for rebellious kids who don't want to be controlled. She'd feed you, give you a hug, and tell you to go home." She slammed the door, his eyes going weary as he sighed. "I don't know where I went wrong with her. Nothing I ever do is right, and nothing I say gets through to her."

"You're the best dad in the world. I think she's just dealing with some stuff," I offered, his tired brown and green speckled eyes lifting to meet mine.

"You think so?"

"Yeah. I'll get Ryder to check in with her. They seem to be friends, sort of, and she'd listen to him. He stands up for her sometimes when other guys talk badly about her."

His eyes narrowed, his jaw tight. "Be honest with me. Are they seeing each other?"

"Uh, no," I laughed, knowing neither of them would choose to date someone. "I know you don't like hearing this, but Tempest is whoring way too much to settle down, and Ryder's not much different. They'd be toxic together and only hurt each other."

He didn't seem to believe me, but his shoulders and jaw relaxed. "He looks out for her?"

"He wouldn't let anyone hurt her, that much I know. They seem to have some kind of understanding for each other."

"I guess I should be grateful he's decent enough to keep an eye out for trouble. I've always had to worry about her way more than I have with you. You've always had Riley and the Donovans, but Temp doesn't seem to have anyone," he said with a frown, lost in thought.

"They all make sure she's okay too. If someone was harassing her or if she was in danger, any of them would help her. I need to go and pack a bag," I mumbled, not surprised when he groaned.

"Okay, but don't take too much. It gives you a reason to come back."

"I promise, I'll come home."

"Good. I don't like it when my girls aren't where I can keep them safe," he murmured before kissing the top of my head and letting me go to my room to pack.

80
100
120
140
160
180
200
220
km/h
240
260

Chapter Eight

Riley

"You're late," Turbo said flatly as I parked in the parking lot beside his Supra, flipping him off as Reid parked on my other side.

"You're lucky I came at all. My dad knows exactly who you are, and he lost his shit about me hanging out with you. If he catches me being involved with any of your businesses, he's putting a bullet in you. Just so you know."

"Everyone knows me," he said as he waved a dismissive hand, but his jaw clenched as I answered.

"My father didn't know I spent time with you until today. He knows enough about you to know you're trouble, and he knows how big this car shit is with you. I might have to skip out on some shit until his suspicions die down. He knows you're not just some kid who races cars like most people, and that you host big stake races."

"You can't just skip races, Donovan."

"No? Would you prefer they show up guns blazing with a bunch of crews to back them up? You'd be dead in seconds, and if they let you live, your entire underground business would be gone. They wouldn't just take down your races, but whatever else you do too. I respect you, so I'm giving it to you straight. I don't want to bring trouble your way," I said firmly, resting my forearm on the open window. "And all it would take is for those guys from the other day at the gas station to open their mouths and blab."

"You didn't mention you had friends in Rawson," he said accusingly, distrust in his gaze. "That's something you should've mentioned."

"I've never met them before, as you could probably tell by our awkward interaction. They're connected to my family though and they know what we do and who's involved. They run a lot of surveillance but I don't know what their business is," I said sharply, narrowing my eyes. "Now, why the fuck are we here? We're not due to race again, and since your bum buddy isn't here and Blake's not coming, I assumed you need us for something else?"

Reid's car door shut as he climbed out and walked around to my side of the car, leaning his butt against it. "Yeah. Why *are* we here? And why'd you tell me to leave Logan at home?"

"You two are discreet, you love the rush, and I know for a fact you, in particular, won't say no to easy money," Turbo replied, his eyes on Reid. "I need help moving something."

"Fuck no," Reid snapped, instantly losing his temper as the muscles in his arms flexed. "I'm not interested in your gangbanger bullshit. I race cars, that's it."

"I'll pay you a lot."

"I don't give a fuck," he spat, his fists clenching by his sides. "I'm not interested in anything to do with weapons, and you already know my thoughts on moving drugs after what happened to Josh."

I had no clue who Josh was, but by the way Reid was

flipping out, I assumed he'd been really hurt or killed in a drug deal gone wrong. It happened regularly in the Heights.

"Thought the money might sway you," Turbo shrugged, sliding his steel-gray eyes to me. "How about you, Donovan? You want to help me move some shit tonight?"

I didn't want to get involved, but the adrenaline rush the risk would bring me was worth it.

"What's the haul? Drugs?"

"Crystal."

"How much?"

"Twenty pounds."

"What's that valued at? Six hundred k?" I asked, amusement flickering in his eyes.

"Didn't think you played into your parents' businesses? Sounds like you know what you're talking about. It's close to six hundred and fifty k."

"Why aren't you moving it yourself?" I asked bluntly, lighting a cigarette and blowing smoke at him. "What aren't you telling me?"

He scrubbed a hand over his face, becoming impatient. "Look, I can't trust Slick, and I need a second set of eyes. It's a lot to move alone and I need someone to watch my six. You feel me?"

"You're not dragging her into your dodgy shit," Reid hissed, giving me a firm look. "You need a rush? I'll race you. Hell, if you're just bored we can get drunk back at Raven's place. You don't need to move drugs for this fucking idiot to get your kicks. It's not like you need the money."

"No, but you do. I'll have my fun then give you the money," I offered, his eyes narrowing to slits.

"I'm not fucking taking money from you."

"Why not? I don't need it, and I'm sure as shit not letting Mr. Wannabe Kingpin over here keep it," I snorted, leaning back in my seat. "Put it towards buying a nicer house or something."

Reid scowled, pushing off my car to point a finger at me. "You know what dirty money does? It gets people killed. It's alright for people like you who have entire crew organizations at your back, but people like me? We don't have shit. I don't want that money near me or the people I care about. Last time one of us got involved in this sort of shit, they got killed. Right there in their own fucking kitchen in front of us."

"I know what it's like to watch someone you love die, Reid," I said gently, knowing his trauma was going to be different than mine. If he really didn't want the money, I'd have to respect that.

"I can't force you not to get involved, but I can't come with you to watch your back and I don't want the money. I'm sorry," he said tightly with a shake of his head, stalking back to his car and slamming the door behind him before taking off with a screech of tires.

Turbo was studying me silently, pulling his lower lip between his teeth in thought.

"You know," I said slowly, blowing smoke out my window as I glanced at him. "If my parents catch wind of this, the pair of us are dead. You know that, right? I just watched my dad set fire to my friend's car because she drove drunk in it. So imagine what he'd do to you for getting me involved with this shit?"

"Live a little," he smirked, tilting his head to the side as his eyes sparkled with mischief. "Chances are high we'll get caught, but I get it if you're too scared."

I scoffed, dragging on my cigarette as I looked away from him. "I have nothing to be afraid of. You, on the other hand, do."

"Leave that concern to me. So, you in?"

"Where's the pick-up and drop-off? If it's in Ashburn, I won't."

"I wouldn't ask that of you," he said seriously. "Kingslake to Crestford. Separate cars. You take the crystal and I'll have your back. Once we get to Crestford, I'll do all the talking and we part ways."

"You're moving rich dude drugs? No wonder you're getting a name for yourself."

"All drugs are rich dude drugs," he deadpanned, tapping his fingers against the side of his car and drawing my attention, my eyes clashing with his dark ones.

"And if we get caught? What happens then? I go to jail for drug trafficking while you play innocent?" I laughed lightly, flicking the rest of my cigarette out the window. "Do you think I'm stupid?"

"No. I just know you like the rush this shit would cause. Your parents might have the Ashburn Valley cops in their pocket, but I have sway with some locals here. Money talks, Donovan. You know that."

"Just how loaded are you?"

"Are you in?" he asked firmly, apparently sick of my shit.

"One time and I'm out, got it?" I said firmly despite the alarm bells going off inside my head, his eyes shining with success.

"Done."

"Everyone knows my car," I pointed out, making him shrug.

"So? It's not like we're waving a flag around saying we're moving drugs. We're less likely to be pulled over if your car's recognizable."

"Unless it's my family who pulls us over," I grumbled,

pulling my hood over my head before starting my engine. "Who's your contact in Kingslake?"

I didn't like the way he was looking at me, laughter in his eyes. "You'll see. Follow me, and make sure your *mommy* isn't tracking your phone."

I switched my location off, not happy to not know the exact details, but it excited me too. There was something wrong with me.

"What the fuck are you doing here?" I demanded as I slammed my car door and stalked towards Zavier Lopez with my bat in hand, his eyes widening a fraction before he cursed. We were at some big fancy house in Kingslake, but it was hidden by trees and was secluded. The perfect spot for corrupt rich dudes.

"I should be asking you the same question."

"I guess you do take after daddy dearest," I said dryly, eyeing him up and down with disgust. "I take it your friends don't know about this shit. Especially after the way Reid just exploded at us."

He frowned, confusion filling his eyes. "The fuck are you talking about? You saw Reid?"

"You put your foot in that one, Donovan," Turbo chuckled as Zavier's eyes narrowed.

"What's she talking about? How do you know him?"

"I guess all the secrets are coming out tonight," Turbo said as he let out a low whistle, annoyance washing through me.

"You didn't need my help, did you? You just wanted to cause trouble. You're such a cunt," I hissed, giving him a shove and causing his lips to kick up into a smirk, giving me my answer. "Let's get this done so I can get home. I won't be letting this go any time soon."

He shrugged, not giving a shit as he walked towards the garage where I could see a few duffle bags were sitting. I glared at his retreating form, but I almost smacked Zavier in the head with my bat as his fingers touched my waist to draw my attention.

"Shit, sorry. I didn't mean to startle you," he cringed, stepping out of my personal space. "Seriously, what the fuck are you doing here? Beckett never mentioned that you guys know Ander."

"She doesn't know him, and I don't want her to know that I do. So keep your big fucking mouth shut, Lopez," I snapped. Convincing him to keep secrets from her was going to be difficult since I was pretty sure he was in love with her or something. He was that far up her ass.

"You want me to keep shit from her?" he asked bluntly and crossed his arms to watch me.

"So Raven and the others know you're some high-end dealer?" I demanded, his face falling. "That's what I thought. I'll stay out of your business if you stay out of mine."

"Are you going to tell me how you know him then? And how Reid knows him?"

"You don't want to know," I warned, but Turbo couldn't fucking help himself, opening his mouth and letting it all out as he dumped bags in my trunk.

"Reid and Riley are two of my best racers."

"Reid races legally on the track, and Riley's family *owns* the damn track. Why would she race on the street?" Zavier argued, making Turbo snort.

"It seems you all like to keep secrets from each other. They've both been racing on the streets for years now."

"No way. If Reid was doing something like that, Logan would know, which means Raven would know and tell me." I watched as his shoulders tensed while Turbo laughed.

"Logan's usually right there in the passenger seat with him."

I slapped his arm to shut him up, turning to face Zavier who looked betrayed. "Raven doesn't know, and they don't want her to know. As you can imagine, it would be bad news for everyone if it was discovered that I was involved too. You can't tell anyone, Zavier."

"Are you going to tell me why you're here moving fucking drugs then? You know Ander's a rival to your family business, right?"

"She's an adrenaline junkie," Turbo answered, going back to the garage to grab the other bag. "The rush gets her off. You should see her behind the wheel on the street. She should've died a good handful of times by now."

"Not helping," I gritted out, pinning him with a glare. "Do you want my help or not?"

"You're not even helping. You're standing around talking," he deadpanned, dropping the last of the bags in the trunk and slamming it shut. "Get in and let's go."

Zavier was silent as I climbed into the driver's seat, but he suddenly walked around to my passenger door and yanked it open. "I'm coming with you."

"What the fuck for?"

He flashed his gun at me, his face serious. "Because I can't let you do this shit with only Ander as backup. You drive, and if we run into trouble I can shoot."

"Stop calling him Ander. It's Turbo," I grumbled, leaning back in my seat and flexing my fingers on the wheel as I assessed him. "I don't need you to babysit me either. Believe it or not, I know how to shoot." Turbo revved his car behind me, telling me to hurry the fuck up, and I sighed. "I guess you know where to go then?"

"Yep. Drive straight to Crestford and I'll direct you from there," Zavier confirmed. "If something feels off, tell me. Chances are high you won't be wrong. If Ander's dragged you along as backup, it means he knows something's up. I don't think he's just causing trouble." I nodded, keeping the music off as I steered us back to the main road, Turbo on my ass the whole time. We drove most of the way in silence, but after a while, Zavier spoke. "I needed the money, okay? Now my father's dead, I don't have to worry about him finding me. I can work and try to make a good life for Raven and the guys. Maybe get them out of the Heights."

"You didn't want to be like that asshole, so what made you decide to move drugs?" I snorted, his face twisting with annoyance in the moonlight.

"I'm nothing like Kristoff Lopez, and I never will be. He was a rapist and a predator. The things he did to Maddox was awful, but who knows how many other kids and women he hurt."

"I know what that piece of shit did to my brother," I huffed, not wanting to be reminded of it. "But I want to know how you got into this drug business in the first place. Are you someone's bitchboy? Or are you running the show?"

His sharp eyes scanned the area around us as we reached the Crestford road sign, his voice dejected. "Bitchboy."

"How long?"

"A few months. You can't tell anyone, Riley. I know you

don't like me, but I can't let the guys and Raven find out. I won't tell Beckett about your shit with Ander, uh, Turbo if you promise me that you'll keep your mouth shut too," he said quietly, finally glancing at me. "I didn't know them when shit went down with their friend, but I know they're still fucked-up from it. They'd probably throw me out."

"Who are you working for? Turbo?"

"That's not something I'm willing to discuss with you. I make sure it stays out of Ashburn Valley though if that's what you're worried about," he grunted, cursing as something pinged off my car. "I fucking knew this wouldn't go smoothly. He never brings backup."

My skin tingled with anticipation and fear at the thought of being chased, my fingers flexing on the steering wheel as I glanced in my rearview mirror to see two sets of headlights behind us as another bullet hit my car. I frowned when we drove under a streetlight and I noticed Turbo's car wasn't one of them, but Zavier wound down his window and gave me a knowing look.

"He'll be following at a distance, that way he could see danger better. He might have brought you along to be a dick, but he wouldn't bail on you. Turn left near the Academy."

I did as he instructed, the headlights following us until we drove along a well-lit street, the Academy looking creepy with the moon behind it. It was a cold, stone building and it was fucking huge. Most people hated that my family decided not to send us to rich kid schools, and some of the Crestford brats talked shit about us for it. I didn't give a fuck, they could keep their creepy school and their fancy uniforms.

No way in hell was I going to be caught dead in that ugly-ass, brown skirt.

Zavier groaned as the cars behind us drove under the lights so he could see who they were. "These fuckers again?"

"Who?"

"Bunch of trust fund babies with too much money and not enough brains," he cringed as a third bullet hit us. "Your family's going to notice bullet holes, you know?"

"I'm aware. Are these guys local or did they follow us from Kingslake?" I asked, glancing in my mirror again as they started gaining speed.

"Local. They're a terrible shot."

"Why are you worried then?"

"Because they're fucking annoying. If I start gunning down rich kids, I'm going to get my ass thrown in prison," he grumbled, but I chuckled and put my foot down harder on the gas.

"Shoot back and scare them, for fuck's sake. If you hurt anyone, I'll handle it. I guarantee my family is scarier than theirs. Besides, Mom knows you wouldn't get me into trouble. We were simply going for a drive and got attacked," I said sweetly, a dry laugh leaving him.

"Oh yeah, like that's believable. You hate me, so why would we be going for a moonlit drive together?"

"Do you have another idea, dumbass?" I barked, not giving him another second to answer before I floored it. I screeched around corners as I made sure to take side streets to lose them, and Zavier somehow managed to lean out the open window and fire some shots at one of the cars that were sticking close to us.

I still couldn't see Turbo, which pissed me off, but my adrenaline was pumping as I sped through Crestford with bullets pinging off my car. They were lucky it wasn't my

Corvette, or I would've pulled over and beaten them to death.

My phone rang from its stand, and I answered it on the hands-free when Turbo's name popped up. "Where the fuck are you, asshole?" I snapped, but he ignored me.

"Turn right just before the bridge to Briar Falls. Turn your location on."

"My parents will track me then, idiot."

"If your phone's on, they can track you. Don't be delusional in thinking they don't check deeper than that little app you guys use," he scoffed, his engine rumbling in the background. "I've got your back, Donovan. Get to that road and don't slow down until you do. Once you're past the stone wall, stop."

"They'll follow me!"

"Trust me?"

"Fuck no."

"Pretend to for five minutes," he grunted out before hanging up.

Zavier sat in his seat properly, giving me a grin. "You haven't seen this side of him before. He sounds like he has a plan and it's not going to be pretty."

Fear pumped through my body as I kept driving, narrowly missing parked cars in the dark. We were moving so fast that I wouldn't be able to see anything in front of me until we hit it.

"Bridge is just up ahead," he warned, and I had no choice but to slow down for the sharp turn, my hands starting to sweat as the two cars behind us continued to follow. At least they'd stopped shooting at us.

Once past the wall, I stopped just in time to see a car roll into the middle of the road, my heart hammering as it exploded. The rich idiots chasing us had no option but to slam on their brakes as the wall of fire spread across the road, my eyebrows shooting up.

"Turbo put explosives in a car? How did he beat us here and set that up?"

"He knows all the shortcuts," Zavier explained casually as if it were no big deal, but his eyes were shining with glee. "He's pretty cool."

"I have no idea how to explain that to my parents," I said and shook my head as Zavier opened the door and climbed out, snatching the bags and quickly putting them in the trunk of another car close by. I frowned when I realized it was Turbo's, and the man himself popped up beside my open window with a smirk.

"Bet that got your panties wet, didn't it?" he teased, giving me a wink. "If you ever want to do this again, just ask."

"Did you even fucking need me or was this just evening entertainment for you?" I demanded as sirens sounded two seconds before I heard a familiar car roaring in the distance. I knew the sound of Skeeter's McLaren anywhere.

"Yep. I couldn't have set this shit up if I wasn't trailing behind. I've gotta go. These idiots are after the crystal, not you. Go yell at them if you want." Then he jumped in his car and took off as if we'd just been hanging out as buddies.

"Dad's almost here," I muttered to Zavier, and I grabbed my bat from my car before taking his wrist to drag him towards the flames. "Let's deal with these assholes."

He pulled his gun out once I let go, and we made our way towards the cars that were still parked on the other side of the carnage.

One guy climbed out with a scowl, but he hesitated when Zavier aimed his gun at his head. If he thought they'd intimidate us, they had another thing coming.

"What the fuck do you think you're doing?" Zavier spat, sounding more menacing than usual. I was kind of impressed. "Do you know you just started a war?"

"With who? You? You're nothing, Lopez," he laughed lightly, but his eyes were focused on me. It was dark, and since my hood was on he probably had no idea who I was. He was in deep shit when Skeeter arrived.

I pulled my hood back and dropped my bat over my shoulder, raising an eyebrow. "You think he was talking about himself? That's cute."

His eyes widened, and I knew when the others recognized me too by the way they went completely silent. One stepped forward, swallowing nervously. "We didn't know it was you. That's not your car."

"Yes, it is. I've had that car longer than my Corvette," I chuckled, holding my bat out to point it at him. "You should do your homework before shooting at people."

"We were told to stop any of Lavaro's drug deals!"

I slammed my bat into the side of his leg, sending him sprawling backwards by the flames as he cried out in pain.

"What fucking drugs?" I demanded, smacking him in the ribs with my bat as Zavier kept the others back with his gun. "I was just driving and you attacked me!"

Dad's McLaren barreled towards us, slamming on the brakes at the last minute, and I wasn't surprised when Caden's Challenger and Slash's Mustang pulled up beside it. I had no idea who was with them, but I kept my eyes on the asshole on the ground. "You fucked up, idiot."

The guy snarled at me out of frustration, and Zavier put an arm around me to hold me back, aiming his gun at him with a growl. "Watch it. I'll put a bullet between your eyes in seconds."

The sirens got louder, and I was jerked to the side as

Slash glared down at me. "Get in the fucking car before the cops get here. We'll talk at home." He turned his glare on Zavier next, looking ready to kill him. "You get yourself out of this mess."

Slash started dragging me towards his Mustang when I suddenly pulled back at his words. "He's coming with us. He had my back tonight."

"It's his fault you're in this mess! I don't know why you're even spending time together, but I don't like it. You two are up to something, and—"

"I'll get your car home," Zavier offered, holding out his hand for the keys. He was a good driver, and as much as I didn't want him driving it, I knew he'd get it home like he said. It was better than leaving it here on the side of the road to get stolen.

I tossed him the keys, pointing my bat at him. "Straight to my place. No joyriding."

"Promise," he nodded before diving into the driver's seat and taking off, knowing all the backroads to get his ass out of here.

"You're in so much fucking trouble," Slash hissed as he pulled me towards his car again, and I could see Skeeter's eyes raking over the rich pricks as they took off. He'd remember all of them and hunt them down later when they least expected it.

His angry green eyes met mine, and I had to admit, he didn't look too impressed. Neither did Caden. I was getting the lecture of the century when we got home.

The moment we pulled into the driveway, we found Zavier sprawled out on the hood of my Supra with a hint of fear on his face, Beckett standing over him with a gun pressed against his forehead. I bailed from the car, knowing she'd shoot him regardless of their friendship.

Family would always come first, no matter what.

"What dodgy shit did you get her involved in?" she demanded as her jaw clenched, making him swallow nervously.

"Beck! It's not his fault!" I explained as I reached them, shoving my bat between them as if that would stop her. "If anything, he's the reason I got out of it."

She turned to me, tapping the side of my head gently with the barrel. "What dumb shit did he have to get you out of then, hmm? What the fuck were you doing in Crestford?"

"If you don't get that gun out of my face, I'll break your kneecaps with my bat," I warned and watched as her eyes narrowed.

"Answer me then. What the fuck are you involved in?"

Maddox's car screeched as he sped into the driveway and slammed on the brakes, jumping out without turning the engine off. "Jesus, Beck. Put that away." She ignored him, and he rolled his eyes, moving behind her to wrap his arms around her to pull her back a step. "I said, put it away."

She finally dropped it to her side, but her angry eyes remained on mine. "Start fucking talking before I lose my shit, Riley. Why were you there, and why the hell were you with Zav? It's the middle of the fucking night."

"I thought someone was following me," I blurted out, making her snort.

"So you called Zavier instead of me?"

"No. I saw him as I was driving through the Heights

and pulled over. I asked him to join me until I got home, but then the other assholes started firing a few shots at us so I didn't want to bring it back here. Zavier said he recognized them as Crestford rich pricks, so we led them there instead to ruin their own town," I said easily, Zavier sitting up and nodding, happily playing along with my lie.

"Yeah. I told her to try and lose them in Crestford so we could get back here through Briar Falls."

"That doesn't explain the burning cars on the road, or why you drove past the bridge to Briar Falls," Skeeter grunted, giving me a knowing look. I shrugged.

"They were on our tail the whole time so I didn't want to risk it. I think they made a trap for us but fucked it up. It went off just after we passed it."

He dropped his hand onto my shoulder firmly, letting me know he wasn't falling for my shit. "Let's talk about this inside, shall we?"

We started walking towards the door, and Caden grabbed Zavier's shoulder, shoving him after us. "You too, Lopez."

I bit back a sigh, knowing I wasn't getting out of this. Especially when we were marched right past Diesel who gave me a disappointed look. He and Slash would've been the two most likely to side with me, and it appeared there was no chance of that happening tonight.

Skeeter steered me into the office and put both hands on my shoulders to gently push me down into a chair at the massive table where they held most of their crew meetings. I placed my bat on the floor by my feet, glancing up at him.

"This is starting to feel like an interrogation," I joked as everyone else crowded around the table, Skeeter's eyes narrowing on me.

"D told us about your little run-in with that asshole in

Rawson Grove the other day. He mentioned you're friends with Ander fucking Lavaro," he said tightly.

My heart beat quickly in my chest at the thought of them being onto me. Being caught moving drugs was one thing, but losing the ability to race? I'd lose my fucking mind without that as an outlet. The track didn't hit the spot like the street races.

I kept my face blank, tilting my head slightly. "Turbo? Yeah. We're friends, I guess. We hang out if we run into each other, but it's not like we go out of our way to party together or anything. Where's Mom?" I had hope that she'd side with me. She was a sucker for my bullshit.

"Was that punk with you tonight?" Skeeter asked instead, and I noticed Marco and Hunter weren't there either. That made me suddenly nervous. Something like this would've made them all gang up on me, so they were either hunting down Turbo, or something else was wrong.

"I saw him earlier in the night," I said smoothly, telling a half truth. "Why? Did he see us being chased and call you guys or something?"

I was pretty sure he was going to burst a blood vessel.

He moved away from me, his jaw set tight. "You have one chance to tell me the truth, Riley. Don't fuck with me right now. I'm seconds away from tearing the Lopez kid's head from his shoulders."

"I'm telling the truth!"

Diesel walked over, resting his hip against the table and crossing his arms. He sighed, his face filled with hurt. "Hunter hacked the cameras in Hawthorne and Crestford. We had eyes on you until not long before the bridge. Ander was tailing you until just before Crestford, then he trailed off to get ahead of you. You were working together on something, and you told me you weren't involved with his bullshit."

"Where's Mom?" I asked again, my voice tight. "No one got me into any kind of trouble. You guys promised you wouldn't spy on us like that without a reason."

"She's at Devil's Dungeon with Hunter and Marco dealing with drunk idiots who tried to break in after closing. Don't change the subject, and we had a reason to spy on you. BG called and wanted to know if we'd heard from you, because he got a call from someone who recognized your car in the Heights. They said you were being followed by someone."

Relief seeped into me at knowing Mom wasn't out there hunting Turbo down to blow his brains out. I didn't need those two worlds colliding.

"What the hell were you doing tonight, Riley? Be honest with me," Skeeter said as he blew out a breath, his muscles relaxing a fraction as he pushed his reddish-brown hair back from his forehead. "Are you in some kind of trouble?"

"Look, I have a lot of respect for Turbo, and we were just hanging out. We'd planned to go and scare some of the Crestford Academy brats who live on campus because we were bored. Things went south and I didn't want to bring you guys into it," I lied, his brow creasing.

"What did the people chasing you want?"

"They assumed, since I was hanging out with Turbo, that we were exchanging goods of some kind. What did you call them?" I asked as I turned to Zavier. "Trust fund babies?"

Everyone's eyes turned to him, and he nodded, more than happy to throw a bunch of rich assholes under the bus.

"I've heard about them a lot lately. Bunch of rich kids

running around with guns, acting like gangsters. They'd been told to keep an eye on Ander's deals. They didn't know Riley was the person with him, and they shit their pants when they realized. They just saw Ander's car and figured it was a job." It was close to the truth.

Skeeter eyed me silently for a while before giving me a single nod. "Alright. Can you give *Turbo* a message for me?"

"I'm likely to stumble across him again soon, so sure," I nodded as if I didn't have his phone number, a dark smirk tugging at Skeeter's lips.

"If I find out he's involving you in his shit, I'll tear him to pieces. Slowly and painfully. We leave him alone since he keeps his bullshit out of Ashburn Valley, but if he drags you into anything? He'll be in my trunk with his hands cut off in seconds." Then he turned to Zavier, narrowing his eyes. "That goes for you too. Drag my kids into anything bad, and you'll cop the same fate. Understood?"

"Understood," Zavier said calmly, fishing my keys from his pocket and holding them out for me. "Here. I'd better head home."

I waved him off, surprising everyone. "Use it to get home. It's late, and I doubt your friends want to climb out of bed to give you a lift."

"It'll get stripped for parts at my place," he grunted as I looked at him, his eyes flashing with appreciation. I didn't like him, but he'd had my back tonight. It was the least I could do.

"Make your friend park his Challenger behind it so no one can steal mine," I suggested, his lips curving into a smile.

"He'll just *love* that idea."

"I'll buy him a new one if it vanishes," I said sweetly

before giving him a serious look. "Just take the damn car. I'll walk you out."

Beckett leaned against the wall as she studied us. She was suspicious, which wasn't good. I needed to get rid of Zavier before she started looking more deeply into our interactions. I'd bet money on her asking Cruz to search cameras, and he'd have no problem showing her evidence of me being involved in Zavier's shit.

No one stopped us as I grabbed my bat and we walked out of the room. I didn't speak until we were safely outside. "I'll come and pick it up later. I'd drive you home, but I have a feeling it would cause too many questions."

He chuckled, unlocking the car. "As if you lending me the damn thing isn't causing suspicion. Aren't you glad I came with you?"

"What do you want? A thank you kiss?" I deadpanned, placing my bat over my shoulder, leaving one arm to hang by my side.

"Yes, actually," he grinned, leaning down and tapping his cheek. "Some appreciation wouldn't kill you."

I rolled my eyes, making it look like I was leaning forward to kiss him, but I swung my fist into his stomach at the last minute, making him wheeze out a breath as I replied. "I'm letting you drive my car home so you don't have to walk back to the Heights or call Reid to come and save you. He'll ask questions. If you want a kiss, you'll have to miraculously grow a pussy."

"You're meaner than your sister," he rasped out as he grimaced. "That's impressive and terrifying at the same time."

"You're lucky I didn't hit you in the cock with my bat. I doubt you even know how to use it anyway," I smirked, lifting my bat to press the end against his groin. "Men like you are the reason I get laid so much."

"You piss a lot of people off, you know?"

"I'm aware. I'm not here to be liked, Lopez. Maybe you should take that advice before you get yourself into trouble and ruin your chance with Raven."

Shadows danced across his gaze as he sighed, leaning against the driver's side door to cross his arms once I removed the bat. "Reid made a promise a long time ago to keep her safe. None of us are good for her, and we'd only fight over her. We agreed not to step out of the friendzone."

"Why would you have to fight over her? Have one of those big poly relationships," I teased, but he shook his head.

"Raven doesn't have any interest in a relationship or sex. We know it would also ruin our friendship with her and we don't want to risk it."

"Why would it ruin it? My family are super close, and there's more than four in that situation," I smiled, but pain filled his eyes.

"We're fuck-ups, Riley. I'm the son of a monster, Logan's a manwhore, and Reid... he won't break his promise," he sighed, giving his head a small shake. "We don't want people talking badly about Raven. She doesn't deserve that. Besides, she has zero interest in any of us like that. We agreed not to put her in a position where she second-guesses our motives towards her. I appreciate your concern for my dick though."

"Asshole. If Reid asks about my car, just tell him I had to ditch it and bail so you grabbed it for me," I said firmly. "He'll know why."

"Give me your phone."

"No."

"Dammit, Riley," he bit out, uncrossing his arms. "Take my number. If you get stuck in the Heights, I can come and help you."

"Don't think for a second we're buddies now just because we shared some gunfire tonight," I warned sharply. "If I find a reason to smash your kneecaps, I will. If I run into trouble, I'll call my family."

He stepped towards me, looking down at me as he spoke in a low voice. "We both know that's bullshit. You'll call Turbo or Reid."

"How about you stay out of my business, hmm? Unless you want me to fuck your girl and tell her about the evening's events we just endured together?" I hissed, standing at my full height and butted my chest against his. "Go home, Lopez. I'll sort out my car later, but other than that, I don't want to see you again. Clear?"

"*Crystal*," he said dryly, not hiding the underlying meaning in his words as he took a step back and opened the car door. "I hope we don't run into each other like this again too."

He climbed in and slammed the door, waiting for me to move away from the car before he started it and drove off.

I stalked back towards the house, not surprised to find Beckett waiting in the shadows on the doorstep.

"You're keeping secrets," she stated bluntly. "Why are you hanging around Zav? And what was that shit about Reid?"

"It's nothing, Beck," I sighed, rubbing my tired eyes. "I swear, I'm not in trouble or anything. I don't demand to know everything in your personal life, so don't do it to me. Please."

She assessed me for a second before her shoulders relaxed and she reached out to give my arm a gentle squeeze. "You'd tell me if you needed help, right? No matter what?"

I nodded, not wanting to speak and lie straight to her face. I'd never drag my family into my own drama unless it involved crews.

This shit would blow over fast anyway.

80
100
120
140
160
180
200
220
km/h
240
260

Chapter Nine

Luna

"Hey!" Riley called out as she jogged towards me in front of the college, confusion in her eyes. "I heard from Ry this morning that you moved out. What happened?"

"Who told him that? I'm just spending a few days at Stan's house," I frowned, surprised that she knew. I'd barely had any sleep, spending most of the night hating myself for upsetting Dad.

Stan had woken me up after a few hours of sleep to tell me I was running late for school, so I was already exhausted.

Riley huffed, raking her fingers through her blonde hair. She looked tired too. "Tempest told him when they were at some party together last night. He told me over breakfast. Why are you avoiding home? Did you and your dad have a huge fight about you driving?"

"It was a last-minute idea for space," I shrugged, walking towards class and changing the subject. "Why do you look like shit?"

She hesitated, her face tightening as she considered

whether or not to tell me. I hated it when she did that because it meant she didn't trust me enough to keep her secrets.

We'd never had secrets until the last few years.

She finally let out a sigh. "I had a long night. Got caught up in some shit in Crestford."

"Are you alright? What kind of shit?" I asked with concern, running my gaze over her as we walked. She didn't seem to be hurt, but Riley was good at masking her pain.

"I was hanging out with a friend who has some dodgy jobs," she answered vaguely, glancing around to make sure no one was too close to hear us. "Some Crestford kids were playing wannabe gangster and followed us. They didn't know it was me until we'd had a major shootout and a car explosion. Then some of my dads arrived, which meant I got one hell of an interrogation when I got home. I'm fine, but the Supra's got bullet holes and some dents from the explosion."

"You sure you didn't get hurt?" I demanded, grabbing her arm and pushing the sleeve of her hoodie away from her skin to inspect it for damage, doing the same to her other arm.

She chuckled lightly, letting me run my hands over her. "Damn, Lou. I'll get shot at more often if it means you'll put your hands on me."

"This is serious," I bit out, but she draped her arm around my shoulders to pull me into her side.

"You worry too much. I didn't get hit. There weren't even that many bullets that hit my car. They sucked at aiming," she laughed as if getting shot at was normal. "But it's adorable that you're so worried."

"Who were you hanging out with in the first place?"

"Turbo. Well, his real name's Ander."

"Never heard of him."

"I'm not surprised. Your daddy wouldn't let you play with someone like him," she teased.

"How do you know him? You've never mentioned him before," I asked as jealousy sparked inside of me, and I almost scolded myself for being rude. If she was opening up to other people, that was a good thing.

I wouldn't feel so bad about spending time with Stanley if Riley had other friends to hang out with, so why did I hate the thought so much?

"He's just some guy. It's not a big deal," she said sharply as she walked ahead, sitting down at her desk and pulling her notebook out. She didn't strike up a conversation again, so I left her alone. It was obviously something that she was going to be secretive about.

She ignored me throughout our lecture, but I couldn't focus on what the professor was saying anyway. I didn't know I'd zoned out until hands dropped down onto my shoulders gently, giving me a squeeze as Ryder's voice reached me.

"Hey, Luney. Is my sister being a bitch again?"

"No. Why?" I mumbled tiredly, glancing at Riley's desk to find her gone. I hadn't even noticed her leaving.

I glanced around the room, finding most people had already left and I was one of the only people still sitting here.

"What's on your mind?" he asked as he dragged a chair closer and sat down backwards on it, resting his forearms on the back of it. "You look sad."

"Are you my knight in shining armor, Ry?" I asked and tilted my head, meeting his gaze. "Here to save the damsel in distress?"

His lips kicked up into a small smile of amusement.

"You're hardly a damsel in distress, but if you need help, I'm at your service. What's up? Is it Riley? Stanley?"

"It's lots of stuff," I admitted, looking away from him. "I feel bad about my fight with Dad yesterday, which led to me leaving. I'm staying at Stan's place for a few days. I'm worried about Riley too after what she said happened last night."

His back straightened, his eyebrows drawing together with confusion. "What happened last night?"

"She was hanging out with some guy and they got shot at or something. It happened in Crestford. We didn't talk about it much because she got snippy about it. She was in a lot of trouble when she got home, apparently."

"Who the fuck was she hanging out with? Why didn't anyone tell me?" he said as the muscles in his jaw ticked with frustration.

"Some Ander guy."

"Ander Lavaro?" he asked with disbelief, and I shrugged.

"I don't know him. She just said his name was Ander. Well, she calls him Turbo. Is he bad? She said Dad wouldn't like me near him," I said slowly. "Is she going to get hurt by him or something?"

"If it's Ander Lavaro, then he's bad news. I've heard shit about him at parties in Blackwater and the Heights. He's into dealing hard drugs and illegal street racing mainly, but he has a chop shop too."

"Riley's not stupid enough to get involved with stuff like that. She knows how dangerous cars can be, and she wouldn't want to get involved with the drugs or she'd join one of the crews," I said confidently, changing the subject. "Can you tell Rory I'm sorry for showing up that drunk the other night? It was a terrible impression for Kate on her first night there."

"Mom knows you're sorry. You sure you're okay though? Do you need a lift home later since Dad wrecked your car?" he asked with a cringe, but I waved him off with a soft smile.

"Stan's going to pick me up. I'm spending the afternoon here in the library to get some studying done. If you see Riley, tell her to call me."

"Sure thing. Don't let her push you around, okay? You're too cute to be sad," he winked before tickling me under the chin. "If she makes you cry, I'll come and cheer you back up."

"I have a boyfriend, Ry," I said dryly, swatting his hand away.

"A door can have a no entry sign on it, but people shouldn't trust me to know how to read," he said with a chuckle.

"I'll see you later," I laughed lightly, getting to my feet and grabbing my books.

"God, I hope so," he threw back playfully, leaving the room to most likely chase down Riley for more information about Ander. There was no way in hell she was getting involved in bad things, so I didn't think we had to worry about it.

"Party tonight," Stanley said the moment I opened the car door to climb in after my study session, making me snort.

"Good afternoon to you too. What party?"

"Sorry. How was your day?" he asked with a small

smile, leaning over to give me a quick kiss. I kissed him back, hiding my confusion as his lips felt sticky.

"It was good," I answered, discreetly rubbing my finger across my lower lip and lifting my finger to my nose to confirm what I thought, my heart sinking. Strawberry lip gloss. "What did you get up to?"

"Watched TV for most of the day. Football was on," he said without missing a beat, the lies leaving his lips with ease. He'd always been so good at that. "Some of the guys want to come around but I told them I had to ask you first."

"Why would you tell them that?"

"It's Raymond and some of the guys from the other night. I wanted to make sure you were okay with it," he replied as he drove out onto the main road and headed towards home.

I couldn't say no now or I'd look like an ass. He was good at twisting things, and I wasn't sure if he did it on purpose or not.

"I mean, I guess. If they keep their hands to themselves," I said quietly, swallowing around the nerves as memories of the last time hit me.

"Thanks, babe. I knew you'd be cool with it. If you don't want to stay, you could always go out," he suggested, my chest tightening at the thought. He wanted me out so he could play strip poker or something. Maybe even sleep with some random girl. I wasn't sure how much longer I could deal with this, but I knew it was me just being needy.

He was a guy, they all did this.

I gave him a bright smile, not letting him know I was onto him. "If you're sure, I'd love to go to the track."

"Sounds good," he smiled back, placing his hand on my knee for the rest of the drive.

I checked my phone to see if Riley had messaged me,

but she hadn't. I hadn't seen or heard from her since she'd left me sitting in the lecture hall.

I pushed thoughts of her aside as we got home, and I quickly had a shower and applied some mascara to make my eyes pop before pulling on a bright yellow sundress and leaving my dark brown hair to fall around my shoulders.

I hesitated when I realized I didn't have a car, so I decided to call Ryder, knowing he'd be at the track.

He answered after the second ring, his teasing voice relaxing me. "Hey, Luney. Please tell me this is a booty call."

"No, but I was wondering if you were going to the track? Stan's having friends over so I thought I'd come hang out and watch you guys race or something," I replied lightly, my stomach sinking at his answer.

"I don't think any of us are going there tonight."

"Oh. That's okay then, I guess."

"If you want to hang out though, there's a party happening. Angel's hosting it, so you can crash the night," he offered. "Riley's coming."

"Sounds like fun. Can you come and get me by any chance?"

"Of course. I'll be ready in about an hour, if that's cool? Where are you?"

I didn't want him pulling up here, or Stanley would get annoyed. He wasn't a fan of Ryder any more than he was Riley.

"I'll meet you at the gas station on the main road when you're ready?"

"Sure thing. I'll text you when I'm leaving," he confirmed before we said goodbye and hung up.

I wasn't sure if Riley would even want me there since she hadn't gotten a hold of me, but I could hang out with

Ryder if that was the case. Beckett would probably let me hang out with her too if she was there and I was alone.

Stanley didn't question me when I left five minutes later, and I hid around the side of the house to watch as people arrived. Sure enough, almost an hour later, I peeked through the window to see him and one of his friends railing some girl on the couch, my heart sinking.

I never understood why people stayed in a relationship when they were abused or cheated on, but part of me didn't want to walk away. I was weak, and I'd loved Stanley since the moment we'd met.

Walking away from him would hurt me, even though I was hurting anyway.

Seeing it with my own eyes made resentment form in the pit of my stomach. I always made excuses for him like he was drunk, but this proved he didn't love me.

I didn't want to face it, so I turned away from the window and shoved it aside to deal with later.

Ryder messaged me to say he was on the way, and I scrambled to make sure I was at the gas station in time, my hair a tangled mess from the breeze as I ran. My sandals made it hard to run in, but I managed to get there with two minutes to spare, Ryder's red Challenger pulling in shortly after.

I climbed into the passenger seat, surprised to find Jett sitting in the back. "Uh, hey."

"Hey," Jett grumbled, making Ryder smirk.

"Don't mind him. He's mad I made him sit in the back so you could have the front. Gotta look after my favorite girl, right?"

My face heated, and I glanced out the window to avoid his gaze. "I'm not your anything, Ry."

"I'm only playing with you," he chuckled, putting his

foot down to propel the car forward, my fingers digging into the leather seat to balance myself. "Put your seat belt on."

"Thank you. For picking me up," I murmured, his striking, green eyes glancing at me as I secured my seat belt.

"I've been hearing some shit about your boyfriend. Is he hurting you?"

"What? Of course he's not. Who's saying things about him?" I demanded, making him sigh.

"It's probably just kids at school causing trouble. You know how they love to gossip."

"What did you hear?"

"That he pushes you around and cheats on you," he said with a growl. "That's not true, right?"

"No. He's never hurt me." I scoffed, disappointment in his tone as he continued.

"But he cheats on you, right?"

I didn't reply, leaning forward to turn the stereo up to avoid answering. He respected my wish to end the conversation, both him and Jett leaving me alone for the rest of the drive.

I didn't know what to expect when we arrived, but I didn't think Riley would straight up ignore me. She was way too moody, and there was no good reason for her to avoid me. If she didn't want to talk about Ander, then I wasn't going to push her, even if I wanted to.

Ryder raised an eyebrow as she breezed past us, letting out a low whistle. "Wow, she's really got her grumpy pants on. C'mon, hang out with me and Emerson." He dropped an arm around my shoulders and led me towards the kitchen with Jett behind us, finding Angel chugging a bottle of vodka as people cheered around her.

That girl could hold her liquor like nobody's business.

We sat at the table and Ryder grabbed us a beer each,

handing me one with a small smile. "Stay by me. If I need to bail, I'll make sure you're with Emerson."

Jett snorted, but his voice was full of amusement. "What if I have to bail?"

"You're with my sister. You don't need to bail for pussy."

"If she wants to get down and dirty, I'm leaving," he replied with a grin. "And trust me. Your twin is one dirty little—"

Ryder gave him a shove, the pair of them bickering like an old married couple for ages while I silently sipped my beer and looked around at the party. My eyes landed on a group of people sitting in the living room, jealousy surging through me as I noticed Riley with her arm around some girl's shoulders.

I guess it was just me she was avoiding.

After a few beers, I'd stewed on my mood long enough. I got to my feet, making Ryder frown. "Where are you going?"

"I can see Riley. I'm going to hang out with her whether she likes it or not," I huffed, making him laugh.

"Put her in her place. She needs to learn she's not the only person who makes the rules."

I nodded, stumbling to my feet and trying to walk in a straight line across the room, knowing I was doing a terrible job at it. I never made a habit of getting drunk, so it was no surprise that I was such a lightweight.

I sat down where a bunch of people were sitting in a circle, Riley's eyes flicking to me with a scowl. "What are you doing? We're playing a game."

"What's the game?" I asked sweetly. "I want to play."

"No, you don't. It's truth or dare," she argued, making me shrug.

"Sounds fun." I hated this game. It was just a way for people to get away with making people do stuff they didn't want to do or for starting gossip. Stanley wouldn't like me playing it either, but part of me hoped someone got dared to touch me. Payback for his cheating ass.

She rolled her eyes, but I sensed her worry as one of the other girls giggled and spoke to me brightly. "Okay, you can play. Truth or dare, Luna?"

These people weren't my friends, and they'd only get me to do stuff that made me look stupid, but the beer was giving me liquid courage, so I smiled. "Dare."

She glanced around the group for a minute before her eyes landed on me again. "I dare you to make out with Riley."

Riley snorted, her voice tight. "That's a dumb dare."

"She doesn't have to play," the girl threw back, tilting her head at me. "So, you going to do it?"

"Why wouldn't I? It's just a kiss," I said confidently, but inside, I was freaking out. I could've been dared to kiss anyone else and it wouldn't have bothered me, but Riley? She loved me. This might hurt her. "She doesn't have to if she doesn't want to though."

Riley's eyes hardened as she got to her feet, moving around to me and getting comfortable on the floor again. "You think a little kiss would bother me?"

"Considering you won't even speak to me right now, a kiss might be pushing it," I joked, not expecting her fingers to grab my throat and squeeze slightly as she stared into my eyes.

"You should be more worried about yourself, Lou. Won't your boyfriend be pissed when he hears about this?"

"I don't care," I said boldly, and she must have seen how serious I was, because her eyes assessed me silently for a moment before her fingers loosened a fraction and a hint of a smile tugged at her lips.

"I hope you know I'm going to consume you then. It won't be a cute little kiss on the cheek."

"I'm not scared of your cooties."

"Remember you said that," she murmured before leaning forward and pressing her lips against mine. At first, it was strange. We'd been best friends forever, and we'd never crossed this line, but as her soft lips moved over mine and her tongue pushed into my mouth, I relaxed and got into it. It felt good, and I let out a soft gasp as her hands went to my waist and pulled me onto her lap.

I didn't pay attention to anyone around us as she forced me to straddle her lap while she deepened the kiss, her thumbs rubbing up and down against my hips, holding me in place.

She smirked against my lips as she went to pull back and I chased her, her teeth sinking into my lower lip and making me squeak. "How much did you have to drink?"

I blinked at her, suddenly realizing everyone watching us as they talked amongst themselves. My face heated as I heard someone whisper my name, but Riley took my chin and narrowed her eyes. "Do you regret that?"

"No."

"Then fuck what people say. Own it, Lou," she said firmly. "How drunk are you?"

"I've had a few," I admitted, making her chuckle.

"I figured. You were way too comfortable with that."

"It's just a kiss," I replied, amusement dancing in her eyes.

"Then can you stop groping my tits?"

I jerked my eyes down between us to find my hand on one of her boobs, embarrassment washing through me as someone snickered. I got to my feet, blurting out that I needed a drink, and I couldn't ignore the light laugh that left Riley as I ran away from her.

At first, I thought she was laughing at me like everyone else, but the moment I joined Ryder and Jett at the table again to take a long drink of beer, arms wrapped around me from behind and Riley's husky voice reached my ears.

"I think you've had enough of that. Don't you?"

I absently leaned back against her, finishing my mouthful before answering. "You're not the boss of me."

"Clearly. It's such a shame too," she teased, my thighs clenching as her teeth nipped at my neck. "What made you grow some balls tonight? You hate games like truth or dare."

Ryder scowled, giving her a dirty look. "Back off and leave her alone. She's not one of your playthings."

"Says the manwhore," she mocked, her lips brushing my earlobe. "Luna's the one who wanted to play with me. Ask her."

Ryder's worried eyes met mine, his voice firm. "Luney?"

"We just played truth or dare. I'm not even that drunk," I scowled, and I would've stumbled if Riley's arms hadn't tightened around me.

"Take it easy," Riley scolded, seeming to snap out of her flirting. "How many of those have you had?"

"I want to sleep," I announced, not listening to her question, and making Ryder sigh.

"She's had way more than normal, and she drank them fast. If she wants to sleep, keep an eye on her."

"You let her have more than one or two?" she demanded, but he simply shrugged.

"She's safe here."

"There are people everywhere! If she's kissing me and not freaking out about it, she's wasted!"

"Wait, she kissed you?" Ryder laughed. "Why are you complaining? You don't mind fucking drunk girls, so—"

"She's different."

I turned in her arms, giggling as I dropped my arms around her shoulders. "Your lips are so soft."

One of the guys snorted, but Riley sighed. "Probably because I keep them moisturized with pussy."

"Should I start putting some on my lips too?" I wondered out loud, making her smirk.

"We'll discuss this in the morning when you're sober."

"Okay."

"Are you ready for sleep?" she asked, taking most of my weight as I sagged against her.

"I'm tired. Can you tuck me in before you run off to chase pussy?" I slurred and her arms tightened around me some more.

"Don't be silly. You're bunking with me. Come on," she replied, saying good night to the guys before pulling me into the hallway. The further into the house we got, the quieter it became, and I couldn't help but giggle as I buried my nose in her hair.

"You smell good."

"Thanks, Lou," she chuckled, opening a door and locking us inside as she flicked a light on. "You always smell good too."

"I do? Is that why you love me?" I questioned, collapsing on the bed as she laid me down. She was quiet for a minute before replying.

"What did you say?"

"Why do you love me?" I asked, shutting my eyes and letting her pull my shoes off. "Is it because I smell nice?"

"I love you because you're my best friend," she said with confusion as she turned the bedside lamp on and switched off the main light so she could climb into bed beside me.

"No. You *love* me," I whispered, opening my eyes to find her frowning at me. I reached out, almost poking her in the eye as I cupped her cheek. "Like how Dad loves Mom."

"Who told you that?" she laughed nervously before pulling back to yank her hoodie over her head and kicking her track pants off. "Someone's teasing you."

"You told me. You tell me lots of stuff when you're drunk," I informed her, snuggling into her side more. "You said you're in love with me."

She froze, her eyes watching me cautiously. "When did I say that?"

"Ages ago. You're a really good kisser," I declared, leaning closer until our lips were almost touching. "Kiss me again."

"Lou—"

"Please."

Riley

"Please," Luna begged, my pussy clenching at her needy tone. I'd waited my entire life to hear her beg for me, but I didn't think she meant it. It must have been the beer talking, and I was trying so hard to restrain myself.

"If I do that, you'll hate me in the morning," I whispered, her eyes filling with tears at my words.

"You don't like kissing me?" Her voice cracked with devastation. Jesus Christ.

I gave her a smile before wrapping my arms around her firmly. "You're the only person in the world I want to kiss forever, but I don't want you to hate me."

"I could never hate you," she whined, and I couldn't help but roll my eyes. She wasn't thinking clearly.

"What about Stan? You know, your boyfriend."

The cutest scowl took over her face, and I was so fixated on it that I almost missed what she said. "He's tag teaming some bitch with his friend right now. If he's mad about a kiss, that's his problem."

"You're kissing me to make him mad?" I hissed while a sigh left her as she pulled away.

"Sort of, but mostly because I want to kiss you. It felt nice, and I wouldn't mind doing it again. He doesn't have to know about this one."

I was a selfish bitch. The idea of getting her plush lips against mine while sending a big fuck you to Stanley made me want to do it so badly that all rational thoughts left me as I grabbed her chin and pulled her face back towards me, slamming my lips against hers.

She moaned into my mouth, the sounds sending tingles through me as I teased her tongue with mine, and her hands grabbed at my shirt. She pulled me on top of her, her dress riding up as she wrapped her legs around me. My heart was hammering with excitement, and I had to remind myself that she'd likely change her mind about this in the morning.

I should've stopped, she was drunk, but I soaked in her desperate kisses like I was addicted.

Her hands ran up the back of my shirt, a whimper leaving her as I pulled back. "Don't stop yet. Can I touch you?"

I groaned, dropping my forehead to hers as I peered down at her. "I'm trying to do the right thing here, baby."

"Say that again."

"Uh, I'm trying to do the right thing?" I repeated with

confusion, a light laugh leaving her as she pawed at my ass, forcing our bodies closer.

"No. The last thing."

"Baby?" I chuckled, her eyes heating in the dim light. "You like me calling you baby?"

"Kiss me and call me baby. I won't hate you tomorrow, I promise," she insisted, sliding her hand up my body to my chest, giving my breast a gentle squeeze through my shirt.

I cursed as she licked her lips, her hands fumbling to push the offending material out of the way to expose my bra.

"Luna, we can't." She was fucking killing me right now.

"Yes, we can. No one has to know," she murmured, those words acting like a bucket of icy water being thrown over me.

I pulled back again, this time my chest tightening. "Is that why you want this so badly? So we can mess around and no one will know?"

"It's just some fun, Riley. I want to see if I like it," she grinned, hurt pushing its way through me as I pushed her legs off my waist and climbed off her. "Where are you going?"

Panic filled her tone, and she scrambled to sit up to watch me through her drunken gaze.

I yanked my track pants and hoodie on, shoving my feet into my shoes. "I'm not some fantasy for you to knock off your bucket list, Lou."

"I know. I just wanted to—"

"No. You're drunk, and you want to hurt Stan like he's hurt you. This was a stupid idea."

"Don't—" I stalked out and slammed the door behind me, cutting off whatever she was about to say once more.

Tears burned my eyes, but I kept them at bay. I didn't cry over girls, and I wouldn't start now.

Everyone warned me about this happening, so I shouldn't have been surprised.

She wanted to fuck a girl because her boyfriend's a cheating piece of shit? She could be my guest. I wouldn't allow her to use me like that though, not unless she genuinely wanted to see if I was what she wanted.

I didn't want her for a night, I wanted her for life.

"Hey, what's wrong?" Ryder asked slowly as he grabbed my bicep the moment I headed through the kitchen. I pulled my hood over my head to give myself a barrier when I found all eyes on me, and kept my voice low as I responded to him.

"I'm leaving. Luna's in the room I usually crash in. Can you stay with her and keep your hands to yourself?"

"What happened?" he asked softly, giving me a small nod of understanding when I stayed quiet. "Alright. I'll crash here and keep an eye on her. Are you okay? Need me to call someone to come and pick you up?"

I shook my head, pulling my phone from my pocket. "It's fine. I've got a lift coming."

Why did I keep lying to people?

"Let me know when you're home safe," he said firmly, kissing the top of my head. "I love you."

"Love you too," I mumbled before slipping away from him and ignoring Angel's curious gaze as I left the room and headed outside, the cool night air making me shiver.

My Corvette was safely locked in the garage, so I wandered down the road for a while until I admitted defeat and scrolled through my phone until I found the number I was looking for. I didn't want to walk home and sulk in my room for the rest of the evening.

Reid answered on the first ring, amusement in his voice. "Evening, Donovan."

"Does that offer still stand about coming and getting drunk with you guys?" I asked quietly, silence greeting me for a moment before he replied.

"Of course," he said lightly, but I knew he wanted to ask what was wrong. He wouldn't though, we weren't like that.

"Can you come and get me?" I chewed on my bottom lip absently, hoping I didn't have to find another way there. I wasn't going to risk driving myself.

"I can send Logan and Zavier to get you. They're just about to leave the docks, and they've got my car," he said without hesitation, relief filling me.

"What are they doing at the docks?"

"Wet Dreams. Logan wanted to watch pussy taunt him, and Zavier's on babysitting duty," he muttered. "Send me your location and I'll make sure they get you on their way back."

"Thanks, Reid."

"Any time." Then he hung up to call his friends.

I sat on the side of the road, sending my location to Reid before laying back on the grass to wait. It was dark, the streetlight above me being the only light in the area. My fingers itched for my bat that I'd left in my car, and I suddenly realized how stupid it was of me to be laying here in the dark on my own without a weapon.

Luckily, a familiar car engine sounded from close by within ten minutes, and I lifted my head to find Zavier sitting in the driver's seat of Reid's Challenger, his eyebrow raised.

"I heard you need a ride?"

"You heard correctly. Where's my pussy pal at? Did you leave him face down in dirty pussy?" I joked as I got to my feet, Logan's face popping into view from the passenger seat.

He was definitely drunk.

"Pussy pals unite!" he cheered, making Zavier sigh.

"He's had a few too many. He's going to climb in the back so you can sit up front."

Logan laughed loudly, unclipping his seat belt and throwing himself between the seats to try and squeeze into the back. He wiggled, his hips getting stuck, making me snort.

"Hey! Did I make it? I can't tell!" he called as I approached the passenger door and opened it, finding his ass in the air and his legs kicking about, narrowly missing Zavier who scowled.

"Stop kicking! You'll smash Reid's stereo!"

"At least I'll get to smash something tonight!" he cackled, kicking his legs around harder while moaning dramatically as Zavier slapped him hard on the ass. "Oh, Daddy!"

"For fuck's sake," he growled, grabbing Logan's legs and giving him a shove, causing him to tumble into the back. I smiled with amusement as I slid into the seat and buckled up, glancing at Zavier as he started to drive.

"Thanks for this."

"You want to tell me what happened?" he asked carefully, surprising me and making me look at him. The car was dark now that the door was closed and the interior light was off but I could make out his expression in the moonlight. He seemed unsure, his eyes focused on the road ahead. He didn't know me so he probably thought I'd want to have a girly vent about my problems. That would've made us both uncomfortable.

"Not particularly. It's gay girl shit," I deadpanned, and

Logan's head popped out from between the seats with a wide grin.

"Like, *really* gay girl stuff?"

I placed my hand on his forehead, shoving him back as my mouth curved into a teasing smile. "None of your business, Donahue."

My phone vibrated and I cringed when I realized it was a text from Ryder.

Ryder: Are you alive? Kidnapped? Or did you get home and forget to fucking message me?

Riley: Sorry. I've gone out, but I'm okay.

Ryder: With fucking who?

Riley: Just make sure Luna's okay, and keep your nose out of my shit.

Ryder: Fine. But only because I like Luney.

Riley: Touch her and die, asshole.

Ryder: I'd never!

The winky face he sent after told me he was full of shit, but he wouldn't do anything with her when she was drunk, which was the only reason I trusted him with her right now. If she was sober and threw herself at him though? He wouldn't push her away.

Maybe it was time I realized she'd never be mine.

80
100
120
140
160
180
200
220
km/h
240
260

Chapter Ten

Luna

"Fuck." I cringed as I woke up, the sunlight blinding me as it peeked through the crack in the curtain. My head was thumping, and my mouth tasted like ass.

"It must be bad if you're cursing," a rough voice rumbled from behind me, making me scream in surprise. I jerked away and almost fell off the bed, finding Ryder's sleepy eyes on me as he winced. "Damn, Luney. Always knew you'd be a screamer."

"What are you doing in here?" I demanded, my head thumping harder from my sudden awakening. "Wait, where—"

"We're at Angel's." He closed his eyes and tucked his arms under his head, making his muscles flex. "You must have been wasted if you don't even remember where you are."

Memories flashed back to me in snippets, my face heating as I remembered kissing Riley during truth or dare. "Where's Riley? Why are you in here?"

He sighed, squinting at me for a second before reaching

out to wrap an arm around my middle, tugging me against him to snuggle me against his heated, bare chest. "I slept in here to make sure you didn't choke on your own vomit in your sleep. You're welcome. Can you be quiet now? My head hurts." I was tense in his hold, and he instantly let go when he realized I wasn't happy about it. I needed space while I tried to get my bearings. "Do you remember anything after you went to bed?" he asked as he peered over at me, his eyebrows furrowing with confusion. "Riley was upset with you. She asked me to keep an eye on you before she left."

I moved back from him, frowning. "She was upset?"

"Yeah. Whatever you did, you hurt her. She wasn't angry, she was sad," he grunted. "If you were a guy, I'd beat you up. It's the only thing that sucks about her being gay. I can't do shit if someone hurts her." I noticed my phone on the bedside table and grabbed it to open the tracking app. I frowned when I realized her location was off. He chuckled, rolling onto his back and dropping an arm across his eyes to block out the light. "I already tried that. She wouldn't tell me where she went. She's probably at home by now anyway." I tried to call her but it went straight to voicemail, so I texted her to tell her to call me. "I don't know what's going on," Ryder murmured, his eyes now on mine. "But don't fuck with my sister. You're sweet, but you hold the power to destroy her. No one in the world has that kind of power."

"She knows we're just friends," I said sharply, his lips kicking up into a smirk.

"Didn't seem that way when you were hanging off her last night after making out with her. Your little game of truth or dare is the talk of the town right now."

I groaned, scrubbing a hand over my face. "People kiss in that game all the time. Why is our kiss circulating?"

He sat up, raking his fingers through his messy, black hair as he continued to smirk. "Because it wasn't just a kiss. I've seen the video. You were in her lap eating her face with your hands all over her tits."

"There's a video?" I asked as my heart rate spiked with anxiety.

"There's lots of videos. Sweet, little Luna Hendricks practically fucking her gay bestie at a party? Scandalous," he teased before his face turned serious. "If you're not into her, don't do that shit again. It's not cute. You want to make out with girls to get a bunch of drunk guys' attention? Then find another straight girl who's not in love with you."

"Ry, I didn't—"

"I know you didn't mean to upset her, but you did. I don't need your boyfriend coming after her either. No doubt he's seen the video by now and is pissed about it," he muttered as he swung his legs out of bed. The door opened, and I found Beckett glaring at me.

"Morning, ugly twin," Ryder taunted, but Beckett ignored him and continued to glare at me.

"What did you do?"

"I don't know," I answered quietly, knowing exactly what she was referring to. "I don't remember her leaving."

Her jaw clenched as she answered sharply. "Get up. You're coming with me."

Ryder groaned, throwing his arms around me defensively. "Please, Beck. Don't take her for a ride in the trunk. She's too pretty to end up as worm food. At least let me bang her first."

Fear trickled down my spine as I realized Beckett could

definitely be here to dispose of me for hurting her sister, but an amused smile tugged at her lips, calming me instantly.

"I'm not here to kill anyone. I know where she is, and Luna's coming with me to face the consequences of her actions."

"Where is she?" I blurted out, her eyebrow quirking.

"Dad tracked her down. She's in the Heights."

"With Ander?" I questioned, making her pause.

"What the fuck do you know about Ander?" she finally asked, crossing her arms to study me. "Does she talk about him?"

I shook my head, climbing out of bed and quickly patting my dress down when I realized I'd flashed Ryder my panties. Embarrassment washed through me, but since he didn't mention it, neither did I. "She just told me about the other night and said she got shot at because people were after Ander."

She relaxed, giving me a nod. "Something like that. She's not with Ander, she's at Raven's."

"Your friend?"

"Sort of," she sighed, becoming impatient. "Just put your shoes on and let's go. I don't have all day." I scrambled to do as she demanded, not wanting to piss her off, and the moment we were in her car and on the way to the Heights, she spoke. "I know you don't have a bad bone in your body, which is why I didn't drag you out by your hair this morning, but that doesn't mean I'm not mad at you."

I glanced at her, flinching as she cracked her knuckles on the steering wheel. "I don't remember much from last night. Ry said there's a video going around, but it was truth or dare. We weren't—"

"It's a video of Riley finally claiming what she wants,"

she cut in, her eyes staying on the road. "Everyone knows she wants you, Luna. Right now, she looks like an idiot."

"Why? She kisses girls all the time," I said as I clasped my hands together on my lap, looking down at them as my eyebrows drew together in thought. I was probably one of the only girls Riley hadn't kissed until last night.

"Because you'll run along home to your boyfriend and she'll get pissed and cause a scene. I hope you're ready for that, by the way."

"What do you mean?" Worry ate at me at the thought of Riley going on a rampage, and it got worse when Beckett replied.

"You think Riley's going to let you go now she's had a taste of you? You know my sister better than almost anyone, so don't act dumb. She's going to do something stupid to claim you," she tsked, and we didn't talk again until we pulled up in front of a rundown house. I frowned when I noticed Riley's Supra in the driveway.

"She drove here while drunk?"

Beckett snorted, giving me a side eye. "Like you can talk after your recent drunk driving display. But no. Zavier's had her car since they got shot at the other night. He was there and needed a way home, so Riley let him take it. Her Corvette's still in Angel's garage."

She climbed out and shut the door, and I quickly followed her. I didn't want to be left alone outside, especially since the neighbor's curtains kept moving as they obviously watched us.

I'd heard bad things about Hawthorne Heights, and I didn't want to get robbed or raped out in the open. I'd be fine as long as I stuck close to Beckett.

She was the type to stab first then ask questions later.

Beckett let out a huff of annoyance as I walked so close

to her that I bumped into her, but she didn't say anything as we reached the door. She knocked on it firmly, waiting for it to open before jutting her foot out to stop it from slamming in her face.

"Morning, asshole. Where is she?" she asked sharply while some guy grimaced before opening the door wide. I recognized him from the track, his name was Reid, but I usually just stuck with Riley and Landon. Since Zane had been hanging around Beckett, we'd been keeping our distance.

"Morning. She's in Logan's room." His amber eyes ran over me curiously, and Beckett snorted as she shoved past him.

"Don't even bother. That's Riley's property."

"Hey!" I snapped, but the guy sighed.

"Yeah, I know all about her. Come in, Luna. We haven't officially met, but I'm Reid. Feel free to follow Beckett."

I thanked him as I chased after her, not wanting to be stuck with a guy I didn't know, but I wasn't expecting to find Riley curled up in bed with another guy. He was spooning her, her blonde hair covering his face.

Beckett glanced at me, amusement lining her tone. "Wow, Hendricks. You messed my sister up so bad you turned her straight. I always knew she'd have bad taste in men."

"I don't think it works like that," I said out loud despite wondering if she was right, making her grin.

"I guess we're about to find out."

I jumped as Reid showed up behind me with Zavier, who seemed just as nervous to see Beckett. From what I'd seen at the track, they were all really good friends with her, so I didn't understand why they were acting so weird right now.

I'd had no idea Riley was friends with them though. She'd always hated Zavier and usually kept us away from him when he was hanging out with Beckett at the house.

"They talked about pussy for hours, got way too drunk, then passed out like this. We figured we'd leave them alone. If Logan tried to touch her, she'd rip his balls off," Reid explained, giving me a frown. "I'm surprised you're here. She wasn't happy with you."

Zavier's eyes widened when he noticed me. "Shit. Luna? No. You can't be here. She's going to rip your tits off."

I guess she liked him enough to bitch about me to him last night.

"Whoever's dick's against me had better get it off my ass before I tear it from your body," Riley mumbled without opening her eyes, making Reid chuckle as he leaned against the door frame.

"I'd get away from it if I were you. You don't know what you'll catch."

Her eyes flew open and she bailed from the bed, glaring at Logan. "Ew. Do you have a death wish, asshole? Why were you in bed with me?"

Logan groaned, peering up at her sleepily. "Is this a dream? Or did I really manage to get Riley fucking Donovan in my bed? And I don't remember it? Aw, man."

Beckett rolled her eyes, but I was frozen in place as Riley turned to face us and her eyes landed on me. She stiffened, hurt swirling in her gaze for a second before she looked away from me to give Beckett her attention.

"You tracked me?"

"Why are you even here?" Beckett demanded, motioning to Logan. "And in bed with that idiot?"

"None of your business. You don't own people, Beck. I'm allowed to hang out with your friends." She turned her gaze to me again before snorting. "And take her home. I don't want her here."

My heart ached at her words, my voice quiet. "Riley, I didn't—"

"You didn't what?" she snapped, glaring at me with frustration. "Didn't mean to make out with me? Paw at me in bed? Or maybe the part where you said you were happy to mess around because no one would know? If you want to feel good, use your fucking hand like everyone else."

"Oh, shit," one of the guys said under their breath, but I stepped closer to Riley with a cringe.

"I didn't mean it like that."

"No? So you've gotten rid of your boyfriend? You're ready to let people know you want to fuck me?" she practically shouted, making me take a step back as my head hammered from the volume. "Fuck you, Luna. You want to get a free pussy trial, then go back to dick? Then you can fuck around with someone else. You know I fucking love you, you said so yourself last night, so don't fucking play games with me!"

"I'm sorry," I choked out as I spun around and pushed past the guys, almost running into someone in the living room on my way out. Raven looked close to my age, her bright blue hair seeming extra vibrant as the morning sun hit it.

I darted around her and yanked the front door open, taking a deep breath as the cool air hit me, my back pressing against the side of the house. Tears streamed down my face as I heard Riley yelling something else, and I jumped when someone thrust a glass of water at me.

I expected it to be Raven for some reason, but when I glanced up, I found Reid watching me with a frown.

"Here." I took it, taking a sip to calm myself, relief

hitting me as he offered me a cigarette. "Sit. It seems everyone got too drunk last night."

I sat on the step and waited for him to light his own cigarette before handing me the lighter. "Thanks."

"It's okay. I know Riley can be like a bomb when she goes off," he said with a small smile. "I've heard a lot about you."

"All bad, I bet," I replied tightly, making him laugh.

"Not at all. I have a feeling you didn't mean to hurt her last night."

I took a drag of the cigarette, blowing the smoke out with a sigh. "I don't even really remember what happened. We played truth or dare and someone dared me to kiss Riley, but the rest? I have no idea."

"She just needs to calm down," he promised, but I was pretty sure she'd need more than that.

If I'd said something like she'd claimed, I was a real bitch.

Riley

The guys left me alone, letting Beckett and I talk in private.

"She really doesn't remember what happened," she said gently, her eyes flashing with annoyance as I sat on the edge of the bed. "I don't like that she said that to you though. You're not her dirty little secret. Take it from someone who had to keep their relationship hidden. It sucks."

"She told me I blurted out my feelings for her while drunk ages ago. She's known this whole time," I huffed, combing my hair with my fingers. "Why didn't she say anything?"

"You're pissed at her about that? Give the girl some slack. She's put up with you pawing at her for years," she scoffed. "Besides, you're the one who played truth or dare with her while she was drunk. A part of that was you being selfish."

"Don't talk to me about self-control. You're the one fucking our brother."

"You can't use that comeback forever," she teased, leaning back against the closed door and crossing her arms. "He's not even our blood brother. Don't make it weird."

I blew out a breath, scrubbing my face with my hands as if to wake myself up properly. I was hungover as fuck. "I'm usually good at taking bullshit, Beck. She hurt me last night though. I don't want to be someone she ticks off her bucket list with and then runs back to her boyfriend."

"Then don't be. Prove to her you can be everything she needs, or let her go. It won't be easy, and as much as I think she's definitely straight, I also believe she loves you more than a friend. You grew up knowing who you were sexually, but if she's starting to second-guess hers, she'll be worried about making a move. You yelling at her won't help."

I clenched my fists, hating to be so out of my element. "I'm good with girls. Why is this so hard?"

She chuckled, giving me an amused smile. "Because you're good with pussy, not love. I found her in bed with Ry this morning."

"I told him to make sure she was alright," I grumbled, my chest tightening with worry. "Do you think they fucked? I'll bash his skull in if they did."

"I don't think so. Ry's an idiot, but he knows what she means to you. She's probably the last girl in the world he'd stick his dick in. Now, go sort your shit out with Luna. The guys can be pretty charming, and I bet she's Logan's type."

I shuddered, hating the thought. "She has a pussy. Of course she's his type."

"Which brings us back to my real reason for showing up," she scowled, her shoulders tensing. "How the fuck do you know these guys so much? Why didn't you tell me you've been hanging out with them?"

"We kept running into each other, so we figured we'd try it deliberately sometimes," I said, telling a half-truth. "I text Reid. We talk about cars and pussy."

She rolled her eyes, opening the door to let me out as I got to my feet and snatched my shoes. "I'm surprised you even like them. I recall you hating Zav."

"Oh, we don't really hang out much. He's still an ass," I answered firmly as we walked down the hallway, and I was annoyed to find Luna on the couch sitting between Logan and Reid. Logan was flirting up a storm, and she leaned back towards Reid more as if he was a safer option.

He'd fuck her brains out too, but he'd be less forward about it.

"I'm going. Thanks for last night," I stated as I glanced at Logan, acting as if we didn't hang out frequently with the racing, his eyes sparkling with mischief.

"Any time, Donovan. You want a pussy pity party another time, you call me."

"Sounds wonderful," I deadpanned, walking towards the door and glancing over my shoulder at the last minute. "You coming, Lou?"

She dove off the couch to follow me as Zavier tossed me the keys to the Supra, and I wasn't surprised when Beckett didn't join us. She'd hang around for ages and grill the guys about our friendship.

I didn't worry about them spilling my secrets since they

were trying to keep those same secrets hidden from Raven too.

I backed out of the driveway, feeling Luna's gaze on me the whole way back to Ashburn Valley, where I finally sighed. "I'm sorry for losing my shit, but I'm not going to humor you while you get the good ol' lesbian college experience then go back to guys."

"I didn't mean it like that. I swear. I was mad at Stan, and I never should've played that game. I don't regret kissing you though."

I frowned, glancing at her as my heart started beating faster. "What do you mean?"

"It was nice," she murmured, her cheeks flushing pink. "You're a good kisser."

"I liked kissing you too, but I have a feeling it meant a lot more to me than it did to you," I said softly as I turned my attention back to the road, but I startled as her hand landed on my thigh. Her eyes clashed with mine as I looked back at her, finding her nervously chewing on her bottom lip.

"I feel... Confused about everything. I liked it, so does that mean I'm bisexual?"

I blew out a breath, not expecting to be giving someone a sex talk first thing in the morning. "I can't tell you how you feel, Lou. You need to figure that out for yourself. I won't lie though, most straight women I've met who said that are usually still straight and they were just curious. They get a taste of pussy, realize it's not for them, then they go back to dick. It's a lesbian's first rule. Never fall in love with a straight chick."

"How's that working for you?" she murmured as her mouth curved into a soft smile, making me laugh.

"You're a little bit sassy this morning considering you

must have the hangover from hell and have an impending argument with your boyfriend." She cringed, my eyes widening with sarcasm. "Ohh. You haven't even spoken to him yet, have you? You ran right to me."

"There's a video going around of us playing truth or dare," she said as she tucked her hair behind her ear. "He definitely knows by now that I had my tongue down your throat last night."

"Wait until I tell him you were begging to sit on my face," I grinned as a groan left her.

"I did not! I'm not that forward in bed!"

"You should be. Always ask for what you want, Lou. Don't be ashamed of your needs or desires."

"Is that why you're so confident?"

I pulled up in front of my house, killing the engine and turning to face her. "I'm confident because I know I'm good in bed. Some girls take forever to get off, but I'm not done until they come on my fingers or tongue."

"What if they fake it?" she asked curiously, making me smirk.

"Trust me, you can tell when they're faking it and when it's real. You just have to be attentive to what their body's telling you. You want a coffee? I need one," I said before bailing from the car, needing to put some space between us.

The house was quiet when we walked inside, but Mom was sitting at the kitchen table with a whiskey in hand.

"Long night?" I asked with a raised eyebrow as she met my gaze.

"I could say the same about you," she replied lightly, her eyes sliding to Luna. "Morning, Luna."

"Beckett's with Reid and the others. She's fine," she blurted out, making Mom's lips twitch.

"Yes. She mentioned going over there to track down Riley, but thank you for letting me know."

"Kiss ass," I muttered under my breath, moving to make us both a cup of coffee before sitting opposite Mom. "How's everything—"

"You want to explain the video that's online everywhere right now?" she cut in bluntly with narrowed eyes, and I shrugged.

"The kissing one? Not much to explain. We played truth or dare, and someone dared Lou to kiss me."

Luna groaned, hiding her face in her hands. "Dad's going to kill me."

"Don't you have a boyfriend?" Mom hummed. "Does he know about this?"

As if on cue, her phone rang, and I snatched it from her fingers with a smirk and hit answer. "Morning, Stanley. Sorry, she's busy right now. Want me to give her a message?"

"Riley!" Luna whisper-yelled, but Stanley was fuming.

"Put her on the fucking phone, you dumb bitch! You think you can get my girl drunk and take advantage of her?" he barked, amusement washing through me.

"You think you can tag team girls with your buddies and she wouldn't find out? I'm a good shoulder to cry on. You know that saying? A shoulder to cry on's a dick to ride on? Well, in this case, a shoulder to cry on's a pussy to glide on. I can still taste her on my lips this morning," I taunted, laughing as Luna yanked the phone from my grip and clutched it to her chest.

"Oh my God, you're the worst!" she snapped, stalking from the room to continue her phone call. "Baby? No. She's just trying to make you mad."

Her footsteps moved further into the house, and Mom pinned me with a glare. "What the fuck, Riley?"

"What? He's an asshole," I said before taking a sip of my coffee, a snort leaving her.

"Why did you kiss her in the first place? Archer's going to kill you."

"You're acting like I fucked her. It was just a little kiss."

"Little kiss? Honey, your tongue was down her throat," she said dryly, a grin tugging at the corners of my lips.

"And her hands were all over my tits. What's your point?"

"You're as bad as your brother," she scolded, but affection flickered in her blue eyes as she swept her black hair back from her face. "But I know she's not just a game for you. Don't get hurt, baby."

"I'll make sure to warm up my muscles first," I teased as she stood and kissed the top of my head.

"You know what I mean. You've hardly been home lately. Do me a favor?" she asked, giving my shoulder a gentle squeeze.

"Anything."

"Come spend some time with your old mom soon. I miss you," she smiled, sadness flicking across her face. "Ry and Marla don't appreciate my company like you do."

"The infamous Rory Donovan's a big ol' softie?" I said, faking a gasp of shock. "Wait until the tabloids hear about this!"

"You're a brat," she chuckled, placing her empty coffee cup on the counter and giving me a wink. "But yes. When it comes to you kids, you know I'm a fucking marshmallow."

"It can be our secret. I won't sell you out," I winked back, feeling bad for not spending time with her lately.

Our housekeeper, Sarah, wandered into the room,

giving me a warm smile. She only popped by occasionally now that she was getting too old to manage the whole house. I was rarely home when she was here. "There you are! Shouldn't you be at school?"

"Shouldn't you be in a coffin by now, you old bat?" I threw back playfully, making Mom scowl.

"Riley!"

"What? I say it affectionately," I smiled sweetly, kissing Sarah on the cheek as I got to my feet. "Right, Sarah?"

"You'll be in a coffin before me if you keep being a little shit," she warned, but her eyes sparkled with amusement. "Put your laundry in the basket and I'll get it done for you."

"Sarah—" Mom sighed, rubbing her temples. "Remember what we said? Those jobs are too much for you now. Besides, I like that the kids clean up after themselves. Having money doesn't mean they have to be treated like privileged little cunts. You've seen those entitled Crestford kids."

Sarah clicked her tongue with annoyance. "I'm not that old. I like looking after this family. Ryder can wash his own bedding though. I draw the line at that."

I snickered, but the amusement slipped as Luna wandered back in, her phone tightly in her hand by her side. She blinked quickly, trying to keep tears at bay. "Um, can you take me to Stan's?"

"What did that prick say to you?" I demanded, surprised when she stood up straighter, her voice firm.

"Nothing. I'm just ready to go."

I went to argue, knowing he'd yelled at her and was making her leave, but Mom spoke up before I could. "I'm heading to the Devil's warehouse to meet Marco. I'll give you a ride since it's on the way." I turned to glare at her, finding her stern eyes already on me. "And you can run an errand for me. Beckett managed to get a deal sorted with the Night Thieves for some of their surveillance equipment. Go pick it up for me."

"I love you, but that sounds like crew business. They're Beckett's friends, so she can get it. She's already in the Heights, she can grab it on her way back," I argued, not wanting to deal with them.

Luna looked worried for me, but Mom shrugged. "It's the only excuse you have to avoid school today. You either do that for me, or you get your ass into gear and go to your classes."

"That's bullshit," I grumbled, a light laugh leaving her as she walked past me.

"That might be true, but the only rules you kids have is to attend school and drive safely. The fact I haven't brought up your recent Crestford incident should also be noticed. You can come with me and discuss that in detail if you want?"

"Send me the address for the Night Assholes," I grunted, hating that Luna didn't give me another glance before leaving the house with Mom talking over her shoulder.

"You're a good girl. Angel dropped your Corvette off too. It's in the garage."

I flipped her the middle finger behind her back and a scoff left her. "I saw that, you cheeky shit."

I swore she had eyes in the back of her head.

At least I had my car back and didn't have to fuck around getting it today.

100
120
140
160
180
200
220
km/h
240
260

Chapter Eleven

Riley

I parked my Corvette right in front of the Night Thieves' compound, rolling my eyes when the door opened and the grumpy fucker from the night at the gas station stalked out to greet me. It was like a fucking army compound, and it was obvious this fucker ran the place.

"Stone," I said dryly without getting out of the car, his annoyed, dark gray eyes on me.

"I don't like you," he announced bluntly, a snort leaving me.

"Any particular reason why? I won't be able to sleep at night unless I know."

He scowled, but Cruz's amused face popped up beside him, his voice playful. "Because we had to clean up a bunch of surveillance that had you on it recently. Your family wasn't too happy to see you speeding through multiple towns being shot at. Cops were sniffing around, so we had to get rid of evidence."

"Oh, I'm sorry. Next time someone's shooting at me, I'll remember to cause less of a scene," I deadpanned, holding my hand out the window impatiently. "Give me this shit for Mom so I can go. I'm busy."

"Got plans with your cute little friend?" Cruz asked, my eyes narrowing. I didn't want them knowing about Luna. They already knew too much about me, and there was no way I'd let them near her. From the way Cruz was looking at me, I had a feeling he was referring to the video of me and Luna at the party.

When I stayed silent, Stone scoffed. "Nothing to say this time?"

"I don't feel the need to waste words," I growled, shoving the Corvette's door open and giving them no choice but to step back as I climbed out, grabbing my bat before locking the car. "I'm here to pick shit up, not chitchat."

"You know that video of you and your friend is in my spank bank, right?" Cruz teased as we walked towards the main entrance. "She looks sweet and innocent, but I bet—" I swung my bat at the back of his legs, not enough to break them, but hard enough that it sent him sprawling across the ground. Stone looked at us like we bored him, but Cruz winced as he peered up at me. "You need a warning label."

I rolled my eyes, continuing to follow Stone inside and leaving his friend where he was, and I was surprised to find it so busy inside. People were everywhere, some cleaning guns while others studied laptop monitors on couches.

It was like something out of a fucking spy movie.

"Avert your eyes and mind your own business," Stone ordered as he shoved open another door to a room full of computer screens and desks, not bothering to hold it open for me as it almost smacked me in the face.

"If you have a girlfriend, I'll be extremely surprised." I watched him yank open a closet and pull a bag out. "You're awfully cranky."

"I didn't think you liked wasting words?" he snapped, a slow smirk spreading across my face.

"They're not wasted if they piss you off."

He fumed silently, shoving the bag at my chest and almost knocking me over from the force of it. I stumbled, glaring at the back of his head as he stalked across the room, practically yanking the door off its hinges and storming off.

If Beckett got along with him, it was a miracle.

"Fucking dickhead," I muttered under my breath as I hoisted the bag over my shoulder and managed to open the door despite having my hands full. My bat was annoying sometimes, but I'd never go into weird places without it.

"Let me take that for you." I glanced to the left to find Cruz, his eyebrows furrowed. "Sorry. Stone's a prick sometimes."

I stepped back as he reached for the bag. "I've got it. But yes, your friend's a prick. Definitely single too. If he does have a girlfriend though, send her my way. I'll save her."

He chuckled, falling into step beside me as I walked towards the front door. "We're too busy for relationships."

"Yeah, I hear you guys steal stuff."

"*Stuff*? This isn't child's play," he huffed as if I'd offended him, pushing the door open and holding it for me as I stepped out into the warm sun. "That's like saying you play with cars."

"If anyone asks, that's *exactly* what you tell them too," I said tightly. Too many people knew my secrets, which was making me nervous.

"Why would someone ask me about you?" he continued lightly, lifting a shoulder in a half shrug. "We don't hang out."

"There's been a lot of close calls this week," I grunted,

opening the trunk and placing the bag inside before slamming it shut. "I'd prefer it if you forgot I existed."

"I don't forget a pretty face."

"You will if I give you brain damage," I smiled darkly, patting my bat affectionately. "I don't get to choose where the races are. I'm sorry if you don't like us tearing up Rawson."

He eyed me as I climbed into the driver's seat and started the engine, his hands going to my open door frame as I lit a cigarette. "I know. How would you like it if we started rolling through Ashburn Valley with our business though?"

I paused, tilting my head in thought before finally shrugging. "To be honest? I don't give a fuck if you come to my town to steal shit. The only things worth stealing are ours, and good luck getting away with it."

"Half of Ashburn is fucking loaded," he said lightly before changing the subject. "Say hey to Donovan... uh, Beckett for me. Tell her I'll stop by this week for a beer."

I raised an eyebrow, surprised by their casual friendship. "You guys actually hang out?"

"Well, sort of," he grinned and stepped back. "I hang out with Jett and she always happens to be there."

"I'm not even surprised that you two get along," I muttered, putting the car in gear and blowing smoke at him. "Enjoy your spank bank."

"I will. I'll be able to think of you every time the bruise on my leg hurts," he said with a mock salute before walking back inside, letting me leave in peace.

I called Beckett on the hands-free, her sharp voice hitting my speakers almost instantly. "The fuck are you doing in Rawson?"

"I miss you too, big sis," I said brightly, switching gears as I got out onto the main road. "Mom sent me to pick up some stuff. Trust me, I don't want to be here. Your friends are assholes."

"Knox is a little bit of a grumpy pants, sure," she said with a chuckle, seeming to relax at knowing I wasn't causing trouble.

"I meant all of them. I don't know who the fuck Knox is, I've only met Cruz and Stone."

I relayed Cruz's message, making her groan. "He's been here more than me this week, I swear. I got home the other day to him napping on the couch with Jett. If I didn't know Jett was straight, I'd swear he was having an affair with that fucker."

I snorted, not at all surprised. "They're scarily similar."

"Yeah. Try spending time with them both at once. You heading back home now? I can meet you there if you want?" she offered, but I had a better idea.

"You feel like a drink? I'll meet you at Harley's Bar in a few hours once I've had a fucking nap. I heard he got a pool table."

"Sold. Text me when you're ready," she replied before hanging up.

I enjoyed the cool breeze as I drove, tapping my fingers on the steering wheel to the beat of the music. I might have loved racing, but a slow drive was nice sometimes.

Once I was home, I dumped the bag in the office, then I trudged upstairs to my room. I needed a nice, relaxing afternoon. It was either that or I stormed through Stanley's house and beat him with my bat for upsetting Luna.

I didn't think she'd appreciate that.

I was furious that he'd cheat on her so easily. She was beautiful, smart, and funny. Sure, she was shy and didn't like big gatherings, but she was insanely loyal and sweet. It was the reason I wasn't expecting her to play truth or dare at the party, let alone go through with kissing me.

There was something fucking wrong with him.

I wished she could love me instead because I'd make sure she got the whole world.

Luna

"Call me if you need me," Rory said firmly as we pulled up in front of Stanley's house to find Stanley standing by the front door looking pissed off. I forced a smile, giving her a small nod.

"I will. Thanks for the ride."

"Any time," she answered, her eyes on Stanley. I hoped he didn't start shouting at me until after she'd left or she'd probably pull a gun on him. She didn't take kindly to violence aimed at women or kids, so if she was worried about me, she'd simply eliminate the threat.

Luckily, she drove off the moment I got to the door and he gave me a tight smile, kissing the top of my head to act like he was happy to see me. "If you want to kiss girls, all you have to do is ask."

I frowned, glancing up at him as he led me inside. "Huh?"

"You want to fuck girls?" he asked bluntly, the door slamming behind him and making me jump. "Then you fuck them in front of me. Literally, any girl you want, you can have, but not that cunt. She's lucky I don't slam her bat up her pussy and tear her to shreds." I tensed, stumbling as he got sick of me being slow and gave me a firm shove into the kitchen. "Everyone's talking about it, you know?" he continued, his eyes blazing with anger. "How Riley

Donovan managed to finally get her hands on you. You're mine, Luna. How could you do this to me?"

I swallowed, looking at the ground as shame washed through me. "I was upset with you and got drunk. I—"

His hand slammed down on the counter, my heart rate spiking. He'd never turned violent with me, but he was scaring me. "What the fuck did I do to you? I let you go to the track, and this is how you repay me? By lying and going to a party to make out with her? Did you fuck her too?"

"No!" I promised, my voice coming out pitchy. "It was just truth or dare and someone dared me to kiss her! I was upset at you because I saw you having sex with that girl when I left!"

His features cooled, a heavy sigh leaving him as if this was all my fault. "Don't you see Riley's just trying to put a wedge between us?"

"I saw you, Stan," I murmured, tears burning my eyes. "Why aren't I good enough for you?"

"You are good enough," he said gently, reaching out to cup my chin, stroking my cheek with his thumb and giving me emotional whiplash. "I just like sex a lot more than you do. I figure this way we can both get what we want."

I bit my tongue so hard that I tasted blood, counting to five before replying. "I can do more. Maybe you can teach me some stuff?"

He chuckled, drawing me against his chest to kiss my head. "This is why I love you. Always so eager to please me."

"I'm sorry about Riley," I whispered, guilt eating at me. "I was just really upset with you. It won't happen again."

"That's okay. I know she pushed you," he said seriously, my stomach twisting from his accusation, but like a coward I kept silent. "I forgive you. I have a killer headache. Can you tidy up for me?"

I glanced around the trashed kitchen, knowing the rest of the house would look the same. I hoped doing as he asked would relax him. "Uh, sure."

"You're the best." He leaned down to kiss my lips softly, his voice a whisper. "We'll go out for dinner tonight, hmm?"

"That sounds nice," I smiled tightly, waiting for him to trudge off to bed before I let out a sigh. I should've told him to take a hike. He wasn't even hiding the fact he was cheating on me regularly, and I'd just accepted it.

What the hell was wrong with me?

Ryder and Riley both slept around a lot, but they didn't date. I was starting to think those people who told me all guys cheat at this age were full of shit. If Stanley wanted to sleep around, why did he ask me out in the first place?

My chest ached at the thought of losing him, and I squashed the pity party I was having. Maybe once I learned some new sex techniques, he'd stay loyal to me. I really wasn't good in bed, he'd told me so himself.

I started cleaning the kitchen, suddenly realizing he hadn't apologized to me for sticking his dick in that girl despite wanting an apology from me.

As usual, I let it go.

The house was spotless by the time Stanley woke up a few hours later, and he rewarded me with a beaming smile. "You're such a good girl. Go shower and we'll go out to eat. It's a little early, but I'm hoping we can come back here and watch a movie. Maybe I could teach you some stuff like you suggested."

"If I do more in bed for you, will you stop seeing other girls?" I asked lightly, hoping I didn't look too desperate. "Can you do that for me?"

He looked annoyed, but he shrugged. "Of course. If I want to get adventurous, I'll let you know. I like those girls because they're up for anything, and I know it's not something you're into. I—"

"We can do anything you want," I blurted out, his lips kicking up into a smirk.

"You say that now, but you don't mean it."

"Yes, I do," I said confidently, standing on tiptoes to kiss his cheek. "I love you. I want you to be happy."

"Remember you said that," he warned, the tone giving me a bad feeling.

I shook it off, giving him a smile before going for a quick shower and getting ready to leave.

The drive into town was short, and Stanley held my hand as we walked into Harley's Bar and found a table.

"Hey, Luna," Landon smiled as he walked over to us. "You want a menu?"

I went to reply but Stanley cut me off. "Nope. We know what we want. Burger with fries, and a burger with salad."

I frowned. He hated salad.

It wasn't until Landon returned with our meals that I realized the salad was for me.

Landon slid the plate in front of Stanley, and he scoffed and pushed it in front of me. "Do I look like I need a salad?"

Landon didn't even miss a beat as he answered him. "Yes."

I held back a snort, but I knew Stanley sensed my amusement as he replied sharply. "Do you want to get yourself fired? It's obvious my girl needs the salad. I like my girl's petite, and she's put some weight on."

Landon frowned, his eyes flicking to me. "Luna's tiny."

"Don't you have fucking work to do?" he snapped back, making me scowl.

"Stan!" I whisper-yelled. "Don't be rude."

"Is there a problem?" Uncle Alex asked as he materialized beside his son, his eyes on me. My uncle was a very patient and calm man until someone fucked with his family.

I didn't want a bar fight to break out because Stanley was being a dick.

"No problem," I said cheerfully, hoping he believed me. "We'll be quiet, I promise."

He hummed, his eyes narrowing as he turned his attention to Stanley. "Are you not happy with the service?"

"I don't appreciate this little fucker flirting with my girlfriend while we're on a date," he replied tightly, making me groan.

"Stan—"

He shot me a glare, and I shut my mouth to avoid an argument.

Alex didn't miss the motion, irritation sweeping through him. "They're cousins, but you should learn to accept the fact people will like your girlfriend. She's lovely, and it's hard not to like her."

"The little weirdo probably wants to fuck her still."

"Maybe we should go," I said slowly and went to get to my feet, but Alex blocked my exit.

"Don't be silly. Have your meal," he said firmly, his eyes flashing back to Stanley. "Enjoy your evening."

They walked away, and Stanley scoffed. "Your family's weird."

I ignored him, picking at my salad, not at all surprised when he ended up eating most of my burger. I'd lost my appetite anyway.

The door swung open and Beckett walked in, Riley not far behind her.

I bit back a groan, trying not to draw attention to us, but it was like Riley sensed us. She always found me in a crowd without even knowing I was there.

Her eyes landed on me, and Stanley rested a hand on my leg, digging his fingers in to draw my attention. "You ready to go?"

"Oh. You don't want dessert?"

He always wanted dessert.

"You don't need it."

Ouch. I had no idea where the hell his attitude had come from, but I didn't like it.

We slipped from the booth and he dropped some money on the table, my stomach twisting as I noticed he didn't leave a tip. He was such an ass.

"Hey, Lou. Date night?" Riley asked flatly, and Beckett paused by the bar to glance back at us, hearing Riley's tone.

"Yeah," I mumbled. "We're—"

"We're just leaving," Stanley bit out, dropping an arm around my shoulders to keep me close. "You're a little homewrecking cunt, Donovan. I don't think you should hang out with my girl anymore. You're going to get her in trouble."

Riley's eyes were on my bare legs, and I knew my dress wasn't hiding the finger marks he'd probably left there a moment ago. She slowly dragged her gaze up to my face, frustration sweeping through her before she looked at Stanley.

"If you weren't such a piece of shit, you wouldn't have to worry so much about losing her. Give her a kiss and tell me how I taste."

He shoved me back and stepped closer to her with his

fists clenched, but Beckett was suddenly between them, her knife against his throat. "I fucking dare you."

I covered my mouth with my hand as if to cram a scream back down my throat, but Alex appeared beside me, his hand on my shoulder to give me a comforting squeeze while he spoke firmly to the others.

"Beckett, you know the rules. You can't just pull that thing out whenever you wish. You're scaring Luna too."

Riley's eyes jerked towards me, but Beckett sighed and stepped back. "It's not my fault. People keep pissing me off. You saying if someone was threatening Landon, you wouldn't do the same thing?"

"Put. It. Away," he ordered, waiting for her to pocket it before continuing. "You're lucky it's only our regulars in here and they're used to your bullshit."

She shrugged. "I don't see a problem then."

Uncle Alex huffed, turning to assess me before speaking. "I'm due at yours in an hour if you want a lift."

Stanley scoffed, grabbing my wrist and pulling me against him. "She's staying with me."

Alex seemed confused, his eyes burning into me to wait for confirmation. Once I nodded, he sighed. "Alright. Let me know when you get there safely."

Stanley rolled his eyes as he practically dragged me out into the cool air, but when I glanced back, Riley was fuming. Landon stood beside her, talking quietly so I couldn't hear him, but I knew he was telling her about what had happened with the food.

That was the *last* thing I needed.

Stanley kept checking his phone as we drove back to his house, my voice quiet as he started texting someone. "Do you want me to drive?"

"I've got it."

"I don't like it when you use your phone while driving."

He glanced at me, huffing as if I were inconveniencing him before putting the phone in his lap. "I'm a good driver. It's not hard to do both."

I didn't reply, I was just glad he put his phone down.

His mood had completely switched by the time we walked into the house, and I quickly messaged Uncle Alex to let him know we made it so he wouldn't worry. Stanley took my phone from my hands when I opened my emails, giving me a smile. "You want to learn new things in the bedroom? You need to put this down."

I wasn't particularly in the mood after the incidents at the bar, but I nodded. "What are we doing then?"

"We'll start with something we've done before," he promised, steering me towards the bedroom and placing soft kisses across my shoulder. I relaxed, appreciating his gentle side.

"Strip for me, baby." I never noticed that my stomach didn't get butterflies anymore when he called me that until now. My cheeks flushed as I remembered Riley calling me baby, and Stanley chuckled, thinking he was turning me on. "You're a naughty girl."

I stripped and crawled onto the bed, his eyes raking over me slowly. I was used to being exposed to him, but discomfort twisted inside me as he studied me.

"Is something wrong?"

"No," he grunted, walking to his side of the bed and opening a drawer. "Lay on your back for me."

I did as I was instructed, excitement washing through me as he pulled out some handcuffs. I liked being tied up, and it was something we'd done a lot at the start of our relationship.

He secured my wrists, surprising me as he pulled out two more cuffs. "You got more?"

He grinned, giving me a wink. "I thought you'd like them. You have small ankles, so this should work easily."

The cool metal tickled my heated skin as he secured my feet to the bed frame, and I shivered as he sat between my legs, eyeing my pussy. "I like you like this. Spread out for me to do what I want with you."

He reached out and teased my clit, making me jerk with a groan. "You're going to tease me, aren't you?"

"Definitely," he laughed, leaning down to place kisses on my inner thigh.

I closed my eyes, enjoying his soft touches as he explored my body, but I let out a squeal as he sharply nipped the inside of my thigh. "That hurt!"

"It wasn't even that hard," he huffed, his fingers pushing inside me a little more forcefully than usual. "I like it rough, Luna. This is what I've been trying to keep away from you. I knew you wouldn't like it."

He went to pull away, but I chased his hand with my hips. "Wait, I like it. I just didn't expect it."

"You're going to let me fuck you how I want, baby? You'd look so pretty screaming for me," he murmured, reaching out to cup my cheek. I nodded, not wanting him to hurt me, but wanting to please him. If this was what other girls did, I wanted to do it too.

I wanted to make him happy so maybe he'd stay.

He was a little harsh with his fingers as he went back to making me come with his mouth on my clit, and before I'd come down from the high, he stripped his pants off and aligned himself with my entrance.

"You ready?"

I nodded, but I wasn't. I thought he'd ease me into it,

but once he slid inside, he immediately picked up the pace. I bit the inside of my cheek to stop myself from crying out, his fingers digging into my waist as he slammed in and out. Tears burned my eyes from the discomfort, and when I finally begged him to stop, I admitted defeat.

I couldn't be like those girls, and I'd never make him happy.

He didn't stop though, not until he'd finished.

80
100
120
140
160
180
200
220
km/h
240
260

Chapter Twelve

Riley

I blew out a lungful of smoke as I leaned against my car in the parking lot in the Heights a few days after I'd last seen Luna at the bar. Between Friday's lectures and helping Mom at home with Kate and some other kids all day today, I hadn't had time to hunt Luna down.

I knew her excuse of being sick was bullshit, and I was still fuming about how Stanley had been treating her.

I eyed Turbo with annoyance as he pulled up beside me. He was late, and I'd been waiting for twenty minutes. He climbed out, giving me an apologetic look. "Sorry. I had to bail Slick out of lockup in Blackwater."

"Why? Should've just left the prick there," I scoffed, giving him the stink eye. "Everyone else is late too, but you're the only one who didn't feel the need to tell me."

"Where's Reid?"

"Fighting with Raven," I smirked, flicking the ash from the tip of my cigarette. "She caught him and Logan sneaking out."

"How has she not noticed until now?" he snorted and I rolled my eyes.

"Women aren't as stupid as you men make us out to be. She would've noticed after the first or second time, but she's probably been waiting to confront them. I guess tonight's the night."

"If they show up with her tailing them, they'll ruin it for the rest of us," he gritted out, lighting his own cigarette. "We don't need the drama."

"No? You don't seem to have a problem creating it. Speaking of which, where the fuck's my money? I sure as shit didn't get shot at for nothing," I demanded, reaching my hand out. "I want interest since it's late."

"The fuck for? You don't even need it," he said flatly, but he was already moving to his trunk to rummage through bags, his cigarette hanging from his lips. He was insane if he was driving around with loads of cash on him.

"It's the principle," I said lightly, keeping my eyes on him. He could've been thinking about pulling a gun out and killing me for all I knew. "Besides, I'm giving the money to Zavier."

"Aw, you got a soft spot for the Heights' kids? That's cute."

"Zavier had my back that night and got my car home, no thanks to you. He earned that money. I got my rush, he'll get food on his table. It's a fair deal. He's not a kid, he's twenty-three, which might I remind you, is a year older than you."

"You wanted a rush, so I gave you one. I kept my end of the deal. It's not my fault you got more than you bargained for, Donovan," he grunted, slamming the trunk and waving a stack of bills at me, dropping it into my waiting hands. "Ten k."

"I wanted interest."

"That *is* with interest. It wasn't a fucking bank heist," he bit out as I tossed it through my open window.

"You're lucky I'm loaded, because my car's going to cost a fortune to fix."

"It's not even that bad, it'll buff out. I think it adds character," he teased, and I quirked an eyebrow in response as I dropped my cigarette butt on the ground to crush it with my shoe.

"You need some character. Want me to put some rounds in you?"

"You don't even carry," he said smugly, seeming surprised when I walked around my car and opened the passenger door, pulling a gun out of the glove compartment.

"I'm the daughter of two criminal street crews and the niece of two others. I respect you, but don't think for a second it's because I'm scared of you. Our friendship can end as quickly as it would take for one of these bullets to pierce your skull," I answered in a low voice, making sure he knew how serious I was.

He leaned back against his car and crossed his arms with amusement as he studied me. "You're something else."

I rested my arms on the roof of my Corvette, giving him a small smile as I aimed the gun at him and shut one eye, acting like I was lining up a shot. "Fuck with me, I fuck you back harder, Lavaro. Remember that."

"You can fuck me if you like," he drawled, heat filling his steel-gray eyes. "I won't stop you."

Cars joined us, and Reid cursed loudly as he bailed out of the driver's seat. "Jesus, Donovan. What are you doing?"

"We're just playing, right, Turbo?" I said dryly, lowering the gun to my side.

"I'd hate to see what your foreplay's like," Turbo grumbled, but he didn't seem fazed by me throwing authority at him. I knew he was humoring me but part of me wished he'd challenge me so I could have it out with him. I was in the mood to hit someone repetitively.

"If you want foreplay, you'll have to bend over for my bat," I chuckled, glancing at Reid. "Where's your boyfriend?"

He snorted. "Pretty sure he's *your* boyfriend. You were the one snuggling with him last week. He still won't shut up about having you in his bed."

Slick slammed the door to his Mustang and stalked towards us, joining the conversation. "You were snuggling with that skinny little fuck? I thought you were a dyke?"

I turned to Turbo, lifting my gun up to remind him I had it. "Unless you want to be left to peel your buddy off the parking lot after I spread his brain matter across it, I'd make sure he stops with the homophobic shit and the gay slurs."

Slick went to argue, but Turbo cut him a glare. "I've already fucking warned you, asshole."

"You won't let her shoot me," he laughed, his face turning thunderous as Turbo aimed his own gun at him that I hadn't known was tucked into his pants. "Seriously? You're siding with *her*?"

"I don't give a fuck what you do in your spare time, but here? Respect everyone," Turbo said flatly, only lowering the gun when Slick snarled and stomped back to his car, shutting himself inside to wait for further race instructions.

Turbo tucked the gun down the back of his pants, lifting an eyebrow at me in question. "Happy?"

"Immensely," I deadpanned, putting my own gun away and turning to Reid. "So, Logan?"

He crossed his arms, giving me a one-armed shrug. "He's at home. Raven flipped out so Logan and Zav are distracting her for me by continuing the argument."

"You know she's going to strangle you, right? She'd know exactly what they're doing."

"If she's safely at home, she can be as mad at me as she likes," he said firmly, growing irritated. "Are we racing? Or can I leave?"

"If you all stopped fucking around, we could get started," Blake said dryly as she put her window down to lean on the door frame. "Lavaro, where's the starting point?"

"We're starting in Stoneleigh," he replied, his eyes on me as he awaited my reaction, knowing it was the Kings' territory.

I groaned, scrubbing a hand over my face and glancing at my car, wishing I'd just brought the Supra. "Really? I'm literally the only person who has a graffiti-painted Corvette. They'll see me and report back to my parents. Hell, Rage will probably chase us down himself and put bullets in everyone. He doesn't like street racing in his town."

"Cops are everywhere in Rawson tonight, and unless you want to end up in Ashburn Valley, this is the only other option," he said on a sigh. "I promised to keep it out of your town, but I can't keep it out of anywhere else."

I frowned. "What's happening in Rawson?"

"Field party ended with someone getting hit in the face with a glass bottle, and some rich girl from Kingslake got raped. This is why we don't hang out with rich kids," he grumbled, giving me the side-eye. "The Donovans being the exception to that rule."

"Why do all the rich kids get assaulted?" Reid asked, rolling his shoulders to loosen his muscles. "Is it because they don't grow up learning to defend themselves?"

"No," I answered easily. "Mostly it's because it causes the most ruckus. The Tabloids get their hands on it and it blows up. Destroys reputations, causes gossip within inner circles, and a lot of the time those rich girls have been saving their virginities for arranged marriages or social status. No one likes a whore. If someone's promised to a man in a business deal as a virgin, the deal is ruined by the rape. She's no longer a virgin, and her name's tarnished by the pompous pricks of society."

Turbo nodded in silent agreement, but Reid stared at me. "That's a thing? Raping rich girls to ruin business deals? And arranged marriages?"

"The life of the rich and famous isn't all diamonds and champagne," I said as he gaped at me. "Why do you think so many famous people overdose? They spend a lot of time wishing they were someone else, in another reality."

"You're not like that."

I held his gaze, lifting my shoulder in a half shrug. "You can take the criminal away from the street, but you can't take the street away from the criminal, if you know what I mean. We might be rich, but my family is based on the underground and the rough side of town. We don't care for fancy parties or the social standard of appearances. You give me money, and I'll put it under my hood before I spend it on something for my closet."

"As much as this is entertaining," Turbo drawled, opening his car door and sliding inside. "Let's go. We've got a bit of a drive ahead of us."

He started his car and eased out of the parking lot, Slick following him with Blake close behind, but Reid hung back with me. He looked uncomfortable, his voice rough.

"Has someone ever assaulted you to make a point to your family?"

I was surprised by the question, but I shook my head. "No. Have people threatened to? Sure. When Beckett was kidnapped by the Demons, they threatened to rape her. My mom's been raped multiple times, and most of her friends have been raped too. It's not always a rich person thing, it's a vagina kind of thing. We're seen as the weaker sex because of it. Street crews don't like women being involved because they're a target."

"Men can be raped too," he said defensively, relaxing when I nodded.

"Yep. It's actually pretty common, but it's shameful for men to talk about, right? People see statistics and assume it doesn't happen because it's not recorded, but a lot of survivors are too ashamed to step forward and report it. It's the same for domestic violence."

He studied me for a moment before motioning to my car, changing the subject. "We'd better go."

"I'll follow you," I answered, making him snort.

"Nope. I'll take up the rear."

"You take it up the rear?" I teased as I climbed in, and he flipped me the middle finger.

"Not likely. Logan's probably into that kinda thing, but I'm not." I wasn't going to argue with that assumption. I got the vibe he was pretty open to bedroom activities. He was extremely comfortable with himself, but I also didn't think that he was actually into guys. "Ladies first." He grinned, waving me ahead as I started my engine and rolled my eyes, taking off after the others.

I cursed as Slick almost ran me off the road. My engine roared as I shifted gears and backed off to let him ahead to save myself from hitting him. The race started on the northern end of town and finished at the start of Blackwater, and we literally had to race through the middle of the whole fucking town.

Rage was going to have my head for this. There was no way the Kings wouldn't notice an underground street race happening right through the middle of their territory.

I darted around a car that was probably on its way home from a night shift, the lights a blur as we zipped through the streets, narrowly avoiding parked cars and drunk idiots who were stumbling around.

Turbo and Reid were right behind me, leaving me and Slick racing after Blake to get in the lead. I couldn't hear the music that was thumping through my car, the whooshing in my ears too loud as my heart rate hammered through me.

I'd already had a close call with Turbo's car a few streets back, and my adrenaline was pumping through me in waves. It was exhilarating.

I jerked the wheel to the right as the map directed me, biting my lip firmly as fear spiked. My tires screeched as they lost traction, my car sliding and only just managing to right itself at the last minute before it could slam into a parked car.

My guardian angel was definitely having a heart attack right about now.

"You piece of fucking shit!" I barked as Slick's car tapped the back end of Blake's when we reached a country road, sending her spinning across the road and into a field. I slammed my brakes on, letting Turbo and Reid past me without hesitation.

I'd have to yell at Slick later, I wouldn't catch him now.

I yanked my emergency brake on and unbuckled my seat belt, not surprised when I noticed Reid's Challenger idling up the road further, his brake lights glowing in the dark as he waited for us.

We'd all been a bunch of selfish kids when we'd started racing together, but we'd slowly formed a friendship over the years. Reid, Blake, and I definitely had each other's back more than the others though.

Blake's car hadn't flipped, but I didn't want to leave her stranded if she'd blown a tire or wrecked something in her steering system.

I jogged across the road and down to where her car sat idling, and I opened the driver's side door to peer in at her. "You good?"

She winced, rubbing her sternum. "Yeah, I think so. Fuck, he's a dick."

"Tell me about it," I grunted, glancing around the interior for damage. She sounded winded, her seat belt probably slamming into her chest. "What hurts?"

"I'm fine."

"Stubborn bitch."

She flipped me off, and I wasn't surprised when Reid popped up beside me with the torch on his phone.

"Hey. Anything broken?" he asked, shining the light at her. She squinted, giving him a scowl.

"Too bad if I had a fucking concussion. Turn that off, asshole."

He averted it from her eyes, but kept the light on her body as I swatted her hand away from her chest, trying to check her for damage. "Let me look."

She argued but let me ease the front of her shirt down enough to inspect her collarbones and sternum, her breath wheezy.

"You'll bruise, and I think you're just winded," I announced. "Are you good to drive?"

"I *did* say I was fine," she grumbled, her lip lifting into a sneer. "You both fucked up your chance at the money tonight. You shouldn't have stopped. I wouldn't have stopped for you."

She was full of fucking shit.

"Sure, you wouldn't. I don't need the money, and if Reid needs some bread and milk throughout the week, I'll treat him to some so he doesn't die."

A smile tugged at her lips despite her trying to remain annoyed with us fussing over her, putting her hands on the steering wheel. "I only sat here because I'm dizzy from the spinning. I'm fine to drive now, but thanks for stopping."

I gently tapped the roof of her car, giving her a grin. "If you need a better inspection when we get back, I'll happily give you a physical."

"You're such a whore," Blake snorted, and I smirked as I stepped back to shut her door, speaking through her open window.

"I can be anything you want, baby."

"I'd like you to be silent."

"Better put your cunt in my mouth then," I cooed, making Reid groan.

"Stop. You can't get mad when I get a hard-on if you say shit like that."

I patted his arm, walking back to my car while speaking over my shoulder. "If I were straight, I'd totally do you, Barron. You're a real catch."

"I hate you."

I snickered, climbing into my car and waiting for him to walk back to his, then I trailed after Blake, not wanting to lose sight of her. If she'd hit her head, she wasn't going to admit it.

Reid drove beside me, pulling ahead then dropping back, his engine revving as he toyed with me to occupy us at the slower pace.

I flipped him off, putting my window down. "I could run out of gas and I'd still beat you."

"You race like a girl."

"I'll take that as a compliment," I smiled, trading insults until we arrived at the end of the finish line to find Turbo waiting for us. Slick was nowhere to be seen, so Turbo must have beaten him.

Slick was a salty bastard when he lost.

Turbo eyed Blake as she climbed out, and he gave her a nod to make sure she was okay, then he met my gaze as I parked beside him.

"You threw the race."

"I'm not that much of a bitch that I'd leave Blake possibly injured on the side of the road," I replied flatly. "And I'm not in this for the money."

"You're a better person than me, Donovan," he mumbled, glancing at Reid who was parked on my other side. "You need money, so why'd you stop?"

"Because I'm a better person than you," he said with a straight face. "And if Blake was hurt, Donovan's little custard muscles wouldn't have been able to carry her out of there."

"I take back every nice thing I've ever said about you," I said as I gave him the side-eye, giving my engine a rev. "My motor's bigger than yours."

"Doesn't mean you know how to use it," he teased, revving his back. "I put mine together myself."

"You think I can't pull a motor apart and rebuild it?" I demanded, leaning out of the window so he could see how serious my face was in the moonlight. "I probably know your car better than you do."

"I won't argue with that." His eyes flicked back to the

road, his brow creasing with concern. "Uh, we've got company."

We eyed the car that pulled in and parked close by, and I bit back a groan as Cruz's head popped out of the driver's side window. "You lose something, Donovan?"

"No," I snorted, but stiffened when Luna stepped out of the passenger seat. It didn't make sense as to why she was here, especially with Cruz.

"You're fucking welcome," Cruz grinned, giving me a salute. "I'll add it to my tab."

"Go fuck yourself, pretty boy," I threw back, my eyes on Luna as she walked towards me. Turbo eyed me with amusement, telling me he knew exactly who she was.

That fucker knew everything and I hated it.

"What the fuck are you doing out here? It's the middle of the night," I scolded as I climbed from the car, my eyebrows furrowing as I noticed the tiny flinch I got in return. She didn't look good, her eyes dull as she met my gaze.

"I wanted to see you." Her voice sounded timid.

"So you tracked me out here and got in a car with a stranger?" I wasn't mad about her finding me, but I was worried that she'd climbed into a car with Cruz. She didn't know him, and it could've ended badly.

If she'd tracked me, it meant I'd forgotten to turn my location off. I was lucky my parents hadn't shown up instead.

She cringed, seeming unsure of herself as she walked towards me, confirming what I thought. "Sorry. You left your location on. I was in the Heights, and Cruz offered to give me a ride. He said he knew you."

"What if he'd been lying, Lou? Jesus. He could've been anyone," I growled, counting to three to calm myself before speaking more softly. "Try calling me next time. I would've picked you up. Are you alright?" I asked, her entire body relaxing at knowing I wasn't angry.

She threaded her arms around my middle and pressed her cheek against my chest, hugging me tightly.

"I am now."

Turbo chuckled lightly, running his eyes over her. "Got yourself a girlfriend, Donovan? Wait, is this the girl from the video?"

"Fuck off, asshole."

"That's not a no."

"Mind your own business," I bit out, hugging her tighter as she went to move back. I'd prefer him to think she was mine so he didn't get any ideas about trying to fuck her. Just because I respected him didn't mean I wouldn't kill him for flirting with Luna.

"You've really gotta give her a stranger danger talk," Cruz called out from his car, laughing as I flipped him off. "Good talk. My job here is done, I guess. I'd better go before the boss comes looking."

"Thank you," I replied tightly, hating to say it, but I was grateful it had been him who'd found her. He ran his eyes over Turbo and the others before leaving, and I knew he'd bring it up if we ran into each other again.

He really didn't like what we were doing.

Blake gave me a small wave, revving her car to get everyone's attention. "I'm heading home. I'm spending time with Kate in the morning so I need some sleep."

"I'll follow you," Reid offered, ignoring her scowl. She could be pissy all she wants, but I was glad he was making sure she got home okay after her little incident.

Once they were gone, Turbo saluted me. "I'll leave you

and your girlfriend to make out here in the dark. I'll call you later."

"Please, don't call," I smiled sweetly at him as he flipped me off before giving Luna one last glance.

"Just answer when I call you," he replied in a droll tone.

"Eyes off, or you'll lose them," I snapped, letting Luna go to take a step towards him. I'd tear his head from his shoulders if he didn't stop undressing her with his eyes.

He chuckled, putting his car into gear. "Always a pleasure, Donovan."

I watched as he drove off, leaving us alone.

I let out a sigh and took Luna's face in my hands, my voice soft. "Are you going to tell me why you're really here?"

"Can I stay with you tonight?" she murmured, her eyes pleading. "I just... I want to stay with you."

It was obvious she wasn't going to open up about whatever was on her mind, so I let it go.

"Of course you can. C'mon, it's getting cold." I ushered her into the passenger seat before I climbed behind the wheel. I didn't want to sit there any longer and risk Rage or Zane showing up.

I kept an eye out for trouble the whole drive back to Ashburn Valley as we talked about school and what she'd missed while being sick, and I was surprised to walk into my house to find Mom sitting at the kitchen table.

I glanced at the time, noticing it was close to three in the morning.

"Why are you awake?" I asked, her eyes flicking between me and Luna.

"I couldn't sleep," she grumbled, her tired eyes running over both of us. "Where have you been?"

I figured she'd properly tracked my phone since Luna had, so I didn't bother lying.

"Stoneleigh. I was with Turbo and Blake."

"You took Luna?" she asked with disapproval, knowing Archer wouldn't like it.

"No. We met up and she asked to stay here tonight," I answered, placing my hand on Luna's lower back to give her a gentle push towards the stairs. "And since it's so late, we're going to bed. You should too."

"I'm the parent, you little shit," she snorted, but her lips tugged into a small smile as I kissed her cheek.

"You're the best parent too. Night, Mom."

"Kiss ass," she mumbled, amusement in her tone.

I steered Luna into my room but froze when she stripped off her jacket and pants. There were marks on her wrists and ankles. I snatched her arm, holding her firmly as she tried to jerk back.

"What the hell is this?" I demanded as something flashed in her eyes before she cooled her features.

"I bought handcuffs."

"That's not really an explanation, Lou." Her skin was bruised, the marks being the sign of a struggle. I'd used handcuffs before but I'd never left bruises on anyone.

Luna laughed lightly, pushing back from me. "I don't like talking sex with you. It makes you mad."

"Lots of people like being tied up and fucked, but those marks are not okay," I scowled, eyeing her ankles. "They look sore. He should've used something softer."

She shrugged, averting her eyes from mine as she rummaged in my drawers for something to sleep in. "I consented to it. It's not a big deal."

"Is this why you've been 'sick' the last couple of days? Did he fucking hurt you?" I snapped as images popped into my head of the things he might have done. She didn't look at me again as she pulled a shirt from my drawers and turned around to give me her back, unclasping her bra and tugging the shirt over her head.

"No. I told you I was sick. Don't be dramatic." She slid under the covers, and I couldn't help it as I ran my eyes up her bare legs, envisioning them wrapped around me as I sank my fingers into her. I bit the inside of my cheek to stop a groan as I caught a flash of her baby blue panties between her legs.

"Are you coming?"

"Definitely," I muttered as my pussy clenched.

"You're terrible," she giggled, making me smile.

"I'm terrible? You're the one in my bed flashing your panties. How am I supposed to behave when you're waving such a gorgeous temptation at me?" I asked, waggling my eyebrows suggestively.

She bit her lip, her cheeks heating. "You don't have to."

"What?" I said with confusion as she blushed harder, my heart hammering in my chest at the thought of touching her again.

"You don't have to behave."

Jesus fucking Christ. What the hell was I supposed to do with that?

80
100
120
140
160
180
200
220
km/h
240
260

Chapter Thirteen

Luna

My face was on fire. I wasn't thinking clearly, obviously.

What the hell was I doing?

Riley stared at me, a dumbfounded look on her face. I wasn't into girls, so I was definitely losing my mind. Then again, I'd caught myself thinking about her a lot this week.

Our previous kiss still sent tingles through me at the thought, and I replayed the memory of her calling me baby over and over again in my head. Stanley thought I was dramatic and a crybaby when I didn't like the things he did to me, but Riley would never make me feel uncomfortable for her own benefit.

The problem was, she loved me, and I knew it wasn't fair to tempt her like this but Riley always made things better. I wanted to feel good, but I wanted someone I trusted to do it. I wanted her to look after me in a way I knew only she could.

I couldn't lie, Stanley was messing with my head. I didn't know if my feelings were wrong, or if I was strange for not liking the same things in bed that he did. I didn't have a lot of experience, but from what he'd been saying, all girls liked it rough.

Why did they like something that hurt so badly?

We'd been at his friend's house in Hawthorne Heights, and when I got uncomfortable and wanted to leave, he refused to go with me. I was angry that he'd let me walk around in the middle of the night alone, and it had definitely been stupid to get in a car with Cruz.

I'd been desperate to get to Riley though, and it had seemed like a good idea at the time. I had tried calling her, but she hadn't answered, so when Cruz pulled up and offered me a ride, I took it.

I'd been hurt to find her hanging out with her friends and ignoring my call, but I'd been so relieved to see her that I pushed it aside.

Now, I just wanted her to make me forget about everything. I was sick of feeling so lonely and hurt.

Riley opened her mouth to speak, and I backtracked slightly. "We don't have to have sex. I just... Shit, I don't know what I'm asking." I fidgeted, and she assessed me for another moment before pulling her hoodie over her head and kicking off her shoes.

"Have you been drinking?" she finally asked, making me scowl.

"No. Why?"

"You're acting weird," she teased, but her voice was strained. "What *are* you asking? You want me to touch you?"

"I don't know what I want," I whispered, holding her gaze. "I just need *something*, Riley. You make everything okay. I can be myself around you, and you never make me feel stupid for it."

I could tell she wanted to ask me what was wrong for

the millionth time, but she decided against it as she finished stripping down to her panties, not caring about being exposed. She grabbed a shirt and pulled it over her head, my eyes lingering on her naked skin and dropping to her thighs as she covered herself. I wanted to feel her smooth skin against mine.

She turned the lamp on before switching the main light off and locking the door, climbing over me to get into bed, and laying down beside me.

"I need more than that, Lou. I don't want to do the wrong thing," she sighed once she was comfortable and placed a hand on my thigh, facing me. My body tensed at her touch and she immediately pulled back, but I reached out to grab her wrist, holding her in place.

"No, it's okay," I insisted, making her snort.

"It's not. You don't want this, and you're not into girls. Trust me, I'd be really excited if you were, but—"

"Kiss me," I blurted out, making her pause. "Like at that party. I liked that."

"You want me to kiss you?" she asked slowly, not seeming to believe me. "Are you sure? I don't want you changing your mind and freaking out on me. What about Stan?"

"Just kiss me, Riley," I said softly. "Please."

"Damn, okay. If you're sure it's what you want," she said as if it were a chore, but heat filled her eyes as I licked my lips nervously. I was surprised when she reached out to cup my cheek before leaning in to brush her lips against mine, keeping her touches light to give me plenty of time to change my mind.

I expected her to be rougher, like last time.

When I relaxed and teased her lips with my tongue, she groaned and opened her mouth for me, placing her free hand on my waist to give me a gentle squeeze. A low chuckle left her as I gasped when her teeth nipped at my lower lip. "You like that?"

I nodded, lifting a hand to her hair to run my fingers through the soft strands. I gave it a light tug and a curse left her lips. "Unless you want me to fuck you for the next three hours, I wouldn't do that if I were you."

"You like your hair being pulled?" I questioned curiously, feeling like a damn virgin all over again as she peered at me with laughter in her eyes. I knew she wasn't making fun of me though. She wasn't like that.

"I like lots of stuff in bed. I'm definitely more of a giver and you've always given me pillow princess vibes, which totally works for me."

"Do I want to know what that even means?" I asked, my skin tingling as she ran her hand under my shirt, her fingers teasing my heated skin just below my breasts.

"You like receiving more than giving," she said with a grin. "There's no shame in that. Lots of people like that."

"Did you just call me lazy in bed?" I asked with disbelief, but she just laughed.

"Hey, I'll never judge you for enjoying laying on your back and getting off a million times. Everyone loves orgasms."

"But you don't? Since you like giving?" I asked as I tried to understand, but she let out a groan.

"It turns me on to make someone else feel good. I've come before while eating pussy. It's so fucking good." I didn't know how to reply to that so I didn't. She seemed deep in thought for a second before tilting her head and looking at me with curiosity in her eyes. "What's with all the questions tonight?"

I ran a hand over my face and she shuffled back, giving

me space. "Maybe this is a bad idea. I don't want to hurt you, and I'm not chasing anything more. I'm in a relationship already, but—"

"How about you tell me what you want, and you let me worry about my feelings?" she scoffed, her tone becoming flat. "If you're willing to cheat on your boyfriend, it means he's being a dick. I'm more than happy to get on board with that kind of revenge plan."

"I don't want to pull you along. I haven't forgotten about the last time when we kissed and I upset you with a similar situation. I don't want you feeling like you're good enough to be a side piece and nothing more." I cringed at how much I was messing this up. "I don't want to talk about Stan right now. I just want to feel good."

"Tell me what you want," she murmured, brushing my hair from my face affectionately.

"Can I touch you?" I eyed her chest, not at all surprised when she pulled her shirt over her head without shame, exposing herself to me without hesitation. She was completely comfortable with her body, and I envied her for it. I hated my body being on display.

She grabbed my hand, pulling it towards her chest, and I gave her a gentle squeeze as the smooth, hot skin connected with my palm. Her lips met mine again, her voice soft as she spoke against them. "You can touch me wherever you fucking want, baby."

Then she kissed me hard.

I kissed her back, a shudder rolling through her as I ran my thumb across her peaked nipple. I did it again, feeling more confident as she cursed into my mouth. I pushed her back so I could wrap my lips around her nipple instead, her fingers threading through my hair as she let out a sound of frustration.

"You're going the right way to get fucked through my mattress." I switched to the other side, sliding my hand along her waist, but I suddenly found myself on my back with her leaning over me, her voice firm. "Lou, I mean it. I'm close to shoving my fingers so deep in your cunt that we'll wake the neighbors."

I blinked up at her, my voice quiet with embarrassment. "You can touch me too, if you want."

Apparently, her willpower was gone because she didn't argue again.

She shoved my shirt up my body and instantly started nipping and sucking at my nipples as one of her hands moved between us, slipping into my panties. The moment she reached my core, she paused, lifting her face to smirk at me.

"I don't even need to warm you up. You're fucking soaked."

"Do I, um. Do I need to warm you up?" I asked awkwardly, but she leaned down to place a kiss on my lips before replying.

"Let me make you feel good tonight, then, if you want to try more another time, you can repay the favor. Deal?"

I nodded, letting her drag my panties down my legs. I tensed as she shuffled down the bed until her face was right in front of my pussy, her warm breath fanning across my damp skin. I panicked at the thought of her seeing me so closely.

What if it looked weird down there?

She'd seen a lot of pussy, and I couldn't help but feel self-conscious about it.

I jerked as her tongue lightly brushed my clit, a breathy moan leaving her. "So fucking perfect."

Then she tongued my pussy, dragging the flat of her tongue up to my clit to tease it before dropping lower again.

I grabbed the pillow beside me to bury my face in it, but she reached up and snatched it, sending it flying across the room. I flinched when she started pushing her fingers inside me and it burned a little, her movements pausing as she looked up at me.

I hated how she studied me, trying to see inside my head, so I forced myself to relax and reminded myself it was Riley. I just had to be honest with her, and she wouldn't push me past my limits.

"Is this okay?" she asked as she crawled up my body more, not pushing any deeper as she toyed with my entrance, her thumb brushing my clit. "And don't cover your mouth. I want to hear what I do to you."

"But someone might hear us," I squeaked out, her face remaining serious.

"Good. I want them to. You didn't answer my question."

I'd liked the idea of just kissing a little, but her fingers and tongue had felt good on my pussy. I wanted her to make me come, and I wanted to touch her too. I doubted I'd be any good at it, but I wanted to try.

"It feels good, we can keep going. Can you be gentle though?" I mumbled, reaching out to toy with the tips of her hair that teased my stomach.

"I'm either going to hell or I'm God's favorite and this is a reward," she answered, pulling her fingers from inside me to slide them between her lips. My heart hammered as I watched her taste me, her eyes never leaving mine as she removed them and dropped them to my pussy again.

I sucked in a breath as she eased her wet fingers deeper, my nipples tightening as she continued to watch me while slowly pumping them in and out of me. If anyone else did this, I'd be uncomfortable, but Riley made me feel like I was the one in charge, and I liked it.

I hadn't felt like that before.

She kept the pace slow as she leaned down to kiss my chest, her tongue teasing my nipples every so often, then she lifted her head to kiss me. I hesitated before running my hands across her back, pulling her closer as she whispered my name. Shivers ran down my spine at the tenderness in her tone, a moan leaving me without permission.

I parted my legs further, lifting my hips as she went deeper and started nibbling down my throat. I took her breast in my hand, hoping I wasn't fumbling like an idiot, but she didn't seem to care.

I grew braver, sliding one of my hands down between us and slipping it into her panties, a curse leaving her as I rubbed at her clit. It felt wrong. Not in a bad way, but I'd only ever done this on myself before, so it felt backwards. I was uncoordinated, but I found the right speed that worked for me, only fucking it up when tingles started forming inside me from her magical fingers.

I didn't recognize the sound of desperation that left me, and Riley tugged my earlobe between her teeth with a groan.

"Grind on my hand, baby. Don't worry about me."

She was curling her fingers inside me in the most erotic way, and I rolled my hips to rub my clit against her palm. My movements were jerky and probably really unattractive, but I was so close that I didn't care.

My muscles locked up as the sensations became stronger, and I completely abandoned her clit, arching off the bed the second the tingles turned into crashing waves of pleasure. I let out a loud moan that was more like a scream, my hands fisting the bedding as she continued to lazily fuck me through it, and it wasn't until she slowed to let me recover that I realized she'd been staring at my face the whole time.

My cheeks flamed and she raised an eyebrow, startling me as she lightly slapped my pussy. "Don't do that."

"Do what?" I panted as I went to tug my shirt down to cover myself, but she forced it back up, laying over me to stop my movements, worry in her gaze.

"Don't hide from me. Are you regretting this?"

Her voice wavered with uncertainty, and I quickly shook my head, relief instantly taking over her face as she relaxed. "No, of course not. You've just been with lots of girls and—"

"And they mean nothing to me," she said sharply, cutting me off. "You're the only person I've touched like this that I give a fuck about. You have no idea how stunning you are, Lou. No one else compares to you. If you don't know that, then your boyfriend's not doing his fucking job right."

Guilt ate at me at the mention of Stanley, reality hitting me like a freight train. Riley had given me more in the past few minutes than he'd given me in the past year, and I hadn't felt uncomfortable for a single second with her.

I'd cheated on my boyfriend with my best friend, and the shameful part was that it had felt right.

Tears burned my eyes, and she cursed before laying down beside me and pulling me against her. "I hate that I always seem to make you cry. I'm sorry. Did I push you too far? I knew I'd fuck this up."

"No, it was good," I insisted, shuffling closer to her and sniffing back the tears. "I'm just a mess tonight."

"We'll talk about this tomorrow, okay? No pressure."

I fell asleep like that, her fingers drawing patterns on my back and her leg draped over my waist to keep me close.

Riley

"Hey. Marco sent me in to wake you up. It's almost lunchtime," Ryder said as he shook my shoulder. "Did you hear me? Wake the fuck up."

I groaned, rolling over to swat at him, and he let out a sound of disgust. "I don't appreciate the titty flash. Where's your company? I heard you two last night and you're lucky I didn't stage a cop raid to shut you two up."

My eyes flew open and I patted the bed beside me, finding it empty. Luna was gone.

I cursed, flying out of bed to my brother's horror as he averted his eyes, and I snatched a shirt, shoving it over my head.

"She's gone? Fuck. Fuck!" I snapped, confusion filling his eyes as he braved a glance at me, finding me covered.

"You don't usually bring them back here. They must have been hot," he grinned at me. "Why are you freaking out? It's a good thing when they slip out before we wake up. We don't have to deal with their meltdown when we boot them out."

"Shut up, Ry," I growled, his biceps flexing as he crossed his arms against his chest. He was in a tank top and shorts, telling me he was about to start a workout or go for a run.

"You're being such a girl right now. It's weird," he muttered as he assessed me suspiciously, but I relaxed as the bathroom door opened and Luna slipped back in. She was only in her panties and shirt, my brain short-circuiting at how good she looked. I couldn't believe I'd fucked her, and it was better than I ever could've imagined.

She paused when she saw Ryder, and I let out a breath of relief. "There you are. I thought you'd taken off."

"I had to pee," she mumbled, her cheeks burning as Ryder chuckled.

"Luna stayed over? That explains the noises that got my cock hard last night."

"Maybe she was eating my cunt and you were jerking off to me?" I bit out with annoyance. "Get out."

"No way in fucking hell. It's way too interesting in here," he argued, and I punched him in the shoulder when he glanced at Luna's bare legs. His pupils were blown, but I didn't bother asking what he'd taken. If he'd been out partying all night and was still high, that was his problem.

"I said *out*, asshole. I won't ask again."

He grumbled as he went, slamming the door on purpose while shouting down the hallway. "I woke her up, Dad! You can pay for my fucking therapy since she was naked with Luna!"

He was such a dick.

Luna's eyes went wide, but I snorted and grabbed her pants off the floor, handing them over to her. "Sorry." She took them, shoving her legs into them as she fidgeted, making me frown. "What's wrong?"

"I don't know how to act around you," she blurted out without looking at me. I loved that she was so innocent, and a small smile tugged at my lips. She'd never slept with someone she wasn't dating, so she was completely out of her element.

"Just like you always do. Is that why you were hiding in the bathroom?" I teased, reaching for her waist to tug her against me. She didn't tense or push me away, so I slid my arms around her, pulling her front flush with mine. "This changes nothing. If you want me to back off, I can. I think we need to talk about it though, but I'm happy to wait until we've had coffee first, or if you need a day to think."

Her soft eyes stared into mine, her voice quiet. "I'm not ready to leave him. I know that's what you'll ask, but—"

It hurt a little, but I knew it was going to be like this. I swore I wouldn't touch her while she wanted him, and I'd already fucked that up, but part of me was enjoying the fact she'd go home to him with my kiss still burning on her lips.

I was petty, but I was looking forward to him finding out I'd had my fingers up her cunt.

I smirked, kissing her neck to relax her, my voice low. "I know. We can figure this out if it's what you want. I told you last night I wouldn't push you, and I meant it."

She melted against me, a content sigh leaving her that went straight to my core. I was pretty observant with girls, and I instantly felt like affection was her love language. Some girls liked gifts, some liked humor, but Luna appreciated soft touches and sweet words.

Stanley used to always hold her hand and say gag-worthy cute shit to her, but she was acting like she was starved of it. I'd give her so much attention that she'd forget his fucking name if that was what it took.

Besides, she deserved it. If he wasn't giving her those things, he could choke on a dick.

"Did your dad say anything about the video?" I asked when she stayed quiet, her body tensing. I knew she wouldn't happily climb into my lap in public and make out, especially if her family wasn't okay with it.

Luna having a relationship with a woman wasn't going to be a problem. Archer would hate his little girl getting on her back for *me* specifically though. He didn't hate me, he simply didn't want me to hurt her like he assumed I would.

She leaned back, moving from my hold to look at the

floor. "He texted me and said he wanted to talk when I got home, but that's it. I haven't been home yet."

I sighed, raking my fingers through my tangled, blonde hair. "You know your sexuality isn't a problem for them, right? Are you avoiding facing him because you're worried?"

"I'm straight," she threw back sharply. "I'm not gay. I don't know what this is, but—"

"Hey, we don't have to label it. You like me and you like guys. That's fine," I replied patiently, knowing she was going to storm off before her eyes even narrowed on me.

"They don't need to know about this. I'm still with Stanley."

"Do you regret it?" I asked, not hiding the bite in my tone as I became defensive, but she shook her head and turned towards the door, speaking over her shoulder.

"I don't, but I cheated on Stanley with you. I don't want it being public knowledge. I need to figure myself out, okay? Let me do that. This is what I was worried about because there's no way you won't get hurt in all of this."

I didn't bother replying as she left the room and shut the door gently behind her. I slid my back down the wall, sat on the ground, and closed my eyes for a moment. I wasn't going to allow myself to get upset, not when I knew this was going to be an uphill battle for a while.

I'd told her to just have fun with me and not to worry about my feelings, so I couldn't be angry with her for running home to her boyfriend.

The only person responsible for me getting hurt right now was me.

The door opened, but I knew it wasn't her. I always knew when she was watching me. The air changed when she was close, and I didn't feel her eyes on me.

Mom slid down the wall beside me, nudging my leg with hers. "You want to talk about it?"

"It's too early for this shit," I chuckled weakly, rubbing my hands over my face before looking at her. I expected her to be frustrated with me since she'd been warning me away from Luna for years, but instead, she looked concerned. "I didn't push her into anything."

"It's lunchtime. You missed Blake's visit with Kate too." She held out a tattooed arm, and I leaned into her to get comfortable. "And I didn't say you pushed her. I wasn't even sure if Ryder was telling the truth or joking until you just confirmed it. You care about her and that's what worries me. Did she break up with Stan?" I snorted, making her groan. "Really, Riley? She's in a relationship and you decided to mess around with her?"

"It wasn't like that," I mumbled, glancing up as someone walked into the room.

Caden looked sheepish, rubbing the back of his neck. "Uh, I don't mean to interrupt, but—"

"Out, Rich Boy," Mom said bluntly, his eyebrow rising with amusement. She'd called him that since they'd met in high school, even though she ended up being richer than him.

"Excuse me?"

"I said, out," she repeated, and I couldn't help but smirk. Mom loved all my dads, but I was the apple of her eye. She'd happily throw them out when we were having girl time. Probably because Beckett and Marla didn't want one-on-one time with her like I did.

I loved spending time with her.

"Rage is in the office," he said as she went to tell him to fuck off like I knew she would, and I did well not to tense. If he'd invited himself over, it wasn't going to be good. He was probably there to tell everyone my car had been seen racing through Stoneleigh.

I was so fucked.

"Angry Man can go home, call me, then plan a time to meet if he has something to talk about," she scowled, but I sat up and got to my feet, holding a hand out for her.

"It's okay. I should make sure Luna got home okay."

She frowned, giving me a weird look. "She's in the kitchen with Jett and Cruz. I didn't know Cruz knew her."

"He doesn't. They met one time," I blurted out before pulling her to her feet and darting from the room. I wasn't going to hang around if they were going to talk about me illegally street racing after they'd specifically told me not to.

I walked into the kitchen to find Cruz leaning against the counter with his eyes firmly on Luna who was being interrogated by Jett. At least she hadn't run from me after all.

"Was it as good as people say? I bet she paid them all to lie so us guys would feel threatened," Jett was saying, glancing at Cruz. "Back me up here, man. Tell her guys are better in bed than Riley. I can't say it without Beckett coming for my balls."

Cruz grinned, crossing his arms. "He's right, Luna. Guys are better. The last time I nailed Jett's ass, he said I was the best fuck he's ever had."

"If we fucked, you'd be the bottom," Jett argued, turning around and smacking his own ass. "See this? This is muscular from all the thrusting. Turn around so we can see yours. I bet mine's firmer. Yours probably has an echo when the air gets inside it from all the poundings it takes."

I was surprised when another guy walked in from the living room, his dark hair spiked at the front to keep it off his face. I didn't recognize him, but since he stopped beside Cruz, I assumed he was one of the Night Assholes.

"Cruz would definitely be a bottom," the guy offered, crossing his arms. "He gives off people pleaser vibes. I wouldn't be surprised if he let Stone fuck him sometimes as stress relief."

Jett cackled, but Luna seemed uncomfortable until she noticed me walking towards them. Her shoulders relaxed, and she pushed a coffee towards me as I rounded the counter. "Here."

"Thanks." I gave her a smile and downed half of it before turning to face Cruz. "You're definitely a bottom."

"Bite me," he chuckled, his eyes drifting to Luna before coming back to me as he raised an eyebrow. "Late night?"

"*Bite me,*" I mocked, repeating his words back to him. He laughed, but he didn't add anything to it. His friend eyed me silently as I dropped an arm around Luna's shoulders to speak in her ear. "Finish your coffee. We've gotta go."

"What for?" she whispered back, leaning into me more and making my stomach flutter.

"I have a bad feeling Rage is about to get me in trouble."

"What did you do?" she squeaked out, and I gave Cruz a dirty look as he snickered.

"Can we just go?" I asked again, relieved when she nodded and finished her coffee. Cruz sighed, glancing at his phone.

"Ry needs to hurry the fuck up. I've got places to be."

I walked towards the hallway but paused, frowning at him over my shoulder. "What are you waiting for him for?"

"We're going running," he said with a shrug before nudging his friend. "Right, Drake? You've been super excited."

Drake grumbled, not seeming happy in the slightest about their impending fitness session.

"Fuck that. Have fun," I answered, taking Luna's hand and tugging her up to my room so we could finish getting ready for the day.

We were in my car five minutes later, the windows down as we smoked in silence, but her soft voice snapped me out of my daydreaming when we reached the main road.

"I'm sorry I got mad this morning."

I glanced at her, pushing my shades onto my head to assess her. She looked uncomfortable, and I had to remind myself that she was new at this. I struggled to understand why sexuality was such a problem since it was so openly spoken about when I was growing up.

I knew lots of kids at school who'd had problems telling their families though.

One guy got his ass beat by his father in our freshman year of high school for coming out as gay. Another guy got bullied badly in our senior year for the same thing. It was ridiculous.

No wonder Landon was happy hiding in the closet.

"It's fine," I said with a small smile, downshifting as we reached the bar. We hadn't had a destination in mind, but the bar was as good as anywhere else. "I'm not about to out you, as much as I'd love to rub it in your smug boyfriend's face." Her eyes went wide, but I took her hand and gave it a squeeze. "I said I won't say anything. Don't worry."

She relaxed, squeezing my hand back before letting go and staring out the window while I parked. We climbed out, and I gave her space as we wandered inside, but her entire body tensed as we noticed her dad at the bar talking to Alex and Harley.

Alex gave us a friendly wave, and the moment Archer's eyes landed on me, they narrowed to slits.

"Shit," Luna murmured under her breath as he started towards us, but I rolled my eyes and nudged her shoulder.

"You're acting guilty. We played truth or dare, relax."

He glanced at her, but turned his attention back to me pretty fast as he stopped in front of us. "Riley."

"Hendricks," I smiled sweetly. "Do you wish to talk with us in private about something?"

"As a matter of fact, yes," he grunted, jerking his thumb at the staff only door. "Walk."

"Yes, Sir!" I saluted, an irritated huff leaving him as I walked towards the door without encouragement. Alex grabbed my arm to stop me, concern in his tone.

"Should I referee?"

"Did you see the video?"

"Yes. So, referee?" he replied with the hint of a smile on his lips. He knew I was in deep shit.

"I don't have my bat, and he's not likely to shoot me so I think we're safe," I answered with a chuckle, shoving the door open, and walking through the kitchen towards the office.

Luna and Archer followed, and we'd hardly shut the door before Archer exploded. "What the fuck, Riley?!"

"You're overreacting." I perched my butt against the desk and tugged my hood over my head, keeping my voice level. "We were drinking."

"So you took advantage of her?" he said flatly, turning to Luna. "Did she push you into it?"

I snorted, crossing my arms defensively. I could smooth talk my way between anyone's legs, but I didn't have to get them drunk to do it.

"Of course not."

He stayed silent, waiting for Luna's reply, and she frowned. "You really think Riley would do that to me? We weren't even really hanging out at the party. I was with Ryder, and I got a little drunk and decided to play truth or dare with some others. Some girl dared me to kiss Riley."

His muscles relaxed, but he still didn't look happy. "It's not like you to play games like that, Luna. Was Stanley there?"

She shook her head, her voice tight. "He knows what happened. We're fine."

"You mean, he saw the video and confronted you," he muttered, glancing over his shoulder as Landon wandered in without knocking, a smirk on his face.

"Hey. It's tense in here."

"Read the room, kid," Archer grumbled, looking at me before pointing at Luna. "See her? No touchy."

"I'll try to keep my hands to myself, but it's difficult," I taunted, and he was apparently over my shit because he stalked out without another word, making me chuckle once more. "She's an adult, Hendricks! You can't keep her safe from me forever!"

"You're dead to me!" Archer called back, and I couldn't help but laugh.

He was so easy to torment.

Landon raised an eyebrow, glancing between us. "Was that about the video? Dad sent me in here to make sure you didn't get blood all over his desk."

"Yeah. I feel like we never hang out anymore," I replied, trying not to draw attention to the fact Luna was now leaning against me, her fingers absently teasing my thigh as she followed the conversation. I wasn't going to stop her from touching me.

I carefully slid an arm around her middle, my fingers

brushing her waist. She didn't move away, so I pulled her into me more.

Landon noticed, but he simply gave me a small smile and acted like he didn't see it. "You two have been busy, and if I'm not working here, my dads have me working the bar at the shed or Devil's Dungeon. It's like they don't want me to have spare time."

"They just don't want you getting in trouble. Jade's probably been speaking to Mom," I snickered. "They don't like the company I've kept lately, so your dads aren't likely to want you around them either."

"Ooh, are they hot?" he smirked, waggling his eyebrows. "Why haven't you told me about them until now?"

"They're guys. Wait, there's one girl. What's her name?" Luna asked, thinking hard for a moment before clicking her fingers and looking up at me. "Blake. Her sister's the one that's living with you, right?"

I nodded, not liking that Turbo and the Night Thieves knew who Luna was now.

"Yeah. Kate's a good kid. She's quiet, but she likes spending time with some of the other kids when she's not at school," I replied, glancing at Landon. "You would've heard of Ander Lavaro, right?"

He groaned, running his fingers through his short, brown hair. "Of course. Harley was talking about him recently, saying the only reason the Psychos haven't dealt with him is because he keeps his shit out of Ashburn Valley. You're friends with him? Isn't he like, some mafia kid?"

"We're associates," I said, waving dismissively at him. "We hang out sometimes. But no, he's not part of the fucking mafia."

"You let Luna near him? He's trouble, Riley."

"She was only near him once, and that was because she

got in the car with a stranger who brought her to me," I scowled, giving her the side-eye. "Right, Lou? You're not doing that again, are you?"

"You got in a random person's car?" Landon snapped, frustration filling his eyes. "Why the hell did you do that? If you needed a ride, you should've called me."

She huffed, crossing her arms and only managing to look even less threatening as she stepped back from me. "He said he knew her. I was walking, and he pulled over and offered to give me a ride."

"Did he have a handful of candy and a white van, by any chance?" he deadpanned, but she frowned, not understanding his sarcasm. "No. It was a normal car. Why would he have candy?"

I rolled my eyes, speaking to Landon. "It was one of Beckett's friends from Rawson Grove, but Luna doesn't know him. She was lucky he wasn't a creeper and he actually brought her to me."

"You're asking to get kidnapped and held for ransom," he muttered, but he pulled Luna against his chest to crush her with a hug. "You're too smart to be that stupid."

"Ugh, thanks?" she mumbled into his chest, relaxing into his hug.

He watched me over the top of her head, and I could sense the worry radiating out of him. Archer and the Reapers of Chaos crew had a lot of enemies, and most of them would love to snatch his baby girl and do God knows what to her to make a statement.

I had to keep a better eye on her.

100
120
140
160
180
200
220
km/h
240
260

Chapter Fourteen

Riley

We ended up hanging out at the bar playing pool and talking for most of the afternoon, and I was enjoying myself until Turbo's name flashed across my phone screen. I considered ignoring him, but I didn't want to deal with him bitching me out later for it.

"Hey, stud. I'm a little busy," I said as I answered, holding the phone to my ear as I handed the cue stick to Landon. He gave me an odd look, but he took his shot and left me alone.

"Get unbusy then. You're coming to the track tonight," he said without saying hello, making me scoff.

"My real question is why the fuck are *you* going to the track tonight? Legal racing doesn't really get your rocks off. There's no high stakes, and most of us use it for bragging rights and fun. You can't make thousands off people there."

Luna lingered close by, and I knew she was listening to me. I couldn't walk off without looking suspicious, so I leaned against the wall and got comfortable. "And I highly doubt my sister will let you in the gate."

He chuckled, a playful edge to his voice. "Your sister's the one who invited me."

I groaned, scrubbing my hand over my face. "What did you do to deserve that? The track's our territory, idiot. It can't be good if she's inviting you. Decline it."

"Nope. I've always wanted to race the infamous Beckett Donovan."

"Wait, you're actually racing her? I'm going to fucking kill you, Lavaro," I hissed into the phone. "If you think I'll show up to be moral support, you're dead wrong. My family comes first, every fucking time."

"If a fight breaks out, I don't expect you to take shots at your big sister. Just be my passenger," he said lightly, and he was lucky I couldn't reach through the phone and punch him.

"What's in it for me then? You know I don't do shit for free," I said more quietly, my eyes on Luna as she moved around me to take her shot. "You promised to keep your world out of mine."

"I meant it too. Problem is, your world's the one slipping into mine. If your family wants to keep an eye on me to make sure you're safe, isn't it in your best interests to play along too? I'll make sure you get a rush."

"You can't race on the track like you do on the streets, asshole," I growled, cringing when Luna and Landon both glanced at me. They definitely heard that. "My brother died on that fucking track, so I won't let you risk my sister too."

"Simmer down. I'm not going to try to ram Beckett off the track. I'm not a complete idiot. How about this for a good deal? You sit your ass in my passenger seat for the race and act like we're buddies, and I'll take your Supra back to mine and fix it for you. I noticed you haven't repaired the damage from the shoot-out yet," he replied, and I could hear the grin in his voice. "You want more money for your boyfriend? I can arrange that too."

I hadn't had the chance to give Zavier the cash from last time, but the track might be a good place to do it.

"Call Z. Tell him to come with Reid. I don't want your money, I just want you to promise me that there's no drama coming," I finally decided. "And keep Slick away. He's not fucking welcome."

"Sold. I'll come find you when I arrive," he murmured before hanging up.

I glanced at my two best friends who were eyeing me suspiciously, knowing they heard enough to know what was happening. "So, do you two want to hit the track tonight?"

"Was that Ander? He's racing?" Landon asked, giving me a stern look. "No offense, but I don't want either me or Luna dragged into that shit."

I watched Luna for a moment before relaxing my muscles, knowing I looked tense.

"Beckett challenged him to a race. He probably just wants to make sure it's not a way for the crews to get to him."

"Don't think I didn't hear you mention the street racing," he muttered, stepping closer so he wasn't talking loud enough for others to hear. "What the hell do you know about his races?"

"Who doesn't know about it?" I scoffed, hoping I didn't look guilty. I hated lying to them, but the last thing I needed was either of them sniffing around that shit. Someone would get hurt.

"You're just going to take his word for it about tonight?" he asked in disbelief. "What if he's full of shit? I'm talking to Beckett about it."

"Go for it," I gritted through my teeth. "I wouldn't let

you two near him if I didn't think it was safe though. So thanks for trusting me."

He met me dead in the eye, his voice flat. "Start telling me the truth then."

I let out a breath, glancing around before replying. "What do you want me to say? That I've raced against him on the street before? I don't want you dragged into it."

He seemed surprised by my honesty, but Luna looked horrified. "You raced on the street?"

"Keep your fucking voice down," I warned. "This is why I didn't want to tell you. It's not a big deal."

"What's not a big deal?" I heard behind us, and I managed to keep my face blank as I found Maddox behind me, Beckett and Zane not far behind him. They all had their crew jackets on, so I assumed they were here for business.

I motioned to Beckett, not missing a beat. "Turbo called me and asked about tonight's race. Apparently, Beckett challenged him."

Maddox's lip lifted in a sneer, his voice sharp. "The fuck did he call you for? To cry about it?"

"No," I huffed. "To see if I wanted to go."

"You're not," he threw back instantly, a light laugh leaving me.

"Uh, yes I am. Are you guys up to something? Why are you worried about me being there?"

"I don't want you near him, Riley," he bit out. "He's going to get you in trouble."

"Says the dude with the Bloody Psychos' jacket on," I smirked, patting his chest. "Whatever you've got planned for Turbo, it won't work."

"Want to bet?"

"Yes, actually." They couldn't do anything to his car if I

was in it, let alone try to run him off the track. Turbo wasn't stupid, and now his demand for me to join him made sense. He knew it wasn't just a race. "You can't hurt him without hurting me. I'm his passenger for the night."

He cursed, clenching his fists before jabbing a finger against my chest, his face twisting with anger. "Why do you have to stick your nose in everything? You don't know what you're messing with."

I swatted his hand away, glaring up at him. "You're the one putting your nose in my shit. Leave him the fuck alone."

"I didn't think you were that close to him? Seriously, stay out of it. If you're just trying to be difficult for the sake of it—"

I gave him a shove, and I heard Beckett curse from close by. I knew she'd get between us any second now.

"Does Mom know about this?" I demanded, spinning around to glare at Beckett before she could pull me back. "If you do anything to Turbo, that makes you as bad as Jeremy Lopez for what he did to our brother. You know that?"

Her muscles tensed as she contemplated knocking me the fuck out, but she knew I was right though.

"What do you know?" she asked, glancing at Maddox. "Did you tell her anything?"

He scowled, motioning to me. "Ander called her. She's his passenger tonight."

"Of course he fucking did," she growled, holding my gaze firmly. "He doesn't give a shit about you if he's willing to use you as a shield."

I snorted, taking the cue stick from Luna's hands and racking the balls. "If you thought you could trick him into being cornered by inviting him to race, you're an idiot. Unless you've got beef with him that you're willing to deal with just by racing each other, don't bother. Mom would burn your Mustang to the ground if you used it as a weapon."

Luna and Landon stood back while we argued, and I could see Alex and Harley exchanging glances every so often.

We must have been getting loud.

Zane joined us and bumped his chest against mine to push me back a step when I got in Beckett's face, and Landon bravely put an arm between us and told him to fuck off.

This wasn't going to end well.

Harley materialized beside us and pulled Landon back, making sure Zane couldn't touch him.

"Enough. What is it with you kids coming to my bar to fight? Whatever the problem is, take it outside. Landon, I don't care what the problem is, you stay out of it," he ordered, defiance shining in Landon's eyes.

Zane chuckled, giving Harley an amused glance as he cracked his knuckles. "I won't hurt your kid unless he hits me first, then all bets are off. I think you should see what the little shit can do. He'll either surprise me or learn to shut his mouth."

"I can take him, Dad," Landon said firmly, but his voice wavered with uncertainty. He had no hope of winning against Zane, and he fucking knew it. He'd try though if it meant protecting me and Luna.

I rolled my eyes, pointing at Beckett. "Keep your bullshit off the track tonight and you won't have a problem. People don't get hurt on our track, we make sure of that. Don't let your emotions control you."

"Stay away from him. I fucking mean it," she threw back, but I flipped her off.

"Fuck you. I don't tell you who you can or can't hang

out with. You have Zane fucking Evans as a best friend, so if anyone here needs new associates, it's you."

"You're a cunt," Zane snorted, but I ignored him and took Luna's hand.

"We're leaving. I'll see you later, Landon," I said over my shoulder, and was surprised when Harley shooed him in our direction.

"Go. You've been here all damn day. Stay out of trouble."

That was unlikely, especially if we didn't keep an eye out at the track later. If it went to shit, Turbo was on his own, but I'd try to prevent it if I could.

Luna

I was nervous. Stanley had called me to find out where I was, and he'd happily offered to come and hang out at the track for the evening. Usually, I didn't mind, but now I had to face him after letting my best friend into my pants.

I leaned against Riley's Corvette beside Landon, both of us watching Riley as she perched her butt on the side of the Ander guy's Supra while she laughed at something Reid said. It was strange watching her hang out with other people, completely in her element.

She'd barely glanced at me since Ander arrived, and Stanley was still on the way, so I hung back with Landon, feeling out of place.

As if sensing my thoughts, her eyes drifted towards us, and she lifted her chin to draw us over. Landon grumbled, apparently not happy with her latest social status either.

"Can you tell if she's faking it? It's not like her to be so talkative unless she's trying to get laid," he said as we walked towards her, and I couldn't stop the snort that left me.

"She's like this with Blake too."

"I guess this is why we haven't seen her much," he grunted, shutting his mouth before we moved beside her. She dropped an arm around my shoulders, and Logan instantly ran his eyes over me.

"Hey."

I smiled and went to reply, but Riley pointed at him and cut me off. "No."

"She's hot!"

"She's taken," Stanley's voice sounded from behind me, and I jumped a mile. He wasn't happy by my closeness to Riley, but he seemed to relax when I moved up to him and threaded my arms around his middle, standing on tiptoes to kiss his cheek.

"You got here fast," I smiled, hoping no one argued now he was here.

"Of course I did," he smiled back. "I had to make sure my girlfriend was in one piece since she snuck out in the middle of the night and didn't let me know she was safe."

I fought not to tense at his lie since he knew I'd left. I really didn't like Raymond, and I was still irritated that Stanley had let me walk around the Heights alone so late at night, all because he wanted to keep drinking with his friends.

"Don't worry, she was fine," Riley snarked, not being able to help taking a jab at him.

"Why am I not surprised that she was with you?" he asked dryly, and I knew he was going to argue with me about it when we were in private.

I was doing a terrible job at hiding my discomfort since Logan was studying me with concern as if I needed saving, and Stanley glared at him, wrapping an arm around my waist to keep me against his side.

"I told you she's taken, asshole. Who the fuck are you?"

Logan let out a light chuckle, and as much as I didn't know him well, I knew he was going to say something stupid from the way Reid rolled his eyes.

"I'm the guy your girl's going to run to when she's sick of your shit. Don't be a possessive asshole. You're not treating her right if you're worried she'll stray."

Stanley's fingers dug into my waist and I cringed a fraction before I could stop it. Reid's eyes dropped to where he was bruising me, and I was surprised when he spoke up. "You're hurting her. Let her go."

Riley's body turned to face us properly as she inspected us, but Stanley laughed.

"Mind your own business. Are you fucking her?"

"Reid," Raven warned quietly, but he ignored her and took a step forward, his fists clenched, and fury written all over his face.

"I don't give a shit who you are, but if I see you hurting a woman, I'll kick your ass."

Riley took my arm and tugged me away from them to keep me safe, and Stanley pointed at her. "Don't fucking touch her, you pussy munching cunt."

She snorted, grabbing her bat that had been leaning on Ander's car to show Stanley she had it. "You think I feel threatened by you? If you get rough with Luna, I'll cave your fucking skull in."

This was going downhill fast, and my heart beat faster as he got in her face. They'd never resorted to violence before, but I was starting to panic at their current exchange.

"You just want to fuck her. Guess what? My girl doesn't want your diseased pussy, Donovan," he spat, and I wanted to smack her when her lips tilted into a small smile. She didn't say anything, but the look on her face said enough.

She might as well have screamed out that she'd fucked me.

She finally pushed him back a step, letting out a light laugh. "You're so easy to rile up, you know? Keep your macho bullshit away from the track. If you want to fight, then get in your car and race me like a grown-up."

"Guys, please don't fight," I said softly, but Stanley gave me a dirty look.

"You're taking her side?"

"No. I just don't want you arguing. You're my boyfriend and she's my best friend. I hate it when this happens," I answered, but he shook his head, taking a step back.

"I'm not putting up with this bitch's bullshit. We're leaving. Get in the car, Luna."

He was testing me to see if I'd stay with Riley or go with him.

Riley rolled her eyes, but she tensed when I took a step towards him. "Can we stay to watch Beckett race?"

"No. Either stay here or get in the car," he snapped, and I knew my only option was to get in the car. He looked furious, and I didn't want him causing a scene.

"Okay," I mumbled, and Riley finally snapped.

"You're seriously going to let him tell you what to do? I hate it when you let people walk all over you. You deserve better than this piece of shit and you fucking know it," she seethed, shoving her hood off her head so I could see how pissed she was. "You're not a lapdog that does as you're told like a good girl. Grow a backbone and stay if you want. We'll take you home later."

Her walls went up as I shook my head and forced a small smile. "It's okay. I want to go."

"I guess you made your choice then," she said flatly, the hint of disappointment flickering in her gaze. "Fuck you, Luna. If you want to side with your homophobic, asshole boyfriend, be my guest."

"Riley—" She didn't let me finish before she stomped off, and I was surprised when Ander eyed me with annoyance before following her.

I didn't feel like this was one of our usual fights. She'd usually flip out, say nasty shit to me, and then paw at some random girl's tits all night until they went home together.

This felt like she'd admitted defeat.

Stanley was stalking towards his car, and Reid dropped an arm around my shoulders to speak quietly in my ear before I could follow. "Do you want my number in case you need help later?"

I scoffed, stepping away from his touch before Stanley could see it and flip out. "He won't hurt me or anything. Even Riley will tell you he's not abusing me."

He didn't look convinced, and Logan popped up beside us with his input. "If you need somewhere to go, you can go to our place. If we're not home, go around the back and use the key that's under the pot."

I scowled, giving them a dirty look. "I'm fine. You guys worry too much."

"I just wanted to give you the option," he shrugged, not fazed by me being a bitch. Reid gave me a nod, and I felt both their eyes on me as I jogged after Stanley before he could leave me here.

I shut myself inside the car, and he wasted no time getting us back onto the road and away from everyone else. He didn't speak until we reached the main road, his voice full of frustration. "I don't want you hanging around her anymore. She's trying to control you, and she's turning you against me."

I glanced at him, guilt nipping at me as I noticed the hurt on his face. I'd been neglecting him, so no wonder he was lashing out. I knew he wasn't a bad person, his mood was because of me.

"I'm sorry," I choked out, his angry eyes landing on me before they softened, his hand reaching out to wipe a tear from my cheek as it fell.

"Hey, what's wrong? Why are you crying, babe?"

"We seem to fight so much when we're together, so I try to stay away and give you space. I don't like that you're mad at me," I replied, my voice breaking. "I want it to be like it was when we first got together. We'd go on dates, you didn't party so much, and we didn't fight. What happened to us?"

He blew out a breath, trying to keep his eyes on the road while glancing over to inspect me. "Are you that miserable with me?"

"No!" I said in a panic, but it tasted bitter on my tongue. I *was* miserable, but I was terrified of leaving him. We'd been together for years, and I didn't want it to be wasted. If we could go back to how we were, I'd do it.

"I don't want to lose you, Luna," he said firmly, placing his hand on my thigh. "Let's spend a few nights alone, okay? When you're done with school through the week, I can pick you up and go for coffee or out for a movie. Sound good?"

I hated that my stomach sank at the thought of being with him so much. Especially when I remembered how good it had felt when Riley was touching me instead.

I was the worst girlfriend.

80
100
120
140
160
180
200
220
km/h
240
260

Chapter Fifteen

Riley

"He's definitely better on the street," Turbo observed as we watched Reid and Ryder race around the track. Landon had happily bailed on me once Luna had allowed Stanley to drag her home, and I'd seen him hanging around with Jett at some point.

If Landon didn't want to hang around Turbo, that was his problem.

I swigged on my bottle of vodka, leaning against the railing. "Say that a little louder, why don't you."

"His girlfriend's not even near us," he chuckled, glancing at Raven as she watched from further down the fence, Zavier speaking in her ear. His palm rested on her lower back as he spoke, and I eyed his thumb as it absently moved back and forth. She leaned into him, nodding at something he said, and Turbo let out a huff. "You're all pussy whipped."

"Are you more of a cock kind of man?" I asked dryly. "Why am I not surprised?"

"Not likely." He turned his attention back to the track

as the cars' engines revved while they flew around the track. "I'm surprised you didn't offer to race Reid."

I waved the bottle at him, rolling my eyes. "I'm drinking. Unless you want to see my sister beat my ass right here on the grass, I won't be getting behind the wheel tonight."

"How are you getting your car home then?" he frowned, peering over his shoulder to look at where our cars were parked. "You can't leave it here."

"Sure I can. No one will touch it. We always leave our cars here."

"Your family has way too much trust in your town," he grunted, pulling his cigarettes out and offering me one. I took it, sparking up and turning around as I sensed someone join us.

Zavier eyed me, and I noticed Raven had vanished.

"She's with Beckett," he said, answering my silent question. "Why'd you want me here? I assume it wasn't just for the company."

I made sure my family wasn't close by, then motioned for him to follow me to the Corvette. I opened the trunk where I'd stashed the wad of cash from Turbo, making sure no one was within earshot before I spoke.

"This is for getting shot at with me. Put it towards your savings."

He slammed the trunk shut, glaring at me. "You want to do this here?"

"What's the problem? It's not like it's a bagful. Stash it down your pants before Reid and the others get back over here, then shove it under the seat when they're not looking."

Turbo crossed his arms, keeping an eye out as he talked, having no problem discussing business in front of me. "When's the next drop?"

Zavier snatched the money from me, shaking his head

as he stuffed the stack of bills down his pants. "I'm not having this conversation here. We can talk about it later."

I frowned, confusion nagging at me as I looked at Turbo. "Why *do* you get crystal from another supplier? Aren't they your competitor?"

Turbo smirked, making me scowl as he dropped an arm around my shoulders to speak in my ear. "Keep the enemy close, Donovan. You know that."

"Why do you think we're friends?" I deadpanned, dragging on my cigarette.

"C'mon, we're real friends."

"Are we? Because I've got the feeling you're using me. That's fine, I don't mind a good business deal, but you've got to be honest with me," I replied bluntly, motioning to Zavier. "And I don't want you dragging other people down for your own personal gain. If your plan with the enemy is going to bring trouble to Zavier's doorstep, speak now."

"We're friends," he said firmly. "And I'm not going to get Lopez killed, don't panic. I didn't think you wanted to know about my business? I recall us having a long conversation about you telling me to keep my shit away from you, and you didn't want any part in it."

"If we're friends and your enemies know about it, then I need to know what I'm in for, asshole. *You know that*," I mocked.

"Since we're friends," he drawled, moving back from me with a grin. "Are you going to tell me what happened earlier with your girlfriend? Why'd she leave?"

Zavier chuckled. "You mean Luna? She's not her girlfriend. Her boyfriend seems to be a real dick though. What's his name? Stanley?"

Thankfully, our conversation was interrupted by Maddox. I wasn't willing to discuss her with either of them.

"You're up, Lavaro."

Turbo grinned, fishing his keys from his pocket. "Sounds good to me. Let's go, Donovan."

Maddox's eyes burned into me as I put my vodka and bat in my car before locking it and walked towards Turbo's, but he didn't say anything. He knew starting an argument wouldn't make a difference.

Zavier vanished, most likely looking for Raven and the others, and once I was in the passenger seat, Turbo started the engine and made his way through the crowd that was gathering.

"Your sister's a big deal around here," he stated, seeming impressed. "It's a shame she wouldn't hit the streets."

"Hey," I growled, giving him a filthy look. "That's my thing. Beck likes the track and the fighting cage while I like the streets."

"What about Ryder? He did well against Reid. Pretty sure he won."

"Ry likes to race, but it's not his passion," I answered, tapping my fingers against my thigh as we got closer to the starting line. "My brother's more into fucking girls and getting high."

"Noted. Beckett doesn't look happy," he said with amusement, giving her a taunting wave.

I was surprised to see Reid in the passenger seat of her Mustang, but I didn't mention it.

"You're good behind the wheel, but this is my sister's domain," I said dryly. "Don't be surprised if you lose."

"I'm aware of her skills. Why do you think I accepted her challenge? I'd like to see if I can beat her on her own turf," he grinned, putting the windows down to let the cool, evening air in.

Beckett revved her Mustang, and I didn't miss the way

Reid glanced at me. He seemed nervous, and that worried me.

The moment the announcer called the race and the flag dropped, we shot off, and it was neck and neck for most of the race. Turbo surprised Beckett when he downshifted and pumped his clutch on the corner, sending us sideways around the curve.

She wasn't used to anyone matching her drifting skills.

I'd seen him drift a lot on backroads, so I knew he'd use it to his advantage here.

It had been a long time since someone had beaten her, but as we inched ahead, I was starting to think Turbo was going to take her crown.

I'd never been in the car with Turbo when he'd raced, and I admired his skills as he drove like it was part of him, slamming through gears and taking corners at the exact right time to drift. I expected him to play dirty, but he didn't try to run her off the road once.

He was genuinely enjoying himself.

People were screaming and cheering from the fence, most of them on team Beckett.

No wonder she had a complex.

I relaxed the closer we got to the finish line, and adrenaline pumped harder as we shot across it just before Beckett and Reid.

Turbo fucking won.

He slammed on the brakes and spun us around to face the other way, turning to glance at me as Beckett parked beside us. "See? I can be a good boy when I need to be."

"I didn't doubt you for a second," I deadpanned, climbing out and facing my sister who looked pissed. I knew I'd ruined whatever plans she'd had for him, but it was probably rubbing salt in the wound that Turbo beat her too.

"Nice race," she grumbled, her gaze flicking to Turbo as he joined me, leaning back against his car.

"We'll have to do it again sometime," he said cheerfully, nudging my shoulder. "You'll have to race me next time. I have a feeling you'd be a good challenge too."

"Sounds fun," I muttered.

Beckett sighed, offering him her hand. "Congrats. Not many people beat me here. You want to stick around for a drink?"

I didn't like that. Beckett wouldn't have decided to be friendly with him without a motive, especially after he'd made her look bad on her own track.

He chuckled, shaking her hand. "Thanks, but maybe another time. I'm not much of a drinker, and I have places to be later."

"Oh? Places with my sister?" she asked lightly, and I let out a groan.

"Let it go, Beck. I've already put up with Stanley and Luna's bullshit tonight, and I don't need yours on top of it."

"It was just a question," she threw back, not taking her eyes off Turbo. "Another time then."

He nodded, stepping back and dropping an arm around my shoulders. "C'mon, Donovan. Let's go for a celebratory cigarette before I go."

Beckett's eyes narrowed as he turned me and opened the passenger door of his car. I slid inside, wondering what the fuck he was up to. He had a look on his face that was calculated, which meant trouble was coming.

He climbed behind the wheel and drove us back to where my car was parked, but he didn't climb out when he shut the engine off. "Tell me right now if you know what your sister's up to."

I frowned, turning in my seat to angle my body towards him. "What do you mean?"

He stared at me for a moment before sighing, his shoulders relaxing. "She's up to something. We ruined her plans by putting you in the car with me, and she's not the type to let things go. She doesn't like us being friends either."

"Trust me, my whole family's pissed about our friendship," I mumbled, keeping my attention on him. "Do you have a bad feeling?"

I was surprised by the tired look in his eyes, his walls dropping just enough for me to see the stress he was hiding. "You know what it's like to be at the top. Your whole family is a target and they have each other to keep an eye out for trouble, but me? I'm on my own. I've learned to read people really well, so when I say your sister's up to something, I mean it. I'll always put myself first, and I won't lie and say I haven't used you as a shield for most of the evening."

"I figured that was the entire purpose of my presence, yes," I snorted. "But thanks for the honesty."

"You were hard to read for a long time," he continued, leaning back in his seat and scrubbing his face with his hands. "You don't show a lot of emotion, and you turn everything sarcastic to hide what you're feeling. I know if you snap, it's because you're really pissed. I also know when you're hurt, you get mad too."

"Where's this going? A therapy session?" I snarked, making him chuckle.

"My point is, I learned to read you. Everyone saw you being an angry friend before with Luna, but I saw how hurt you were. I pay attention. Now, your sister? She doesn't hide her emotions as well as she thinks. She's trying to get me away from you."

"What the fuck do you want me to do then? Piggyback

you everywhere?" I asked dryly. "Or am I supposed to have sleepovers with you?"

He rolled his eyes, smirking with amusement. "No. Then again, I'd like to see you try to piggyback me. You're a whole foot shorter than me."

"Am not, asshole. It's only a few inches," I growled. "And I told you earlier, if I have to choose between you or my family, you're on your own. They'll know something's up if I show my loyalty to you over them. My family is everything to me, and nothing will get in the way of it." That was a lie. I'd already shown them that I was struggling with my loyalty just by getting in his car and ruining their plans, but until they gave me a damn good reason for targeting him, I'd make sure they left him alone.

He nodded, taking his eyes off me to stare out the window. "Chances are high I'll die at the hands of your parents, I've always known that. When you first stumbled across my races, I was stupidly excited. I wanted to make you trust me, and I was going to use you as a way to get to them if I ever needed to."

"You're not painting me the prettiest picture right now."

"That *was* the plan, but things changed," he admitted, scrunching his face with frustration. "I like you, and I respect you. I don't know where I'm going with this, but I just wanted you to know that."

"Knew you were a fucking marshmallow." I leaned forward to smack his shoulder. "Where'd your balls go?"

"Where are yours?" he said bluntly. "You let some asshole drag your girl away, and you got mad at her over it. Do you honestly think she would've left if she felt like she'd had a choice?"

"Don't change the subject," I snapped, his eyebrow raising.

"You hit like a girl."

"This has been fun." I reached for the door to let myself out, but he grabbed my hoodie and tugged me back. I went to slam my elbow into him, but his voice stopped me.

"I'm tired, Donovan. Everyone's my enemy, but you're not. Right? I don't have to watch my back with you?"

"I'm not your enemy unless you turn me into one," I said, warning in my tone. "If you give me a reason, I'll turn on you like the world's biggest snake."

"Noted. Do you want to get out of here? I'll help you kill that asshole and steal your girl back?" he offered, and I would've laughed if he didn't look one hundred percent serious.

"Ander," I said with defeat, using his real name so he knew how serious I was. "She's not my girl, and as much as it pains me to say this, she never will be. It's scary how similar you seem to my sister right now. That's some psycho kinda shit that she'd say."

"Nothing makes people bond faster than burying a body together," he confirmed. "You know, it sucks that you're not into guys. We could've been a power couple."

I laughed, pulling back as he went to tuck my hair behind my ear. "Don't make this weird, or I'll break your nose and you'll never find anyone to love you. I'll fuck your face up so bad."

"Is violence your love language? Are you flirting?" he teased, laughing loudly as I gave him a shove. "No? What a shame."

"If I saw your cock, I'd probably throw up," I replied, faking a gag. "Have you actually taken a good look at one? They're gross."

"Why do you think I like pussy?" he joked, but his attention was on something across the field.

Beckett and Maddox were talking with Zane, all of them watching us like hawks. I had to find out what they were up to, but not right now. They wouldn't do anything while I was there. Not because they didn't want to upset me, but because they weren't sure whose side I was on.

How bad would it look if I caused a scene in front of everyone, protecting someone from my own family?

"You know what?" I chuckled as I looked away from them, giving Turbo the side-eye. "I say we go get drunk. Wanna go to Wet Dreams?"

"You want to go to the strip club?" he asked slowly. "That's owned by the Reapers, right?"

"Well, you can't come back to my place. Mom wouldn't let you through the door," I smirked, grabbing the seat belt and buckling myself in. "If you have a better idea, I'm all ears. I just want to get drunker."

"Wait.," he said with a frown, opening his door and holding out his hand. "Give me your keys."

"Why?"

"Just do it, Donovan."

I handed them over, watching him suspiciously as he rummaged in my car, and relief filled me as he returned with my bat, handing it over along with the keys. "We can't leave without that. I have a feeling you're going to get me in trouble and we're going to need it."

"Me? Trouble? Unlikely," I grinned and clutched my bat. "But thanks."

He smirked, starting the car and turning the headlights on. They lit up the field in front of us, shining off parked cars and drunk people as they looked in our direction, but my eyes were on Beckett. Her fists were clenched by her sides, and I didn't miss the gun in Zane's hand as he glanced at her, motioning to it.

If he thought I'd put up with being shot at to stop me from leaving, he'd have another thing coming.

Turbo revved the engine and gave them a wave out his window, driving towards the road carefully, not wanting to run anyone over. I noticed Landon leaning against his car with Jett and Logan, and I called out a goodbye to them so they knew I was leaving on my own accord.

Landon would probably call the cops and say Turbo kidnapped me.

"Hey! Where the fuck are you going?" Jett demanded, glancing back from where we'd come. Beckett was probably following us to try and stop me from leaving.

"We're going to go party," I answered with a grin. "No, you can't come."

"Is this about Luna? Because—"

"What about her?" I snapped, not surprised when Turbo sighed and braked to let me talk. "She went home with her boyfriend. Am I supposed to just sit here in case she comes back?"

Logan scowled, stepping towards my door and resting his hands on the top of the frame to lean in. "How drunk are you?"

I grabbed the front of his shirt and pulled his head through the window, speaking quietly so the others didn't hear me. "I'm safe with Turbo, and you know it."

"Where are you going?" he asked, pretending like he didn't hear me. "I don't need Beckett flipping out and going on a murder spree."

"Oh, so this is about Beckett? I guess this is you showing your loyalty card." I pushed him back out the window, my chest tightening. I wasn't usually sensitive about this kind of thing, but I was a little drunker than I thought.

I'd assumed Logan and Reid were more my friends by now than Beckett's, but apparently, I was wrong.

"Dammit, Riley. It's not like that," he said quietly, but I didn't want to hear it. I put my window up like a child and turned to Turbo. "Let's go."

He smirked, revving his car loudly, the sound bouncing around the field from the volume of it. "Shots and titties it is then."

He floored it, the vodka threatening to come back up at the sudden violent surge as I was thrown back in my seat, a light laugh leaving him as he pumped the clutch and spun the wheel, causing us to slide sideways out onto the main road before he put his foot down hard, sending us flying along the road.

Beckett was probably freaking the fuck out, and if I was sober, I probably would've felt bad for scaring her. Yes, she seemed like a reckless driver, but she only pushed her car as much as she knew she could handle. She didn't trust Turbo to keep me safe, that much I knew.

He drove like a maniac until we reached the docks, and he gave me a wide smile when he finally parked and glanced at me. "How long until your sister shows up?"

"She won't. I've turned my location off."

"Turn the whole phone off." He glanced over at me like I was stupid. "I've told you before, that app isn't what keeps you hidden."

"If you wanted to hide, you should've told me. Lexi always tells Mom when I'm here, and she'll definitely call her once she sees I'm with you," I threw back, opening the door and climbing out, keeping my bat in my grip. "I thought you were busy tonight anyway?"

He followed, giving me a wink. "No offense, but I just didn't want to hang out with your sister."

"I don't blame you. You probably had an appointment with her knife," I said seriously as we walked through the door, the Reapers that were on security giving Turbo a once-over. They'd know who he was, but since he was with me, they didn't say anything.

I walked up to the bar, leaning my arm against it to get the bartender's attention, not surprised to see that Angel was on shift.

"Hey! Two tequila shots and—" I glanced over my shoulder at Turbo, making him snort.

"Scotch. Neat."

I turned back to Angel, relaying what he wanted. "Scotch, neat, and vodka on the rocks."

Angel ran her gaze over me before doing the same to Turbo, her voice hard to hear over the music that pumped from the stage as two naked girls put on a show.

"Who's your friend?"

"None of your business," I replied, waving my credit card at her to hurry her along. She rolled her eyes, making our drinks silently before pushing them towards us.

"Penny's here tonight if you were after a dance," she stated, motioning towards the back of the room to where a smaller stage was. Penny was grinding on the pole in nothing but a thong as she kept her audience entertained.

"Why isn't she at Devil's Dungeon?" I asked. It was rare Hunter sent entertainment here. They usually only helped out with bar staff or security.

"Lexi had a girl quit right at happy hour. Hunter asked Penny to help out, so she did. If you're bringing that bat in here, you know the rules. No bar fights," Angel warned, shooing us away to serve other customers.

I dropped down into a booth in the corner, keeping

Penny in my sight as Turbo slid into the seat opposite me with a big grin.

"From the way you're watching her, I can only assume she makes you come hard?"

I smirked, turning my attention to him. "She's pretty good."

"I didn't think you had regulars."

"If they keep it casual, I don't have a problem with seconds or thirds. Penny likes to fuck, and she doesn't like strings attached. It works well for both of us," I explained, pushing a shot towards him. "Bottoms up."

"I don't like tequila," he scowled but he picked it up anyway. "No lemon or salt? Are you a fucking psychopath?"

"Yes," I grinned, downing my shot without hesitation and savoring the burn it left down my throat. "Don't be a pussy."

He grimaced but did as he was told, making me chuckle as he screwed up his face. "That's nasty."

"Shut up and drink your scotch, fancy-pants." Grabbing my vodka, I let out a laugh and took a large mouthful, the burn intensifying.

"You got a dancer to recommend?" he asked as he sipped his drink and glanced around. "I don't come in here much."

"It depends who's working," I shrugged, scanning the room until my eyes landed on Peaches. The girl looked sweet, but she was ridiculously kinky behind closed doors. She'd let you do almost anything to her.

She caught my gaze and I curled my fingers to motion her over, a soft smile tugging at her lips as she started towards me. Turbo snorted, giving me a weird look. "That one? She looks—"

"Trust me, she's not sweet. I know most of the dancers

and sex workers in this town. Peaches? She's in my top three. You want to fist-fuck her? Have a gangbang? Maybe you like hot wax? She's your girl. Hell, if you want her to put her fist up *your* ass, she'd do it without question."

I'd heard some stories, and she was definitely worth the money.

I shuffled to the edge of my seat and took Peaches' hand once she joined us. She instantly perched her perky ass on my lap, tucking my hair behind my ear.

"Hey, baby. I haven't seen you in a while," she smiled, glancing at Turbo. "New friend?"

I took her hand to stop her playing with my hair and raised an eyebrow. "You miss me?"

"Of course. I have a feeling you're not wanting my services yourself tonight," she said lightly, not taking offense to me pushing her hand away.

"Sorry, babe. This is my friend, and he asked for a recommendation from me. Can you look after him for me?" I murmured in her ear, not understanding why my body didn't react to her like it usually did. She always got me hot for her, but not today.

It seemed no one did anything for me since I'd gotten my hands on Luna.

"Are we talking the whole deal? Or just a dance?" she asked, but Turbo interrupted.

"Just a dance, babe. I'll pay you for both though."

That surprised me, but I didn't voice it.

She kissed my cheek before climbing off my lap to straddle his instead, and I wasn't surprised when Penny made her way over a few minutes later. She was giving me a naughty smile, her hips swaying in their usual tempting motion, but she was going to be sadly mistaken if she thought she was getting fucked in the dressing room.

"Did you know I was here?" she asked, sliding onto my lap like she always did. Turbo seemed amused by her boldness, but he kept his attention on Peaches who was rolling her body against him, encouraging his hands to move to her waist.

If he didn't fuck her before we left, he had to be gay. Peaches had talent.

"I'm not here to play tonight, babe. Sorry," I answered, running my arms around her. She was sweaty from her dance, but I didn't mind. If someone thought sweat was gross, they were obviously having the wrong kind of sex.

If the bed wasn't soaked by the time you were done, you didn't do it right.

Penny pouted, her lips grazing my cheek as she spoke in my ear. "I'm feeling needy. It won't take long."

"I'm not in the mood."

"You're always in the mood," she said with a laugh, and irritation swept through me. Saying I wasn't interested should've been enough, especially since I told her I wasn't here for her.

"You're on the clock, and I'm busy tonight," I replied firmly, leaning back to look up at her face. "I don't need Lexi or Archer mad at me for distracting you from paying customers."

"Pay for a dance then," she giggled, threading her arms around my neck to nibble my earlobe. "It's not like you can't afford it."

I wanted to shove her off me, but assaulting one of the dancers was a bad idea, even if we knew each other.

"Penny, you're here to work," someone said sternly from close by, and I peered around her to find Milky standing there with his arms crossed, his Reaper's jacket on like it always was.

He was Archer's second in charge, and I heard he got his nickname from being busted sucking on some ladies lactating tits. "Penny," he repeated when she didn't move, and I gave her a gentle push of encouragement.

"Sorry, Milky. I did tell her I wasn't interested," I said as she got to her feet, giving me a dirty look.

"Fuck you, Riley." She stomped off in a huff, her heels clacking over the music.

I guess she just took herself off the casual list since that reaction didn't seem too casual.

Milky glanced at Turbo, a frown tugging at his lips. "Who's your friend?"

"Don't ask like you don't know," I said dryly, reaching for my vodka and taking a mouthful. "I don't like people dancing around their questions."

"Hey, I just wanted to make sure *you* knew who you were with," he snorted, his eyes flicking back to Turbo. "I know exactly who he is."

"Good. Me too. Milky, this is Ander. Ander, this is Milky," I deadpanned, resting my elbows on the table. "Yes, Mom knows we're friends."

"Does she know you're here with him?" Milky asked tightly, not seeming impressed when I rolled my eyes.

"No. She doesn't track my movements. I'm not a kid anymore."

He glared, leaning down to growl at me. "You're also not legally allowed to drink here, remember that. Just because your sister's working the bar, doesn't mean you get let off the hook. We've had cops in here lately, and it's obvious you're drunk. They'll think you've been here for hours. That Logan kid's been in here lately too, so tell him to fuck off until his birthday."

"Are you asking me to leave?" I said with a small smile,

knowing he wouldn't. If they wanted Logan gone too, they would've kicked him out themselves. Even Logan knew not to start a fight with them over some tits.

Milky pointed to my drink, his voice low. "No more."

"Yes, Sir," I mocked, flipping him off once he'd walked away.

Peaches was laughing at something Turbo said, but I wasn't paying them any attention.

Not when Luna had just walked in the door with Stanley.

80
100
120
140
160
180
200
220
km/h
240
260

Chapter Sixteen

Luna

I huffed as I walked through the doors of Wet Dreams, the smell of sweat, sex, and beer hitting my nose. I hated being in the club and it always made me feel uncomfortable.

I wasn't close with the workers, and even though clients usually knew who I was, that didn't stop them from leering at me.

Tempest, on the other hand, loved it here for the same reasons.

I'd expected a quiet night with Stanley at his house after the drama at the track, but he got a call from one of his friends, insisting we had to come out for drinks. Well, Stanley could drink, but I couldn't.

His rules, of course, and he needed a sober driver to get us back to his when he was done.

Not that he even seemed to remember I was with him by the way he was walking towards his friends at a quick pace, leaving me to trail behind.

"Luna? What are you doing here? Are you meeting up with Riley?" Milky asked as he stepped in front of me and cut off my view of Stanley. I frowned, glancing around the room.

"Riley's here? I'm here with Stan. His friends wanted him to catch up with them for an hour or two."

"You know Arch doesn't like you here. It's late," he replied, but I gave him a small smile.

"I'm also twenty."

"It was only yesterday that you were five and climbing onto my lap to steal my fries. There's no way in hell you're twenty, or that means I'm really old," he grumbled, narrowing his eyes. "Didn't you just start high school?"

"Nope. I'm in college," I laughed lightly, my eyes finally landing on Riley in the dimly lit room. She was sitting in a booth with Ander, the pair of them having a conversation while he got a lap dance.

My chest ached as the dancer moved towards Riley and straddled her lap, confusion hitting me. I had no reason to feel hurt by it, but something nagged at me.

I eyed some of the other dancers around the room, and I felt nothing for them. I didn't care that their tits were out on display, or imagined touching them.

Looking back at Riley, my heart picked up the tempo, and my body heated at the thought of her fingers sliding into my pants as her lips trailed across my neck.

"Luna," Milky said sharply, snapping me out of my daydreaming. "I asked if you were going to stand there all night or sit down?"

My face flushed, and I started walking towards Stanley's friends, speaking over my shoulder. "Sorry, it's been a long night."

His eyes burned into me until I sat down beside Stanley, and one of the guys rolled his eyes.

"Dude, you brought your girlfriend?"

"Don't be a dick," Stanley threw back, my heart warming until he added, "Her parents own the club. They'll probably give us discounts if she's with us."

The guys all whooped and cheered dramatically at that, making me scowl.

"It doesn't work like that. Those girls keep a decent percent of their tips, so Mom won't give you a discount because it's stealing from the staff."

"They're just strippers, Luna. If they wanted good money, they should've gotten a real job, like when your mom met your dad and he stopped her whoring around. He gave her a *real* job. I'd never let you dance or get on your back in a place like this. It's disgusting. It's for desperate, single moms who are too lazy to work," Stanley snorted, his friends snickering and making jokes about throwing tinned food on the stage instead if they needed to feed their kids that badly, and I snapped.

"Don't talk about people like that," I demanded, hoping my voice sounded firm. "Their jobs are really hard. They work really long hours in awful shoes, they put up with men assaulting them regularly, and they pay taxes just like everyone else. My mom liked being a dancer, and for your information, she didn't give it up because she met my dad. They grew up together and he let her work here when he bought it. He gave it to her because she loves this place."

It was a little lie. Dad signed it over to her due to crew problems before I was born, but Stanley and his friends didn't need to know that.

Stanley scoffed, sneering at me. "You can't assault someone who's waving their tits in your face. They're literally begging to be touched. Of course your mom liked being a sex worker. She got paid in piles of money and orgasms. I feel sorry for your dad now though. He probably can't even feel the sides anymore when he fucks her."

They all laughed, tears pricking my eyes. "Why would you even say that? Of course a sex worker can be assaulted. My mom was raped and—"

"That's theft, not rape," one guy piped up. "Unless they paid."

I got to my feet, and Stanley grabbed my wrist firmly. "Where are you going? Don't be so fucking sensitive."

"Sensitive?" I hissed, trying to pull back but he wouldn't let go. "You're calling my mom a whore and being a dick. You always get like this in front of your friends."

"You're causing a scene," he said in a threatening tone, his fingers biting into my skin as he tightened his hold. "Sit down and stop being dramatic. I don't know why I put up with you when you get like this. You can be such a baby."

"I don't know why I put up with you either," I spat before I could think about it. "Let me go. We're done."

"Are you breaking up with me?" he laughed dryly, but I saw frustration flash across his eyes. "This is because of your fucking cunt of a friend, isn't it? She's brainwashed you."

"It has nothing to do with Riley. It's because you've become such a massive asshole. It's like I'm dating a completely different person!"

"You want to leave me? Fine. Your timid pussy's not even that good anyway." His eyes gleamed with cruelty, making his friends chuckle.

I yanked back again, this time almost landing on my ass as he let me go.

I turned before he could see the tears fall, moving across the room quickly and almost running into Milky who grabbed my biceps to steady me. "Hey, what's wrong?"

"Can I sit in the office until closing?" I choked out,

knowing he was going to ask questions but not wanting him to cause a scene.

His muscles tensed as he glanced over at the table of laughing men, his voice turning cold. "What did the jackass do to you? Did he fucking hurt you?"

"No, he's just showing off in front of his friends, so I broke up with him. Please, can I—"

"Of course you can. Lex is doing paperwork so she's in there." He dropped his arm around my shoulders to steer me in the direction of the office, his voice softening. "You swear he didn't hurt you?"

"He didn't. He's acting stupid in front of his friends like he always does. I'm just over it," I whispered. I looked to where Riley and Ander had been sitting, only to find them gone. It was probably a good thing or she would've caused a crime scene.

Mom got to her feet as we entered the room, her voice sharp when she noticed the look on my face. "What the fuck happened?"

I didn't want her to know the shit they'd been saying about her, but I had to tell her something to stop her from losing her shit. I went to speak, but Milky beat me to it, his voice gentle as Mom wrapped her arms around me tightly.

"She's here with Stan and his friends. She just broke up with him and wants to sit in here with you until you go home."

"Do I need to call Arch to deal with them?"

"She said they didn't hurt her. I'll tell them to leave though," he said firmly, leaving the room and closing the door behind him to give us privacy.

Mom took my face in her hands, wiping my tears with her thumbs. "Was he being an asshole? Showing off in front of his friends?" I nodded, a sigh of disappointment leaving her as she pulled me close again, her fingers combing through my hair. "I'm sorry. Boys can be such pricks. I'm proud of you for not letting him get away with it."

"I'm going to have to get my stuff from his house," I sniffled as she gave me a small smile.

"Trust me, we'll send your father with you to make sure you get what you need and leave without a problem. If you want to go home instead of hanging around here, I can drive you home then come back."

I shook my head, pulling back to try and get my shit together. "No, finish your work first. I can wait."

"You sure?" She asked, motioning to the couch in the corner when I nodded. "Alright. Get comfortable. I'll try and be quick, but I still have a lot to do."

"It's fine, Mom. If I really want to go, I'll tell you," I smiled before walking towards the couch to get comfortable. It was going to be a long night, and my chest ached the more I thought about Stanley. I loved him, but I had to learn to love myself more, no matter how selfish that made me feel.

If I really loved him as much as I thought, then why was I finding my thoughts drifting to Riley instead?

"You sure you don't want me to tip a little whiskey in it?" Angel grinned as she handed me a glass of coke. "I won't tell on you. Boys suck."

I smiled, giving my head a small shake as I took the cool glass, speaking loudly over the music and laughter from people around us. "Drinking when you're upset just makes it worse, you know?"

"Huh. I usually get really happy, horny, then laid," she

chuckled before glancing over my shoulder. "Hey. I didn't know you were still here. Where'd your friend go?"

I glanced behind me to find Riley there, her hoodie slung over her shoulder and her bat in her hand. I thought she'd left too, and part of me wished she wasn't here. I wouldn't handle her yelling at me when I was feeling so shitty.

After the issues at the track earlier, I knew she was pissed at me. I should've told Stanley to shut his mouth when he started the lesbian slurs, but I always kept my mouth shut to avoid conflict.

I was such a bitch, and I hated that I couldn't stand up for my best friend because I was a pussy.

Her eyes raked over me, but she didn't speak to me as she turned her attention to her sister. "We've been in a private room talking. He's still in there."

"You paid for a room just to talk to your friend? Wasn't Peaches with you?"

Riley shrugged, stepping forward to lean on the bar beside me. "Yeah, she was with us for a while. Ander paid for her time, but he let her nap for the hour. She's tired."

"We're all fucking tired," Angel grunted, motioning to me. "Luna's practically dead on her feet."

"Your boyfriend too busy choking one of the workers with his dick that he can't take you home?" she scoffed, her eyes softening slightly as Angel scolded her.

"Don't be a bitch. She broke up with him earlier, so she's waiting for Lexi to finish for the day so she can get a ride with her."

"You actually dumped his ass? The fuck did he do?" she asked tightly, angling her body to face me. "Do I have to rearrange his face?"

"No," I mumbled, not meeting her gaze. "He was just being a dick like he was at the track, and I got tired of it."

"Why didn't you call me? Even if I'd left, I would've come back for you." Her forehead creased with concern as she studied me, and I completely relaxed at knowing she wasn't holding our argument against me. "I get so fucking angry when you let him walk all over you, and that's why I snapped at you. Probably didn't help I'd been drinking a lot too."

"It's fine."

"It's not fine, Lou," she said with a sigh. "I need to learn to bite my tongue sometimes, but nothing makes me wilder than someone treating you like shit. I don't know why you put up with it. Sure, I understand you love him, but some of the shit he's said and done would've made anyone else leave a long time ago. What did he do this time that made it different?"

I cringed, and she took my hand and gently pulled me to my feet. She laced our fingers together before grabbing my drink. "Let's sit down, okay? There's too many people here and it's hard to talk."

I nodded, letting her lead me into a darker corner where she slid into a booth and pulled me into her side, wrapping her arm around my shoulders to keep me close so we could talk.

I explained most of what had happened with Stanley and his friends, and when I was done, she was scowling.

"He's such a piece of shit. I can't believe he'd say shit about your mom like that. Men are pigs. They couldn't dance for ten-hour shifts in those shoes. They say it's disgusting, but they have no problem coming in and watching the show. Assholes."

"I'm really sorry for how he spoke to you tonight," I

murmured, resting my head on her shoulder. "I'm the worst friend in the world for letting it happen."

She was quiet for a moment before speaking, her voice low. "Tell me the truth. Are you scared of him? You let him have so much control over you. Has he hurt you for not doing as he says before?"

I sat up, frowning. "No. He's never hit me or anything. I'd never stay with someone who did that."

"I just wanted to make sure. To be honest, lots of people in domestic violent relationships stay for multiple reasons. It's not as easy as just walking out or breaking up. Some get stalked and abused more, some end up killed by their partners, and some are so manipulated mentally that they believe they deserve the abuse. I just had to make sure, because if he was hurting you—"

I took her hand, giving it a squeeze. "I promise. He's never hit me."

"Good. Otherwise, I'd kill him," she said without hesitation, her eyes serious. "Do you need help getting your stuff? Is it safe there without you? I can call Ryder and Maddox to come and help get it if you want."

"Dad can take me there tomorrow. Milky kicked Stan and his friends out, so they're probably all there partying." I winced at the thought. "I don't want to deal with them tonight."

"I know what will cheer you up," she smirked, getting to her feet. "Let's dance."

"I don't really feel like it," I snorted but followed her as she tugged me from the booth.

Riley was a good dancer, and she didn't give a shit about people watching her. She was the complete opposite to me.

I much preferred hiding in the corner and watching everyone else have fun.

Wet Dreams was one of the biggest strip clubs in the country. It had multiple stages, private rooms, and a lot of lounge areas for people to sit and drink while getting dances or watching shows. The dance floor was large too, and as much as people thought it was weird to have a dance area for the public when they were supposed to be there watching shows, it was actually really smart.

People loved to dance, and lots of women walked through the doors because of it.

Riley laughed at the look on my face, her arms sliding around my waist as the song switched to *"Boyfriend"* by Dove Cameron.

"Pretend it's just us here, Lou. Dance with me. Follow my lead."

I was awkward, having zero rhythm as she swayed her hips to the music and sang along, giving me a wink as she put my thigh between her legs to grind on me. "Relax. You're overthinking it."

My face heated when I noticed Angel watching us with amusement from the bar, but Riley ran her fingers through my hair and pulled it gently to get my attention. "Close your eyes and feel, baby. Put your hands on my hips."

I did as she said, my eyes fluttering closed as I tried to feel her movements and follow them. It was easier without people's eyes on me, and I became more confident as she helped guide me.

I didn't flinch when her thigh pushed between my legs more, her core grinding on me and making my breath hitch.

She didn't push for more, she just let me dance against her as sweat beaded on my brow, her lips tickling my ear as she leaned in to speak. "Get yourself off on my leg. I can tell you're close. Do you think you can come without screaming the club down?"

"No," I huffed but ground down harder as we danced, the bass pulsing through me as the lights heated my skin. My body was on fire, and it buzzed as my release got closer.

"Then scream, because I have no problem letting everyone know what we're doing," she teased, her arms going around my neck to stop me escaping. "I love it when you come for me, Lou. It's the second hottest thing I've ever seen."

"What's the first?" I asked, my voice strained.

"The look you gave me when I first slid my fingers into your tight cunt," she murmured, my pussy clenching around nothing as I came hard. My knees almost gave out, but she kept moving our bodies to prolong it, her voice so quiet against the music that I barely heard her. "Fuck, I'm going to come too."

My body was screaming at me to stop from being overstimulated, but I bit my lip and tried to keep grinding, her breath suddenly sharp near my ear and she cursed, her body tensing.

I slowed, knowing I was panting but not caring. "Jesus, Riley."

She chuckled, her heated gaze meeting mine for a moment before she turned me around to draw my back against her chest, moving us as if we didn't just get each other off in the middle of the dance floor, and snaking her arms around my middle to rest them on my stomach.

"Please say you'll stay with me tonight. I know I shouldn't be selfish, but I really want you on your back with my tongue in your pussy. If you just need me as your friend right now, just say so. I know you're confused about how you're feeling, so if you just need to be held tonight, I'll respect that."

I tilted my head to the side as her lips teased my skin, her tongue tempting me as she licked a path to my earlobe.

"I don't have a car here, and you've been drinking."

"Ander's only had a couple. He can drop us at my place, but you'll have to sit on my lap in the car," she replied, making me cringe. I'd already gotten in trouble for drunk driving, so being in a car without being secured would make my dad lose his shit.

As if sensing my hesitation, she chuckled. "Or, I could call someone to pick us up. I'm not likely to keep my hands to myself in the car though."

"That sounds like a better plan," I replied, preferring to be safe. She'd been drinking a lot by the smell of her, so I had to make sure we made smart choices.

Ander popped up beside us, his shirt unbuttoned and lipstick on his neck. The dancer from before wandered out of the private rooms, looking freshly fucked and content with herself.

"Why do you look like you just came?" he asked, laughter sparkling in his eyes as he ran them over us, and Riley snorted.

"Says the one with the sex hair. I'm bailing on you, and I'm not even sorry about it."

"I figured. You need a ride?"

"I'll get someone to pick us up. Feel free to take Peaches home and fuck her brains out all over again," she teased, making him roll his eyes.

"I'm glad you have so much faith in my stamina. Just because you don't need recovery time doesn't mean the rest of us don't."

I scoffed, pulling away from Riley but keeping hold of her hand. "I definitely need recovery time."

He laughed, giving me a wink. "Good luck with that. I

doubt you're getting any sleep tonight. You sure I can't give you a ride home?"

I shook my head, and Riley let my hand go to pull her phone from her pocket. "Everyone else is probably still at the track. They can come get me."

"Suit yourself. Have fun," he winked, following Peaches towards the dressing rooms.

I turned to Riley, finding her glaring at her phone. "What's wrong?"

"I was a bitch at the track and left with Turbo, and Reid's being a dick about it."

"What did you do?"

"They didn't like me leaving with him, and since Turbo's an asshole, he drove us out of there like it was one of his street races. I'm probably going to get yelled at. Beck had a plan of some kind to hurt him, I think, so me being glued to him all night ruined it."

I wasn't surprised. Especially if he was involved in as much bad shit as I'd heard.

"So, he won't pick us up?" I asked, making her snort.

"Oh, he's coming. He dropped Raven and Zavier at their place and was heading back to the track with Logan when I messaged him. Let's go say goodbye to Angel and let your mom know you're staying with me for a girl's night."

I hoped to God she hadn't checked the cameras while we'd been dancing, or there was no way she was letting me leave with Riley.

I poked my head into the office, noticing the paperwork still piled up. "Uh, I'm going to stay at Riley's."

"How are you getting there?" she asked without looking up.

"She's called someone to pick us up. I'll come home

tomorrow to organize getting my stuff from Stan's," I promised, her eyes finally lifting to mine.

"Be careful."

"I am. Riley's car's not even here."

"That's not what I meant," she replied with a raised eyebrow, tapping the monitor on her right that was connected to some of the cameras. My face heated, and she let out a sigh. "I'm not judging how you drown your demons, baby, you're an adult. Just be careful."

"You're not going to grill me about it?" I mumbled as her lips kicked up into a smile.

"I'm not your father, but I know you'll come to me if you want to. I'll see you tomorrow, alright?"

"Love you, Mom."

"Love you too."

I shut the door before walking towards the bar, Riley instantly taking my hand to hurry me along, her bat in the other. "C'mon, Reid's almost here."

"Bye, Angel," I blurted out as I was dragged away, the sound of her laughter behind me as we walked outside and into the cool night.

100
120
140
160
180
200
220
km/h
240
260

Chapter Seventeen

Riley

Reid's car was idling out front, and Logan climbed from the passenger seat to put his seat forward for us as we approached. "Just so you know, we only picked you up because Luna's with you."

"Thanks, asshole," I scoffed, encouraging Luna to slide in before me, and I patted Reid's shoulder as I followed. "Hey, thanks for this."

He grunted, glancing over his shoulder as Logan fixed the seat and jumped back in to shut the door. "Your sister's pissed at you." He ran his eyes over Luna, his tone a lot sweeter to her. "Hey, Luna."

"Hey, can we go?" she blurted out.

"In a hurry?" he asked as he started driving out of the parking lot, raising his eyebrow in the mirror.

"Uh, sort of," she mumbled, her face flushing in the moonlight.

I grinned, shuffling closer to her to cup her chin. Her eyes bounced between mine nervously, but her hand rested high on my thigh. "You're really impatient, you know?"

"I'm aware," she practically squeaked, and I probably

shouldn't have been so forward with her until she was ready, but I really had drunk a lot.

I pulled her mouth to mine, a soft gasp leaving her and sending tingles straight to my pussy. She was tense for two seconds, but then she literally dove at me, knocking me back against the seat as she claimed my mouth.

I groaned as she straddled me, her hands squeezing my tits firmly.

"How the fuck am I supposed to drive while you're making porn in the back?" Reid snapped, but Logan shushed him.

"Shut up, bro. You drive, I'll tell you what happens."

I forced myself to push her off me, my entire body protesting. "Seat belt. We're not fucking in the car."

"Why not?" Logan whined, but I ignored him, keeping my gaze on Luna who was panting.

She thankfully did as she was told, and Reid blew out a breath. "Do I even want to know?"

"Nope," I snorted. "Mind your own business."

"Stop waving your business around my car then," he threw back, glancing at Logan. "Put your fucking seat belt on too, dumbass."

I struggled to keep my hands to myself until we reached my house, and once the guys had dropped us off, I dragged Luna through the quiet house and up to my room, locking the door behind us.

I didn't waste time taking it slow. She'd happily mauled me in the car in front of the guys, so I pulled her shirt over her head, yanked her pants off, and walked her backwards toward the bed.

Her hands were all over me as I stripped myself, and for once, I wanted to give up control and let her have her wicked way with me.

She attacked my mouth with hers, her fingers in my hair as her free hand dipped between my legs.

"Fuck, Lou," I groaned as she pushed a finger inside me the moment her back hit the mattress, and I braced myself above her as she explored. I wasn't used to this, but I wasn't complaining. It had been a dream of mine to have Luna's hands on me, so I wasn't about to stop it.

Her lips tickled my neck as she added a second finger, her voice soft with nerves. "I don't know what I'm doing. I want you to like it."

A light chuckle left me, and I peered down at her. "If your hands are on me, then I like it."

"I want to make you come again," she said more firmly, her eyes widening a fraction as my pussy tightened from her words, her fingers slowing as if she was unsure. "You like dirty talk?"

I smirked, leaning down to nip her lip lightly. "You can talk dirty to me if you want, I won't say no."

"Can I go down on you?"

She was going to fucking kill me.

"Fuck yes, you can," I replied, dropping onto my back beside her. She rolled over to face me, holding my gaze despite her face burning with embarrassment as she lifted her fingers to her mouth and sucked my juices.

I cursed, not being able to take my eyes off her as she licked them clean.

"You taste good," she whispered, and I could feel my self-control slipping away.

"If you don't touch me soon, I'm going to flip you onto your back and fuck you for the next week," I growled, hating to sound desperate but beyond caring.

"What if I suck at it?" she asked, biting her lower lip.

I tugged her on top of me, parting my legs to make room

for her to lay over me. "I'll help you, but you'll be fine. You're not supposed to know what you're doing when you've never done it before."

"You'll direct me?" she asked with relief, her shoulders relaxing.

"You want me to boss you around in bed? Sold," I grinned, running my fingers through her hair and pulling her down to kiss me. "Take your time. I promise you'll make it feel good."

She nodded, kissing me and teasing my lips with her tongue as she slid her hand between my legs again. She eased two fingers inside me, and I couldn't help but arch slightly at the delicious intrusion.

She studied my face as she figured out which pace worked for her, my hips jerking as she brushed across my G-spot. "Right there?"

"Yeah, curl your fingers a little. Oh, fuck," I gasped as she did as directed, my body already tingling with need. "Tease my clit. You're doing so good."

She surprised me when she shuffled down my body, only hesitating for a second before wrapping her lips around my clit to suck it into her mouth. I instantly tangled my fingers in her hair, probably pulling too hard, but she didn't move away.

She pumped her fingers in and out, curling them every so often as she tongued my clit, and I couldn't hold back the loud moan as I came hard, the sound more like a fucking scream that everyone in the house had definitely heard.

I ground my pussy against her face, easing up my grip on her hair as I started to come down from the high. "Fuck, sorry."

Her pupils were blown as she looked up at me, wiping her mouth with her hand. "Was that good?"

I reached for her, pulling her over me to give her a kiss. "So fucking good. Do I get to fuck you until you pass out now?"

"Is that possible?" she asked skeptically, squealing as I flipped us over so that I was laying between her legs instead.

"You've been having the wrong kind of sex if you've never passed out. If you want more than my fingers, let me know. I don't really care for toys other than vibrators, but I know some people like feeling full."

"You don't like dildos?"

"It's not that I don't like them, I just prefer fingers and a mouth. It's fun to change things up sometimes though. If you need something to help get you off, just ask," I promised, her brow creasing with confusion. When she didn't voice her thoughts, I stroked my fingers across her forehead to smooth the creases. "Tell me what's on your mind."

"I'm going to sound rude and arrogant."

"Never. Just ask." I chuckled, not surprised by her next question.

"If lesbians don't like guys, why do some still like dildos?"

"Because we're simply not attracted to men. If it takes the feeling of being filled and fucked deep to get someone off, that's okay. They can still be gay. Have you seen some of the weird sex toys on the market? There's tentacles and everything. Doesn't mean they want to actually fuck a damn octopus though," I smirked and slid my hand between us to pinch her clit lightly, making her jerk. "So if you need a vibrator, dildo, or even a finger in the ass in order to come, don't be afraid to ask for it. All I care about is getting you off and making you feel good. You won't hurt my ego or anything."

She seemed surprised, but she nodded and got comfortable.

Since she'd wanted it to be gentle last time, I started with light touches, brushing my thumb over her clit every so often as I slowly teased her pussy with my finger, pushing it in a little just to withdraw it and going deeper on the next stroke.

"I—" she said softly but hesitated to say anything else. I continued to tease her, leaning down to graze my teeth over her pebbled nipple before speaking.

"Be open with me. If you want something, then ask. If it's something I'm not into, that doesn't mean we can't do it. Right now, we're making you feel good, not me."

"No, I was just going to ask you to use your mouth and maybe go a little faster with your fingers," she blurted out. I rolled my tongue around her nipple and blew cool air on it, making her squirm as I picked up the pace.

"You want me to eat your pretty cunt until you come on my tongue, baby?"

Her breath hitched, and I smirked. I was enjoying learning what she liked, and it seemed a filthy mouth was one of them.

I dragged my lips down her chest and stomach, pulling her legs over my shoulders once I was comfortable. I kissed the inside of her thigh, licking a path back to her center and pushing two fingers deep as I rubbed her clit with the flat on my tongue.

She whined, lifting her hips to encourage me deeper, but I didn't go harder until she was begging me to. The last thing I wanted to do was scare her off.

Her thighs squeezed my head as she got closer, and her fingers were gripping my hair hard enough that she was definitely pulling strands out. The fact I could hear her despite her thighs pressing firmly against my ears meant she was being extremely loud.

She was grinding furiously against my mouth as she chased her release, a growl of frustration leaving her. "It's right fucking there! I need more."

I loved that she was losing it enough to curse.

"I've got you," I mumbled. "Harder?"

"I just need more," she choked out, jerking as my tongue teased her clit. She was so sensitive, it wasn't going to take much to push her over the edge. I added a third finger, moving faster and harder with my hand. "Fuck, fuck, fuck."

She almost shot off the bed when I sucked on her clit, her pussy gripping my fingers like a vice as my name rolled off her tongue between more curses. I kept going, her muscles locked tight as she tried to push my head away.

"Riley, oh my God, stop!"

I eased off, waiting for her to relax before going again and forcing a second one out of her. My hand was soaked, and I licked it clean with a smile as I climbed up her body to find her panting.

"You know I'm only warming you up, right?"

Her eyes almost bugged out of her head, and her voice was squeaky. "Are you joking?"

"No," I said with a chuckle. "I'm fucking you until you pass out."

She seemed to consider it for a moment, her eyes brightening. "Can I do it to you again? Do girls actually do the scissors?"

"Do girls scissor?" I repeated correctly, making her nod. "Yeah. Why? You want to?"

"Not right now, but maybe next time. I like what we're doing at the moment," she replied, reaching out to grab the back of my neck to pull me down. "I definitely want to kiss you again."

I didn't argue. I wanted to kiss her again too.

I woke up to my body tingling and a wet tongue on my clit, a groan leaving me. I threaded my fingers through Luna's tangled hair, her tongue eagerly licking and sucking at me until my bones turned to jelly, leaving me breathless.

I lifted the blanket to peer down at her, her body climbing up mine as a satisfied smile spread across her face. "Morning."

"If you're going to wake me up with orgasms, you can stay over every night," I joked, cupping her chin to drag her down for a kiss. "Morning, baby." She completely melted against me, straddling me and rubbing her hot pussy on my skin. "Shit, no more. If we keep going, we'll never get out of bed," I laughed, giving her one more kiss before sitting up and keeping my arms around her to stop her escaping my lap.

Her cheeks were pink, and I could see the uncertainty flash across her pretty eyes. "Am I supposed to take you out for breakfast or something?"

I rolled my eyes, running my fingers up and down her spine. "No. We can go out for breakfast if you want though."

"Can we start with coffee, then figure the day out?"

"Of course. C'mon, get your cute butt out of bed and cover it up before I bend you over the edge of it and fuck you so hard that you squirt all over the floor," I winked, her mouth dropping open.

"Riley!"

"What? You don't think I can make you squirt?" I asked with fake offense. "I'll hold a vibrator against your clit while I slam my fingers into you. I bet you'd gush all over the place."

"That sounds gross," she laughed nervously as she climbed off my lap, getting to her feet as I greedily ran my gaze over her exposed skin. She really was stunning.

"You're not one of those people who think sex with food is weird, are you?"

She giggled, grabbing her panties and pulling them up her slender legs. "What kind of food?"

"I'm definitely filling your pussy with skittles and eating them as you come," I groaned, her nose scrunching.

"That turns you on?"

"You'd be surprised what you'll discover you're into if you branch out into new things," I replied, swinging my legs out of bed to snatch my panties from the floor. "I definitely have a fantasy of fucking you on the hood of the Corvette."

"That one sounds okay," she mumbled, not meeting my gaze as she started pulling her clothes on. I left her alone to think while I got dressed, but hooked my fingers in the back of her pants to tug her towards me when she went to leave the room.

"Am I allowed to touch you in front of people? Or do you need more time? Logan's probably told everyone about last night, but I'll give you space if you need it."

Her face softened, a small, shy smile on her lips. "You can touch me. I don't know what to say if people ask about it though. I have to deal with Stan, and I don't know what I'm supposed to feel right now. I'm not into girls, Riley. This is weird. I know we talked about this before, but—"

"Hey," I murmured, cupping her cheek. "No labels,

remember? If you want to just tell people we're figuring things out, then do that. I don't want to pressure you. I really want this, but I can't force your feelings. If we try this and you decide it's not for you, of course it'll suck, but I'll understand."

I'd do everything in my power to make her want me, but I wasn't going to say that.

"I like that. We're just figuring things out," she said slowly with a nod, letting out a sudden sigh. "Dad won't like the sound of that."

"I'll look him right in the eye and tell him we're besties who like to fuck. I'll handle him," I offered, a groan leaving her as I opened the bedroom door and took her hand.

"That's what I'm afraid of."

We padded down to the kitchen, and Luna's fingers tightened in mine as everyone glanced at us. It seemed we were late for pancakes, and literally everyone was sitting around the table eating.

Their conversations died, and I rolled my eyes before tugging Luna towards the coffee machine. "Don't everyone talk at once."

Slash scowled, his voice sharp. "No."

I paused, turning to face him. "No, what?"

"Whatever this is," he said and waved his hands dramatically at the pair of us. "Just no. I don't need Hendricks kicking the door down."

"Aw, are you scared of him?" I teased, turning back to the coffee machine to finish our drinks. A chair scraped, and Lukas appeared beside us.

"I've got the coffee. You two eat before Ryder eats it all."

Luna stayed silent as we sat at the table, and she refused to meet anyone's eye as I put some pancakes on a plate for her. I sighed when it remained silent around the table, and I motioned between us.

"We're figuring some stuff out, in case you were wondering."

"She's got a boyfriend," Tyler muttered, but Hunter shook his head.

"They broke up last night. Lex messaged me to make sure she was alright. I told her she was fine. Well, I assume she was from the sounds we were hearing," he grumbled, giving me a dirty look. "The only thing I hate about you being into girls is that I can't chase them away with the threat of violence."

I grinned, shoving a forkful of pancake into my mouth. "I'm sorry."

"No, you're not," Skeeter huffed, taking a large mouthful of coffee. "You want to explain about you being in a car with that maniac last night?"

"Your favorite child ratted me out?" I snorted, but I was surprised when he shook his head.

"I don't have fucking favorites, and you know it. You had no interest in guns or fighting as a child, so you can't be annoyed that Beckett got more of my time. If I remember correctly, you occupied Slash and Hunter a lot." He motioned to Ryder, throwing him under the bus. "Your brother's a rat though."

"Ry!" I snapped. "What did you say?"

Ryder shrugged, leaning back in his chair to push his empty plate away. "I just said you hung around Ander after the race and you left with him."

"And?"

"*And* he tore out of there sideways like hellhounds were on his ass, and you were drunk as fuck," he smiled tightly. "I don't like him. Sorry."

"You're a petty bitch."

"I'm just worried about you," he sighed dramatically before narrowing his eyes when I glanced at Marco.

"You know, while we're all concerned for each other, I think it's time we shipped Ry off to rehab. I saw him shoving powder up his nose last night like he was storing it for the winter."

"Where?" Ryder demanded, glaring at me as I replied with a straight face.

"Off a set of tits. *Before* your race."

"Ryder," Diesel bit out. "You said you'd stopped."

"I'm going out," Ryder announced as if that would stop him from getting in trouble, shoving back from the table and stomping towards the door, slamming it behind him.

Everyone looked back at me, and I shrugged. "What? He shouldn't throw stones while sitting in his fancy-ass, glass house. I'm not afraid to smash it."

Slash rubbed his temples, his voice flat. "You kids are turning me gray."

"Hey, at least you don't have to worry about unplanned babies with me," I said sweetly, turning to Luna who was silently picking at her food. "We'll get my car from the track and I'll take you home so you and Hendricks can get your things. I'd offer to come along, but I have a feeling he won't let me."

She snorted, the hint of a smile on her lips. "You think?"

"I'm going to get the Supra fixed today too, so I'll—"

"It's fixed," Hunter said as he got to his feet, making me frown.

"Since when?"

"Since two days ago. Tell your friend he's getting the bill next time."

"He was going to fix it for me," I huffed. "But thank you for doing it."

He eyed me, looking ready to argue, but he simply nodded. "You're welcome. Behave today."

"Always."

"Fucking liar," he grumbled under his breath as he leaned down to give Mom a kiss, saying goodbye to everyone else before heading to the warehouse.

Skeeter was still eyeing me, and I waited to finish my food before meeting his gaze again. "What?"

"I don't trust that Lavaro kid. I've asked around, and he seems to be a lone wolf. He's got a lot of connections, but he doesn't seem to have an inner circle. I don't know if that makes him cocky or stupid."

"He's got businesses to run. He doesn't have time for much else," I said lightly, waving dismissively. "You know what it's like to be at the top. There's always someone who wants to use you or knock you down. He simply doesn't risk it by trying to let people in."

"I didn't think you two talked business," he scowled, and I couldn't help but roll my eyes as I finished my coffee.

"We talk about lots of stuff, but he knows I have zero interest in being part of it. If I wanted to be involved in that kind of thing, I'd join the Devils. Drugs, guns, and fistfights don't do shit for me."

I was such a fucking liar sometimes, but they couldn't find out about my involvement.

Diesel gave me a fake, dirty look. "You'd join the Devils? Why not the Psychos?"

I smirked, motioning to Marco's Devil's jacket. "Because it looks cooler."

"Fuck yeah, it does," Marco replied, leaning over the table to give me a high five.

Mom rolled her eyes, turning her attention to Luna. "Do you need a hand today getting your things? Is Stanley likely to be civil?"

"Um, he should be. I doubt he'll even say anything mean since Dad's coming with me," Luna said softly, peering over at me. "I think less people will be easier."

I bit my tongue to stop myself from being a bitch, and Mom gave me a stern look. "When do you intend on going to some of your lectures? I've let you slack off lately, but you can't keep doing it."

"I've only missed a few days."

"So don't miss too many more. What are your plans for tonight?"

"I have a feeling you're about to tell me," I said dryly. "What do you need me for?"

She chuckled, standing to start clearing the table. "I don't need you for anything. We're expecting a big turnout for fight night, and I was hoping you'd want to come."

"Who's fighting?"

"Beckett's fighting Grim, Maddox's fighting Zane, and some dumbass challenged Skeet so it could be an interesting evening," she answered, surprise hitting me.

"You're letting Zane and Maddox fight?"

"They both want to, so I don't see a problem. Beckett will beat them both up if they take it too far," she smirked, piling up a stack of plates and taking them to the counter. "There's a lot of interest in it, no surprise."

I frowned, starting to help her clear the table too. "I thought you guys were laying low? Hosting a huge event is just asking for the cops to raid it."

"They won't show up. With Zane fighting, it means the Kings will all be there. Three of the biggest street crews congregating together? Yeah, no cop will want to go near the place. BG's already told me they're basically hoping those gatherings lead to us having a shoot-out so we take each other out."

Luna looked horrified, but Skeeter shrugged. "Hey, sometimes it's tempting, but other times I remember how useful the Kings can be."

"You all love each other, you softies," I teased before moving behind Luna's chair to run my fingers through her hair. "We should probably get ready to go."

She fidgeted with everyone's eyes on us, but she nodded and stood. "Yeah. Dad's probably waiting for me."

I slid my arms around her middle from behind, kissing her shoulder. "Text him and let him know we'll have a shower and then we'll leave. You can take the Supra once I get the Corvette."

"Probably don't tell him you're showering together," Skeeter grunted, getting to his feet and leaning down to drop a quick kiss on Marco's lips. "I'm going to head to the shed to start setting up early. Holloway, D, Ty, you're with me."

Caden was already on his feet, knowing he'd be called upon, but Diesel and Tyler pulled a face, not impressed with the early start.

Caden dropped a kiss on my head, mumbling about behaving and not stirring shit up with Archer, and once they were all gone, Lukas let out a loud sigh. "They'll literally do anything to get out of doing the dishes."

Slash snorted, glancing at his phone. "You and Jense chose to be stay-at-home-daddies, so that's on you. I need to meet with the Soldiers this morning, and then I'm dealing with something with Mikey. If anyone needs me, don't."

Marco pushed to his feet, stretching with a yawn. "I don't have to be at Devil's Dungeon until later, so I'll help clean up. I'm not ready to deal with drama yet, but I also need to stop by Angel's place. She had some weirdo follow her home last night from Wet Dreams."

Mom paused with whatever she was stacking in the sink, turning around with a scowl. "Why is this the first I'm hearing about it? I'll go around there right now if she needs me to."

Marco gave her a look like she was crazy. "She's got them tied up in the basement. Mikey already checked to make sure it was secure and said it could wait."

"Jesus fucking Christ," Mom hissed, snatching her keys and pulling her Psychos' jacket on. "I'll handle it. Luna? Tell your father if he needs help today with Stan to just call. If I can't come, I can get someone else to."

"Thanks," she mumbled as I tugged her towards the stairs. I'd already reached my socializing limits, and it wasn't even midmorning yet.

80
100
120
140
160
180
200
220
km/h
240
260

Chapter Eighteen

Luna

Riley gave me the Supra for the day so I could drive myself around, and once she'd driven off in the Corvette, I left the track and drove towards my parents' house.

It felt good to be behind the wheel again, and I took my time to enjoy the morning. I couldn't wipe the smile off my damn face as I thought about Riley, my stomach doing weird flips that I hadn't felt in a long time.

My body ached in the best way, and as much as I still felt confused by what we'd done, I didn't regret it. Riley was making me feel things that I didn't think were possible, and I couldn't deny my attraction to her.

It was definitely more than friendship now.

Her giving me control and letting me explore her body had meant a lot to me because I knew she didn't do that for anyone else. I was pretty sure she never made a habit of letting the other person top her either.

I parked in the driveway behind Mom and Dad's cars, locking the Supra and making my way inside the house.

They were sitting at the kitchen table, Tempest nowhere to be seen, and Dad instantly got to his feet with a sharp tone in his voice. "What did that fucker do to you? I'll kill him."

"Good morning," I said dryly. "It's lovely to see you too."

"Good morning," he said tightly, trying to calm himself. "Seriously, what happened? Lex said he was being an asshole and you'd just had enough."

I nodded, hoping he didn't want details. He'd strangle him for talking about Mom.

"He was showing off in front of his friends, and when I called him out on it, he acted like a prick. It's fine, people break up all the time. That doesn't mean you have to kill them all."

"When it comes to you and Tempest? Yes. I will kill them all," he muttered, glancing out the window with a frown. "Where's Riley?"

"Oh. She lent me the Supra today. She didn't think you'd appreciate her joining us because she won't bite her tongue around Stan," I answered, a scoff leaving him.

"She can taunt him all she likes. If he was a prick to you, he deserves her pissing him off."

I cringed, combing my hair with my fingers absently before deciding to tell him about Riley. It was obvious Mom hadn't told him anything or he would've exploded by now.

"Uh, Dad? I need to tell you something, and I don't want you to get mad."

Mom sipped her coffee, trying to hide her smirk behind the cup, and Dad narrowed his eyes.

"Why's your mother finding this funny? Why does she already know what you're about to say?"

"I'm seeing Riley. Like, we're not dating, but we're

figuring some stuff out," I said more confidently, glancing at Mom for support. She was smiling, her voice full of warmth.

"That's wonderful, babe. Right, Arch? Isn't it lovely that your daughter's seeing someone who respects her?"

Dad seemed to go through a million emotions before raising an eyebrow. "Respect? Does that mean she's agreed to take it slow and keep her hands to herself until she marries you?"

My face heated, and Mom laughed. "This isn't the fifties. A healthy sex life can be—"

"I don't want to know," Dad grumbled, but a sigh left him. "Is this what you really want? You broke it off with Stan last night, and you're already moving on. That's a little fast, right? I'm worried this is a rebound kind of thing, and you'll ruin your friendship. Can you hold off on the touching stuff until you're sure?"

I snorted, not being able to help myself. "I had more sex last night than I've had in my entire life."

"Forget I said anything," Dad groaned, grabbing his keys. "We'll talk about this more later, and I'll try not to strangle Riley when I see her. See? I can be supportive like your mother."

"Proud of you," Mom teased, grabbing the front of his Reaper's jacket to tug him down for a quick kiss. "Remember, they're twenty."

"Stop reminding me," he mumbled, kissing her back before walking towards the door. "Let's go while I'm still feeling calm. I'd hate to take my mood out on Stanley."

Mom gave me a wink, and I followed Dad outside towards the cars. He motioned to the Supra, defeat in his tone. "I shouldn't be letting you drive today, but I can't punish you forever. You drive."

"I really am sorry," I winced as we reached the car and I unlocked it, his eyes meeting mine over the roof.

"I know."

We drove in silence for most of the way to Stanley's, but he eventually spoke, his voice flat. "So, you're into girls?"

"Why do you say that like it leaves a bad taste in your mouth?" I asked softly, peering over at him to find him already watching me. "Am I not allowed to?"

"Fuck, I'm doing this wrong. I'm just confused because you've never shown interest in them before. Your mom made it very obvious that she liked them, so this is new to me. You can like whoever you want. Whether it's got tits or dicks, I still don't like them touching you."

I chuckled, going back to watching the road properly. "Well, no. I don't like girls. I'm still trying to figure it out myself. I just like Riley."

"She's not being too pushy with you? I know she's extremely open and confident with her sexuality," he frowned, seeming to relax as I shook my head.

"She's letting me take the lead with most of it. It's at my pace, and she's really good at reading me. She's also trying not to scare me away."

"You're not doing it just to make her happy, right? If she was a real friend, she'd understand."

"She's aware this might not stick, and she's okay with that. She loves me, but she also knows she can't make me love her," I answered, turning onto Stanley's street. "We're making sure we communicate about it."

"I'm worried about you, but I'm also worried about her. She's a good kid, and you two have been thick as thieves since you were born. If this break up with Stanley becomes temporary—"

I was surprised he was taking it so well, but I didn't need him to worry.

"It's not temporary," I said firmly, parking in the driveway and shutting off the engine, not surprised to find multiple cars everywhere. "He was being a jerk. If he's going to choose his friends over me, then I don't want to be with him."

He gave me a proud smile, patting my arm. "You're a good girl. Don't put up with anything less than what you deserve, and you deserve someone who thinks you're their world."

I smiled, opening the door and climbing out, while hoping the house wasn't too bad when we walked inside. Unsurprisingly, it was.

Dad walked in behind me, the smell of cigarettes and weed hitting us hard. Beer cans littered the floor as we walked into the kitchen, and people were passed out in the living room on the floor.

It looked like a damn crack house.

Dad's jaw was so tense I was surprised he didn't break it.

Raymond stirred, rolling over on the couch and giving me his usual creepy smile. "Hey, babe. What are you doing here? I knew Stan wouldn't throw you out for long."

I knew Stanley would spin some story despite there being witnesses to me leaving him, but I didn't care. These people weren't my friends, and I didn't care what they thought of me.

"I'm just picking up my stuff," I said lightly. "Where's Stan?"

"Fuck knows. Probably in bed," he mumbled, squinting at Dad. "This your new boyfriend? He's a little old for you."

"This is my dad, asshole," I scoffed, his eyes going wide.

"Wait, your dad's in a gang?"

Dad was done spectating, and he stepped forward with a glare. "I run the Reapers, you little shit. Stop looking at her like that."

Raymond sat up, rubbing his eyes. "Sorry. She's hot."

I took Dad's wrist, tugging him along the hallway towards the bedroom before he could throw his fist at Raymond's face, and I wasn't surprised to find Stan and some girl asleep naked in bed. She was his usual, and she could have him.

I grabbed a bag and started shoving my stuff in it, the girl waking up with a shriek. "Hey!"

I didn't bother glancing over my shoulder, continuing to pack things. "Sorry, don't mind me."

"I'm naked!"

"You usually are," I muttered, making Dad frown. I knew he'd question me about it later, but he wouldn't in front of company.

Stanley rolled over, fury filling his eyes until he noticed Dad lingering by the door. "Uh, hey, Luna. I was wondering if you were coming over today."

I turned, crossing my arms and raising an eyebrow, giving him some attitude. "I just came to get my stuff."

He seemed to remember the girl beside him, panic filling his eyes. "Shit, I—"

"It's okay. We broke up, Stan. You can sleep with whoever you want," I shrugged, knowing he was staring at my neck where Riley had branded me with a hickey. I could tell he wanted to demand answers, but he wasn't stupid enough to fight with me in front of Dad.

He didn't say anything else as I handed the bag to Dad before making sure I got everything else from the bathroom on my way out.

Dad took everything out to the car while I grabbed some loose items from the kitchen, and I jumped when I turned to find Raymond directly behind me. "Jesus. You scared me."

He reached out, his fingers tracing the hickey as he chuckled. "If you wanted a rebound, you should've come to me. I would've fucked you within an inch of your life."

I didn't doubt that, and it sounded awful.

I swatted his hand away, trying to look firm. "Not interested. Move. My dad's waiting."

"Does he know his daughter's a cock-loving whore?" he murmured, pressing against me as my back hit the wall, his breath tickling my ear. "You'll do anything to make a guy happy. Stan's told me how much you try to please him."

Panic started bubbling in my chest, but I calmed when I heard the front door open and Raymond stepped back just before Dad walked in. His eyes narrowed on our closeness, but he didn't voice it.

"You ready?"

"Yep. Bye, Raymond," I said as I slipped past him, his sleazy smile in place again.

"See you later, babe. We'll catch up soon."

Doubtful.

Stanley didn't leave the bedroom to say goodbye, and that was fine by me. As long as I had all my things, that was all I cared about.

I climbed behind the wheel of the car, and once we were shut inside, Dad spoke.

"Do his friends always harass you like that? I know you really well, believe it or not. He makes you uncomfortable."

I backed out of the driveway, trying to make light of it. "He's weird, that's all."

"I saw him crowding you through the window. Has he

touched you? If he has, I'm going to go back in there and put a bullet in him," he snapped, my heart rate spiking. I didn't like the guy, but I didn't want Dad losing his shit like that.

"He hasn't touched me. He thinks all girls like him being a cocky prick. The other girls in their group swoon over it, and he thought he'd take his shot with me since I broke it off with Stan. I told him I wasn't interested, and he backed off," I lied, heading towards home. "Girls are into some really weird shit. Why do they like being pushed around?"

"Are you opening this conversation up to a sex talk? Because I'm really not comfortable explaining these things to you," he groaned, scrubbing his hands over his face. "But I'm glad you're not into that stuff."

"Why? I've heard that Mom likes that kind of thing. She likes it when you hit her too," I said, frowning hard. "You hate it when men hurt women."

"Shit," he cursed, looking extremely uncomfortable. "This is not how I thought I'd be spending my morning. Look, I don't hit your mom in a way to hurt her. Where did you hear that?"

I changed gears as we reached the main road, giving him a sheepish look. "Me and Riley were eavesdropping on Rory, Mom, and Aunt Charlie when we were younger. They were talking about sex stuff. Mom said you slap her sometimes."

"Jesus Christ," he muttered, his neck turning a tinge of pink. "I don't abuse your mother, Luna. I swear to God. I'd never want to hurt her. You need to talk about this with her because I don't know how to fucking explain it."

"I'm an adult. I'm aware my parents have sex and like weird shit," I snorted despite my embarrassment. "Wouldn't it still hurt her though? And Aunt Charlie said—"

"Nope," he growled, giving me a pleading look. "I don't want to know what Rage fucking Evans does to my baby sister. In my head, she's still a sweet little girl that was never corrupted by the devil."

I stayed quiet, both of us way too uncomfortable, and he happily changed the subject after a moment. "I know I said I wouldn't push you with your studies, but you've had time off and I'm worried you're going to fall behind."

"I'll catch up easily. Riley's had some time off too, so we'll study together or something."

"Sure you will," he said slowly. "I have a feeling Riley won't study for long."

"She doesn't have to, but I actually want to pass," I grinned, turning onto our street. "Maybe I should set up a reward system for her."

"I love you, but please stop," he begged, bailing from the car the moment I parked in the driveway. I snickered, climbing out to help him carry my things inside, and the moment I was alone in my room, I let out a sigh of relief.

Everyone left me alone to unpack, so I savored the peace and let my mind drift to Riley.

A stupid smile spread across my lips, and I let out a huff of amusement.

Was I really going to date my best friend? She was pretty and knew how to light my body on fire like no one else could, but what if Dad was right?

What if it was a rebound? Was I clinging to her because she was safe and made me feel comfortable?

I sat on my bed, thinking hard. I was attracted to her, and my body heated just from the mention of her name.

Yeah, I was a goner for her. There was no way these feelings weren't real.

Riley

"Good morning," Turbo smirked at me as I climbed from the Corvette at the abandoned warehouse in Hawthorne Heights, my bat in hand. "You look well fucked."

"Says the guy with his pants undone," I deadpanned. He was resting his butt on the hood of his car, his ankles crossed and a joint hanging from his lips. He'd called me not long after I'd picked up the Corvette and said it was important.

It didn't look too fucking important to me.

He chuckled, reaching down to zip up his jeans. "I was in a hurry. Sue me."

"She fuck's good," I replied with a nod, but let the annoyance reflect in my tone. "Why did you drag me out here? Can't you go a day without me?"

"She was the one screaming my name, not the other way around," he scoffed, a hint of a smile on his lips. "I thought we bonded yesterday. Why are you being a bitch? Did you know your brother's a druggie?"

That got my attention.

"You've been watching my fucking brother? Stay away from him. I mean it," I bit out, and he rolled his eyes, taking a puff of his joint.

"I didn't go looking for him, no. So, you know he's in the drug scene?"

"Yes, he's always liked his pills and powder. Why?" I demanded, getting defensive. We'd all taken pills or snorted cocaine once or twice in our lives, but Ryder did it regularly. The fact people were taking notice and referring to him as a druggie was pissing me off though.

"I was buying smokes at the gas station a couple hours

ago and he hit me up for LSD and Molly," he answered, raising an eyebrow. "Why would he come to me when he has a million drugs at his fingertips through your family business?"

"You fucking sold to him?" I spat, gripping my bat tightly as my jaw clenched. Our parents would strangle him for buying drugs from another business. A lot of people were greedy, making shitty batches for higher profit, but we kept ours pure.

Ryder knew not to touch anyone else's supply.

"I didn't say that. He hit me up for it, but I told him I didn't have anything," he scowled. "I don't turn down business from anyone, so I hope you can see how important our friendship is now. I could make a killing off him, you know? He wanted a lot."

I blinked at him for a second before replying, the anger burning away only to leave confusion in its wake. "You turned him away?"

"Of course I did. He's your brother. If he wanted weed, I'd sell it to him, but I don't want to be responsible for your brother fucking himself up. Do your parents not like drugs? I was under the impression that you guys can do whatever you want."

I pulled out a cigarette, lit it, and blew out a puff of smoke. "We can do coke and weed in moderation if we get it through them so they know it's pure. My parents also specialize in crystal, but they don't allow us to touch that. They don't tend to care much for party pills though. The main clients for that are rich kids and frat houses, which they won't sell to. Do you feel bad selling to kids who'll take too many and die?"

He shrugged, looking away from me. "Everyone who takes drugs can die, Donovan. I don't sell to young kids, but high school seniors? They're old enough to know what they're doing. They know the risks they're taking. Do your parents feel bad for selling to addicts who will most likely end up dead? It's just business."

"Aren't you worried about rich kids dropping dead and their families blaming you?"

"I rarely sell directly to my clients. I have runners, or I do drop-offs. Not many of my customers know who I am. There's a reason I'm one of the biggest players in the game," he winked at me before finishing his joint and squashing it under the toe of his shoe. "Anyway, I just wanted you to know that your brother's sniffing around other dealers. He needs to be careful."

"He's the son of some of the most notorious criminal street crews in the country. I doubt anyone's going to sell to him," I laughed but immediately stopped when he cringed.

"That's the problem. Nothing would knock your family down like your brother taking a hot shot or a bad batch of pills. Take it from someone who's supposed to be their enemy. Killing Ryder would send a message, and you already know how much it ruined your family when Zavier's brother killed Lloyd. He shouldn't even accept a bottle of water from anyone else because there's always someone ready to strike."

Chills ran down my spine, and I shook my head. "Ry's not stupid. We grew up knowing not to trust anyone outside our circle."

"I don't mean this to be a prick, but drugs make a person stupid. If he's hooked, he'll do anything for a fucking fix. Just because he's not injecting crystal yet, doesn't mean he won't. All it can take is the promise of a good high from someone he thinks he can trust, and he'll take it." His face was void of emotion as he shoved his shades over his eyes and stood up straight. "Enough of that, it's getting depressing. You want to race for pink slips tonight? I had a guy drop out and I need someone to fill their spot."

I took a drag of my cigarette, glaring at him. "You think I want in on that shit? I'd never risk my Corvette like that."

"Use the Supra. You're a good racer, you'd win," he replied with amusement. If they wanted to risk it all, they could be my guest. No amount of adrenaline rush was worth losing my baby over.

"Fuck no. I'm not the best, my ego isn't that big," I scoffed, flicking what was left of my cigarette at his feet. "And I'm giving the Supra to Luna."

"You're obsessed with that girl."

I flipped him off when he laughed at me.

"Mind your own business. I can't race tonight even if I wanted to. It's fight night at the Psychos' shed, and Mom wants me to attend."

"Big fight?"

"Seems that way. Beckett's fighting Grim, and Maddox is up against Zane Evans. I'm kind of hoping someone challenges Mom so I can watch her flatten them," I smirked. "I'd offer for you to tag along, but I doubt that would be a good idea."

"I'm not interested in watching people beat each other up for sport, but thanks," he said dryly. "Are you taking your girlfriend?"

I wanted to be annoyed with him for bringing up Luna, but I liked hearing her being referred to as my girlfriend. I'd never given a shit about a relationship before, but I wanted to shout it from the rooftops with her.

"She usually comes along, but it's not really her thing either. It makes her nauseous to see so much violence and blood," I answered as the ghost of a smile tugged at my lips. "I never force her to go though."

"True love then?"

"Bite me, Lavaro. I'm leaving before I hit you with my bat," I replied and waved it in his direction. "And thank you for not selling to my brother. I'll talk to him."

"Vouch for me if your parents ever come for me. Tell them about this day," he joked, but I could hear the worry in his tone. I doubted they'd go after him since he stayed out of Ashburn Valley, but I understood his concern.

"Will do. If you call tonight, I won't answer."

"Understood," he answered before climbing behind the wheel of his Supra and starting the engine, peeling out like his ass was on fire.

I rolled my eyes, starting my car and moving towards the main road, only to curse as I entered Ashburn Valley to find Beckett's Mustang flying towards me in the rearview. I considered putting my foot down and leaving her in the dust since I was a lot better at navigating the roads at high speed, but it wasn't smart to show that skill to her after the latest accusations.

She stuck to my ass the whole way home, and I'd barely stepped out of the car before her fist hit my face.

I stumbled, catching myself on the Corvette to avoid ending up on the ground. I glared at her, refusing to give her the satisfaction of clutching my face. It fucking hurt, she was trained way more than I was, but she didn't need to know how badly it was burning.

"What the fuck was that for?" I spat, watching the fury in her eyes as she tried to tower over me with the tiny height advantage she had, a muscle ticking in her jaw.

"That was for leaving the track drunk as fuck last night and letting that asshole drive like a dickhead," she scowled, her knuckles cracking as she balled her hands into fists. "I can't believe you got in his car and left."

"Why wouldn't I? We're friends!" I snapped, bending down to grab my bat that I'd dropped when she'd hit me. "If I hit you every time you put yourself in danger, you'd be unrecognizable. I get it, you're scared of losing me, but I'm sick of you trying to control me. You're not my mommy, Beck."

"Are you trying guys? Is that it? Are you into Ander or something?" she demanded, and I lost it. She'd never said something rude about my sexuality before.

I swung my bat at her, narrowly missing her head as she ducked out of the way. "Fuck you! You think I'm in the closet about being *straight*? He's just my fucking friend. Aren't I allowed to have those?"

She pulled her knife from her pocket, and I hadn't even heard the front door open, but Jensen was suddenly standing between us. "What the fuck, you two? Knock it off!" he barked, his back to me as he stared Beckett down. "Put that away."

"She—"

"Beckett!" he shouted, making her pause. Jensen never yelled. He was always so calm compared to most of our dads. He cleared his throat, speaking more quietly. "If you two want to deal with an issue, you don't use weapons."

Beckett put her knife away, but I wasn't going to let go of my bat. I could fight with my fists if I had to, but I wasn't risking it.

"I think she's fucking Ander," Beckett said flatly, making Jensen chuckle.

"Excuse me? Your gay sister's sleeping with a guy?"

She huffed, starting to calm down but sticking to her argument. "She has to be. She doesn't give a fuck about anyone and she never sticks her nose in people's business. She's had his back a lot lately, and she spends a lot of time with him. Straight girls have a tendency to be curious by girls, so gay girls could get curious about guys, right?"

"Trust me," I said flatly, giving her a blank expression. "I'm not interested in dicks. Not even a little bit. Do you know how arrogant you're sounding right now? I'm friends with Turbo. That's it. Why would I lie about that? If I did get curious by some guy, I'd just say so. I don't give a fuck what people think of me and I have nothing to hide."

"Shit," she mumbled, scrubbing a hand over her face, the anger vanishing completely. "I'm sorry. I shouldn't assume shit, you just freaked me out last night and it's strange that you'd take his side over mine like you have been."

Jensen moved to stand beside us, disapproval in his voice. "If you have questions about sexuality, you know Riley's an open book. I don't know what the hell is going on with you kids, but you're all divided at the moment and I hate it. What's going on?"

I sighed, pulling my hood over my head and crossing my arms. "Mikey moved out and married Poppy, Lloyd died, Angel moved out, Beckett and Maddox moved out, Marla's about to run away to college, and Ryder's on some permanent drug-induced bender. We're all on our own paths, Dad. Things happen, we disagree, but we're still family."

"You're keeping secrets, Riley," Beckett murmured, hurt in her gaze. "I want to know how bad it is since you can't trust me with it."

I didn't deny it, but I started walking towards the house, speaking over my shoulder. "You were nailing our brother behind my back and didn't tell me. Don't get mad when I don't want to tell you everything in my life, because it's not like you're always honest with me either."

She cursed but she didn't follow me.

Our family had been falling apart for a while now, and I had a feeling this was just the tip of the iceberg.

80
100
120
140
160
180
200
220
km/h
240
260

Chapter Nineteen

Riley

I parked in Luna's driveway behind the Supra later that evening, barely shutting the driver's door before she threw her arms around my neck and kissed me, my ass smacking into the side of the car from the force of it.

I wasn't expecting it, but I instantly slid an arm around her waist, pulling her closer.

"Hey, baby," I murmured against her lips. "You miss me or something?"

She stepped back, her face flushed. I loved how awkward she could be, it was cute.

"Of course I did. Was I allowed to do that?"

"If you want to fuck me against my car right here in the open, you're allowed," I smirked, raking my fingers through her silky, brown hair to keep it off her face. "We go at your pace, remember? If you want something from me, take it."

She frowned, pushing my hood off my head and gasping when she saw my bruised eye. "What happened?"

It hurt as she softly ran her fingertips over it, but I didn't push her back. I liked that she was worried.

"I had a disagreement with Beckett, it's fine. Are you ready to go?"

She looked sheepish, glancing towards the house. "Uh, Dad wants to talk to you."

Amusement flickered through me, and I took her hand. "You told him that I fucked your brains out?"

"Riley," she whined, meeting my gaze with worry. "Please don't say that."

I tugged her towards the house, laughing lightly. "I'll try to contain myself."

Her hand was tight in mine, and I could tell she was freaking out. I had no idea how her parents had reacted when she'd told them, so I didn't know what Archer's mood was going to be like right now.

Luna opened the door, stepping inside and keeping a tight grip on me as if I was going to run away and leave her there to deal with the carnage. She dragged me into the living room to where Lexi and Archer were watching TV, and he instantly muted it and turned to me.

"Sit."

I sat on the couch, pulling Luna down beside me. "Am I in trouble?"

"Have you done something you shouldn't have?" He raised an eyebrow, not sounding mad. Yet.

"Nope."

"Then you have nothing to fear. Luna tells me you two are seeing each other."

"Is this one of those talks where you ask what my intentions are with your daughter? Because I don't think you really want to know," I smiled at him, making Luna scowl at me.

"You said you'd behave."

"I said I'd try to contain myself," I corrected, glancing at

Archer. "We're all adults here. Look, I can't knock her up, I understand consent, and I won't let anything bad happen to her. Isn't that enough?"

Lexi leaned forward, giving me a wink. "Let him get his stern father stuff out of the way. You know we love you, Riley. I'm glad you two are together, even if I think it's a little too soon after Stanley."

I glanced at Luna, not being able to help the grin on my face. "You said we were together?"

She panicked, her eyes widening. "No! I said we were just figuring things out!"

"That's a shame. I was getting all excited to brag about my hot girlfriend," I teased, tucking her hair behind her ear. "I can wait until you're ready though."

She looked unsure, and Archer let out a sigh. "I never thought I'd see the day that Riley was bursting at the seams to announce she's off the market while my sweet little girl wants to just have friends with benefits."

"Maybe the benefits are just really good?" I drawled, giving him a sly glance. Luna groaned, and Archer rubbed his temples.

"I'm done with this conversation. The main reason I wanted to speak with you is about tonight. You know I don't like my girls at the shed, but I'm trusting you to keep Luna safe. I'm trying to relax my rules with her because I'm aware she's an adult, so don't make this hard for me. I want to know if she's staying at yours or coming home, and I need you to promise me you're not drinking if you're driving. I won't budge on that."

I turned serious, giving him a nod. "I promise. If I decide to drink, I'll make sure one of my parents can take us home."

"No drugs."

"I don't do drugs. I tried powder once or twice and didn't like being high," I said firmly. "And I'd rat Luna out if she even thought about taking any herself."

That made him relax.

He leaned back in his recliner, relief on his face. "Good to know. Don't get her in trouble, and keep her safe. Those are my rules."

"She's staying at mine," I said without checking with her. "I'll bring her home tomorrow."

"Thank you," he mumbled, turning his attention to Luna. "Call me if you need me. I don't care if it's three in the morning, alright?"

"I promise," she agreed, getting to her feet. "Let's go, Riley."

I said goodbye before letting her lead me out to the car, and once we were inside, she let out a deep breath. "That went better than I thought."

I chuckled, starting the engine and backing out of the driveway. "I can't believe you told him so fast."

She cringed, fiddling with her hands on her lap. "I was worried he'd hear about it from somewhere else and flip out."

I switched through the gears before placing a hand on her thigh, giving it a gentle squeeze. "I'm really proud of you. I know it can be really scary to admit something like that."

She gave me a blinding smile and laced our fingers together. "I'm glad we don't have to hide it. I'm still terrified of my feelings, but I think it's going to be okay. If Dad can cope with it, then no one else should be a problem."

I didn't dare tell her the world was full of people who hated people like us or that I'd been dealing with a lot more homophobic shit than she saw. I didn't want to scare her away, not when she was still trying to understand her feelings.

We'd talk about it once she was more comfortable.

We talked about school for the rest of the drive, and I laughed when she told me about the reward system she'd told her father about. I wished I'd been there to see it.

I parked beside Maddox's Charger and climbed out before walking around to Luna's side. I offered her my hand, waiting to see if she'd take it.

If she didn't want to get too close and personal here, I wouldn't push her.

To my surprise, she only hesitated for a second before taking it with a deep breath. "I'm nervous."

"Do you want my hoodie? You can hide in it," I offered, moving to pull it over my head for her, but she stopped me with a hand to my chest.

"No, it's fine. I just—" She looked uncomfortable, and I gave her hand a squeeze after letting go of my hoodie.

"Hey. I won't maul you in there, okay? We can just hold hands, or not. I don't want you doing anything you're not comfortable with."

"I'm not ashamed of you. I'm just really nervous about it," she murmured, relief filling her eyes in the dim light as I gave her a reassuring smile and let go of her hand.

"You're allowed to be nervous. I won't touch you. We can go in there as friends like we always do, and if you decide you want to hold my hand, you can."

"Are you sure?" she asked, but I could hear the nerves leaving her voice. "I suck at this, don't I? I don't even know what I'm feeling, so explaining it to other people is going to be hard."

I pinned her with a firm look, wanting her to see how serious I was. "If anyone says anything, you can tell them to mind their own business. No one has the right to know your personal shit. You only give people answers if you're comfortable with it."

She nodded, starting to walk towards the door. "Let's get inside before we miss anything."

I'd hoped she'd at least hold my hand, but I had to let her lead. She'd be in my bed when we left, so I didn't exactly have anything to mope about.

I kept my hood up as we wandered inside, and my hand itched for my bat. I knew I wouldn't need it in here, but that didn't mean I was comfortable without it. It was in the trunk just in case though.

I scowled as someone's arm snaked around my middle, noticing Luna pause as hurt crossed her face. I had no intention of seeing anyone else, even if we weren't technically dating.

I grabbed the arm and pushed it off, turning to find Penny. The woman was like a fucking leech all of a sudden, and I thought I'd made myself clear at Wet Dreams the other night.

"Penny—"

"I don't know why you're so grumpy with me, but let me fix it," she pleaded, pawing at me like a desperate bitch. "Let me make you feel good."

"Don't fucking touch me," I snapped, not giving a shit about upsetting her. "We're done with the casual hookups."

"Why?" she demanded, her eyes narrowing. "I thought we were having fun?"

I blew out a breath, knowing Diesel and Hunter were at the bar close by, watching our exchange. I'd been warned against fucking our employees, and this was why.

"Does this feel fun to you?" I snorted. "But I'm just not interested. I'm seeing someone."

I swore her jaw almost hit the ground. "You're dating someone?"

"No, I'm seeing them. Like, it's casual but I hope it becomes more," I said firmly, not wanting to say who since Luna wasn't ready for anyone to know quite yet. "I don't want anyone else."

"Whoever they are, they won't last. It takes a lot of woman to keep your interest," she threw back as I started walking away. I wasn't going to waste my breath arguing with her. I'd told her no, so it was her fault if she didn't want to accept it.

I was surprised when I reached Luna and she instantly slid her hand into mine, pulling me against her front. "Are you okay?"

"You're fucking her?!" Penny screamed, drawing most eyes in the room to us. "Over me?!"

I kept my face blank, tightening my hand in Luna's to let her know it was fine.

"You want to know why I'd choose Luna over you?" I asked dryly, not stepping back from Luna who was gripping my hand tightly. "Because I could never love someone like you when I have her in my life. I've always made it very clear to you that we were casual, nothing more. You were fine with that. I never tricked you into my bed, and I've never lied to you about my intentions. It was just sex, Penny. But this?" I held up mine and Luna's clasped hands. "Means more to me than getting laid."

She took an angry step in our direction, and Mom was instantly between us, her arms crossed. "Either calm down or leave. It's the only warning you're getting."

"But—" Penny sputtered, her back going straight as surprise covered her face.

"Don't make me throw you out," Mom said quietly,

making Penny instantly shut her mouth and stalk off to sulk elsewhere. She wasn't stupid enough to argue with Mom.

Mom turned to me, waggling her finger at us. "Does Hendricks know she's here?"

"Yes. I picked her up, got the third degree about keeping her safe, and he knows she's staying at ours tonight," I said as I ticked the list off with my fingers. "And I told him if I'm drinking, someone will drive us home."

"I bet that was fun." She let out a chuckle, motioning to my eye. "Is that from Beckett? Jense said you two had an altercation."

Luna let my hand go, so I stepped back to give her some space as I kept talking. "Yeah, we're fine now."

"Good. I'm sick of you kids attacking each other. Let me know when you two leave so I know you haven't been kidnapped or anything."

"Okay. Love you." I gave her a smile and her expression softened.

"I love you too. Behave while you're here."

I motioned for Luna to follow me towards some of the seats in the back, and the moment we sat down, she spoke softly. "We're not together, so if you want to see Penny—"

My head snapped around to face her, irritation washing through me. "You think I want her when I have you?"

Her face turned red, and she shifted uncomfortably as she averted her gaze from me. "I just thought—"

It was dark where we were sitting, so I didn't hesitate to grab her waist and haul her into my lap to make her face me, ignoring her squeak of protest. She didn't try to get back in her seat, and I couldn't help the smirk that spread across my lips as her hand flattened against my chest to keep distance between us.

"I'm not even holding you in place. Don't act like you don't like this."

She bit her lip, glancing over her shoulder nervously. "What if people see?"

"Want me to put you back in your chair?"

"No."

"Then what's the point in your argument?" I teased, placing my hands on her butt to pull her closer. "I hope all the women here see you on my lap and know they don't stand a chance."

She wrapped her arms around my neck, leaning close to rest her forehead against mine, hiding us in my hood. "I like that you don't want anyone else."

"You have no idea how much I fucking love you, Lou," I whispered, tightening my hold on her. "Having you on my lap makes me stupidly happy."

She giggled, leaning back to meet my gaze. "You make me happy too, even if I don't know what these feelings mean."

"Just promise me you won't run if you get scared. You'll tell me?" I asked, not hiding the vulnerable tone in my voice. "I couldn't take that."

"I promise."

Luna

I winced and leaned into Riley's side as we watched Maddox and Zane fight, bile sitting in my throat as Zane landed a solid hit to Maddox's eyebrow, splitting it and causing blood to spatter on the second hit.

Riley's arm went around my shoulders, but her eyes

were glued to the fighting cage. I honestly didn't understand how anyone liked watching people beat each other up.

We were standing closer to the cage than where we had been sitting earlier, and I could smell the blood in the air from the previous fights. They'd been brutal, and I was sure Skeeter had killed his opponent.

Riley assured me the guy was fine, but he didn't look like it.

I tensed as Beckett materialized beside Riley, her voice low. "I actually think Evans might have this fight."

Riley didn't look at her, but she sighed. "Yeah. Maddox needs to get his head in the game. What's his problem? I've never seen him so unfocused in the cage."

"Him and Jett had a fight earlier."

"What about?"

Beckett snorted, annoyance on her face. "Laundry. It was Jett's turn, but he didn't do it because he was too busy gaming with Cruz and Drake."

Riley finally turned to her, not letting go of me as disbelief filled her tone. "They got in a fight because Jett didn't wash some clothes?"

"Yes," she grunted, her eyes running over me before her lips quirked into a grin. "You look ill. Why do you keep coming to watch if it makes you sick?"

"Because it's important to Riley," I said without hesitation. "And I like spending time with her."

Riley frowned, holding my gaze. "If you really don't like it here, you don't have to come along. I can always grab you on my way home and hang out."

"No, it's okay. I like being able to support Beckett and Maddox," I reassured her before jumping as there was a loud thud over the music.

We turned our attention back to the cage, finding Maddox on top of Zane as he slammed his fists into his ribs.

"Get him, babe!" Beckett screamed, moving away from us to get closer. "Show him he's your bitch!"

Riley chuckled, wincing as Zane somehow bucked him off and landed a fist on his nose, definitely breaking it. "This is going to be nasty by the time they're done."

They were going hit for hit, the pair of them covered in blood, and it wasn't until Slash stormed past us while cursing that we knew it was over. They were going to kill each other if it wasn't stopped.

It was labeled a tie, and they had to call a break to clean the cage before letting Beckett and Grim fight. The blood was everywhere, and I fought a gag as both guys walked past, actually laughing at each other as they accepted small towels from Beckett to try and stop the bleeding.

"You two are ridiculous," she said as if she were bored but there was amusement in her eyes. Maddox shrugged, cringing as he pressed the towel to his nose.

"It was going well until it wasn't."

Zane scoffed, pulling the towel from his face to give him a dirty look, his eye already swelling under the blood. "You didn't stand a chance, idiot. You were distracted as fuck in there."

"Bite me, Evans."

"Uh, Riley?" I frowned, noticing people arguing by the door. "Isn't that your friend? Blake?"

She glanced over, letting out a huff of annoyance. "Yep. Let's go see what the fuck she's doing here."

We walked over, and she kept a firm grip on my hand to avoid losing me in the crowd. People were amped up from the fight and getting rowdy.

"Donovan!" Blake snapped when she saw us, trying to

pull away from the Bloody Psycho who was working security. "Don't you know how to answer your fucking phone?"

Riley tensed, not liking the attitude being thrown at her. "I told that prick I was busy tonight."

I had no idea who she was talking about, but my stomach sank as Blake continued. "Logan's been trying to fucking call you for the past hour. Slick ran Reid off the road to avoid losing. He's in the hospital."

"Reid was racing for pink slips?" she bit out, not seeming to care about people hearing her. I didn't know the whole story behind the street racing, but I had a feeling there was a lot going on. If Reid was in the hospital, it must have been a bad crash.

"Slick taunted him into it and talked a heap of shit about Raven. C'mon, let's go," Blake said desperately, fear in her voice. "I don't know if he's going to make it, Donovan. It was bad."

Riley turned to me, not hiding the concern. "I'll go with Blake. I'll give you my keys and—"

"No," I bit out, keeping a tight grip on her hand. "I'm coming with you."

She looked ready to argue, but Blake growled. "Are you coming?"

"Shit, okay. Luna's coming too," she answered, tugging me out into the cool night air. She yanked her phone from her pocket, cursing at all the missed calls. She sent a message to someone before unlocking the Corvette, pointing to the passenger seat. "Buckle up tight. I'm breaking some road rules, just so you know."

I made sure I was securely in my seat, and my stomach did a flip as Riley put the car in reverse and floored it, peering over her shoulder to see where she was going. I was both impressed and horrified.

Blake tore off into the night ahead of us, and we followed at a slower speed until we were away from the shed, then she put her foot to the floor and we sped through town. I'd been in the car with her on the track, so I was used to the speed, but not on the road. I had no idea how she was missing parked cars and signs that seemed to come out of nowhere in the dark, confirming that she'd been racing on the road for a long damn time.

I watched her in the dim lighting to try and distract myself from the panic bubbling to the surface from the dangerous driving. She looked angry, her jaw set tightly and her fingers flexing on the wheel, but I wasn't sure who it was aimed at. Reid, for racing, or the Slick guy for causing the crash.

The drive didn't take long, and I was grateful when we arrived in one piece. Riley flung the door open and bailed out without a word, and I had to jog to keep up with her. I wasn't surprised to find Ander by the reception desk with Blake beside him.

His jeans and gray hoodie were covered in blood, his hands stained red as they trembled by his sides. He looked withdrawn, ignoring everyone around him as he stared at a mark on the floor, but I heard the pain in his voice as he spoke when he noticed us. "They've had to bring him back once already. He died in the fucking ambulance. Jesus, Donovan. I—"

I gasped as Riley punched him in the cheek, glaring daggers at him and not giving a shit about the receptionist threatening to call the cops.

"This is why I told you to bring rules in. The only person to ever cause accidents is Slick, but you won't do anything about it."

"He's banned," he said firmly, clearing his throat. "I told

him tonight that he's not welcome back. If he can't race fairly, then he's not racing at all."

"It's a little bit late for that, don't you think?" she snapped, making Blake flinch. I took Riley's hand to calm her, and she jerked away from me angrily. I stepped back and tried to ignore the hurt I felt, but she blew out a breath before reaching for me. "Sorry, baby."

"It's okay if you don't want me to touch you when you're mad," I protested, but she shook her head and pulled me against her chest, burying her face in my neck.

"No, I want you to touch me."

I hugged her tightly, looking at Ander over her shoulder. "Where's Logan?"

"In the waiting room with Raven and Zavier. Raven's hysterical," he murmured, glancing at Riley. "We've managed to keep your name out of everything so Raven doesn't know about you being part of this shit."

"I *wasn't* part of this though. I was at the shed supporting my fucking family, but now I'm missing Beckett's fight because of that cunt. I'm assuming you're out here because of Raven?" she growled, waiting for him to nod. "I'm going to check on them. You'd better mean what you told Slick too. I don't want to see him again."

"He won't be racing through me," he promised, and I was surprised when Riley patted his shoulder before taking my hand to lead me through to the other room, leaving Blake with Ander.

Logan sprung from his chair when he saw us enter, not hiding the heartache on his face. "That fucker—"

"I'll get him, don't worry," she mumbled, not letting me go. "I'll break his fucking kneecaps."

I waited for her to reassure me she was joking, but she didn't. My stomach twisted uncomfortably at the thought of her going after the guy, but I forgot about it when Raven threw herself at Riley, not hiding her tears.

"He fucking died. They brought him back but he's not stable and—"

I let Riley go, leaving her to console her friend as I sat in a seat to wait. Zavier's hair was sticking up at all angles as if he'd been running his fingers through it repetitively, and Logan dropped into the seat beside me. I hesitated before threading my fingers through his, and even though he didn't look at me, he gave me a small squeeze.

We all sat in silence for a while, and it wasn't until the doctor came out and Riley threatened him with violence, that he said Reid was now stable and resting.

The sob of relief that left Raven broke me, and I couldn't help it as a tear escaped the corner of my eye. It seemed she had no idea that he'd been racing on the streets, and by the way she was clinging to Zavier and not Logan told me she was pissed at him too.

100
120
140
160
180
200
220
km/h
240
260

Chapter Twenty

Riley

I was glad that Logan was finding some kind of comfort from Luna. She barely knew him, but she stayed glued to his side for hours. Raven was a mess, and when the guys mentioned coffee, I dragged her outside for a cigarette, thankful that Ander's car was gone.

Blake's was missing too, but I wasn't surprised. She wouldn't want to stick around in case the cops showed up for any reason.

"I'm so fucking angry at them," Raven scowled, lighting her cigarette and shaking her head. "I can't believe they've been racing like that. I knew they were sneaking off to do something, I've caught them a few times now, but that was the last thing I expected."

"I know you're angry, but don't shut Logan out," I said carefully, pulling my hood off so she could see my face properly. "He's not to blame, and he's hurting too."

"He knew!"

"So you're going to punish him? Make him think it's his fault? I know you and I aren't besties, but I do give a shit about you. You're important to the guys, you're their family.

Everyone makes mistakes, you know?" I answered, her face pinching as if in pain.

She silently smoked for a while until speaking again, her voice tight. "Did you know?"

I met her gaze, not being able to lie to her. "Yes."

"Were you fucking there?" she spat, relaxing when I shook my head.

"No. I was at the Psychos' shed. Maddox and Beckett both had fights tonight. You can ask them if you don't believe me."

She eyed me, her voice becoming so quiet that I barely heard her. "But you've been before, right? That's how you know the guys so well?"

I was starting to panic. She'd tell Beckett, there was no doubt about it, and I'd be fucked.

"I like cars, Raven. I don't race for pink slips like what tonight was about, but I do enjoy feeling the power under me as I race. There aren't any rules on the streets, unlike the track, and sometimes that means assholes show up. The guy that caused this has done it before. He's a sore loser too. It's not all about racing though," I sighed, grateful when she didn't argue. "Sometimes it's where a bunch of us meet up for a beer and admire cars. Sometimes we just hang out and talk shit."

"Beckett doesn't know, or your car wouldn't be on all four wheels," she stated, blowing smoke in my direction. "You need to stop, Riley. Or the next time it might be you lying in a hospital bed. Promise me you'll stop, and I'll keep my mouth shut."

As I studied her, I saw her eyes filled with irritation. She looked ready to punch me for not telling her about the guys, but she respected Beckett too much to go through with it.

"I'll stop." I intended on stopping one day, so I technically wasn't lying. It would probably be in a year or two though.

We finished our cigarettes in silence, and I groaned as I heard Beckett's Mustang roaring up the road. "Shit. I shouldn't be here."

"Why? You're friends with the guys," Raven frowned. "And you had her as an alibi so she'd know you weren't racing too."

"My sister's got it out for Ander, and she's angry we're friends," I said dryly. "She's going to be savage towards me."

As if on cue, the Mustang tore into the parking lot and braked hard, the door slamming as Beckett climbed out. "What the fuck are you doing here? Why didn't you tell me?"

I didn't have an answer for the second part. I should've told her when Blake first showed up at the shed.

"Sorry, I didn't think. Blake came and got me and I—"

"Raven said he was fucking street racing. Is that how you all know each other?" she demanded, her eyes on me as realization spread across her face, making her angrier. "You all race together, don't you?"

I was going to have to lie to her and pray Raven kept her mouth shut. I was so sick of the lying, but I wasn't ready to give up the rush the racing brought me. Not yet.

"They were racing for pink slips. You know I'd never risk my cars like that. Besides, I know how those races work. You're either in them all, or not at all. I was watching the fights when this shit happened tonight, so obviously I wasn't there," I said confidently, hoping she wouldn't call me out on my bullshit.

She snorted before turning to Raven, dismissing me. "How is he?"

I left them to talk and headed back inside to find Luna,

not surprised to see her talking to Logan quietly. Zavier sat on Logan's other side, his arm dropped around his shoulders for comfort as he silently listened to whatever Luna was saying. Kids that grew up in the Heights together were usually more like family, so I knew just how badly this was tearing them all apart.

I knew their pain all too well from Lloyd's accident.

"Where were they racing? And how come you weren't in the car?" I asked as I joined them, sitting cross-legged on the floor in front of them. "I assume the Challenger's still at the crash site?"

Logan nodded, raking his fingers through his hair. "Yeah, it's still there. Slick argued and tried to say having a passenger was cheating because I could help navigate, so Turbo suggested I stayed behind while they raced. It was short, and it was only one on one, so I hung back with Blake and some of the others. He wrecked on the edge of Rawson Grove and the Heights. The car flipped and rolled, it's a fucking mess."

"Cops investigating?"

"Majorly. They know it was street racing," Zavier murmured, flicking his gaze to me. "They're going to come down on Ander hard after this."

Logan glanced at him with confusion. "You know Turbo?"

I steered the subject away from Zavier's business deals with Turbo, not needing that problem to come to light yet.

"I can get the cops to hurry it along so I can get the Challenger towed. I don't want it left there for people to steal parts off. I'll see what I can salvage from it," I offered, his face pinching with discomfort.

"That sounds expensive."

"Don't worry, I've got it," I said as I waved off his

concern. "I'll help with his medical shit too. Then again, I should force Slick to pay up since it was his fucking fault."

"It's not your problem, Donovan," Logan replied tiredly. "But we appreciate the offer."

"Put your pride aside, asshole. I've got money, so take it. You don't owe me shit," I huffed. "I don't mean this in a nasty way, but do you even have the money to cover it?"

"We'll figure it out. We always do," he scowled but relaxed when I reached out to give his knee a friendly squeeze before dropping my hand again.

"And I figured it out for you. Let me help."

"Reid will appreciate you saving what's left of his car. I'll be sure to tell him," he said quietly, glancing at Luna. "And thank you. You're sweet."

Her face heated at his praise, and I fought not to roll my eyes. She was way too innocent to fit in with anyone in our circle, but I wouldn't want her any other way.

"Stop flirting with my girl, Donahue," I teased as a small smile tugged at his lips.

"You don't think I could steal her if I wanted to?"

"Not after I showed her just how much better women can be. Keep your useless dick away from her," I threw back, giving her a wink. "Right, baby?"

"Oh my God, stop," she whined, her face burning even more. "How are you guys so open about this?"

"About sex?" Logan chuckled, leaning back in his seat. At least he was smiling for five minutes. "Because sex is good. We like to swap tips and tricks and compare dick sizes."

"Mine's bigger," I laughed, and he flipped me off.

"You wish. Mine's magnificent."

Zavier snorted, eyeing us like we were crazy. "You guys are fucking weird. Stop making Luna uncomfortable."

I got to my feet, dusting my pants off. "Yeah, we should get going if we're going to sort out Reid's car. Text me with any updates, and when the asshole wakes up, tell him to call me."

Logan nodded, and Luna stood to follow me out. We didn't get far before Zavier appeared, stopping us. He winced, flicking his gaze to Logan who was slumped in his seat again.

"Thank you," he said softly, looking back at me. "I could pay for some of it, but it's going to use all of my savings and I don't want them asking questions about where it came from. That's our ticket out of the Heights, you know? I've worked my ass off to try and make our lives better, but—"

I put my hand on his arm, giving him a smile. "Don't beat yourself up about it. I've got it covered, alright? Are you okay?"

He blew out a breath, giving a half shrug. "I'll be fine. It's just been a rough night."

"Beckett's outside with Raven. She'll probably stay here all night with you guys."

"Can you let me know when you're done with Reid's car and you're home?" he asked, rubbing the back of his neck awkwardly. "I just want to know you both got home okay."

I understood his worry, car accidents did that to people. My family was proof of that.

"Give me your phone," I nodded, taking it from him as he offered it to me, and I added my number to his contacts before sending myself a text. "Now you have mine and I have yours."

"Drive safely," he replied before walking back to Logan. I turned to walk away, finding Beckett and Raven walking towards us. Beckett's eyes burned into me as she glanced between me and Zavier's retreating back, but she didn't mention it.

"Leaving?"

"Yeah. I'm going to get Reid's car towed so the scavengers don't take what's left," I replied, not bothering to hide it. She frowned.

"You're going to get it towed?"

"Yeah, might as well use my money for something good. I like Reid, he's nice," I shrugged and she gave me an amused snort.

"We'll finish this conversation later, because there's more to it."

We said goodbye and I took Luna's hand, pulling her out into the cold night air, and I couldn't help but feel like this was only the beginning of a whole pile of drama.

Luna

It was close to four in the morning by the time we got back to Riley's house. Hunter was only just getting home himself, fatigue written all over his face. He frowned as we walked towards him where he stood by the front door with a joint between his lips, not seeming happy to see us.

"Where the hell have you been?"

"Dealing with some stuff," Riley said lightly, trying to move past him but he blocked her from entering the house.

"Was it to do with the street racing fatality?"

"He didn't die," I mumbled, his eyes flashing to me with frustration.

"She took you to a fucking street race?"

Riley's fingers threaded through mine, her shoulders tense. "No. We weren't there. You know we were at the shed when that happened. Blake was there and she came and got me because I'm friends with them. It was Reid, Beckett's friend from the Heights. We were in the hospital talking to Zavier and Logan, then Beckett showed up so I got the cops to hurry up and got the car towed so no one could take parts off the wreck."

He blinked at me silently, concern in his voice when he finally spoke. "It was Reid?"

"Yeah. One of the racers is a real prick apparently. He and Reid were racing for pink slips, and he was losing. So he caused Reid to crash."

I zoned out as they talked everything over, and I was relieved when Hunter finally let us inside so we could go to bed. I was exhausted, and wanted nothing more than to sleep.

I left Riley in the kitchen to keep chatting while I walked up to her room, pausing when I heard the familiar sound of Ryder banging some girl as I walked past his bedroom door. I had no idea how they all lived together and listened to that kind of stuff all the time.

Maddox had been just as bad before he'd started dating Beckett.

I sighed, knowing I wouldn't be able to sleep, but a door up the hall opened and Skeeter stalked out, hardly glancing in my direction before bashing his fist against Ryder's door.

"I'm sick of having this conversation with you, Ry. Shove a pillow over her fucking face or go to her place. I've got to be up in two hours for work."

There was a giggle, but Ryder hissed at her to shut up before replying. "Sorry!"

"Little shit," Skeeter grunted under his breath, turning to face me. "Did you and Riley just get home?"

I tried to keep my eyes on his face, not wanting him to

think I was checking him out. He was in nothing but his boxers, and I could feel my face heating.

"Uh, yeah. One of Riley's friends was in a car accident tonight, so we went to the hospital to check on them and got their car towed," I blurted out, his eyebrow arching.

"That was nice of you both." When I stayed quiet, he motioned to Riley's room. "Are you going to bed, or are you going to stand there cluttering the hallway?"

He gave me a teasing grin, making me relax. "It's a nice hallway. I'm just enjoying the view."

I didn't realize how bad that sounded until I remembered he was in his underwear right in front of me, and pure horror raced through me.

I didn't hear Riley approach until she let out a gag. "Ew. Are you flirting with my dad?"

My entire face was on fire, and I spun around to glare at her. "No. What the fuck?"

She smirked, reaching out to touch my heated skin with the back of her hand. "Aw, you totally were, you're burning up for him. You're so defensive that you even swore."

"I love you Riley, but you're a dick," Skeeter grumbled. "Go to fucking bed." Then he stalked back to the bedroom and shut the door.

"I hate you," I scowled as I walked into her room, her dry chuckle following me as she locked us inside.

"You totally asked for it. I was only joking."

She startled me as she pushed my face down onto the bed, her breath tickling my ear as she straddled my ass. "If you've got daddy issues, baby, I can work with that. You can call me daddy if you want."

"Don't be weird," I said, laughing lightly before moaning as she leaned down and sucked my skin between her lips, branding my neck with another hickey. "You can't seriously want to get naked again."

She pulled back, admiring the mark she'd left on me before running her hands down my spine, her fingers teasing my waist. "If it were up to me, you'd never put clothes on and my tongue would never leave your pussy. Are you sore?"

"A little bit," I admitted awkwardly, twisting my head around to peer up at her. "We can mess around if you want though."

She eyed me for a moment before dropping down beside me, sliding an arm around my waist. "No. You don't feel like it."

"It's not that," I said with a cringe. "I'm just tired and—"

"I don't care," she replied firmly, cutting me off. "If you're tired or don't feel like it for any reason, then that's a no. Was that asshole making you fuck him when you didn't want to?"

Violence shone in her eyes, and I quickly shook my head. "No. Forget I said anything."

She didn't believe me, but she sat up and stripped off, undressing me before pulling the blanket over us and curling her body around mine to spoon me.

"Sleep, Lou. You look beat."

She didn't have to tell me twice.

It was Tuesday, and I'd been pleasantly surprised when Riley had decided to go to school with me.

Some of the other students had been glancing at us all morning, so I knew they'd heard gossip about our friendship becoming more. I ignored them, and Riley wasn't acting any differently than she normally did.

I wrote notes throughout the lecture, rolling my eyes when I noticed Riley was napping. It drove me insane that she didn't give a shit about her education. She was smart, but even smart kids fell behind if they missed too much, and we'd both been slack lately.

I studied her, her chin on her chest and her hood over her head. Her arms were crossed, and I watched her chest as it rose and fell with each breath.

"You're not being very discreet," Landon murmured in my ear, startling me. I turned to him, finding curiosity in his blue gaze as he glanced between us.

The professor dismissed everyone, but Landon stayed in his seat, waiting for me to speak. I knew he wouldn't tease me about Riley, but it was nerve-wracking to say it out loud more publicly. Other people would hear us since they were definitely lingering, and they'd definitely tease me.

"Me and Riley are seeing each other," I finally decided to blurt out, cringing at how loud it was as one of the girls across the room snorted. Landon's eyebrows almost hit his hairline, not hiding the surprise in his voice.

"No shit?"

"Nope. We're labeling it as *figuring it out*," I shrugged, trying to sound confident but failing badly. One of the girls across the room made a gagging noise, and anxiety rushed through me. I knew this was going to go through the school like wildfire now that I'd confirmed the gossip.

I shouldn't have been embarrassed, but I couldn't help it.

I was about to be the talk of Ashburn Valley.

"So you guys are taking it slow?" Landon continued,

ignoring my freak-out. I went to speak, but Riley's amused voice cut me off.

"Fast, slow, it depends on our mood at the time and how tired my wrist gets."

I snapped my gaze to her, finding her smirking under her hood, still in the same position. I couldn't see her eyes, but I knew they'd be sparkling with humor.

She'd definitely been holding that comment in until I outed myself.

"I'll add that mental image to the spank bank for later, thank you," Landon deadpanned, dropping his arm around my shoulders supportively. "I'm happy for you guys, but uh, aren't you dating Stanley?"

Riley pushed her hood from her head and narrowed her eyes at the mention of his name, so I quickly shook my head. "I broke up with him. He was being a dick. I know it's fast, but—"

"Nonsense," he scoffed, smacking a kiss on the top of my head. "If it's the right person, then don't waste time. You two have known each other forever, so it's not like a random hook up."

I squealed as I was hauled onto Riley's lap to face her, her arms banding around me as her lips skimmed across my neck. Landon gave us an amused grin, and I struggled to keep the discomfort off my face when the other students finally left, gossiping as they went.

"What happened to keeping the PDA to a minimum?" I scolded, making her pause. She loosened her grip slightly, her voice low.

"Fuck. Sorry. I'm not used to giving a shit about people's opinions, and since you practically shouted your love for me across the room, I assumed you wouldn't mind."

"It's okay," I said weakly as a wave of anxiety washed

through me, getting to my feet. "I'm taking a study session this afternoon. I'll see you later?"

She frowned, knowing my reason to escape was more about our PDA, but nodded shortly after. I felt like an asshole when I grabbed my things and hightailed it out of there, but I was getting overwhelmed.

It got worse as I wandered through the halls, noticing people glancing at me and snickering. I avoided eye contact, keeping my head down as I made my way to the library, but jerked back as I ran into someone, my eyes going wide as I realized it was Penny.

She glared at me, clenching her fists. "You."

"Me, what?" I asked slowly, taking a step back. She followed, fury in her eyes.

"You took Riley from me."

"You two weren't together," I squeaked out, swallowing nervously. "I didn't do anything."

She shoved me back against the wall, knocking the wind from me as she got in my face. "You probably don't even know how to get someone off. You're a meek little girl with no tits, and you can't possibly keep her attention for long. Do you think she'll keep you around when she has someone like me? Look at me, Luna. I'm a woman, while you've got the body of a ten-year-old boy."

Tears pricked my eyes, and I flinched when she raised her hand to slap me. When it didn't connect with my face, I opened my eyes to find Beckett's fist in Penny's hair, holding her tightly in her grip. The nausea that had started pooling in my stomach ebbed away knowing Beckett wouldn't let anyone put their hands on me.

"What's going on?" Beckett hissed, her attention on Penny. "What makes you think you're allowed to bully Luna?"

"Get off me," Penny threw back as she struggled, but Beckett just tightened her hold on her, shoving her chest against the wall beside me.

"If my sister decided she doesn't want to fuck you anymore, that's hardly Luna's fault," she spat, violence in her tone. "Leave her the fuck alone."

She gave her a shove away from us, glaring at her until Penny gave me a scathing glance and took off in a huff. Beckett turned to me, her face softening a fraction. "Are you okay?"

"I'm fine," I said quietly, trying to keep the shake from my voice but failing. I jumped as an arm dropped around my shoulders, but relaxed when I realized it was Ryder.

"What's going on?" he grunted, glancing at Beckett for an answer. "I saw you chase Penny away."

"She was bullying Luna. She's been doing the whole stage five clinger thing with Riley," Beckett replied, rolling her eyes. "Where the fuck have you been? You weren't in class this morning."

"I was busy," he shrugged, giving my shoulders a squeeze as a smile spread across his lips. "C'mon, Luney. I'll walk you to wherever you're going."

"I'm just going to study group," I replied softly, and he started walking along the hallway with me still in his hold. I blurted out a thank you to Beckett before we turned the corner, and she gave me a mock salute before she vanished from sight.

"I'll take you then. I'll fight the hordes of angry women for you."

"Kind of you," I joked, but was grateful to have him take me. "Are you okay, Ry? I haven't seen you much lately but I've heard some stuff."

"Like what?" he asked lightly, but I could hear the annoyance in his voice.

"Just tell me if you're okay," I answered, a sigh leaving him. He seemed withdrawn, and even though I was just his sister's annoying friend, I hoped he knew I cared about him. He'd always looked out for me and I didn't like knowing that he was struggling.

He didn't speak until we reached the library, where he leaned against the wall and slid his hands into the front pockets of his jeans. "I'll be alright. I'm just dealing with some shit right now. You're the first person to ask me though, you know? Everyone else just talks down to me like I'm a piece of shit."

My heart hurt for him, and I reached out to squeeze his arm gently. "I'm here if you ever need to talk. You probably have your own friends, but—"

"No, I really appreciate it," he said, cutting me off. "And I think it's cool you and Riley are seeing each other. She's loved you forever, you know?"

"Yeah, I know," I smiled, clutching my books to my chest. "I'd better get inside. I'll see you later."

"You call me if you need me too, okay?" he said seriously while ruffling my hair lightly. "I know I'm a jackass and like to piss off Riley by acting interested in you, but I honestly see you like a little sister. I want to make sure you're alright too."

"Aw, you big softie," I teased, laughing as he playfully swatted at me with a grin.

"Cheeky shit. Don't tell anyone or you'll ruin my bad boy rep."

"I'll be sure to tell all the girls you kick puppies and steal candy from children in your spare time," I deadpanned, making him bark out a laugh as he turned to leave. "Hey, Ry?"

He glanced back at me, amusement on his face. "Yeah?"

"You're the best big brother, you know? And thank you for giving a shit about my sister. I know she's a hot mess, but you care for her. That means a lot to me."

He gave me a weird look, but he nodded. "Have a good afternoon, Luney."

I walked into the library, relieved to find only a couple of people in here studying. I sat at a table and made myself comfortable, knowing I'd probably be here until dinnertime.

80
100
120
140
160
180
200
220
km/h
240
260

Chapter Twenty-One

Riley

Giving Luna space was harder than I thought. I wasn't surprised when she bailed for study session, because I'd told her I'd let her set the pace but then went against my promise and publicly pulled her onto my lap.

It was late, and I scolded myself as I checked my location app to check where she was, finding her just arriving at her house. I never wanted to become one of those people who needed constant reassurance, but I was silently freaking out that I'd fucked things up already.

I'd spent the afternoon checking in with Reid at the hospital to take my mind off of Luna. He still hadn't woken up, but he was more stable, which was a relief.

I had to admit I was worried about him.

Luckily for me, Turbo called early in the evening and required my presence, giving me something else to focus on.

I was parked by the abandoned warehouse in the Heights, tapping my fingers on the steering wheel and checking my phone like a lovesick idiot. I dove at it when a message came through, a small smile tugging at my lips when Luna's name popped up to let me know she was home.

I quickly replied to her to thank her for letting me know she was alright before sliding my phone into my pocket as headlights shone across my car. I stepped out with my bat in hand, flipping Turbo off as he flashed his lights at me multiple times before switching the engine off, plunging us into darkness.

He stepped out, the sound of gravel under his shoes as he approached and the moonlight bright enough to see the shape of him in the dark. "Donovan."

"Lavaro," I answered, leaning back against my car. "What can I help you with?"

"We've got a tiny problem," he grumbled, resting his butt against the car beside me, mimicking my pose. "A Slick kind of problem."

"What's the fucker done now?"

"He's joined up with one of the car enthusiast groups. A bunch of V8 and performance car pricks. You know those assholes from that big joint car meet we did last year?"

I nodded, my teeth grinding. "Yeah. They do meet-ups in Briar Falls and Blackwater, right?"

"Yep. Well, he's somehow gained their trust stupidly fast. We need to keep an eye out because I have a bad feeling they're going to cause us trouble. I haven't heard anything yet, but I just know something's coming," he said tiredly.

My eyes were adjusting to the dark more, and I could see his hand raking through his hair with frustration. For someone who claimed they didn't like anyone, he was doing a bad job at proving it.

Guilt was eating at him over Reid, and he'd already confessed he gave a shit about me. I didn't know how to feel about that, but I was starting to appreciate having him on my side.

"I'll keep an ear out. I'll make sure Mom and my dads let me know of anything too, if you want?"

"Is that a smart idea?" he asked dryly, glancing at me. "I know I've been a dick about you attending races, but if you want out, Donovan, just tell me. It's not fair to keep you in the middle of this mess."

"I'm pissed at you for not reining in Slick's behavior before now, but Reid's accident wasn't your fault," I admitted, staring out into the dark to avoid his gaze that was burning into me. "Reid's an adult. He chose to race and he knew the dangers. It wasn't fair for me to pin the blame on you. It's Slick's fault and that's it."

"I've been thinking of shutting this shit down, you know?" he murmured, the gravel crunching under his feet as he shifted. "It's pathetic, but the races are the only social thing I have that doesn't consist of asshole dealers or clients. I get to race and enjoy cars like a normal person."

"You know," I started, a chuckle leaving me as I glanced at him. "If you want to hang out, we can always get the others together at the bar or something. We don't have to risk our lives to illegally race cars in order to hang out."

He snorted, not convinced. "You might be willing to do that, but the others won't. Blake only talks to me when she has to, and Reid might not even be alive by the end of the week because of this shit. Logan won't want to hang out now either."

"Are you lonely?" I teased, nudging his shoulder with mine. "People don't hang out with you outside of these races because you've made it that way. You don't like friends, remember?"

"Maybe it's time for a change," he said on an exhale, wariness in his voice.

"Are you going through some kind of midlife crisis?" I joked but patted his shoulder to show him I wasn't serious. If he wanted out, I couldn't blame him.

He let out a light laugh, the tension easing from him. "I'm only twenty-two."

"Our lifestyle means a shorter life expectancy. We'll all be lucky to reach fifty," I muttered, discomfort washing through me at the thought of leaving Luna behind.

She needed me, and if something happened to her?

I couldn't think about it.

"You mean *my* lifestyle," he said bluntly. "You try and keep yourself separated from all this bad shit."

"And how's that working for me?" I grumbled, absently tapping the toe of my shoe against my bat. "My family's a bunch of criminals, my friends are all criminals, and I'm an adrenaline junkie. I get a kick out of doing dumb shit and risking my life."

"You need a different kind of adrenaline rush," he suggested, sounding thoughtful. "Get your girlfriend to choke you in bed or something. Much safer."

"Hey, I'm in charge in the bedroom," I argued as he let out a bark of laughter.

"Don't be afraid to change things up. If you really don't like that idea though, you could always go to those places that let you jump out of planes. Or just join up with one of the crews. They get shot at all the time."

"Would you like to have dinner tonight?" I asked randomly as the idea popped into my head, a huff of annoyance leaving me as he gave me a gentle shove.

"I mean, I guess. I won't tell your girlfriend you asked

me out. Shit, do I have to put out for you? Just a heads up, I haven't shaved my nuts this month."

"You're a dick. I'm going to see if Blake wants to come too. Luna might come if she hasn't eaten already," I said as I thought out loud, giving him the side-eye. "But if you want to eat all by yourself—"

"No, I'd like to go," he said quickly, making me smirk.

"That's what I thought. Get to know Blake better. She'd be a good friend for you to have."

"It wouldn't work," he sighed while jiggling his keys, a sign he was ready to go.

"Why not?"

"Because I'd spend too much time trying to fuck her," he said without hesitation, zero humor in his tone. "She's fucking hot. You know that."

"Hey, I heard girls think you're hot. Maybe if you showed interest in her outside of the races, she'd be up for a roll in the sheets. I bet she's a screamer," I stated, a groan leaving him.

"Let's get going. You call both of them. If I ask Blake to come out for dinner, she'll hang up on me."

"Can you behave tonight? Or should I not invite Kate?"

"Her sister? I doubt she'd want her near me," he said tightly, but I waved him off and opened my car door, leaning in to start the car.

"Trust me. If you show that you're happy to spend time with her sister too, she'd like you more. Kate means everything to her, and family is important to both of them. If I invite her and say Kate's welcome to come along, I can pick Kate up from my place on the way and meet you all at Harley's Bar," I suggested. I had no idea why I was making such an effort to make him feel better. If he didn't have any friends, that was his own fault.

He studied me for a second before nodding. "Fine. I have something to do, but I can be there in an hour."

"I'll text you," I replied, climbing behind the wheel and driving towards home, calling Blake and Luna to see if they wanted to go. Blake took some convincing, but she finally agreed, and I was relieved when Luna instantly said yes. I was such a sucker for her.

I'd never been the needy type, but if I could spend all my time with her, I would.

I found Mom the moment I got home, pulling her aside to talk in private. She wouldn't like my plan, so I knew I'd have to convince her.

"Can I take Kate out for dinner?"

She frowned, suspicion on her face. "Where to, why, and with who? You hardly know her."

I cringed. "I'm meeting Luna, Blake, and Ander for dinner. I told Blake I'd bring Kate."

"Riley, that's not your call to make," she said with a sigh. "And I don't want Kate near Ander."

"I'm trying to show him he can have friends and family. He's lonely, Mom. He's a really nice guy," I huffed, her gaze softening.

"Baby, it's not your job to fix people."

"I know," I said with annoyance. "But he's my friend. How can people like him find a way out of the lives they're burdened with if they don't know the way? You don't like what he does, but this is why he won't change. He's had no reason to until now."

She crossed her arms, tapping her finger on her bicep for a moment before nodding. "Fine, but Kate is your responsibility. She doesn't get in anyone else's car and she doesn't leave your sight. Understood?"

"Understood. I'll make sure we check in with you too," I promised. "And maybe another time, Ander—"

"Don't push it," she said firmly, kissing the top of my head. "Kate's in her room. See if she wants to go and make sure she's ready. Just dinner, right? Don't take her anywhere else."

"I'll bring her home first if I end up with other plans later," I agreed, heading towards the hallway.

I walked upstairs, poking my head into Kate's room to find her lying on her bed, staring at the ceiling. She didn't seem to want to play like most nine-year-old kids, but she'd been raised on the rough side of town where most kids had to grow up too fast.

"Hey. Do you want to come have dinner with me? Blake, Luna, and our friend, Ander, will be there," I offered, her eyes darting over to me as her face lit up.

"Blake's going?"

"Yeah. I told her I'd bring you along so you guys could hang out. So, you want to go?"

"Yes!" she squealed, leaping off the bed and grabbing her jacket. "Can we get ice cream too?"

I chuckled, tilting my head to watch her yank her arms through the sleeves and shove her feet into her shoes. "Possibly. C'mon, we'll go see what the others want to do."

Kate ran ahead of me, but I paused outside Marla's room, giving the door a light knock before entering.

Marla was at her desk like always, her head buried in a book from school. As much as we weren't that close, she was still my sister and I'd miss her when she left for college.

"Hey," I murmured, her eyes flicking over to me silently. "Did you want to come to Harley's Bar for dinner? Me and some friends are going there and I'm taking Kate too."

"No, thank you." She motioned to the books in front of

her, fatigue written all over her face. "I have an exam in the morning and I really need to study."

"Do you want me to bring you back some pie if Harley has any?"

"Cherry?" she asked hopefully.

"Yep. If he has any, I'll put a slice in the fridge for you."

"Thanks." She gave me a smile before turning to her book again to dismiss me.

I made my way down to the kitchen to find Kate waiting for me, and she happily followed me out to the Corvette once Mom had repeated her rules to both of us. I knew her concern was because Kate was being fostered, which meant any little fuck up could get her taken away.

I was glad the foster kids we had were well cared for and got to feel what love was like. So many from other places didn't have such luck.

We spent the evening eating and just hanging out at the bar, Blake and Kate playing pool together while the rest of us stayed at our booth. Luna had been uncomfortable at first since she didn't know anyone well, but she was happily chatting to Turbo now that he'd proven to be a nice person.

"You should bring Luna with you sometime," Turbo said as he sipped his coke, eyeing me over the rim. "I think she'd enjoy it."

Luna frowned, not understanding what he was referring to, but I snorted.

"There's no way in hell that's happening. It's dangerous for starters, but if we do get busted by the cops, I'm in a lot of fucking trouble for dragging her into my mess."

"Are you talking about the car stuff? Can't I come and

watch without being in the car?" she asked, a sigh leaving me. I dropped an arm around her shoulders, keeping her close so I didn't have to talk too loudly. Harley and Alex would definitely tell on me.

"It's not like the track, Lou. We race through towns and side streets. We sometimes start somewhere like Stoneleigh, then end up in the Heights. It changes each night."

"That doesn't sound very safe," she mumbled, making me snort.

"It *isn't* safe. You remember that Reid's in the hospital right now fighting for his life, right? That could've easily been me."

Her eyes widened, but Turbo waved his hand dismissively. "Stop scaring her. You'll be fine."

"Don't make promises you can't keep, asshole," I scoffed, eyeing Luna. "It's dangerous and completely illegal. That's why I don't tell anyone about my involvement. It's not really your thing either, and I don't want to risk your life in the process."

"But you'll risk yours?" she snapped, making me cringe at the volume. Alex glanced our way with a frown, and I knew I had to calm Luna down before she got me in a world of trouble.

"It's hard to explain. We'll talk about it more later, okay?"

"Whatever," she bit out, getting to her feet. "I need to pee."

I let her out of the booth, watching her stalk off to the bathroom before I turned to glare at Turbo across the table. "Thanks, asshole."

"Just go and shove your fingers in her. She can't stay mad at you then," he smirked, making me roll my eyes.

"Here? In the bar that her uncles own? Doubtful."

"Just tell her that at the end of our race season, you're done," he offered, my eyes narrowing.

"I don't want to lie to her."

"Who's lying? I think the next few races will be it for me," he replied lightly, sipping his coke. "Too many people know that it's me behind all this shit. Those two worlds don't need to collide, and my other businesses are taking too much of my time. A lot of people have died or been seriously hurt while participating in my races, and it's becoming too much of a cop magnet. If I draw too much attention, it's going to start becoming problematic for my other stuff."

"You really want to shut it down?" I asked with surprise, realizing how serious he was.

"I think it's time, don't you?" he murmured, eyeing Luna as she walked back towards us. "Besides, it would be a shame for you to die now that you're happy."

That would be just my luck too.

Luna

Riley didn't bring up the conversation of street racing over the next few days, and as much as I enjoyed being able to be with her in public, anxiety was constantly eating away at me. People whispered wherever we went, and I knew Riley was sensing my impending freak-out.

My feelings were still all over the place, but I knew she made me happy. Was it love though? Or was I just clinging to her?

That was the question I kept asking myself.

I'd spent my entire Friday being gossiped about at school, and Penny had tried to corner me again on my way to the parking lot. Luckily, Ryder had spotted her coming a mile away and materialized by my side to get rid of her before she could create too much of a scene.

It was now early evening, and I was sitting in Riley's Corvette at the track with her, watching everyone wind down after a long week, and I tensed when Riley's low voice hit me after we'd been silent for so long.

"Are you going to tell me what's on your mind, or do I have to guess?"

I didn't glance at her, my finger tapping on my thigh nervously.

"What do you mean? There's nothing on my mind."

She snorted, and I could sense her gaze on me. "You're the world's worst liar. Just tell me."

I peered over at her, letting out a soft sigh. "I'm still trying to figure out my feelings. You make me happy, and you make me feel good, but I don't know if it's because the lines in our friendship are getting confused. I don't know how to handle everyone watching us like we're some kind of entertainment either."

Her face stayed blank, but panic flashed across her eyes for a second. "Have I been too pushy? If I'm making you uncomfortable—"

"No, I like what we're doing," I assured her, reaching out to take her hand. "I'm just unsure if it's a temporary Band-aid from me being hurt. I don't want to waste your time."

"Come here," she murmured, tugging my hand to encourage me towards her, and I climbed over the gear shift to straddle her lap, my dress keeping me covered. There wasn't a lot of space, but we made it work. "You're not wasting my time. I want this so badly that it hurts, but I really can't force you to feel something for me."

"But—"

"Be open with me about your feelings. I just don't want to be left in the dark," she said softly, her hands sliding around my middle. "I love you, and part of me wants to be selfish and make you love me too, but I also know it doesn't work like that."

I rested my forehead on hers, closing my eyes to savor her hold on me. "What if I'm not enough for you?"

"You'll always be exactly what I want," she promised, running a hand through my hair to hold the back of my head. She pulled my mouth to hers, kissing me lazily, just how I liked it, and she seemed to relax as I placed a hand on her cheek to hold her in place.

I kissed her harder, a groan leaving her. "Baby—"

"Fuck me," I murmured against her lips before I could change my mind, gasping as she instantly tugged my panties to the side without argument. She dipped her fingers into my pussy, pulling them out once they were wet with my juices so she could rub my clit.

"I think I'm addicted to making you curse," she chuckled, her lips finding my neck as she nibbled at my skin. "It's fucking hot when you beg me."

She slid her fingers lower, teasing my pussy and making me let out a huff of frustration. "Don't tease me."

"You're being loud. Do you want people to come and investigate?" Her words made me tense, suddenly reminding me that we were parked in the middle of the field, surrounded by other cars and people. She licked my neck, her breath cooling the damp skin. "You're covered. I'll keep your tits away, I promise."

"Don't let anyone see me," I whispered, and she leaned back to meet my gaze, her eyes serious.

"No one gets to see you like this. You're mine. It's dark and the windows are tinted. You're safe."

I nodded, trying to relax as she pushed her fingers inside me deeply this time, her thumb brushing my clit lightly and making my thighs clench. She always knew how to turn me into a puddle.

We'd only slept together a handful of times, but it was definitely the best sex I'd ever had. She could be rough, gentle, fast, or slow, and each time I'd come so easily. I couldn't tell if I'd hit the jackpot, or if sex was supposed to be like this all the time.

My nails bit into her shoulders as I tried hard to contain my scream when I came, but I was failing badly. People definitely would've heard us if they were near the car.

Sweat was forming on the back of my neck as she fucked me through it, and I wasn't surprised when she grabbed my throat firmly to pull my mouth to hers again, swallowing the sounds I was making.

Her fingers slowed when I begged her to stop, and I sagged against her as I tried to recover.

"I fucked myself last night while imagining your mouth on my cunt," she said breathlessly, a shudder rolling through me as she pulled her fingers from me and lifted them to my lips. "Open." I sucked them into my mouth, licking them clean as she watched me with heated eyes. "You're so good for me."

I dipped my fingers below the elastic of her pants, letting out a huff as she stopped me.

"I want to touch you too."

"Later," she promised, kissing me before giving me a small smirk. "Do you want to stay in the car when I race?"

"I thought you didn't want me in the car because it's not safe?" I asked with surprise, but she shrugged.

"I don't mind if we're on the track, but not on the streets. I like you beside me here."

I climbed back into my seat, fixing my dress, and reaching for the cigarettes. I was getting a terrible habit of having one after Riley had blown my mind. "Who are you racing?"

"Some preppy Crestford dude. He has no respect for his car," she grunted, shaking her head slightly. "Him and his buddies regularly lose, so I don't know why they keep coming back."

I lit a cigarette and handed it to her while looking out the window as I watched a group of girls crowding Ryder, his usual cocky grin on his face as he ate up the attention. I hoped he'd find someone who would see his worth because, underneath that playboy mask, he was sad and lonely.

"Do you think he's high again?" I murmured, not meaning to say it out loud, but it was too late to take it back. Riley was staring at me, her eyes burning into the side of my head, but I kept watching Ryder as he stumbled around.

"Probably," she finally said slowly. "Why?"

"I'm worried about him."

"He's fine, Lou," she muttered, but my eyes widened when he stumbled again, this time landing on his ass. Riley groaned as I opened the door, speaking over my shoulder quickly.

"Race without me this time. I'll get Ry some water and make him sit down so he doesn't hurt himself." I ran over to him despite Riley shouting back that I was wasting my time, the girls around him not pleased with me joining them.

They all cooed over him, acting like they gave a shit, but they didn't. They only cared about guys like him because of their money or social status. Some of the girls had Crestford

Academy uniforms on, while some I recognized from the Heights.

I had to stop myself from rolling my eyes as they all pawed at him.

"Luney!" Ryder laughed when he spotted me standing off to the side, reaching his hands up and opening and closing them like a child wanting to be picked up. "You came to help me!"

I stepped closer, noticing how blown his pupils were. He was definitely high. I offered him my hands, bracing my feet in the dirt to help pull him to his feet, and he stumbled into me with a hoot. "How about you come home with me? Riley doesn't have to know."

"Don't be an asshole," I warned tightly, hating it when he got like this. He was such a show pony.

He slid an arm around my waist, holding himself up, and I tensed as his hand dropped to my ass. "You know I'd look after you," he said quietly in my ear, kissing my cheek. I went to pull back, but he just leaned into me more. "You might have to drive us to mine though. I don't think I should be in control of a vehicle right now."

I smacked his chest hard, seeming to snap him out of it a little. "You're being a dick, Ry. Stop it."

"You care about me," he huffed as I started dragging him away from the hoard of girls and towards the bathroom to put cold water on his face. "You wouldn't use me like everyone else."

"I'm like your little sister, remember?" I grumbled, a bark of laughter leaving him as he wrapped his arms around me firmly, giving my ass a squeeze.

"You sure don't feel like a sister."

"Don't touch me like that," I scolded, panic starting to

climb inside of me as he did it again, burying his face in my neck to bite my skin gently.

"C'mon. I bet there's a bad girl hiding under all that cute shit you do. Relax and—"

I'd never been afraid of Ryder. He'd always been the one to keep girls safe from assholes, and I never thought he'd be the person I'd be trying to get away from.

He kept holding onto me to stop me escaping, and I let out a sob as I drew my hand back and slapped him. He stumbled, letting me go to catch himself. He looked confused by my violence, but his voice held so much worry that it was hard to believe he was the same person from a few moments ago.

"Fuck. Luna, I—" He reached for me, and I stepped back with a shake of my head, tears streaming down my cheeks.

"Don't fucking touch me. What the hell is wrong with you?"

Shame filled his eyes, his voice breaking. "I'm sorry."

Sobs wracked my body as I became overwhelmed with emotion, and I let out a squeal as someone grabbed my wrist. I found Beckett beside me, her jaw tight as she took in the state I was in.

Jett and Cruz were with her, but I didn't see Maddox.

"What happened?" Beckett asked firmly, glaring at Ryder when I just kept crying. "Ry? What the fuck did you do to her?"

"Luna, I—" I didn't let him finish. The second he tried to step closer again, I pressed closer to Beckett, my voice shaking.

"He kept touching me. I told him to stop it but he didn't listen. He—"

Beckett went rigid beside me, but Jett suddenly had

Ryder by the front of the shirt, shoving him back against the bathroom wall. Ryder let him, his arms hanging by his sides in shame.

I was terrified of what might have happened if no one had noticed us walking this way in the dark.

I didn't want to think he'd rape me, Ryder wasn't like that, but he also never would've touched a girl without their permission before either.

"The fuck is wrong with you? You touched her?" Jett hissed, giving him a firm shake when he didn't reply. "Answer me!"

"I didn't mean... I said sorry. Fuck!" he yelled, trying to get free but Jett didn't let him go.

"You're sorry?" he threw back, glancing at me before turning back to him. "Look at her! Do you think sorry's going to fix that?"

My hands were shaking as everyone seemed to assess me, and Beckett stepped in front of me to block their view. "One of you get Ryder the fuck home. He's in no state to drive, and there's no point dealing with this tonight while he's that fucking wasted. I'll stay with Luna until he's gone. We don't need Riley losing her shit here."

"What do we tell your parents?" Jett grunted. "Should we take him to ours instead?"

"No. If Riley wants to beat his ass when she gets home, she can. I just don't want it happening here," she replied, dropping an arm around my shoulders.

Maddox jogged over, his eyes instantly narrowing when he saw me. "What—"

Jett gave Ryder a shove in his direction, his voice low. "Get your brother in the car. He fucked up. Keep Riley away from him."

"Are you hurt?" Maddox asked me firmly, relaxing

slightly as I shook my head. "I'll deal with him. You stay with Beck, okay?"

I nodded, trying to control my tears as they walked away from us, and once I heard Maddox's Charger leave, I let my muscles relax.

"Riley's going to kill him," I choked out, making Beckett snort.

"The prick deserves it. I love my brother, but that doesn't mean I'll step in to save him when he does something stupid." She seemed deep in thought for a second before her voice turned soft. "Was he trying to rape you?"

"No," I said quickly, wiping my eyes. "He just kept grabbing my ass and kissing my neck. He scared me when he kept doing it."

"I'm sorry. We'll handle it," she promised, cringing when Riley's voice came from close by.

"What are you guys doing?" I turned to face her, and anger instantly covered her face as she reached for me, pulling me close to thumb the tears from my cheeks. "Who was it? I'll kill them. Did someone say something to you? Are you hurt?"

I couldn't tell her that it had been her brother. I didn't want to be the person to break her heart like that.

"You need to get her out of here," Beckett said without hesitation, not sugarcoating anything. "Ryder assaulted her."

Riley stilled, her eyes hardening. "Excuse me?"

"Well deal with it later, Riley. Just get Luna home," Beckett snapped, motioning to me. "Can't you see she just wants to leave?"

I expected her to throw a fit and storm off in search of him, but she kissed the top of my head, keeping me close. "Where is he?"

"What did I just say? Don't worry about him right now," Beckett scowled as Riley snorted.

"I'm not going to go looking for him. I just don't want to take Luna back to mine if he's there."

"Maddox and the others took him back to yours, yes. You can't take her back to her place like that," Beckett cringed. "Archer would lose his fucking shit."

"I'll take her to Angel's place," she answered, tucking me under her arm and fishing her keys from her pocket. "Let's get you out of here."

We went to leave but Beckett stopped us. "Angel's got Mikey and Poppy over with some of their friends."

"I'll figure it out," Riley growled, leading me across the field in the dark towards the Corvette.

She sat in silence for a few minutes as we drove, and I peered over at her to speak softly, wanting to ease some of her worries.

"He didn't rape me."

The tension in her shoulders eased, but she didn't look at me. "I should've followed you. I was on the phone with Zavier. Reid woke up. When I hung up, you two were gone. I—"

"Why would you need to follow me? He's your brother, so I didn't think it would be a problem," I whispered, finally drawing her attention. "He needs help, Riley. That wasn't him, he's high as a kite."

"Tell me what happened."

She listened while I explained everything from start to finish, and by the end, her fingers were white from the grip she had on the steering wheel.

"Where are we going?" I asked, suddenly feeling exhausted. I just wanted to curl up in bed and sleep.

Even though Ryder had scared me, I couldn't help but

worry about him. Part of me wanted to check on him, but that was a bad idea. Riley would most likely kill him.

"I was just going to drive until we figured it out. I can take you to Beckett's if you want, but she's probably got a houseful. Cruz usually stays there if he's been at the track with them."

"I like him. That's fine," I said quietly, relaxing as she turned the car around. "Thank you."

She kissed the back of my hand before letting it go to call Beckett, and we didn't speak again until we pulled into her drive.

"They're still at mine," she said when I frowned at the empty driveway. "She told me to let myself in and take the spare room. Cruz is sleeping on the couch tonight so we can have the room to ourselves."

I felt bad for him losing his bed, but I didn't voice it.

I hadn't been to her house many times before, so I followed Riley as she switched lights on and opened a door at the end of the hallway, and I immediately dropped down onto the bed.

Riley chuckled, taking my feet to pull my shoes off. "Do you want me to find you something to sleep in?"

"No. I'm fine like this," I mumbled, yawning as she stripped down to her shirt and panties before sliding in beside me.

"Sleep, baby. Wake me if you need me."

I slept like the dead the moment my eyes closed.

80
100
120
140
160
180
200
220
km/h
240
260

Chapter Twenty-Two

Riley

I was beyond furious. I didn't get any sleep as I laid beside Luna all night, my mind going a hundred miles an hour. Ryder was the guy who beat people up for touching others without consent, so I had no idea how the fuck he'd ended up assaulting Luna.

She'd woken up and wanted to shower alone, so I headed into the kitchen to make us coffee, finding Cruz and Maddox talking in low voices at the table. They glanced up when I walked in, Cruz getting to his feet.

"How is she?"

"She slept most of the night. She's having a shower," I replied, glancing at Maddox. "I'm going to kill him."

"Join the club," he grunted, flexing his fingers and drawing my attention to his knuckles. They were a mess from his fight with Zane, but he'd re-split some it seemed. "He'll have a nice fucking black eye this morning."

"What did you tell Mom?"

"Nothing. No one was home, so I put the prick to bed. Never seen him cry so much before," he scowled, clenching his jaw. “He was asking for her, you know? He’s a fucking mess.”

“I don’t give a shit what he says. He’s not seeing her,” I spat, stalking towards the coffee machine. Maddox joined me, dropping an arm around my shoulders.

“Whatever drugs he’d taken was making him hallucinate. He was having a conversation with Lloyd in the kitchen at one point.”

“That doesn’t excuse his behavior,” I snapped despite my heart aching. “He scared the shit out of Luna. If he can’t control himself, he should stay sober. What if he’d raped her?”

“I’m not excusing him. I’m just warning you that he was really fucked up last night. He’s probably just as bad this morning. I don’t think he would’ve taken it that far, but who knows,” he mumbled, his eyebrows drawing together as he became deep in thought.

I didn’t give a shit how bad Ryder was. He’d be lucky if I left him breathing by the time I was done with him.

“He shouldn’t have even tried to touch her, let alone asked her to go home with him. She’s my fucking girlfriend for starters, but she told him no and he kept going,” I threw back, frustration burning inside me. “She cares about him a lot, and he fucking scared her, Maddox.”

He muttered his agreement, gently pushing me out of the way as I stared out the kitchen window. “Sit. I’ll make your coffee.”

“Thanks,” I said quietly without argument, moving towards the table to sit beside Cruz. He pulled his phone out, mumbling something about needing to check in with Stone as he got to his feet and headed outside, giving us a moment alone.

Maddox took his seat, sliding my coffee in front of me

and meeting my gaze. "What are you going to do? I know it's not something you'll let go of. I'm insanely pissed with him, but I can't let you kill him."

"I still can't believe he fucking touched her," I answered, trying to wrap my head around it. "He's always joked around with her, but he's never made her uncomfortable. He's never crossed a line like that with anyone."

He snorted, leaning back in his seat to watch me. "You sure? I'm starting to think we don't know what he's like when he's not around us. I love him, he's our brother, but I can't just forgive him for this. We save girls from monsters all the time, so for him to become the monster? I just can't deal with his ass right now. Did Luna really sleep okay?"

"She slept right through," I confirmed, hearing the water switch off, signaling her shower was finished. "Are Beck and Jett still in bed?"

"Nope. Slash needed Beckett's help with something and Jett wanted to give Luna some space this morning," he answered, leaning forward on his elbows. "So, how are you handling Ry?"

"I'm not too sure yet," I admitted, taking a sip of my coffee and tugging my hood over my head. He eyed me silently for a moment before sighing.

"Want me to come with you to speak to him?"

"You'd do that?"

"Of course I would. You're my baby sister," he smiled, reaching forward to ruffle my hair, making me scowl.

"I don't want to take Luna there."

"I think that's up to her," he said lightly, glancing over his shoulder as Cruz walked back inside.

"I can hang out here with Luna if you need to deal with your brother," Cruz offered, and I cringed a little.

"She might not want to stay with you since you're a

stranger. I can ask though. Thanks." I didn't know him myself, but if Beckett and Maddox trusted him, I knew he was safe.

I had a cigarette and finished my coffee before Luna joined us, and she seemed more than happy to sit beside Cruz, a warm smile on her face. "It's you again."

"It's me," he chuckled, pushing a coffee towards her. She sipped it, seeming surprised when it was exactly how she liked it.

"Don't think too much of him," I joked, motioning to Maddox. "He's the one who made the coffee."

"You're a liar," she said with a fake gasp, Cruz's lips quirking into a smirk.

"A thief, but never a liar. I just stole his credit, that's all. I never said I made it."

I rolled my eyes, getting to my feet. "Did you want to stay here while I go to my place for a while, Lou?"

She frowned, cradling the cup in her hands. "You don't want me to come with you?"

"Unless you want to witness me beating my brother's ass, then no," I muttered, panic flashing in her eyes.

"No, he—"

"Don't make excuses for him!" I bit out, glaring down at her. "He had no fucking right to touch you. Maddox and I are heading over there. If you don't want to deal with the confrontational shit that I'm about to throw at him, I can either take you home, or you can hang out here with Cruz."

She glanced at Cruz, her voice soft. "I don't need a babysitter. He probably has better things to do with his day."

"What's better than hanging out with a pretty woman? My other option is to go home to Stone and deal with his shitty mood, so trust me, you're my preferred way to spend the day," he grinned as a small smile brightened her face.

"You sure?"

"Fuck yeah. We can get out some wine, gossip about the Donovans, and I'll even paint your nails." He winked my way, relaxing me slightly. He was flirty as fuck, but I had the feeling he had a really soft side. I'd almost bet money on him being serious about painting her fucking nails.

"Sold," she said with a laugh before reaching for me to pull me closer as she turned serious again. "Don't hurt him too badly. He really wasn't himself."

"Don't worry about it," I murmured, leaning down to drop a kiss on her lips. "Call me if you need me."

She nodded, not seeming happy to let me go, but she didn't stop me when I walked out the door with Maddox. I heard her laughter a moment later, so I knew Cruz was doing a good job of distracting her.

We took my car, and Maddox didn't seem too worried until we parked and I grabbed my bat from the trunk. "Uh, Riley?"

"What? You thought I was just going to slap him and swear a little?" I scoffed, slamming the trunk and dropping my bat over my shoulder. "I'm going to break all of his fucking fingers and carve his damn eyes out."

He cursed as he followed me, and I knew I wouldn't have long to handle shit before one of our parents stepped in. It seemed most of them were home from the chatter I could hear in the living room, but Ryder stood in the kitchen by the fridge, talking to Jett whose muscles were tense.

It looked like he was going to punch him.

Ryder's gaze lifted to me as I approached, and he swallowed nervously. "Riley, listen to me. I—" I wasn't going to let him worm his way out of it. I swung the bat hard, smashing him in the ribs and causing him to stumble as he grunted, his voice sharp. "Riley! Stop!"

I swung the bat again, slamming it into his back and legs like a crazy woman, but I was jerked back before my aim for his head could connect.

"What the fuck is going on?" Caden barked as he snatched my bat away from me and tossed it behind him to let it roll across the floor. Hunter pulled Ryder to his feet, lifting the back of his shirt to check the damage, but he paused when I tried to lunge at Ryder with my fists. Caden grabbed my hood, almost choking me as he hauled me back again. "Riley! That's enough!"

"He fucking deserves it!" I shouted, trying to twist from his grip but failing. "He's lucky I don't gut him!"

"Calm down and tell us what happened," Caden asked patiently. Jett stood beside me, crossing his arms and giving Ryder a dirty look.

"She's not lying. He does fucking deserve it."

"Would someone tell me what's going on?" Hunter demanded, his gaze bouncing between the three of us, but he went completely still as I motioned towards Ryder.

"This piece of shit got so drunk and high last night that he sexually assaulted Luna. He scared the hell out of her."

"Ryder?" Caden said slowly, loosening his hold on me. "What the fuck is she talking about?"

Ryder nursed his ribs, wincing as he pressed his hand against them, his voice hoarse. "I didn't mean to scare her. I—"

"You don't just accidentally assault someone, asshole!" I growled, my knuckles cracking as I clenched my fists. "What's next? Will you accidentally rape her?"

"I'd never do that to her," he choked out, his voice breaking. "I love Luna. She's family to me."

"Yeah?" I spat, not giving a shit that I was hurting him. "I never thought you'd touch someone without their permission either. She told you no, Ryder. It doesn't get much easier to understand than that. Did you fucking touch her at Angel's that night? When she was passed out?"

The thought made me sick. I'd left her alone with him, completely vulnerable, and he could've done anything to her.

His eyes widened, and he took a step towards me. "No! I swear, I didn't touch her! Riley, please. I need to apologize to her."

Caden cursed as I slipped from his hold, slamming my fist into Ryder's face as hard as I could. My chest was heaving with anger, and I wasn't surprised when Beckett materialized beside me, dropping an arm around my shoulders to pull me back a step. She didn't say anything, but a muscle ticked in Hunter's jaw as he turned to Ryder, disappointment on his face.

"What did you do to her?"

He sighed, his face pinching with pain. "It's a bit blurry. I was being a dick, and—"

"He kept groping her ass and trying to convince her to fuck him while mauling her neck," I supplied, crossing my arms tightly to keep control of my fists. "Ask Beckett how terrified Luna was. She was the one who found her last night while she was trying to get away from him."

Marco appeared out of nowhere, his voice firm. "Beckett? Is this true?"

She nodded, her voice cold. "She slapped him and it seemed to snap him out of it, but he can't take back what he's done. She was a fucking mess, and he's lucky I didn't stab him. Maddox, Cruz, and Jett got him home last night before Riley found out. I didn't want us airing our shit at the track for people's entertainment."

Marco had apparently heard enough, his face void of emotion as he pointed a finger at Ryder. "You're done."

"You're kicking me out?" Ryder forced out, panic filling his face. If they kicked him out, he had no one to blame but himself.

Hunter eyed him for a second before glancing at Marco, having a silent conversation before he answered the question. "No. You're going to fucking rehab."

"It was one time! I won't get like that again!"

I scowled, giving him a dirty look. "You don't think Ander told me about you trying to score a shitload of LSD and Molly from him? It's not just a bit of weed or a line of powder anymore. You're popping pills like they're your lifeline."

He looked like he was about to argue, but Maddox stepped in, finally speaking up. "You were a mess last night, bro. You were having an entire conversation in the kitchen with yourself, thinking it was Lloyd. You need to get some help."

"I'm fine," he croaked, but Hunter snatched his chin firmly in his grip, peering into his eyes before scoffing.

"You're high right now. It's not even nine in the morning. Give me your keys."

"No, you're not taking my car," Ryder threw back defensively, but Caden walked up to him and fished the keys from his pocket, holding them in front of Ryder's face.

"If you want to keep your car safe, you'll temporarily surrender it. If we catch you driving it while wasted, it'll go up in smoke. Clear?"

Ryder looked ready to break, and the stupid part of my

heart hurt for him. I knew something was going on with him, and I wished I'd seen it sooner, but he'd dug his own grave now as far as I was concerned.

He stared at me hopelessly, his voice soft. "Can you just tell her I'm sorry? I really didn't mean to scare her."

"Sure, but stay the fuck away from her," I said flatly, turning and stalking up to my room, slamming the door behind me. I couldn't go back to Luna until I'd calmed down but if I had to look at Ryder any longer, I was going to tear him apart.

Luna had apparently had an awesome morning with Cruz. He had, in fact, painted her nails, and I walked in the door to find them both sitting on the couch watching a romance movie. Cruz looked genuinely invested in it too.

Maddox had stayed with Beckett and Jett, but I knew they'd be home soon.

"Hey," I chuckled as I leaned against the wall and crossed my arms. "You ready to go?"

"It's not finished," Cruz whined, waving his hands at me dramatically. "Twenty more minutes."

Black nail polish on his fingers caught my eye, and I snickered. "You let her paint your nails too?"

"Yep," he said with a grin, holding them out to show me. "I think it looks badass."

"It does," Luna said as she reached her hand out to me, taking my wrist and tugging me down beside her. "How's Ry?"

I scowled, giving her a flat look. "It doesn't matter. He doesn't deserve your concern."

She was quiet for a second before meeting my gaze, her voice so quiet that I hardly heard her. "It matters to me. He's spiraling, and I know he's just messed up from drugs and alcohol. He wouldn't have touched me otherwise."

I glanced at Cruz, and he took the hint, clearing his throat as he paused the movie and got to his feet. "I'm going for a cigarette. I'll be back in a minute."

Once he'd left us alone, I sighed, scrubbing my face with my hands. "He's going to rehab."

"When? For how long? I need to see him," she blurted out, frustrating me. She was way too good for any of us. He'd abused her trust, yet she wanted to make him feel better.

"Lou, he assaulted you."

"Don't say it like that."

"That's what he did. It's sexual assault," I growled, hating that she wasn't taking it seriously. "I don't care if he's my brother, I'll call him out for his bullshit. He's sorry for scaring you, but I've told him to stay away from you."

"That's not your call to make," she argued, fire burning in her eyes. "When's he leaving?"

"In a few days, I think. My parents were having a discussion about it earlier. Diesel and Marco are addicts from their younger years, so they've suggested a ninety-day program to see how he does. He won't be allowed visitors for a few weeks, but if he shows improvement, that will change."

"I want to see him and let him know I don't hate him," she said softly, her voice breaking. "I don't want him thinking he's a bad person."

I leaned my back against the armrest, spreading my legs out and pulling her on top of me to cuddle her. "He needs to realize things need to change. If you make it out like it's not a big deal, he won't get better. Maybe write him a letter or something once he's settled into the facility, okay?"

She didn't seem convinced, but she finally nodded, closing her eyes and snuggling into me more. "Mom called me not long after you left this morning. She's demanding a family dinner, so I'll have to go home tonight. I think she's trying to rein in Tempest. She's been a little crazy lately."

"No offense, but your sister's always been crazy," I mumbled, combing my fingers absently through her silky, brown hair. "I bet Mom will want to do something similar since Ryder's leaving. Beckett mentioned going to the track and Mom gave her a dirty look for it, so I doubt any of us will be allowed to go anywhere tonight."

"Your mom's probably freaking out."

"She is. She feels like she's losing us," I said as guilt nipped at me. "I should probably spend more time with her. We haven't had a girl's night in ages."

"I haven't spent much time with my mom either," she sighed. "Maybe we spend the next few days doing family stuff, then we can plan on having a sleepover or something?"

I slid my hand up the back of her shirt to tease her skin and brushed my lips across hers, my body heating at the thought of getting her into my bed to strip her bare. "Why? You want to get me naked again?"

Her cheeks flushed, but she gave me a quick kiss instead of pulling away like I expected. "Yeah. I'd like that."

I kept her close as I devoured her with a kiss, loving it when she moaned into my mouth and tugged on my hair. She was building confidence, which was exactly what I wanted.

"Can you two *not* fuck on my couch?"

Luna flew back from me as if we'd been busted doing

the wrong thing, but I smirked and tilted my head back, finding Beckett behind me.

"Do you blame me? I've got a hot girlfriend."

"Then fuck her on your own furniture," she grumbled. "Mom said dinner's at six. Be there or plan your funeral."

I sat up, peering behind her but not finding the guys there. "Where's Maddox and Jett?"

"Outside with Cruz," she answered, dropping down onto a recliner. "Ry's going to miss too much school to graduate."

"He can catch back up next year," I shrugged. "Maybe he'll agree to go to Harvard with Marla. It won't take long for people to find out he's in rehab. He might not want to come home to deal with it."

Luna excused herself and went outside with the others, and Beckett instantly changed the subject. "Have you spoken to Marla much?"

I frowned. "Not really. Why?"

"She's really upset Mom. After you left, they got into an argument. She's close to being able to do her final exams already, and she's told Mom she's leaving the moment she graduates."

Marla had been a brat lately, but there was no reason for her to be a bitch to Mom and make her feel bad.

"Where the fuck does she think she's going? And why?" I bit out, not understanding why our sister seemed to hate us so much. Some days she'd hold a conversation with me but usually, she'd avoid all of us.

Beckett cringed, running her fingers through her black hair. "She kind of exploded. Screamed about how we're all criminals and no one gives a shit about her, and that she's leaving for Harvard early so she can settle into her own house and make some friends before she starts. I've never seen her so angry."

"She thinks no one cares about her? How fucking dramatic," I scoffed, but Beckett shrugged.

"To be honest with you, I saw this coming a long time ago. Marla's not like us, Riley. She's never enjoyed cars, violence, or even social gatherings. She doesn't feel like she fits in with us, so I understand her need to find her place in the world."

"She's family. We'll make her fit," I argued. "Why didn't she say anything earlier if it's been bothering her?"

"She's always told us she's leaving the moment she could. She's been saying that for as long as I can remember. She made some good points, and I think it's why Mom's so upset about it. We're all targets due to the crews and our enemies, and Marla would be the perfect kid to take for revenge. She's sweet, has a good future ahead of her, and she probably wouldn't see it coming unlike the rest of us. She's sick of always looking over her shoulder, so she wants out."

"Family's not a subscription that you can just cancel."

"I know, but it's not fair to make her live like that," she said with defeat as she leaned back.

"So she'll turn her back on all of us just so she can marry some religious do-gooder and live in some cute little cottage or something?" I huffed, but she gave me a sad look.

"She's not happy here. If she wants that kind of life, then who are we to stop her?"

"This family's fallen apart, you know?" I murmured. "I wish Lloyd was still here. He'd know how to fix it."

"I'm worried about you more," she admitted, her green eyes pinning me in place. "I know whatever you're hiding from us is bad. I can take on anyone to keep you safe, but I can't help you unless you tell me."

I gave her a small smile, getting to my feet to stretch. "I'm not in trouble. I promise. No one's forcing me to do anything, no one's blackmailing me, and I'm alright."

"I can't lose you too," she said on an exhale, her shoulders tense. "If it's not bad, why won't you tell me?"

"Because it's just going to disappoint a lot of people," I said truthfully. "I'm handling it, and it won't matter soon."

She nodded, her smile not quite reaching her eyes. "Okay."

"I'd better get my girl home. Unless she wants to keep hanging around me doing nothing for the rest of the day," I joked, and Beckett rolled her eyes.

"You two always do nothing together. I'm not that good at the whole dating thing either, but I know Luna's the type that enjoys the little things. Take her for coffee or buy her flowers."

I gave her an amused glance, my lips curving into a smile. "You're giving me dating advice?"

"She's always had shit relationships with stupid guys that can't read her. You've always been good at that, so you know she appreciates small gestures of affection and dates. Take her for lunch or something," she replied. "Prove to her it's not just about sex."

"You act like I fuck her all the time. It's not as common as you think."

"Why not? You're a sexual person, and she knows that. She's probably doubting herself if you're holding back. And just a heads up? Penny's been harassing her at school. You might need to set that girl straight."

"Luna hasn't mentioned it." Anger burned inside of me

at knowing she was being bullied. "What's she been doing to her?"

"Just pushing her around and saying nasty shit to her."

"How do you know and I don't?"

"I've stepped in a time or two. Talk to Luna about it. And take her on a fucking date," she scolded. "You always call her boyfriends pieces of shit for not spoiling her, so you'd better spoil her yourself."

"I'll see you for dinner," I grumbled, heading outside to where the others were.

Cruz was still bragging about his nails, and Luna giggled as Jett practically swooned over them.

"Honestly, they'll definitely get you laid, man. They look awesome. Luna did those? I think blue would look good on me, right, Maddox?"

"Totally," Maddox replied with a straight face, glancing at me. "You leaving?"

Luna's bright smile fell a fraction, and I knew Beckett was right. I needed to spend more time with her.

"Yeah. I've got a hot date with my girl," I grinned, taking Luna's hand. She seemed confused, her brow creasing.

"You do?"

"Yeah. I'm taking you out."

"On a date?" she asked nervously.

"I suck at this," I chuckled, pulling her against me to kiss the tip of her nose. "Yes, a date. I'm sorry we haven't done stuff like that. I'm changing that right now."

Maddox snorted. "You wouldn't know romance if it bit you on the ass."

"I'm learning, you fucker," I threw back. "See you at dinner."

"Looking forward to it," he deadpanned, the other two saying goodbye to us so we could leave.

Once in the car, I gave Luna a serious look. "When were you going to tell me about Penny giving you trouble?"

She cringed, clicking her seat belt into place. "Never."

I started the engine, backing out of the driveway, and giving her a sweet smile. "Well, we have some time to kill on the way to lunch. So start talking."

80
100
120
140
160
180
200
220
km/h
240
260

Chapter Twenty-Three

Luna

It was late on Friday night, and Riley and I were sitting in her Corvette at the track. The place was like a ghost town, which surprised me. There were usually a handful of kids hanging out there when races weren't on.

I'd stayed at her house the previous night once Ryder had left for rehab, and she'd tried to explain the street racing to me. I didn't see the appeal of tempting fate, but her face lit up with excitement as she talked. I was terrified of her ending up in a hospital bed like Reid, or worse, dead.

I had to take my mind off it or I was going to send myself crazy.

"Can we mess around tonight?" I asked lightly, hoping my nerves didn't carry in my voice. "I want to learn what you like."

She looked over at me from the driver's seat, her eyes studying me in the moonlight.

"I like anything you do to me."

"I know, but there has to be some things that you *really* like," I replied. "C'mon, tell me your fantasies," I insisted, keeping her hand in mine. She smirked, making me squirm.

"You already know I want to spread you out on my hood and make you scream."

"How can we do that without people seeing us?"

"It's always a risk when you're fucking out in the open," she said with a chuckle. "But if you're wearing a dress, no one would see anything they shouldn't. They'd definitely know what we were doing though."

"No one's here now," I offered, peering out at the darkness surrounding us. "And I'm wearing a dress."

"You want me to fuck you on the hood right now?" she asked in disbelief. "Where'd my good girl go?"

"Good girls will be bad for the right person," I said with an innocent smile, and she was suddenly out of the car and racing around to my side, yanking the door open to haul me out. I giggled, my arms going around her neck instantly. "You really wanted this, didn't you?"

She didn't answer me as she pressed my back against the door, kicking it shut and consuming me with a kiss while I tangled my fingers in her hair.

It was as if she was going to die if she didn't get to touch me, and that made me feel stupidly horny. Out of all the girls in the world, how had she fallen in love with me?

She hardly broke our kiss as she lifted me and moved around to the front of the car, dropping my butt onto the hood. She pushed me back gently, snagging my panties and tugging them off, leaning over me with a wicked grin as she tossed them aside.

"Let me know if you want to stop."

"Hurry up," I teased, wiggling my hips. "It's cold out here."

"Bossy." She didn't seem to mind though, pushing me further up the hood so that I couldn't slip off. She vanished under my dress, and two seconds later her hot, wet tongue started rubbing circles over my clit, making me moan. I couldn't grip her hair like I wanted to, so I clenched my fists against the hood, jerking when she hit the right spot.

She pushed a finger inside me, and my butt left the hood as I arched slightly. "Oh, shit. Right there."

She kept the same pattern with her tongue and finger until I let out a loud curse, my nails probably scratching her car as I tried to cling to something to ground myself.

She moved back as my body started to calm, her hands tugging me further down until I was perched on the edge with her standing between my legs.

"You have no idea how hot that was, baby," she murmured, sliding her hand between us and easing a finger inside me again. "But I'm not finished."

"I don't need a second one," I insisted as I tried to catch my breath.

"Who said you were only getting two?" she murmured, adding another finger before her lips were on mine. I gasped, her thumb brushing my sensitive clit as she pushed her tongue into my mouth to let me taste myself.

She fucked me hard, whispering encouragement and dirty words against my lips until I was seeing stars and screaming her name, and it wasn't until I heard someone speak that I realized we had company.

"Donovan."

I squealed, and Riley fixed my dress, glaring at Ander who stood close by, leaning against his Supra. I hadn't even heard it, which was concerning since it was a loud car.

"What the fuck, Lavaro?" she snarled, helping me off the hood with one hand as she sucked her other fingers into her mouth to lick them clean before adding, "Can't you see I'm busy?"

He barely spared me a glance. "I can see that, but I've been trying to get hold of you. A race has been called."

She snorted, but I could see her interest. "What race? You vs me? Slick's been booted, Reid's currently sitting in a hospital bed with no car, Logan's only a passenger for Reid since he doesn't have his own car, and I doubt you'll run a race just for us and Blake."

He cringed, his voice dropping. "Some prick from Kingslake called it. He's just a rich dude with too much money and not enough brain. He and his guys vs us and Blake. It's a shorter race than usual, and it's only from one end of Rawson to the other. Bring your girl if you want since you don't have to worry about Slick anymore."

"It's still fucking dangerous, idiot," she hissed, not even looking at me. "You have no idea what these guys want. It could be a trap and they're working with the cops for all you know."

"They're part of the Kingslake car club. They're legit. I've done background checks on them all too."

I stepped beside Riley, hoping I sounded confident. "I want to come."

"Like fuck," she snapped, but I gave her a glare.

"Why not? I want to try and understand why you like it so much. If it's that dangerous, then you shouldn't be doing it either."

"It's not just the danger that worries me," she scowled, her jaw tight. "We could get arrested if we're caught, and both our parents would kill us. I don't want to get you in trouble."

"Let me come. I'm used to fast cars because we race here," I insisted, motioning to the quiet track in front of us. "And I know you're a good driver."

She blew out a breath, eyeing me silently for a moment before nodding. "Fine. But you're not going to like it."

"You don't know that."

"Yes, I fucking do," she growled, turning her attention to Ander. "Where's the meeting point?"

"Northern starting point."

"We'll meet you there," she grumbled, turning and walking towards the driver's seat with tense shoulders. I scrambled after her, getting into the passenger seat before she could change her mind, and she was surprisingly quiet for most of the drive, other than telling me to switch my phone off.

I was nervous when we finally arrived to find multiple cars parked close together, but I relaxed a little bit when I noticed Blake amongst them. She looked tense, so I assumed the others were the rich pricks. One of the guys was shamelessly flirting up a storm with her, not that she seemed interested.

We parked beside them and climbed out, my skin crawling as the rich pricks checked us out. Ander walked over and stood beside Blake, speaking for everyone to hear him.

"You'll all receive the map once you're in your cars and we're ready to go. No deliberately running each other off the road, and if you're arrested, that's on you. No ratting each other out either."

"You expect us to race a bunch of girls?" One guy scoffed, making Ander chuckle.

"You're scared to race girls?"

"They probably don't even know how to reverse park, let alone race," he threw back, eyeing me with amusement. "And what about her? She looks like she's on her way to fucking church. Hey, sweetheart. How about you come sit next to me and blow me while I drive?"

Ander was fast as he grabbed Riley's wrist before she could lunge at the guy, his voice firm. "Donovan, don't."

"Why the fuck not?" she seethed. "You think it's okay for him to speak to my girl like that?"

"It's fine," I said softly, not wanting them to fight. "Just do your race so we can go."

The guy's eyes lit up, and he tilted his head to run his gaze over me. "You're a pussy licker? What a shame. I bet I could change your mind."

He grabbed his crotch and licked his lips, but Ander shot him a dark look.

"Shut your fucking mouth. You're wasting our time."

Riley was fuming, but I took her hand and pulled her back, keeping a tight grip on her. "Ignore them."

Once everyone was in their cars and ready to go, we moved into position and Riley set up a tablet on her dash. It was surprisingly fancy.

"How does everyone afford that?" I asked. "Reid and Blake couldn't buy one, right?"

She glanced at me, not answering for a moment until she let out a sigh. "Turbo supplied them. We all pay them off though."

"They look really expensive."

"They are." I frowned, trying to figure out why anyone would go into debt just to race, and Riley chuckled dryly at my confusion. "Just because I race for the thrill of it, doesn't mean other people do. There's a lot of money in it if you win."

"How much? Is it worth dying for?" I replied, her fingers flexing on the wheel.

"To people like Reid and Blake? Yes. They can pay

something like three grand to race, and end up taking home twelve grand if they win. That's a lot of money when you're desperate."

"What do you do with the money if you win? You don't need it," I said curiously, and her jaw tightened at my words.

"I give it to them. I race for the fun of it and have no need for the cash. You think I keep it?"

"Don't get mad at me," I mumbled, staring out the window at Blake's car as she revved her engine. "How am I supposed to know? I didn't even know this side of you until recently, and I only found out by accident. It's not like you told me because you wanted to."

"I didn't want you dragged into this, that's why I never told you sooner," she answered, her voice strained. "I didn't want to ask you to lie for me if anyone started questioning what I was doing."

"When are you going to realize I'd do anything for you," I said quietly, not looking at her.

"Lou—" Numbers started flashing on the screen, and she let out a sigh. "Hold on. This isn't like the track, and you're likely to shit your pants."

I didn't reply, but my body went tense as the countdown hit zero and she slammed her foot down on the gas, sending us forward so fast that my stomach did a flip. My fingers dug into the seat as fear started seeping into me, and I closed my eyes tightly when we almost got hit by Blake as she passed us.

I had no idea how Riley thought this was fun, it was terrifying.

We were way too close to the others as we moved through narrow streets, taking the turns way too fast. One of the Kingslake guys almost ran into us on one corner, and I started to freak out.

"Slow down!"

"Do you know how a race works?" she threw back, darting around parked cars in the dark. "If I slow down, I'll lose."

"If you don't slow down, you'll fucking kill us!" I snapped, hearing her huff.

"Once we finish, I promise to never bring you with me again."

"I want to get out. Right now," I begged, her hands tightening on the wheel as one of the rich pricks hit the gravel and sent their car skidding across someone's front lawn, slamming into a parked car and a fence.

"I can't just pull over and let you out," she hissed, passing Ander and almost hitting his side mirror. "There's also a car on my ass and if I slow down, he'll hit us."

Tears pricked my eyes as we skidded around a corner and the back tires slid out. My heart hammered as Riley managed to correct it, but I was done. If she wanted to die so badly, she wasn't taking me with her.

"Let me out, please," I repeated, not giving a shit that I was crying. "Stop the fucking car!"

She slammed on the brakes, moving off the road to let the others pass, and I flung open the door and scrambled out on shaky legs.

I heard Riley curse as she slammed her door, joining me on the side of the road. "I told you you'd hate it. This is one of the reasons why I don't bring you with me, apart from it being dangerous."

I turned to face her, not hiding how upset I was. "You find this fun? You're going to die, Riley!"

"We can't sit here arguing. The cops will be on their

way to deal with the asshole who crashed," she warned, but I shoved her away when she reached for me.

"Don't fucking touch me!" I shouted, knowing we were probably waking people up. I started walking, and she grabbed my wrist to pull me back.

"Where the fuck are you going? Get in the car and I'll take you home," she growled, and I was surprised to see Ander's car idling not far away. He must have seen us stop and decided to throw the race to make sure Riley was alright.

"I'm not getting back in the car unless you promise not to race again," I said firmly, her eyes widening.

"I can't just stop racing. It doesn't work like that. There's a handful more to go and then Turbo's calling it quits, so once that happens—"

"You're going to choose racing over me then?" I asked bluntly, wiping my eyes as hurt filled me. "I don't want you to die."

"I'm not going to fucking die."

"You can't make that promise!" I snapped, glaring at her. "You could've died multiple times tonight. I don't want a girlfriend who's going to risk her life just for thrills. How do you think it makes me feel to know you might not come home to me? This isn't racing, Riley. This is stupidity."

"Once the races finish, I'll stop," she said weakly, and that was the first time I'd ever heard her lie to me. She got too much of an adrenaline rush from racing on the street, so once Ander stopped running races, she'd find someone else.

I couldn't live in fear of her not coming home to me for the rest of my life, and if she really loved me like she claimed, she wouldn't want to risk leaving me if she died.

Realization hit me like a freight train, and I shook my head as she reached for me again. "I can't do this."

She stared at me silently as she processed my words, her voice coming out as a whisper when she finally replied. "You don't want to be with me?"

"No. I don't," I bit out. "Because it's not fair for you to expect me to be okay with this."

"Jesus. I'll see if I can get out of racing then if it's going to upset you that much," she said firmly. "You're more important to me than racing."

I scoffed, starting to walk again as I spoke over my shoulder. "That's the second time you've lied to me tonight. Also, if I meant more to you, you would've chosen me straight away."

"I can't lose you, Lou," she choked out, but I kept walking, refusing to turn around and see how upset she was or I'd crumble.

"You just did."

I walked past Ander's Supra, and he poked his head out the window with a cringe. "Do you want a ride?"

"Fuck off," I said sharply, hating that I was being a bitch, but I blamed him too.

"Okay," he winced, putting his window up and letting me walk off in peace.

I didn't get far before a car pulled up beside me. I knew Rawson Grove was a little rough at times, so I panicked for a second that I was about to be kidnapped but relaxed when the window went down and Cruz leaned out with a grim look on his face. "Hey. Get in."

I glanced back to find Riley standing by her car still, watching me as if I was going to run back to her. I deserved better than someone who didn't give a shit about life or death.

I opened the door and climbed in, securing my seat belt

as Cruz started driving. "Thanks. How did you know I was here?"

He handed me his cigarettes and lighter, giving me a small smile. "We have access to every surveillance camera in town. I saw Riley racing and figured I'd keep an eye on her. I didn't know you were with her until you got out of the car. Are you alright?"

I shook my head, biting the inside of my cheek to stop myself from crying. "She chose cars over me, so I broke up with her."

"Do you want me to drive you home? Or you can stay at my place. It's only a few streets away," he offered, and I fiddled with my hands on my lap awkwardly.

"I don't think I'd be allowed to stay at yours. My parents are really strict on strangers."

"Call them. See if they're okay with it, and let them know Beckett can vouch for me if they're unsure. I can drive you home first thing in the morning and I'll even introduce myself to them so they know who I am," he shrugged, making me snort.

"You're brave. Dad's likely to aim a gun at your head."

"Wouldn't be the first time someone's done that," he replied with a chuckle. "Call them so I know where I'm taking you."

I turned my phone on, finding messages from Mom asking where I was. She hated it when she couldn't see my location.

I called her, not surprised when she answered on the first ring. "Where are you? I've been trying to get hold of you for hours," she scolded, but she paused when I choked on a sob. "Luna? What's wrong?"

"I'm in Rawson Grove. Can I stay at a friend's house

tonight?" I forced out, trying to control my emotions. "You don't know them, but they're nice."

"Who? Weren't you staying with Riley? Where is she?" she demanded, and I started crying more.

"I just broke up with her. I don't want to come home tonight, so can I just stay here? His name's Cruz. He's friends with Beckett if you want to check with her."

"Oh, babe, what happened?"

"We got in a fight and I broke it off. I'm in Cruz's car right now, and he can bring me home if I'm not allowed to stay here, but—"

"Hold on. I'll ask your father," she sighed, and my stomach sank, knowing he wouldn't let me go. I bit back a groan when Dad demanded I put the phone on speaker. He was going to embarrass the hell out of me.

"Cruz? Can you hear me? It's Archer," Dad growled, and I relaxed slightly as Cruz answered politely.

"I can hear you, Sir."

"Don't *Sir* me, you fucker. Don't act like you don't know me." That made me pause.

"You know my dad?" I asked with disbelief, and he gave me a grin.

"We've met once or twice. I don't know how much business he tells you though, so I don't want to put my foot in my mouth."

"You listen to me, Cruz Lennox. Don't touch my daughter. She gets her own room, and for fuck's sake, keep her away from Drake. You'd better get her chocolate, and make her laugh too, or I'll kill you," Dad said sharply, and I wiped my tears to pull myself together.

"I can stay with him?"

"Are you fucking him?"

"What? No!" I said with horror, ignoring Cruz's smirk. "We're just friends!"

"Good. Keep it that way," he grunted. "And, Luna? Where's Riley? Because I'm going to go and strangle her."

"Leave her alone," I begged, taking the phone off speaker and pressing it to my ear. "We just had a disagreement and broke up. She didn't hurt me or cheat on me."

He was quiet for a second before replying, his voice gentle. "Whatever she did to make you leave means it wasn't simple. Please stay safe, and if you need me to come and get you, call me. I'll come running, okay?"

"Thanks, Dad."

"You'll always be my first priority. I promise. Get a good sleep, I'll see you tomorrow. I love you."

"I love you too. Good night," I murmured before hanging up, and Cruz gave me a wide grin.

"So, slumber party?"

He had no hope of that happening. I was definitely going to sleep the moment we got there.

Riley

"Do you want to talk about it?" Turbo asked as he walked towards me with Luna vanishing in the dark in Cruz's car. I was glad she wasn't walking in the dark alone because I knew she wouldn't have gotten back in my car, but I was mad that she'd left with him.

"We're not girl besties. Go away," I said quietly, not having the energy to fight with him. My heart was breaking, and I had no one to blame but myself. This lifestyle I'd created had become an addiction, and I'd just let it ruin my relationship with the one person I could ever love. Turbo stood quietly, and I finally looked at him with annoyance. "Why'd you stop? You could've beaten those assholes."

"Blake will beat them. I was more worried about you. You wouldn't stop racing unless something was wrong," he said casually as if it wasn't a big deal. "You're more important than a race."

His words practically hit me in the face, and I fisted my hair tightly out of frustration. "What the fuck is wrong with me?"

I expected a smart-ass remark, but he replied gently, understanding in his tone. "Giving something up can be hard. You didn't expect her to leave, so you made a choice that you thought wasn't going to be such a big deal."

"How much did you hear?" I scoffed, his lips lifting into a smile that looked more like a grimace.

"You two were yelling pretty loudly. We need to get out of here before the cops show up. You head home, I'll make sure Blake's alright. She's probably freaking out that she hasn't seen us."

I nodded, silently getting back into my car and driving towards home, trying to figure out how to fix things with Luna. I'd never seen her lose it like that before, so I knew this wasn't going to be a simple fix.

By the time I arrived home, I was a fucking mess. I parked in the garage, walking inside to find most of the house in darkness. It was quiet, and the pit in my chest only grew when I realized just how empty it was becoming here.

Everyone was leaving, most of my parents were probably still at work, and it wouldn't be long before Marla left too. I never worried about it because I'd had Luna, but now I had no one.

Tears burned my eyes as I made my way through the dark and into the kitchen, finding Mom straddling Lukas' lap at the table as he fed her candies. He was laughing at something she said, but his face turned serious when he noticed me.

"Riley? What's wrong?"

Mom glanced over her shoulder, her brow creasing with concern as she got to her feet.

"Mom," I choked out, tears escaping as the emotions hit me all at once. "She left me. I fucked up."

"Come here, baby," she murmured, holding her arms out for a hug, and I immediately wrapped my arms around her and held on as I let it all out. I couldn't tell her why we'd broken up, but I knew she wouldn't pry.

Lukas excused himself to give me some space, and Mom led me outside to the back porch. I lit a cigarette, taking a drag before speaking. "I didn't put her first."

She crossed her arms, giving me a frown. "With what?"

"I don't want to talk about it," I mumbled, staring at the glowing tip of the cigarette. "But I don't know how to fix it."

"Where is she? I haven't heard from Lex, so I assume they don't know."

"She didn't go home?" I asked, pulling my phone out to turn it on and my stomach twisted when it showed her at the Night Thieves' compound. I thought he'd just take her home, but apparently not.

Would she rebound with him?

Mom peered over my shoulder, surprise in her voice. "What's she doing there?"

"We were in Rawson and we had a fight. She wouldn't get back in the car, and Cruz showed up to save her," I grumbled. "They're basically besties now."

"You're mad that she has friends?" she asked slowly, but I shook my head, wiping my cheeks.

"No. I'm mad at myself. She hates me," I answered, making her snort.

"I highly doubt that. She's probably just overwhelmed by whatever happened between you two. Give her some time to herself and maybe she'll be open to talking about it," she suggested. "You've known her your whole life, so you know how she processes things. She just needs time."

"What do I do if I can't fix it?" I said softly, hating the pity in her gaze as she took my hand and gave it a squeeze.

"You get through it."

We sat outside for ages until she decided it was time for bed. She offered to sleep in my room, but I declined. I wasn't going to get a lot of sleep, and I ended up spending most of the night staring at my phone to see if Luna ended up leaving Cruz's.

She didn't.

80
100
120
140
160
180
200
220
km/h
240
260

Chapter Twenty-Four

Luna

I woke up to hear a door closing and peered over my shoulder to see Cruz creeping around in the dim room. The sun was shining through the curtains, so I knew it wasn't too early.

He heard me moving and gave me an apologetic glance. "Sorry. I need to grab some fresh clothes for the day."

"It's okay," I mumbled, sitting up and rubbing my eyes. "What time is it?"

"Almost ten. I know your dad told me to keep you away from Drake, but he's in the kitchen making breakfast if you want some. He's on a health kick again, so it's probably avocado and spinach on toast or something weird like that."

I was wearing Cruz's shirt and gray sweatpants, so I swung my legs out of bed and got to my feet, my stomach rumbling. "I'm starving, actually, and avocado on toast is good."

"Give me two seconds to get changed and I'll come with you so he keeps his hands to himself. He thinks he's charming, but he's not."

I laughed, leaving the room and standing outside the

door to wait for him, and once he was changed, I followed him down the hallway until we reached the huge open space that he'd brought me through when we'd arrived. It had been a ghost town, but now it was bustling with people and activity.

People gave me a curious glance, but no one said anything until we reached the kitchen.

There were a few people lingering around the table, and a guy looked up at our arrival and scowled when he saw me with Cruz's arm draped over my shoulders. "What the fuck, Cruz?"

"What?" he replied bluntly, steering me towards a chair and pulling it out for me to sit in before he gave me his attention again. "Coffee? Milk and two sugars, right?"

"Thanks," I smiled shyly, not liking everyone's attention on me.

The moment Cruz moved away to make my coffee, another guy sat beside me with a smirk on his face. I remembered him from Riley's place one time, and I was pretty sure it was Drake.

"How did Cruz manage to get you into his bed, huh? You're not his usual type."

"Why am I offended by that?" I snorted, but Cruz scowled.

"Leave her alone. She's just a friend, not a hookup, and I don't fucking have a type, asshole." Drake reached out to touch my hair, and I jerked back to avoid it. My heartbeat started thumping harder when I realized I was in a place I didn't know with a bunch of random guys. I trusted Cruz, but none of the others. "Hey!" Cruz barked, smacking the back of Drake's head firmly. "Don't fucking touch people without asking. Besides, I wouldn't touch her if I were you.

For starters, her and Riley broke up last night, but secondly, she's Archer Hendricks' daughter."

My cheeks heated, but the grumpy guy from earlier spoke up. "And *that* is my problem with the whole thing. Why the fuck would you bring her here? He's going to burn our compound down."

Cruz rolled his eyes, placing my coffee in front of me. "He's fine with it as long as I keep her away from Drake."

"How's that going for you?" the guy deadpanned, assessing me like I was a problem to solve. Drake was rubbing the back of his head, the playful mask slipping from his face as he watched me with concern.

"Sorry. I forget that not everyone's way of expressing themselves is touch. Do you want breakfast? I can make you anything you want."

"It's okay," I said softly. "What are you having?"

"Sliced avocado and tomato on toast. You don't want it."

"I'd love some, actually," I replied. He chuckled lightly, but a smile took over his face at my answer.

"You need to help these other pricks learn to eat properly. They think it's gross," he scoffed as he got to his feet. "Knox tolerates my menu sometimes, but it's rare. Stone would die if he didn't get his bacon for breakfast."

"How are you guys all fit if you eat garbage?" I asked with disbelief, making who I assumed was Stone, raise an eyebrow.

"We don't eat garbage. We just don't eat the bullshit cleansing crap that Drake does. There's nothing wrong with eggs and bacon before a workout. If you like eating rabbit food, go for it."

"Ignore him," Drake said cheerfully as he started slicing up a tomato. "He hasn't been laid in forever and it's fucking with his mood."

"Taking it up the ass regularly isn't something you should brag about when we have a guest," Stone grunted, making me frown. If Drake was gay, then why was he flirting so badly with me?

"Do you have a boyfriend?" I asked curiously, amusement filling Drake's eyes.

"Yes, but if you ask him, then no. Right, Knox? You don't like that label. It feels too gay for you."

One of the guys at the table growled, glaring daggers at him. He'd looked ready to murder me the moment I walked through the damn door, but he'd stayed silent until now. "Shut the fuck up."

"He's a little touchy about it, but don't worry, he doesn't let me touch his butt. Thought you should know so you don't think he's too gross," Drake said sarcastically, my heart hurting for them. If people were being mean to them for choosing to be together, that wasn't fair.

Drake didn't seem bothered by it, but Knox looked ready to bury me so I couldn't tell the world his secret.

"You can do who you want. It's nobody else's business," I said, turning to Knox. "You look mean enough to knock anyone out who talks shit anyway. Why are you so worried?"

Cruz snickered, sitting beside me and motioning to my coffee. "Stop while you're ahead, Hendricks. Drink your coffee."

"I'm just saying," I shrugged, lifting the mug into my hands. "I've been sleeping with Riley, but I'm not gay."

Drake sighed, placing a plate in front of me before moving around the table to sit beside Knox with his own plate. "It's fine. I like him grumpy. Angry sex is awesome."

I cringed, remembering the few times Stanley had fucked me while mad. It was painful, not enjoyable. I couldn't imagine how awful it would be to take it in the ass like that.

"If you're dating Knox, then why are you flirting with me?" I asked flatly as I raised an eyebrow. "I don't want him getting angry at me as if it's my fault you have no self-control."

"That's easy," Drake grinned, shoveling some of his food into his mouth and dropping a piece of tomato on the table before speaking around his mouthful. "We still fuck girls."

Knox got to his feet and stalked off, but no one mentioned it or went after him.

I continued to eat my breakfast silently as the guys talked, and once I was finished eating, Cruz led me back to his room. My dress was freshly washed and folded on the bed, surprising me. "Who did that?"

He glanced at the small pile, a snort leaving him. "Probably one of the girls."

"There's girls here?" I asked, not hiding the surprise in my tone. I hadn't seen any, so I'd assumed the Night Thieves were all guys.

"Of course. There's hundreds of people in our organization, and we don't discriminate. It's definitely male-dominant, but there's a handful of girls here who are some of our top members. They probably heard you were here and snuck in while you were sleeping so you had fresh clothes. Sorry."

"No, it's okay," I said quickly, not wanting him to think I was ungrateful, even if it made me uncomfortable to think someone had been able to sneak in while I was asleep.

I sat on the edge of the bed, touching the fabric of my dress with a sigh. I wouldn't be able to look at it without thinking about Riley banging me on the hood of her car.

"You okay?" Cruz asked gently as he lowered himself

onto the bed beside me, drawing my attention. "You haven't mentioned much about last night."

"There's not much to say," I mumbled, holding his gaze. "I asked her to choose me over racing, and she couldn't."

"I don't know her that well, but I don't think she's intentionally selfish. She's just not used to having to think about other people. She's been racing for years, Luna. I'm not saying you're wrong, but some people just need to be eased into things," he replied lightly. "You definitely shouldn't have been in that car with her though. Who's idea was that?"

My shoulders sagged, my voice soft. "Mine. She was against it, but I really wanted to see why she liked it so much. We'd had an amazing night, but it was ruined. Those races are terrifying."

He gave me a small smile, hesitating before reaching out to playfully tug on the ends of my hair. "It takes a lot to scare a Donovan from what I've heard. If fear is keeping her going, I get it. I get a rush out of my hobbies too."

His touch didn't bother me since I felt like we'd formed a friendship at Beckett's, but I was grateful when he pulled his hand away, not letting his touch linger or making it weird.

I shuffled back on the bed more and placed my feet on the mattress, resting my chin on my knees as I watched him. I didn't want to talk about Riley anymore, I wanted to get to know him better. It was the least I could do since he seemed to give a shit about me. "What hobbies do you have?"

"If you ask Stone, we do surveillance and protection. In reality though? We're trained thieves. Don't tell him I told you that. It's a bit obvious though when everyone calls us the Night Thieves, not that they know it's actually us."

"You steal things for fun?" I asked in disbelief, but he gave me a cocky smirk.

"Technically, yes, but it's our job. People pay us obscene amounts of money to break into places and steal shit. Sometimes we steal things just for us, but usually, we're hired to. Rare paintings, jewelry, artifacts, and the occasional car. It honestly depends on the job."

"You enjoy that?" I scoffed, and he rubbed his hands together with dramatic glee.

"It's the best rush. There's always a chance we'll get caught and end up in prison, but I think that's half the fun."

I stared at him for a moment before blowing out a breath and shaking my head. "You people are weird. I swear I'm the only normal person I know. Everyone's an adrenaline junkie or enjoys the chance to go to prison."

He laughed and then nudged me. "What do you like then? You must have something you enjoy."

"To be honest, I usually just do what other people are doing. I hang out with Riley and my cousin, Landon, or I'm at home with my family. I only go to the shed to watch the cage fighting because of Riley. I don't have something that's just my thing, you know? I like cars, but not as much as Riley. Apart from studying, I guess the only other thing I do is watch romantic comedy movies," I said, sounding confused. I'd never noticed how much I followed people around instead of finding things I enjoyed.

"Maybe you and Riley needed some time apart so you could find yourself, so to speak," he suggested. "Everyone needs a hobby."

"I'm not getting back with her," I stated bluntly, narrowing my eyes at him. If he was only helping me to try and convince me to forgive Riley, he was going to be sadly mistaken.

"You don't have to but take this time to find something you enjoy doing. If you want to learn guitar, I can help with that," he said with a grin, relaxing me slightly. "If it's art or something you want to try though, you're on your own. I don't have a single artistic bone in my body." I chewed on my lip as I tried to think of something I could do, but came up blank. I didn't have many interests. "Stop that," he murmured before pulling my lip from my teeth. "You don't have to think of something right now."

"I've always been her shadow," I answered with defeat as his face softened.

"You're not. You'd be surprised how bright you shine if you actually took a long, hard look."

"You think?" I asked hopefully, and even if he was full of shit, I appreciated him trying to cheer me up.

He tucked my hair behind my ear before tickling me under the chin to make me smile. "I know."

When the door opened, I assumed it was going to be Drake, so I wasn't expecting Beckett and Riley.

Cruz lowered his hand, letting out a sigh. "I don't want you guys fighting. Stone will lose his shit."

Riley kept staring at me, and I was confused as to why she looked like I'd just shattered her heart until I remembered I was sitting in Cruz's room in his clothes. It was obvious I'd stayed here, and it probably looked really bad.

She ran her eyes over Cruz before silently turning and walking back out, but Beckett was furious as she glared at me. "What the fuck, Luna?"

"It's honestly not what it looks like," I blurted out in a panic, flinching as she scoffed.

"You're going to try that excuse? Is this why you left her? You decided you missed dick too much?"

Cruz groaned, getting to his feet. "C'mon, Donovan. I

just let her sleep in here because she was upset and Archer told me to make sure she had her own room. I slept on the couch."

"Fuck you," she spat, stalking closer to me. "I can't believe you'd do this to her."

"I didn't do anything!" My voice was pitchy, fear sweeping through me at knowing she was likely to beat me for this. She was a machine in the cage, so I knew I had no hope if she started swinging.

"She loves you, and you tore her fucking heart out last night, then ended up in bed with Cruz!" she snarled, but Cruz stepped in front of me, blocking her from most likely strangling me.

"You've got it all wrong," he warned, having no problem standing up for me. "Did Riley even tell you what happened last night?"

My heart was hammering in my chest. Apart from the likelihood of getting beaten, if Cruz told her the truth, Riley's secret would be out. Her family would lose their shit.

"She said she and Luna had a fight and Luna bailed from the car and broke up with her. Now move before I fucking make you," she threw back, but he shook his head, standing his ground.

"Riley didn't put Luna first last night in a situation that she should have. I saw Luna walking in the dark on the cameras in Rawson, so I went and picked her up and offered to take her home. She didn't want to go home, so I let her sleep here with her father's permission. You think I'd treat Luna like one of my hookups? You know me better than that."

She was quiet for a moment before speaking to me, her

voice low. "What did you fight about? You two fight all the time, but breaking up is a little bit dramatic."

"If Riley didn't tell you, then I won't either," I said confidently, crossing my arms as I watched her from my spot on the bed.

"Tell me or I'll kick your ass," she threatened, making me swallow nervously. I might have been angry with Riley, but I'd never sell her out like that. She'd been my best friend since birth, and I'd never be petty enough to rat her out when she'd trusted me to keep it to myself.

"You'll have to kick my ass then because I'm not spilling her secrets."

"You two drive me fucking insane," she growled out before turning and leaving the room, slamming the door behind her. Relief flooded through me at knowing I wasn't getting hit, and the sick feeling in my stomach from the fear slowly started leaving me as I dropped my face into my hands, my elbows on my knees.

Cruz glanced at me, letting out a breath. "I'll leave you to get dressed. The door locks. I'll wait in the hallway."

"Thank you," I murmured, waiting for him to leave before getting changed, trying to take my time. I knew Riley wouldn't have just left, and I wasn't ready to face her.

Especially if she thought I'd spent the night here banging Cruz.

Riley

"This was why I was mad at breakfast," Stone said sharply, giving Beckett a dirty look. "You and your people need to stop coming here demanding shit and slamming my doors. I'm close to throwing you all out permanently."

I was only half listening, my chest aching at the image of Luna in Cruz's clothes on his bed. Beckett said they didn't fuck, but I wasn't sure if I believed it. I hadn't even wanted to come here to get Luna, but Beckett insisted on dragging me here by threatening Luna.

She obviously didn't know the whole story, and I'd been worried she'd do as she'd said and end up beating her. As much as I was angry about finding her and Cruz so close in his room, I never wanted to see her hurt.

Luna and Cruz entered the living room, and she kept her eyes on the floor as if waiting to be scolded.

I hated to admit it, but if she'd rebounded with Cruz, it was my fucking fault. She'd been right in calling me out for my bullshit last night, I'd been lying right to her face.

"I'll be back soon," Cruz said to Stone as he jiggled his keys. "I'm taking Luna home."

"Make it quick. You've got a job this afternoon with Knox," Stone growled. "And after this morning's bullshit, I don't want to hear a single complaint."

"Yes, boss," he muttered, turning to Luna. "Come on, Hendricks. Let's get you home before your father murders me."

"Thanks for letting me stay," she said softly to Stone, a snort leaving him.

"I didn't let you do shit."

"Don't be a dick," Cruz warned, giving me a pointed look before leading Luna outside, leaving us behind.

Once they were gone, Stone turned his annoyance to me. "If you don't want your girl ending up under someone else, don't be a cunt. It's simple."

"So I'm supposed to do everything she says?" I argued weakly, his eyes narrowing.

"You act like she demands shit from you all the time.

You wanted a relationship, so now you have to learn to sacrifice shit you like and meet her in the middle. This is why I don't date. I'm not giving up anything for anyone, and I'm too damn busy."

Beckett let out a huff of annoyance, absently toying with her knife in her hands. "How come everyone seems to know what happened except me? What the hell did you do, Riley? If you fucked up, why are we here? You acted like she ran off for no fucking reason."

"You're the one who dragged me here," I grunted, giving Drake a scowl when I realized he was staring at me. "What?"

"You're so stupid," he said with a chuckle, leaning against the wall. "Get your shit together or I'll give her a shoulder to cry on."

"Drake," Stone bit out, not wanting his friend to escalate the situation. "Shut your fucking mouth. Stay away from Luna. Knox would eat her alive."

"He needs a soft woman to soothe him," Drake replied lightly, not taking his eyes off me. "And she needs someone to obsess over her because she deserves it. I thought you were, but it appears you're only obsessed when you want to be."

"Go choke on your boyfriend's dick," Beckett deadpanned, sliding her blade into the pocket of her jeans. "We're leaving. Hunter and Diesel are stopping by this week to buy some more tech. Just a head's up."

Stone grumbled his fake excitement before asking what they wanted, and I pulled a cigarette out and waved it at Beckett. "I'm heading outside."

"I won't be long," she nodded, and I quickly left the massive compound, standing in the sun to get a good look at the property while I smoked. It was massive, and part of it had multiple stories, looking more like a hotel than a compound.

I didn't know much about the Night Thieves, but they definitely had money. I found that strange since they didn't seem to flaunt it.

Their cars were flashy but not brand new, their clothes weren't expensive, and they seemed pretty humble.

I noticed a large truck parked beside the house, and I watched as people unloaded whatever goods were inside.

"Let's go," Beckett said sharply as she materialized beside me. "Stone doesn't like it when we snoop."

"No offense to your friends, but I don't give a shit," I snorted, moving towards the car anyway. "The only nice ones are Drake and Cruz. The rest are pricks."

"Stone's in charge, so he has to keep up appearances of being an asshole. Besides, can you blame them for being wary? They're running a huge criminal organization here of stolen merchandise," she replied dryly, climbing into the driver's seat and starting her Mustang, the engine roaring to life.

"Have you spoken to Reid?" I asked, changing the subject. "I've been meaning to visit him. I heard he's awake."

She drove out the gate and towards the road, not glancing at me as she spoke. "He texted me this morning complaining that he was bored. They were concerned because he had swelling in his brain but it's under control now."

"Do they know when he's allowed to go home?"

"Do you actually know how badly he was injured?" she asked with a scoff. "Just because he's awake, doesn't mean he's okay. He has multiple fractures and breaks in his leg and arm, his head injury is still being monitored, and he had a collapsed lung and internal bleeding. He can't just get to his feet and walk out any time soon."

"I just figured he could heal at home," I sighed, staring out the window. "Turbo's tried to see him, but Raven loses her shit every time."

"Can you fucking blame her?" Beckett snapped, unsurprisingly taking her friend's side. "That prick almost got Reid killed."

I turned to face her, narrowing my eyes. "No. *Reid* almost got himself killed. He knew the risks and still chose to drive in that race. It's not Turbo's fault."

"Then why isn't *Turbo* paying for the medical bills? I bet he's too busy running races to even notice Reid's missing."

"He's devastated about Reid getting hurt," I said angrily, sick of her talking shit about him. "He's closing the races down once the current events are finished."

"He's full of shit. I don't see why you like the guy," she grumbled, and I couldn't help but laugh.

"Says the person who's besties with Zane Evans."

"Zane's got my back. That's different," she said lightly, pissing me off even more. Our entire family was untrusting of others, and for good reasons, but she couldn't tell me Turbo was a problem when she trusted the Devil.

"Yeah, and Ander fucking Lavaro has mine. Just because you don't know him, doesn't make him a bad person."

"Does he know what happened last night?" she asked flatly, and I was suddenly so fucking tired. Tired of the arguments, the secrets, the divide in my family. All of it.

"He witnessed our fight, or he wouldn't know about it. It's not a competition between you two, Beck. I'm not deliberately doing shit to piss you off. I don't want to fight with you, and I don't want to talk about Luna."

She placed her elbow on the window frame, her face twisted with frustration. "I don't mean to take my mood out on you. I'm worried about you, but it's the closest thing I can try to understand compared to everything else. The shit with Ry, Marla bailing, Lloyd. It's too much and I feel like I'm going to lose it. Now you and Luna are fighting, you've been keeping secrets, Reid almost died, and I had a fight with Jett last night on top of everything."

I frowned. It wasn't good if Beckett and Jett were already having problems. They'd only just gotten together.

"What did you fight about with Emerson?"

"Logan. Well, I guess Drake and Cruz too. One of them is always over, and as much as they're good guys, I like my space. Jett sits up gaming with them half the night, then comes to bed and wakes me and Maddox up in the process. I'm sick of it," she huffed, turning onto my street. "I don't mind them coming over, but not every fucking day."

"Want me to chase them out with my bat?" I offered, making her laugh.

"Don't tempt me. Maddox stayed at Mikey's the other night because he's sick of it too. Jett's not selfish, but he always needs company. If Maddox and I are doing crew stuff, I understand why Jett would invite them over for pizza and gaming, but we've been home a lot lately and they're still there."

"Why are relationships so hard?" I mumbled, checking my phone in hopes that Luna had messaged me, but she hadn't. I checked her location to see she was at home, and I wondered if Cruz had dropped her off or if he'd stuck around.

"Cruz isn't into her," Beckett said as if reading my mind. "He likes her, but only as a friend."

"How do you know?"

"I know Cruz pretty well now. If he was interested in her, he'd already have her under him. He works fast," she chuckled, parking out front of the house and shutting the engine off. "I think it's whiskey o'clock, don't you?"

I groaned, getting out of the car as she did the same. "I'm really not in the mood today."

"Please? I'm not ready to go home yet," she joked, but I had a feeling she was serious. I hadn't gotten to spend much time with Beckett since she got out of prison a few months ago, so I bit my tongue and nodded, following her inside the house.

"Alright, but if you're hungover tomorrow after trying to keep up with me, that's your own fault."

80
100
120
140
160
180
200
220
km/h
240
260

Chapter Twenty-Five

Luna

"You don't have to come inside," I said almost too quickly, making Cruz smirk.

"Why not? I'd like to make sure you get inside okay. Trust me, your father would prefer that than me driving off like a little bitch."

"He might shoot you," I warned, completely serious. I'd seen him chase off guys before, and I didn't want him hurting Cruz who'd shown nothing but kindness to me.

"He might not," he teased, opening the car door and climbing out to wait for me to follow.

We hardly got to the door before it was jerked open and Dad was staring at us with suspicion, his voice rough.

"You've got balls, kid."

"I don't want to talk about my balls in front of Luna," he said with a smile before ushering me inside. "She slept alone in my room, she's had breakfast, and Drake didn't fuck her."

"Cruz!" I gasped as my cheeks heated, but Dad snorted.

"Like I said, you've got balls. Come in, I want to talk to you."

I went to argue, but Cruz waved me off. "You worry too much. If the guys you bring home run from your dad, then they're not man enough to protect you from anyone. Choose someone who your dad can respect."

Dad tried fighting a smile but failed, pointing to the kitchen. "Exactly right. Tempest is home if you want to see her."

"Oh, I'm not leaving you alone with Cruz," I said flatly, moving towards the table to get comfortable. "If a girl's not going to protect you from her dad, then she's not worth your time, Cruz."

He chuckled, sitting beside me and ruffling my hair. "Good thing I don't make a habit of meeting the parents then."

I zoned out as they talked business, and I didn't realize Tempest had walked into the room until her fist hit my nose. I cursed as pain spread across my face, blood starting to drip as I glared at her while trying to stop myself from crying.

"What the fuck, Tempest?" I choked out as Dad shot to his feet and grabbed her around the waist to yank her back before she could hit me again. Cruz didn't hesitate to pull his shirt over his head and swat my hands away from my face, gently pressing the material to my nose. I winced as he pinched my nose slightly, and he gave me an apologetic grimace.

"Sorry, Hendricks. Lean forward."

I did as he asked, but Tempest snorted. "Everyone knows you're supposed to tilt your head back to stop a nosebleed."

"No," he scoffed, keeping his eyes on me as he started cleaning my hands with the other end of his shirt. "That causes the blood to run down your throat. If you fill your stomach up with that, you'll end up vomiting."

"Who the fuck are you anyway?" she huffed, giving me a dirty look. "Does your girlfriend know you went and got a boyfriend on the side? And you think I'm a whore."

I could tell Cruz wanted to tear into her but respected Dad too much to push it. I didn't give a shit if Dad got upset with me or Cruz right now. She'd literally just punched me in the face.

"This is Cruz. He's my friend, not boyfriend. Riley and I broke up. I don't think you're a whore, but you seem to keep proving that you enjoy sex with random people so don't get mad when people call you out for it. Now we've caught up on everything, you want to tell me why the hell you just hit me?" I asked, my voice coming out muffled from the shirt that Cruz was still holding against my face.

"What the hell is wrong with you?" Dad growled, keeping a firm grip on Tempest as she tried to come at me again. "Stop it!"

"It's her fault Ryder's gone! She lied and got him sent away! As if he'd want her!" she shouted, and Cruz finally looked at her flatly.

"Ryder's that fucked up on drugs that he has no idea what he's doing. He needs to get clean. Luna wouldn't lie about something like that."

"He wouldn't touch her!"

"Why not? Druggies would hump the grass when they're high if you let them. He was out of line, and he wanted to go and get himself straight. No one forced him. Why would you take his side over your sister's?" he asked with irritation.

"This is why Riley left you," she spat, trying to throw salt in the wound to make me feel like shit. "Even she saw how pathetic you are."

"Enough!" Dad barked, starting to drag Tempest

towards the hallway while speaking over his shoulder. "I'm sorry. Let me deal with this."

"It's fine, I've got Luna," Cruz replied, giving me his full attention as Dad removed Tempest from the room. She'd never turned violent before despite our fights, and Cruz said something I was wondering myself.

"Pretty sure she's on drugs too."

"I think that's what she and Ryder have been bonding over," I mumbled, staring at the blood-soaked material on my face. "I've ruined your shirt."

"It's just a shirt," he shrugged, pulling it back carefully to look. "I think it's slowing down."

"It hurts like a bitch," I grumbled, making him wince.

"Yeah, a hit to the face usually does. I don't think it's broken, which is good. It's going to swell though."

"I figured. Ugh, I can't go to school like this," I complained, but he just smirked.

"Sure you can. Just tell everyone you got in a fight and you won. They'll leave you alone if they think you'll beat them up."

"I basically cry when yelled at, so no one's going to believe I'd inflict violence."

"I'll teach you to throw a good punch," he offered, but I sighed.

"I don't like violence. It makes me feel sick."

"If someone attacks you, it's good to know you can try to hit them to escape. You don't have to fight in the cage or anything like Beckett," he explained with amusement. "Trust me, it's helpful to learn self-defense."

He talked about it for a few more minutes until my nose stopped bleeding, and by then, Dad had joined us with a firm look on his face. He looked frustrated, and I couldn't blame him.

Tempest was out of control.

"Let me look," he sighed, grabbing my chin to keep my head still as he assessed my nose. "I don't know what's gotten into that girl. She's not usually violent."

"I'm fine," I said as I pulled back, getting to my feet to wash my hands in the sink. "Cruz thinks I should learn self-defense."

Dad groaned, running a hand over his face. "Just what I need. The two of you beating each other up in the living room regularly. I think Cruz just wants to spend more time with you."

Cruz smiled, leaning back in his chair and showing off his tanned abs and the tattoo across his chest. It was a skull with crows flying towards his shoulders. He was cute, but he didn't give me butterflies when he smiled at me or anything like that.

I was more than happy to keep him in the friend zone.

"I love spending time with Luna. She painted my nails, see?" He held his hands out that had some of my blood on them, and I cringed.

"Wash your hands, you weirdo."

"I was hoping to make it look like I got ambushed on the way home and had to fight my way out. I'm supposed to be on a job with Knox, remember?" he said with amusement, getting to his feet and moving towards me, nudging me out of the way with his hip so he could reach the water. "I don't think he'll be pleased when I get home."

"I'm surprised Stone hasn't tried calling you."

"He has. My phone's on silent," he grinned, scrubbing his hands as I handed him the soap.

I sensed Dad eyeing us, but I ignored him and dried my hands on the towel on the counter while scolding Cruz.

"He's your boss. You're going to be in trouble."

"It's not like he can fire me. I'm one of the best he's got and his fancy tech is mine," he replied smugly, taking the towel from me when I was done. "I'd much prefer to hang out with you than Knox."

"I don't pay your bills," I pointed out, making him laugh.

"Neither does that fucker. I pay my own bills. I should go though. You sure you're okay?" He studied me, acting as if Dad wasn't right there to help me if I needed it.

"Yep. Thanks for bringing me home and for letting me stay last night." I gave him a smile but he waggled a finger at me like a naughty child.

"And next time you need me, call me. I gave you my number for a reason."

"I promise."

I walked him out to his car and said goodbye, and I wasn't surprised to find Dad still waiting for me when I walked back inside. He looked worried about me, so I knew I'd have to give him some kind of explanation for my breakup.

I gave him a loose version of the fight, and as much as he was annoyed at Riley, he didn't lose his temper about it like I expected, which was a relief.

I pulled my phone from my pocket as a message came through, and I glanced down at it to find Stanley's name on the screen. I opened it, a chill running down my spine at the message. He'd been sending me drunk messages lately, and since I kept ignoring him, he was getting angrier with me by the day.

> Stanley: You think you can ignore me, you stupid cunt? Just wait until I get my hands on you.

I doubted he'd actually touch me, he wasn't violent, but everyone seemed to be proving me wrong lately, and that scared me.

"What's wrong?" Dad asked, snapping me from my thoughts. He'd go on a rampage if I told him Stanley had been bothering me, so I kept it to myself and forced a smile.

"Nothing. I might go and study for a while."

The look he gave me told me didn't believe me, but he let me leave the room without argument.

Riley followed me around school on Monday like a lost puppy. I assumed she'd act unbothered by me and go back to climbing all over the other girls, but I was wrong. Everywhere I went, she was there, and she begged me to talk to her twice despite having an audience. She was freaking out from me telling her to go away, but she didn't keep pestering me, giving me the space I wanted.

She'd always laughed at others who chased someone around desperately, so I could only imagine what people were saying behind her back.

Riley didn't chase anyone, so I was surprised there wasn't an article in the damn newspaper about this.

She was demanding to know who'd hit me too, but I told her to mind her own business and that I was fine. I didn't want her storming over to my place to beat up my sister.

"Hey," Landon said as he jogged towards me, glancing at Riley who was sulking by her car with a cigarette between her lips. It was the end of the day, and she knew I wouldn't let her follow me home.

"Hey," I replied, giving him a small smile. "How are you?"

He snorted, giving me a dirty look. "Don't try to make small talk with me. What the fuck happened between you and Riley? Did she do that to your face?"

"You honestly think Riley would hit me?" I scoffed and watched as his shoulders relaxed, knowing it wasn't her.

"I had to ask. All she'll tell me is that she fucked up. Did she cheat on you?"

"No. Can we hang out at yours and talk? I don't want people here to know anything," I mumbled. We used to hang out at his house all the time, but in the past year or two, we'd been drifting apart. I hated that.

"Of course. Did you drive here?"

"No. I left the Supra at Riley's and haven't organized a new car yet. Mom dropped me off on her way to Stoneleigh this morning," I shrugged, peeking over my shoulder to find Riley's car gone.

Landon took my bag with a smile, his voice cheerful. "Mom's probably at home, but she'll leave us to talk. C'mon, I'll take you to mine for the afternoon and I can drop you back home when you're ready."

I followed him through the parking lot until we reached his deep blue Corvette, and he filled me in on what he'd been up to while he drove. He'd been working his butt off still, and he said his parents were worried about him being overworked. They gave him days off from working at the bar, but he'd show up anyway to help in the kitchen, or he'd end up at Devil's Dungeon offering to help wash glasses or run drinks to people if it was busy.

I was starting to think he was avoiding having five seconds alone. He knew he could talk to me if he needed to, so I didn't question him.

The moment we walked into his house, Jade wrapped me in her arms for a hug. "I've been wondering where you've been! It's good to see you. What happened to your pretty face?"

"It's good to see you too, Aunty Jade. It's still pretty. Tempest just got a cheap shot in," I joked as I sank into her embrace, ignoring Landon's huffing about her being embarrassing, her fire truck red hair tickling my cheek.

The house smelled like cookies and coffee, and she gave me a knowing look when I glanced around the kitchen.

"You're definitely still pretty. Would you two like something to eat? I made cookies a few hours ago."

"I won't say no to your baking. Can I make a coffee?" I asked as I stepped towards the machine, but she hooked her arm in mine to pull me back.

"Nonsense. You two go and hang out. I'll bring you a plate of cookies and coffee when they're ready," she scolded, shooing us from the room.

Landon led me up to his room, where we both laid back on his bed and stared at the ceiling like we used to as kids.

"You know how Riley's involved with the racing stuff?" I murmured after a few moments of silence, making him grunt.

"Yeah. What about it?"

"I went with her on Friday night."

He rolled over to face me, a glare in place. "She fucking took you to a race?"

"Keep your voice down," I hissed quietly, glancing at the door to make sure we were still alone before continuing. "It was awful. People crashed, Riley wouldn't slow down, and they were darting around cars in the dark. It was really dangerous and scared the hell out of me."

"Why did she take you?" he demanded, making me wince.

"She didn't want to, but I begged to go. I wanted to see what it was like."

"So you guys broke up because you didn't like it?" He frowned at that, his brow creasing. "I don't understand."

I sighed, turning to face him. "It took forever to convince her to stop the car, and when I told her I didn't want her to die and to stop racing, she made excuses. I don't want to spend my nights wondering if she's going to come home in a body bag. Since she wouldn't choose me over her death races, I told her I was done. I hadn't figured out my feelings for her anyway, so it was probably for the best."

Jade wandered in shortly after with a tray of coffee and cookies, but she didn't hang around like I thought she would. She used to make excuses to hang around and listen to our conversations. I hoped she couldn't hear us from outside the bedroom, because she'd tell Rory or Marco everything.

Landon was quiet, but he finally took my hand and gave it a quick squeeze before letting go. "I don't think you're into girls, but I've seen you with Riley. You definitely see her as more than a friend."

"I've been bullied at school a lot over it," I mumbled, sympathy filling his eyes.

"I've heard a few rumors. Is it just the girls who Riley bailed on?"

"It's mainly Penny, but others find the whole thing a joke. Riley's a player, and I'm the good girl. It's not supposed to work," I said slowly, but he chuckled, giving me an amused smile.

"Says who? You're not just some girl, Luna. Riley's been in love with you forever. It's not just sex between you two.

From what I heard, Riley threatened Penny for harassing you. She's left and I doubt she'll be back."

"I didn't know that Penny left. It's weird talking about sex with my cousin so let's not," I grumbled uncomfortably. We always talked about everything when we were younger, but now we were adults, some things seemed weird to tell him.

A vulnerable expression crossed his face and he cleared his throat. "Can I tell you a secret? Something that only Riley knows?"

I shouldn't have felt hurt that she knew something that I didn't, but it was hard. I'd always been the first person he told secrets to, but I guess things had changed.

"Of course."

He let go of my hand, rolling onto his back to avoid my gaze. "I'm gay."

"But you've slept with girls?" I said slowly with confusion as I processed his words, his face heating.

"No. Girls made up rumors and I just didn't stop them. There were one or two in early high school, but I didn't like it. It did nothing for me. It wasn't until I met up with some guys that I realized why." He swallowed nervously, still refusing to meet my gaze. "I got into trouble one night. The guy was too rough and he was an asshole. I didn't have my car with me, and I didn't want to call my parents to pick me up because they'd want an explanation."

Understanding dawned on me. "So you called Riley."

He nodded, his voice quiet. "I knew I could openly tell her without judgment, and she's still the only person to this day that knows. Well, other than you now."

"You really haven't told your mom? She'd support you, you know?" I offered, but he shook his head, finally meeting my gaze with shame.

"I don't want her to be disappointed with me. She sees me finding a wife, having kids, and she always asks if I've got a girlfriend. She'd support me, yes, but I don't want her to be disappointed."

"She wouldn't be. She just says that stuff because she assumes that's what you're into. What happens if you meet a guy you really like? Are you just going to keep him a secret forever and marry a woman to keep up this ruse?"

"I haven't figured that part out yet," he murmured. "How did your parents react to you and Riley?"

We talked for a few hours before he took me home, and I scowled as I checked my location app out of habit to find Riley tailing us from a distance. How was I supposed to stay mad at her when she was trying so hard to fix it?

I kept telling her to leave me alone but that didn't mean she was going to stop following me to make sure I was okay.

I wanted to see her, I missed her, but I had to stand my ground.

I said goodbye to Landon and headed inside the moment we arrived, not wanting to get cornered by Riley in the front yard. Mom gave me a concerned once-over as I pressed my back against the door once it was closed and I let out a breath.

"Are you okay? Is someone out there?" she asked with worry, glancing towards the drawer beside me where I knew there was a gun hidden.

"It's just Riley. She's become the stage five clinger that she always bitched about," I said dryly as Dad walked in, his face blank.

"I can go out there and tell her to fuck off if you want."

"She's not hanging around the door. She's just following me in her car as if I don't know she's there."

"I'll make her own mother threaten her," he grumbled,

pulling his phone from his pocket and sending a text. I had no idea what he sent, but he seemed satisfied with the response he got back.

"Where's Tempest?" I asked, his eyes going straight to my swollen nose.

"Considering she's grounded, that's a good question."

"There's a bunch of parties on tonight. She's probably at one of those," I shrugged before glancing at Mom. "Are you working tonight?"

"I was supposed to, but if you want me to stay home, I can get Milky to cover for me," she said straight away, making me smile.

"I'd like that. We can have a movie night."

"You girls have fun," Dad said as he put his phone to his ear and jiggled his keys. "I'll tell Milky he's in charge tonight. I have to meet up with the Soldiers for a few hours, so I'll be home later."

Mom groaned. "Can you and Axel play nicely?"

"The little bitch is sending his guys to deal with me. He can't even face me," he scoffed. "I still owe that fucker a bullet for that time he shot me."

"Oh good. Then you can be twins with matching scars," Mom deadpanned. "Behave."

"Make me," he teased as he shut the door, leaving us to have a girls' night in peace.

Riley

"Riley," Mom called out sharply from the other room as I finally trudged into the house after dark. I'd spent most of the afternoon following Luna around, but she'd made it obvious she didn't want to speak to me. It hurt, but I respected her wishes.

She'd told me not to speak to her, but she'd said nothing about following her.

"Yeah?" I called back as I walked into the living room, finding Mom, Hunter, Skeeter, and Marco watching a movie. Mom didn't look happy as she glared at me with her head on Hunter's lap, and she sat up to point at the chair beside their couch.

"Sit."

"Whatever it is, I didn't do it," I snorted, doing as I was told.

Skeeter sighed, running a hand through his hair as he assessed me. "We understand you're dealing with some shit right now, but—" Mom didn't let him finish, cutting him off as she scowled at me.

"Stop following Luna around. I get it, you're upset right now, but you need to leave her alone."

"She called you?" I demanded, but Hunter shook his head.

"No. She knew you were following her home tonight and when Archer found out, he texted your mother and asked us to politely get you to back off."

"He should be grateful that I'm keeping an eye out. Someone hit her in the face, you know?" I growled, making Marco cringe.

"Her sister did it."

"What the fuck for?" I spat as anger consumed me. Tempest was always a cunt, but I was surprised she'd used violence.

"She's blaming Luna for Ryder's current whereabouts," he answered calmly, but I could tell he was irritated by the whole situation. "She thinks Luna lied about it."

"Tempest's fucking obsessed with him. Luna wouldn't lie about something like that!" I exploded, considering getting back in my car and tracking Tempest down to beat the shit out of her.

"Everyone knows that, but Tempest is struggling with some personal shit, I think. I have a feeling she and Ry had a few struggles in common, and he was someone she trusted to talk to about it. Now he's not here, she's probably just freaking out."

"They don't even see each other much!" I threw back, but Mom gave me a look to shut up.

"I think they text a lot, but Ry's also been spending a lot of time at parties outside of Ashburn Valley lately. They might be hanging out at those and you just don't know."

"She's probably just trying to get knocked up by him so she can live a comfortable life with lots of money," I said flatly, crossing my arms tightly. "She's a gold-digging whore."

"Riley," Skeeter warned, but I snorted.

"What? She is. She sleeps around, wants all of her shit paid for, and—"

"If I do recall, before you started seeing Luna, you slept around regularly," Mom cut in, disappointment in her eyes. "It's unlike you to judge someone for their sex life."

"I fuck people because I like making people come. Tempest sleeps around in hopes it secures her for life. You watch, she'll have a baby daddy in no time."

"Just stay away from Luna, alright? You can't force her to love you," Mom said softly, patting my leg. "She's probably just feeling overwhelmed. If it's meant to be, she'll come back to you."

"Can I go to bed?" I asked, knowing I was being rude, but not wanting to talk about it anymore. I knew I couldn't force her to love me, but I wasn't ready to lose hope that she would.

They excused me to finish their movie, and I headed up to my room through the quiet house. It was strange not hearing Maddox or Ryder yelling at their games or banging random girls, or hearing Beckett working out in the gym.

It was just quiet, and it felt empty now that they were all gone.

Obviously, Ryder would be back in a few months, but that wasn't the point.

I had a hot shower to wash away the day, and once I'd climbed into bed, I checked social media and did one last check of the location app to make sure Luna was safely in bed.

I frowned when there wasn't a marker at her house showing she was home, but my heart sank when I realized she wasn't in the system at all.

She'd blocked me.

80
100
120
140
160
180
200
220
km/h
240
260

Chapter Twenty-Six

Riley

I stood outside of the hospital the next afternoon, smoking and avoiding going inside for twenty minutes before Logan walked out. Luna had been ignoring me, and since chasing her around wasn't weakening her towards me, I figured it was time I visited Reid.

I should've visited him sooner, but Raven didn't like me hanging around now that she knew about my involvement in the races, and I honestly didn't know what to say to Reid. His car wasn't going to miraculously be repaired despite all the money I could throw at it if I had to, and I wasn't sure if he was blaming Turbo or not for allowing it to happen.

That was a stupid thought though because Reid knew what the risks were before he'd climbed behind the wheel.

"Hey," Logan said with surprise when he saw me, walking in my direction. "We were wondering if you were ever going to stop by."

Guilt ate at me, and I blew out a breath of smoke, keeping my hood over my head. "Sorry. I don't have an excuse, other than not wanting to piss Raven off and I've been preoccupied with Luna. I should've visited by now."

He watched me for a moment before replying, leaning against the wall to light his own cigarette. "Raven's only just started speaking to me, so it's probably not a bad thing that you've stayed away. She's really touchy about the whole racing thing. Reid would prefer you spent time with your girl instead of staring at his useless body right now anyway," he chuckled before a crease lined his brow when I sighed. "What? Trouble in paradise?"

"I'm surprised you haven't heard the Ashburn Valley gossip," I muttered. "She doesn't want to be with me, and she's been avoiding me for a week now."

"Did something happen, or did she just decide she's not into pussy?" he asked casually, and I relaxed. He was the first person to not just accuse me of fucking it up, even though I technically did.

"I took her to a race."

"I haven't heard of any races," he scowled, taking offense. "Are we kicked out now or something? Why hasn't Turbo kept us in the loop?" Surprise suddenly took over his face, his jaw dropping. "Hang on, you took her to a race?"

I squashed my cigarette under the toe of my shoe and leaned back against the wall to cross my arms.

"It's not that you're kicked out, but Reid's not exactly in racing condition, and he doesn't have a car. Some pricks from Kingslake wanted to race us, and since Luna was with me when Turbo tracked me down, she asked to come with me. I should've said no," I grunted before shaking my head. "It scared the hell out of her, and she ended up forcing me to pull over and let her out."

"She left you because the race was scary?"

"No. She left me because when she asked me to give it up for her, I didn't put her first. It's fair enough, but I can't just drop out, you know? There's a process."

Logan snorted, calling me out on my bullshit with ease. "It's not like you'd need the refund, it's pennies for you, but Turbo would let you go without a problem. You two have formed a friendship, and he's always respected you. If you wanted out, he'd allow it. You're just terrified to let go of the races because they're the only times you feel that rush you crave."

"That's not true," I mumbled, but he rolled his eyes.

"If the only joy you have in your life is chasing the devil in a death machine, then you really should ask yourself if your feelings for Luna are real or not. Raven told me if Reid and I want to keep racing on the streets, then we can leave. It was an easy choice for us to give it up because as much as we need the fucking money, she's more important. I'd live in a cardboard box if it meant keeping my family together. The moment Luna asked you to choose, you should've turned the car around and gone home with her."

I frowned with confusion. "If you already told Raven that you'll stop racing on the street, then why did you just have a tantrum about being kept out of the loop?"

"Because it just proves the point that Ander Lavaro doesn't have friends unless they're making him money. We haven't heard from him since we ended up here." He seemed bitter, his face twisting with frustration. "And don't change the subject. This is about you."

"You think he doesn't give a shit?" I asked, tilting my head to assess him.

"Why would he?" he replied as if it didn't bother him, but I could tell he was annoyed at the thought.

"You know he tried to visit regularly, right? Raven flipped out every time and he decided it wasn't worth upsetting her. He feels like it's his fault, and to be honest, I think he's a little traumatized from it. He doesn't think you guys will want to see him," I said slowly as he sighed.

"I won't lie, it's going to be hard to see him without Raven assuming he's luring us back into the races. I doubt he'd want to just hang out though," he chuckled, only to pause when I gave him the side-eye.

"He'd love to just hang out. Me, you guys, Blake. He thinks we only want to spend time with him because of the money."

"Oh," he said with a frown. "Maybe we could start hanging out at the track or something. We could still race there. Or just meet at parties for drinks."

"There's no way Beckett will let him hang out at the track after he won against her and made her look stupid in front of everyone," I grumbled. "But yeah, it all sounds like a good idea. How's Reid?"

"Grumpy," he replied, shrugging his shoulders. "He'll appreciate your company though. Pretty sure he's sick of mine."

"Bullshit. Your company's probably keeping him sane," I scoffed. "Has Zavier been by to see him much?"

He finished his cigarette, motioning for me to follow as he walked towards the front entrance of the hospital. "Yeah, but I think he's up to something. He's been bailing at weird times, and some gangster-looking dude was talking to him in the parking lot the other day."

"Considering you hate being judged for being from the Heights, you'd think you'd know not to judge someone for their appearance," I said lightly, but I knew Zavier was probably just trying to run drugs between visiting hours.

If Raven found that out, she'd probably have a fucking mental breakdown.

"It's a habit we pick up from living in our town," he

replied dryly, glancing at me as we reached the elevator. "When someone that looks like they're part of a gang is hanging around, we know something's happening. I didn't say they're a bad person, but even you can admit what your family does is trouble."

"True. It's okay, I'll threaten Zavier," I grinned as we stepped inside the elevator. "Is Raven going to throw me out?"

"She's not here. Zav took her home an hour ago, so you're safe."

He filled me in on Reid's healing process on the way to the private room, and I knew Reid would be losing his shit about it.

He wouldn't be running around for a long time with his fucked leg, let alone everything else. He'd be getting around like an old man for a while, that was for sure, and he definitely wouldn't be driving.

We walked into Reid's room and he gave me a smile. "I was starting to think you'd forgotten about me." He sounded relieved to see me, making me feel like an even bigger bitch. He probably thought I didn't give a shit now that he was out of the races.

"How can I forget an ugly face like yours?" I joked, sitting in the chair beside his bed, and pulling my hood off. "How are you feeling?"

He tried to sit up more, grimacing at the pain. "I'll be doing marathons in no time. How's my car?"

I cringed. "Uh, it's fucked. You can probably salvage some of it, but not much. We'll figure it out though, and you have plenty of time until you can drive again anyway."

"I'll drive myself home. You can't stop me from driving," he chuckled, but his face fell when I snorted.

"With what car?"

Logan huffed, crossing his arms as he dropped into the chair in the corner. "Even if you had your car, you can't drive with your leg."

They bickered like a married couple for ages until I groaned. "You two are ridiculous. You're lucky to even keep your license."

Reid frowned, eyeing me suspiciously. "Yeah. How exactly did that happen?"

"You're welcome."

"Seriously, how did you manage to stop me getting my ass thrown in prison?"

"I'm a Donovan, I get what I want," I said seriously, resting my elbows on my knees and leaning forward. "I did what all entitled rich fuckers do. I paid them off. It was a nasty, unfortunate accident. Nothing more. Pretty sure a cougar ran across the road and caused you to crash."

"Donovan, we don't have cougars here," he deadpanned, making me shrug.

"Maybe he was on a drunken adventure? You know how easy it is to end up in weird places when that happens."

"There's no way in hell the cops filed the report as a cougar issue," Logan cackled, the shadows under his eyes lifting slightly as his cheeks brightened. "How much money did you fucking give them to say that?"

"Okay, so maybe the big kitty cat part wasn't true, but it's still an accident, and I'm not going to tell you what it cost. You'll think badly of me," I said tightly, knowing what people thought of rich pricks throwing their money around as if it was confetti.

"Just how rich *are* you guys?" Reid grumbled, suspicion in his eyes. "It would've cost you thousands for my medical stuff, the car, paying the cops off, and whatever else you've paid for."

"Hundreds of thousands," I corrected, his eyes almost bugging out of his head. "You're in a private room with around-the-clock care, and the cops don't take bribes unless it's worth the risk of going to prison."

"Donovan!"

"Just shut the fuck up and say *thank you, Riley. You're my best friend,*" I said sweetly, cutting off his argument before he could start.

Logan nudged me, a teasing smirk on his lips. "So, do you give out loans?"

"Bite me, Donahue. Loans are only a way for the rich to get richer by taking advantage of those who are desperate. Loans come with interest, which also leads to missed payments and late fees," I reeled off, his eyes going wide.

"Chill, dude. I was only joking."

"You want to know how my family manages to stay rich despite our terrible spending habits?" I offered. "It wasn't too hard for my parents once Mom got her father's money when he died. It was a shitload, including the house and a heap of fancy cars and stuff. They invested a lot into businesses, which is how we have so much power in Ashburn Valley."

"What do you guys own?" Reid asked curiously, making me snort.

"What don't we own is probably an easier question. The real estate companies, two of the main construction companies, gas stations, investment properties, a heap of the stores in the mall, and most of the food joints. Pretty sure they're starting to branch out into other towns, too. I know you guys are getting a new community hall in the Heights, and I think they're helping upgrade the schools."

I could tell they appreciated it, but Reid's smile was sad. "It's a waste of their money. Someone will just burn it down or smash it to pieces."

"They know, but Mom lived in the Heights when she was younger. I think it's her way to try and help other kids that suffer," I replied. "Maybe we should place an MC in the Heights to help clean it up."

Logan gave me a look as if I was crazy. "You think bringing a criminal organization into it will clean it up?"

"Yep. The main issue in the Heights is poverty and kids running around out of control. If we shake things up with a clubhouse and sort out the community center, it will force things to change."

"Or, kids will just join the bikers and you'll lose control of the club," Reid pointed out, wincing as he coughed. "Fuck, that hurts."

We kept talking about random shit until Reid started looking really uncomfortable, and I got to my feet to stretch my legs. "I think I'd better get going. You look like you need a nap and some pain meds."

"I'd argue, but you're not wrong," he grunted, appreciation flickering across his face. "Thanks for stopping by. Next time bring me some real food if you can. This hospital shit sucks."

"I'll keep that in mind," I chuckled, saying goodbye to both of them before heading back down to my car. I automatically checked Luna's location before remembering she'd blocked my access, and there was no point driving past her house since she didn't have a car.

I'd tried to make her keep the Supra, but she refused.

Maddox was fighting at the shed later in the evening, so I grabbed an early dinner at Harley's Bar and hung out with

Landon in the kitchen while he worked, and as much as I wanted to ask about Luna, I didn't. I knew they'd been hanging out a lot lately, but it wasn't fair to put him in the middle.

If he was going to take a side, I knew it would be with Luna since they were family.

I was pretty sure he was waiting for me to ask too since he didn't seem to relax until I was leaving.

Luna

It was Saturday, and Dad had been stressing about Tempest all week. She kept vanishing, but this time I stumbled across someone's Facebook live video which had my sister drunkenly stumbling around a party wearing a skirt so short that her butt cheeks peeked out the bottom.

I didn't want to worry Dad, so I'd asked Mom to borrow her car with the excuse that I wanted to go to the store for sanitary items.

I hated lying, but I wanted to bring Tempest home without Dad causing a scene like he'd done in the past.

The party was on the border of Ashburn Valley and Hawthorne Heights, so it was easy for me to find. Loads of people from school were posting about it online, and the address was even public.

I parked out on the road so no one could block me in, and quickly made my way across the lawn and into the party, the dim lights making it hard to see. People ran into me as they moved around and danced, and I ended up finding the kitchen where the lights were on so people could see the drinks they were pouring. Some were playing beer pong, while others did shots and stumbled around with their friends.

I really didn't see the appeal.

"Excuse me," I murmured to a guy who was pouring a beer from a keg. "Have you seen Tempest?"

His eyes ran over me for a second before he shrugged. "She's probably in one of the bedrooms. You her friend?"

"She's my sister."

He was lifting his drink to his lips but paused when I said that, his eyes running over me again before he snorted. "There's no way in hell you're her sister."

"Why not?"

"She's got tits and an ass," he said without hesitation before walking off, my face heating with embarrassment. A girl walked past me and snickered as she chased after him, but another girl stopped beside me thoughtfully.

"You're looking for Tempest?"

"Yeah. I saw a video of her online and she's wasted. If Dad sees it, he'll show up and cause a scene," I sighed, her lips kicking up into a smile.

"I can take you to her, but she's probably, uh, naked."

"Why?" I asked without thinking, the girl laughing lightly as she motioned for me to follow.

"She's a creature of habit. Get drunk, get laid. She's been getting drunk for hours now, so she's probably found a dick to occupy herself with for a while."

I cringed, hating that people just knew her as the girl who got wasted before sleeping with random people.

She stopped outside of a room that didn't even have a damn door on it, and I peeked inside to find Tempest between two guys. She was riding one while another took her from behind, and when the guy behind her glanced over his shoulder, my breath caught.

Raymond looked way too happy to see me, and he let out a dark chuckle as he slowed his thrusts. "Look what the cat dragged in, Stan."

My heart hurt as Stanley's face came into view, but I wasn't upset at him, I was upset that Tempest would want to sleep with someone I'd dated. I'd told her what an ass he'd been to me, and she'd had the decency to look offended on my behalf.

That was probably the only time she'd been nice to me in a long time, but now here she was, riding him like nothing mattered between us.

Raymond got to his feet, facing me without bothering to cover his dick. "I knew you'd come crawling back to him."

I snapped out of it, taking a step back. "I didn't know you guys were here. I'm here to get my sister," I said firmly, glancing at Tempest to find her glaring at me.

"What the fuck are you doing here?" she spat, her voice slurred. "You think I'll leave with you?"

"C'mon," I begged, not wanting to be here anymore. "Dad's wondering where you are, and there's videos and photos all over the internet of you here. I'm trying to get you home before he shows up and loses his shit. I'm trying to help you."

The girl who'd brought me here had vanished, apparently not wanting to deal with our drama, and Raymond thankfully grabbed his pants and yanked them on.

"You're such a stick in the mud. I have no idea how you and Temp are related. She's a blast."

Stanley was watching me, but he let Tempest continue to ride him like I wasn't even here.

I tensed as Raymond dropped his arm around my waist, his lips against my ear as he spoke. "I don't know what Riley sees in you. You're so fucking bland. Did you know that me and her are basically besties? You're honestly not her type," he chuckled, looking over at Stanley. "Right, dude? The pussy licker loves me."

Stanley snorted, returning his attention to Tempest as he started thrusting up into her. "I don't want to talk about that stupid cunt."

I tried to move away, but Raymond tightened his hold on me. "Where do you think you're going?" He grabbed my waist and tossed me over his shoulder, making me scream as panic took hold.

"What are you doing?" Tempest asked, managing to sound concerned, but Stanley grunted as he finished, pushing her off him.

"We just want to scare her. We won't hurt her," he said lightly, grabbing his pants to get dressed. "Thanks for the ride."

"Wait, we're done?" she growled, and I could see her glaring at me from my awkward angle. "You ruin everything."

"Don't let them take me," I begged as tears burned my eyes, but she scoffed and got dressed, stumbling towards the door.

"They can fucking keep you for all I care. If they want to scare you a little, I'm not going to stop them." Then she was gone.

I fought and screamed until Raymond scowled and dropped me, my arm burning as I hit the floor. "Would you shut the fuck up for a minute? Or I'll shove my cock down your throat."

I scrambled backwards, crying out as Stanley grabbed my hair and hauled me to my feet.

"You think you can leave me for that bitch? You might

have brought your daddy to protect you last time, but he's not here now."

"What do you want me for?" I croaked as I stared at him. "You don't even love me."

He didn't release my hair, making sure I couldn't escape. "I fucking needed you. You only had to stay for six more months and I could've let you go."

"What the hell are you talking about?"

"I picked you because you were placid and sweet. You weren't likely to start problems or get in my way," he hissed, slamming his fist into the wall beside us and making me jump. "Six more months and that money would've been mine, but you fucked it up!"

"Money? What money?" I whimpered, and he let my hair go to shove me against the wall with frustration.

"My money! I only had to prove I was in a steady relationship for three years and my grandfather would hand over what was meant for me! He refused to hand it over to someone who had a sex and drug problem, so he said if I cleaned myself up and got into a steady relationship, he'd give it to me!"

The fact that he'd never loved me stung more than it should have, and I felt stupid for believing it had all been real. I'd just been a cover-up for his partying lifestyle.

"You were only with me because of money?" I mumbled, staring at him and realizing I never really knew him. "Why didn't you tell me?" Pain spread across my chest at knowing I'd been used, and I ignored Raymond as he snickered from close by.

Stanley laughed, his eyes full of hatred. "You honestly think that Riley would've been okay with it? Watching someone use the woman she's obsessed with? There's no chance. You're no use to me, but Raymond has a use for you."

My skin prickled as Raymond moved behind me, his voice low. "I've got some payback to give someone who fucked me over. Don't take this personally."

Stanley drew his fist back and then hit me in the head, knocking me out.

80
100
120
140
160
180
200
220
km/h
240
260

Chapter Twenty-Seven

Riley

I was driving to Devil's Dungeon in the Supra to hang out with Angel when my phone rang, and I answered on the hands-free as Turbo's name flashed across my screen.

"Whatever it is, I don't want to know. I'm about to get ridiculously drunk and—"

"You have to get to the Heights," he blurted out in a panic, making me sigh.

"Not tonight. Are you okay? You sound weird."

"It's Luna."

That had me instantly turning around and putting my foot to the floor towards the Heights.

"What the fuck is she doing in the Heights? Is she hurt?" I asked as fear trickled in. "Where in the Heights is she?"

"Our meeting point at the parking lot. I don't know how he found her, but you have to race to keep her safe, Donovan. I'm not there yet, he called me and—"

"Who called you? What the fuck happened?" I shouted, gripping the steering wheel.

"Slick. He's taken her and won't let her go until you race him. I tried to convince him to let her go, but he's refusing," he bit out with frustration. "You know this is a trap, right?"

"Of course it is," I spat, my engine roaring as I pushed it harder. "I won't leave her with him. Fuck knows what he'd do to her."

"Be careful," he warned before hanging up, and I smacked my fist against the door angrily, barely slowing to turn the corner. I couldn't waste any time. I had no idea if she was hurt, but I knew Slick would've done something to her. It was in his nature to cause fear and pain on the women around him, and if he knew what Luna meant to me?

She could've been black and blue by now.

My tires screeched as I navigated my way through the Heights, and my anger only grew the closer I got to the parking lot. I was going to tear his head from his shoulders when I got my hands on him.

No one fucked with Luna and got away with it.

I sped into the parking lot and slammed on the brakes, only stopping millimeters away from Slick's black Mustang. Turbo was there arguing with him, and Blake stood off to the side looking helpless. I had no idea why she was there when I didn't see her car, but then I realized she must have come with Turbo.

I got out of my car and stalked towards them with my bat in hand, my eyes landing on Luna who was curled up in a ball by Slick's feet, her hair a mess and her dress torn and dirty. Pure hatred filled me, and I turned my attention to Slick who was looking way too smug as Turbo shouted at him.

I appreciated him having my back, but this was between

me and Slick. If he wanted to race, I'd give him one, but only if he let Luna go.

"Let her fucking go before I paint the parking lot with your intestines," I growled, Luna's eyes flashing up to mine as she heard my voice. Her lip trembled, and she sat up with a wince as tears trickled down her face.

"Riley, don't. He's going to hurt you."

"Shut the fuck up!" Slick snarled, not hesitating to knee her in the cheek and make her choke on a sob to get his point across. "This is why Stan can't stand you. You never know when to mind your own business."

"What the fuck does Stan have to do with this?" I demanded, a sly grin spreading across Slick's face.

"He's my best buddy. It's a shame I never got to take Luna for a ride like we'd planned. At least I got to touch her tits, right?"

My eyes dropped to Luna as shame filled her eyes, telling me he wasn't lying. He'd fucking touched her without her permission.

"You're dead!" I snapped as I started towards him, but he chuckled and pointed a gun at Luna, his eyes remaining on me as she started begging him not to shoot, giving me no choice but to stop moving. Turbo was cursing at him but he stood back, not wanting to cause Slick to pull the trigger, while Blake stood silently with her hand over her mouth to stop a scream.

"You want her safe? Then fucking race me. Just you and me."

"Why are you doing this just to race me? Are you that upset I got you kicked out of the races?"

He snickered, tilting his head. "Who knows? Maybe you'll have an unfortunate accident."

I knew my chances of finishing this race unscathed were slim to none, but I had no choice.

If it kept Luna safe from him, I'd risk it all.

"You think you scare me? Do you have any idea what my family will do to you if something happens to me? You'd be tortured for weeks," I hissed. "If you wanted to race me, you didn't have to bring Luna into it. You should've just asked and I would've happily come and beaten you."

I was fighting to stand my ground, wanting to go to Luna and stop her from crying instead.

"You think you can beat me?" he laughed, his eyes narrowing to slits when I smirked at him.

"I usually do."

"Stop wasting time then and get in your car. Let's go," he growled, making Luna sob loudly.

"Raymond, stop it. Leave her alone."

"Get in the car," he ordered, terror filling her face.

"What? No! I don't like going that fast!"

He went to kick her, but he stopped when I called out to him. "Just you and me, asshole. She stays with Turbo and Blake."

"You'll just drive off," he scoffed, a dark chuckle leaving me.

"It's cute that you think I'm scared to race you."

He sighed, glancing at Turbo. "You honestly want to babysit this brat?"

"Just let her stay with me and get going. Riley won't back out of a challenge," Turbo scowled, slowly stepping towards Luna while keeping his eyes on Slick and the gun in his hand.

He let him approach, and once Luna was tucked under Turbo's arm by his Supra, Slick motioned to my car with his gun.

"Get in then. If you fuck me over, your girl's dead, Donovan."

"All this talking is making me think you're trying to delay our race," I taunted, glancing at Turbo and giving him a nod. "Get her the fuck out of here. Get her to your place or something."

Luna's eyes went wide, and she tried to reach for me in a panic, but Turbo kept a gentle but firm hold on her to stop her running towards me. "Don't do it! Please, Riley!"

I opened my car door, giving her a reassuring smile. "Go with Turbo, okay? I know what Slick's capable of. He's the reason Reid's in the hospital."

I slid behind the wheel, but she spoke again, halting me from closing the door.

"I love you. Please don't race."

I peered over at her, giving her a confident wink that I hoped hid my concern. "I love you too, baby. Which is why I have to do this."

I was grateful when Blake moved to her other side to calm her down, and I knew Luna was in good hands. Blake and Turbo had become really good friends of mine, and as much as I struggled to trust them in the past, I knew they'd keep Luna safe for me.

I closed the door and put my window down to speak to Slick as he started his car and drove closer to me. "Where's the start and finish?"

"We start here, and it ends at the Rawson Grove sign. No rules," he smirked, making me roll my eyes.

"Obviously. The only way you can beat me is by cheating, after all."

"When you're lying in a ditch bleeding out, I hope you know I'm going to fuck your cunt until your last breath," he snarled, a snort of amusement leaving me.

"We all know you can't fuck girls without them being intoxicated or unconscious, so there's no need to brag."

He started cursing me out, but I wasn't paying attention. I kept my eyes on the others who were watching us with worry. Turbo was murmuring something quietly to Luna, but her eyes were on me. I hated that my world had collided with hers like this, and if I had the opportunity to take Slick out, even if it put me at risk, I'd take it.

We lined up and Slick made Blake call the race, and the moment she shouted go, I slammed my foot down on the gas and yanked my foot off the clutch, my car jerking forward as I started shifting through gears. I didn't pay attention to Slick until we were on the main road, and he caught up to me.

My phone rang, and I glanced at the screen to find Cruz's name, so I quickly hit answer on the hands-free. "I'm a little busy, dude."

"You didn't turn your location off. I just got a call from Beckett, and they're coming out here to beat you up for racing. Hunter's watching you on the Height's surveillance."

I cursed, narrowly avoiding a parked car that seemed to come out of nowhere in the dark.

"Tell Beckett to stay home. I don't want her to see how this is likely to end."

"What the hell does that mean?"

"I need you to do me a favor," I continued, my tires screeching as I took a corner too fast and almost lost control. "I need you to go to Luna. Turbo and Blake are with her. She's going to need you."

"Tell me what the fuck is going on, Donovan," he snapped, his car keys sounding in the background as he barked orders at someone.

"Slick took Luna to force me to race him. I'm not stupid, I know he'll have plans for me like what he did to Reid. Go to her, Cruz. Please. She trusts you. We're finishing the race at the start of Rawson, but I don't know if we'll make it that far. If you see us, keep fucking driving to her, alright? I'm counting on you."

Slick's car tapped the back of mine, but I managed to keep it on the road despite my impending heart attack.

"I've got eyes on you. We can cut you guys off and stage some bullshit that won't seem like you're involved," Cruz said quickly, starting his car. "It's hard to set something up in the dark that you'll be able to see yourself in time, but—"

"No, go to Luna," I demanded, dodging a few late-night drivers as we sped through suburbia. "Tell Beckett to back off too." Then I hung up.

Slick and I were neck and neck as we reached the next road, and this time when his car clipped mine, there was no saving it.

Tires squealed as they skidded on the road, and panic consumed me as I started rolling. I couldn't hear anything else other than my heartbeat and the crunching of my car turning to scrap around me, and all I could think about was it was all because I hadn't played my music.

I knew that was what kept me alive every other time.

My vision blurred as my head smacked into the window, and blood pooled in my mouth as I bit my tongue. If Cruz and Turbo didn't keep Luna safe for me, I was going to come back from the dead and kill the pair of them.

The last thing I saw before blacking out was Slick's car on its side close by, turning the air around us silent.

I'm sorry, Lou.

Luna

"Riley's going to kill me for this," Ander grumbled as he drove after them, making me growl.

"I don't give a shit. I want to make sure she's okay." I was sitting on Blake's lap since his car was only a two-seater.

"I'll remember you don't care about my life when you need my help next time," he threw back lightly, but there was no anger behind it. He was just as terrified for Riley as I was.

We were driving a lot slower than they'd been going, but I knew we'd find them eventually. Riley hadn't turned her location off, so it was easy for Ander to track her. He frowned the closer we became, his voice wary. "Why the fuck did they stop there?"

A sick feeling seeped into me, but Blake was the one to speak. "Drive faster."

I held on as he gained speed, my stomach twisting as fear spiked. I had no idea how any of them could go this fast in the dark without hitting anything, but that was the last thing on my mind the moment we drove onto the road that Riley was stopped on to find a car engulfed in flames.

"Fuck," Ander cursed, driving closer before parking, all three of us bailing from the car. It was dark here, only the flames lighting the street up, but as we ran towards the car, we noticed another one further away. Relief hit me as I realized Riley's car wasn't the one on fire, and before I could run to her door to try and yank it open, an arm banded around my middle to haul me back.

"Hendricks, don't."

I glanced behind me to find Cruz, his face twisted like he was in pain. "I need to help Riley!"

"You girls stay back. We'll get Riley out," he promised,

and Blake took my hand to keep me beside her, leaving the guys to inspect the damage. Cruz had Drake with him, and all three of the guys managed to get her door open despite it being a mess. I waited until Blake released her tight hold on me, and the moment she did, I started running towards the wrecked Supra.

She cursed and chased after me, but I got to the car in time to see blood in Riley's blonde hair, a sob leaving me and making the guys glance back. Cruz cursed, but then I heard Riley's voice, my heart practically stopping at the sound.

"I thought I told you to get her back to your house?" she scolded Ander, and I shamelessly shoved him out of the way to see inside the car properly, finding her bleeding from the head, but very much alive as she glared at Ander.

"I thought you were fucking dead!" I snapped angrily as I tried to control my emotions, a slow smirk spreading across her bloodied lips as her eyes shifted to mine.

"You sound upset that I'm alive. If you need me to do a better job next time—"

Sirens filled the air, and engines revved in the distance, signaling the arrival of her family. There was no mistaking Beckett's Mustang or Skeeter's McLaren.

Cruz gently patted my shoulder, his voice low. "We need to get her out. Can you move, Donovan?"

"You can't move her!" I exclaimed. "She might have spinal injuries!"

"I'll risk it," Riley said dryly, offering Ander her hand. "Help me out, asshole."

"Since you asked so nicely," he deadpanned, gently easing her from the car until she was on her feet. She swayed slightly, leaning back against Ander so he could help hold her up. Her legs were like jelly, and he sighed before bending down to pick her up, ignoring her protesting. "Shut up. Let me carry you away from the car so you can sit down somewhere. It's not safe here."

They argued as he carried her towards the road, and Cruz's arm dropped around my shoulders to stop me from looking at Slick's car as it burned to a crisp. He wasn't lying around injured, so I assume he'd burned to death, just like Lloyd had.

We didn't get far from Riley's car before flames from Slick's wreck ignited the Supra, and I jumped as the explosion rang out around the street.

Tires skidded close by and I glanced up to see Beckett running towards us, pure terror on her face. "Riley!"

Ander turned, and Riley instantly tried to calm her sister down. "I'm okay. You can't get rid of me that easily."

"You're dead to me," she threw back, but she gently touched Riley's head, inspecting the injury. Skeeter, Rory, and Tyler joined us, and the moment Tyler took Riley from Ander, Skeeter snapped.

He grabbed the front of Ander's shirt and held a gun to his head, a scream leaving both me and Blake.

"I've warned you, you little punk," Skeeter snarled, but Riley fought against Tyler's grip until he cursed and put her on her feet.

"Don't hurt him. He just saved me!" she shouted almost hysterically, telling me just how close to losing it Skeeter was. Riley sounded scared, which was rare.

Ander appeared to be calm, but fear flashed in his eyes, giving him away.

"You wouldn't be in this mess if it wasn't for him! You promised us you weren't involved!" he bellowed, not removing the gun from Ander's head. "And this motherfucker—"

Everyone shut up as loud sobs left me, and Skeeter cursed before putting his gun away, letting Ander go. "What the fuck are you doing here? Were you in the damn car?"

I shook my head, struggling to get air in as I kept crying, and soon found myself pulled against Riley's chest.

"It's not your fault, baby. It's okay," she murmured softly before glancing at her family. "We need to get out of here. We can discuss this at home."

Rory snorted, her eyes blank of emotion. "If you think the cops won't know that's your car, you're mistaken. You might as well stay here and save them the hassle of showing up on our fucking doorstep later."

Ander looked torn before speaking, his voice calm. "Riley had no choice. Slick took Luna and would only let her go if Riley agreed to race him. He ran her off the road and caused the crash, just like he did to Reid. I won't lie to you, Riley's raced at my events before, but this wasn't something I'd planned. It was all Slick."

Skeeter turned thunderous, his voice sharp. "Why the fuck would you allow someone to act like that in your races? He almost killed Reid, and now my daughter. Why did he challenge her? Where is the prick?"

It was quiet for a second before he replied. "He didn't get out of his car. He's gone, and he wanted to hurt her because, after Reid's accident, Riley made me kick Slick out of my events. There's no rules on the streets, but we all raced fairly, except for him. He blamed Riley and thought he could hurt her and get away with it, but he must have lost control himself."

Everyone stared at the burning car, and I eyed Beckett who was looking pale, but Maddox appeared out of nowhere, pulling her against him to let her draw strength from him. She seemed to calm down instantly, and envy burned inside of me.

They were soulmates, and I hated to think I'd never have that. I snapped out of it as Riley kissed the top of my head, tightening her hold on me, and suddenly realized that I'd calmed from her touch too. I hadn't been lying when I'd told her I loved her before her race, but I wasn't sure if we could mend what we'd broken.

The sirens grew closer, and Skeeter pinned us all with a glare. "No mention of street races. We'll handle it. If you're asked directly, this was a onetime thing, got it?"

We all nodded, and Riley kept her hold on me as the ambulance, fire truck, and police cars arrived, filling the rest of our night with endless questions and interrogations. Ander was taken to the station for questioning due to his street racing connections, and Riley was ordered to go to the hospital.

I didn't want to let go of her, but she needed to get her head injury checked out properly. She was lucky to be alive considering the state of her Supra.

Tyler stood beside me as Rory went in the ambulance with Riley, and Skeeter was still trying to deal with the cops. Cruz, Drake, and Blake stayed with me, and Tyler let out a sigh.

"I'd better get you home. Your father's going to fucking kill me, then you."

"Hey," Cruz said firmly, trying not to draw attention to us. "She had no say in this. She was fucking kidnapped."

"You want to tell me why you and Drake are here? How are you involved?" he replied without reacting, keeping his eyes on the cops. "I doubt this incident was a surprise to you."

"Beckett called me to say she was coming to get Riley, so

I called Riley to warn her. She told me to look after Luna, so I jumped in the car with Drake who was keeping tabs on Riley on surveillance. We got here just after the crash, and Turbo, Blake, and Luna arrived too. We don't get involved with other people's personal business, so yeah, we knew Riley had been racing. She's an adult, so it wasn't our problem, no offense," he said with a shrug. "We've hacked the cameras so any recording will just play repeats of the street instead of tonight's events. You're welcome."

Tyler finally turned, his jaw tight. "How long has she been racing? And thanks, I doubt Hunter was worried about hiding evidence after watching our daughter almost die. He's a little preoccupied."

"You'll have to ask Riley that. She won't lie now that she's been caught," he said lightly. "And I'll take Hendricks home. I promised Riley I'd look after her."

He raised an eyebrow, giving me the side-eye. "You know her father's going to strangle you, right? Look at her, she's all roughed up and dirty."

"Archer loves me, I'll be fine," he said confidently, turning me towards his car. "Give me a call if you need something wiped."

"Except your butt," Drake grinned as he fell into step with us, speaking over his shoulder. "You can handle that yourself."

I slid into the back seat, and Blake popped up beside the car, giving me a small smile. "Tell Donovan to call me when she's got a moment. I want to check up on her."

I nodded, motioning to the spare spot beside me. "Do you need a ride?"

"Nope. Ander gave me his keys to make sure his baby got home okay," she said dryly, jingling the keys as if to prove it. "I hope you're alright. Slick's an absolute asshole."

"I'll be fine. Get home safely."

She gave us a wave and walked towards Turbo's Supra, and we waited for her to leave before we pulled away, heading towards Ashburn Valley.

Cruz glanced in the rearview mirror, concern in his gaze. "He didn't touch you, did he? I've heard bad shit about that guy."

"Not today," I grumbled, his eyes narrowing.

"He's touched you before?"

"He was best friends with Stanley, my ex. He has a habit of sharing girls with him, and he let him get a little handsy with me one night. He's never raped me or anything if that's what you're worried about," I offered, a snort leaving him as he returned his eyes to the road ahead.

"He had no right to touch you at all. You have a bit of a bump on your temple. Did he hit you?"

I absently reached up to touch it, wincing at the tenderness. "Stan hit me to knock me out. That's how Raymond, uh, Slick, got me in the first place."

"They knocked you out? You might have a concussion," Drake said as he peered over his seat at me. "You should get checked out."

"Dad will probably keep me up all night, so it's fine," I said, waving off his concern. "You can just drop me off and—"

"We're walking you inside. End of story," Cruz cut in. "You think he'll be pissed that we showed up with you? I'd bet money on his being even angrier if we just dumped you and took off. We'll stay with you while you explain what happened, then we'll leave."

"You're going to make a really good husband one day, you know?" I murmured, amusement filling his face as he glanced in the mirror at me.

"My chances of marriage are slim to none. My luck, I'd probably get caught stealing the damn ring from somewhere and get locked up again. Juvie sucked so I really don't want to go to prison."

"Stop stealing things then."

"It's way too much fun," he said with a chuckle. "And besides, I'm a one-night only kind of guy. I don't need a relationship."

"I find it hilarious when guys say dumb shit like that. Those who do are usually the sweetest guys in the world and low-key hate not having someone they can dote on," I said with amusement, noticing his fingers tighten on the wheel slightly. "It's a shame too because you really are a nice guy, Cruz. You're basically waving a banner above your head that says *boyfriend material*."

Drake let out a sigh, staring out the window. "There's no point getting close to someone and bringing them into our world. No one wants to live at the compound, and we basically work twenty-four-seven. It's not exactly romantic."

I was silent for a second before replying, hoping I didn't offend him. "Is that why you and Knox have a thing?"

"I love that bastard, but it's complicated," he replied. "If Knox was given the option of me or women, he'd cut me off in a heartbeat."

I frowned, but Cruz rolled his eyes. "This got depressing real fast. Play *I spy* or something."

"It's dark," I deadpanned.

"You'll have to look really hard then," he teased as we entered Ashburn Valley.

We talked about random things the rest of the drive like my classes and some jobs they went on, despite me knowing Stone would kill them for telling me, and I wasn't surprised when we walked into my house to find Dad sitting at the kitchen table looking ready to explode.

I hesitated, but Cruz gently pushed me forward with his hand on my back, apparently having zero fear towards my father.

"It's three in the fucking morning," Dad said sharply, his eyes running over me. "What the hell happened to you? And why are these assholes with you when you were with Stanley?"

I tensed, eyeing him suspiciously. "What do you mean?"

"Your sister said you were at a party with Stanley and his friends. It's the only reason I didn't chase you down and murder you for not letting me know where you were. She brought your mother's car home, by the way."

Tears burned my eyes, and Cruz led me towards a chair to sit down as I replied. "I was at that party to bring her home so she didn't get in trouble. She was banging Stanley and Raymond when I found her." I took a deep breath, looking away from him as I continued. "They finished and decided to torment me, and Tempest let them. Once she ran off, they knocked me out and Raymond kidnapped me. I don't know how she got the keys from me."

Dad's eyes flicked between the guys, his voice low. "These two helped you?"

A tear fell, and I quickly swiped at it. "Raymond took me to get revenge on Riley. She was involved in some street racing stuff, and she got him banned because he's the guy who almost killed Reid."

I jumped as his fist slammed down on the table, his voice loud enough to wake up the whole house. "This is Riley's fucking fault?!"

"No. It's Raymond's fault. He took me and said the only way he'd let me go was if Riley raced him. He wanted to hurt her, so he ran her off the road. I thought she was dead," I choked out, his expression softening as worry crept into his gaze.

"Where is she?"

"The hospital. She walked away from the wreck, but she's got a head injury and she's in bad shape. Raymond crashed too, and he burned to death like Lloyd did," I whispered. "Ander kept me safe, but now he's been arrested, and Riley's parents are blaming him. Riley had no choice, she wanted to keep me safe from Raymond. I told her not to, but—"

He took my hand from across the table and gave it a squeeze. "It's okay. Are you hurt?"

I explained the knock to the head, and my legs were grazed from being thrown on the ground at the parking lot when we'd arrived.

Once I'd answered all of his questions, he turned to Cruz. "Thank you for bringing her home. Again."

"I don't mind. I wanted to make sure she got here okay," he replied with a shrug and nudged Drake. "We'd better go. We bailed on the boss when we found out what was happening, and he was a little pissy at us."

I thanked them again, and Cruz gave me a wink before saying goodbye, Drake following behind and quietly shutting the door.

Dad ran a hand over his face, seeming tired all of a sudden. "Have you been going to the street races with Riley?"

"No. She never wanted me involved, but I begged her to take me one time. I hated it, and we had a huge fight. I told her to quit, and she said she had to finish the races first," I said quietly, wrapping my arms around myself.

"That's why you broke up," he stated seriously, waiting

for me to nod before he sighed. "I'll speak to Tempest in the morning. She shouldn't have left you or lied to my damn face."

"Can I go to bed?" I asked, fatigue hitting me. "Please? Wake me every few hours if you're worried about me having a concussion but I really need some sleep."

"Fine, but don't go anywhere tomorrow, okay? Not without letting me know."

"Promise," I mumbled, getting to my feet and padding to my room.

I didn't even get changed before curling up in bed and passing out from exhaustion.

80
100
120
140
160
180
200
220
km/h
240
260

Chapter Twenty-Eight

Riley

I hated it when Mom was silent. It meant she was plotting murder or something equally terrifying. The hospital had wanted to keep me in for twenty-four hours to monitor me, much to my annoyance, and Mom wouldn't leave me alone in case I ran off.

It was nine in the morning, and I hadn't slept because she kept watching me like a hawk. My body was aching, but I was on some good pain meds, so it was bearable.

I was definitely more comfortable now that Jensen had dropped me off some clean clothes.

"You can go home," I grumbled from the bed, making her snort.

"I want to keep my eyes on you. You're grounded for life."

"I'll move out," I sassed, not surprised by her answer.

"I'll fucking follow you," she grunted, her face falling slightly. "Am I that much of a bad mom? Marla hates me so much that she's running away, everyone keeps moving out, Ry's in fucking rehab, and now you're trying to kill yourself on the road."

"You know the rush you get when you're in a shootout?" I murmured, holding her gaze. "The power you feel with the hint of fear? That's what I feel behind the wheel. The track doesn't bring the adrenaline rush I crave, but the streets? It's the best rush of my life. Beckett likes to race on the track and fight, Marla likes to read, Ry likes to party, and the others are all out doing their own thing. I don't want to die, and it's really hard to explain to someone who doesn't get a kick out of it."

"You should've called me the moment Ander told you Luna had been taken. We would've shown up and gotten her back without you having to race," she said with frustration. "You were the one kid who always came to me when you were in trouble. What changed?"

I looked down at my hands, toying with them on my lap. "Lloyd died. No one's been the same since."

She seemed to think about it before getting to her feet, and moving to sit on the edge of my bed. "I know I pulled back from you kids when he died, and I'm sorry for that. I had no idea how to process it myself, let alone help you through it."

"It wasn't that," I said softly, reaching out to take her hand. "I'm an adult now. I needed to learn to figure out my own problems, and you needed to grieve him without worrying about us. We don't like to bother you."

"Baby, nothing you kids need help with will ever be a bother to me," she promised, sincerity in her gaze.

"We know you tried to act as strong as possible when he died," I whispered, my voice cracking with emotion. "But we'd hear you crying when you thought you were alone. If you didn't have to worry about our grief, you could focus on yours. You might be a mom, but you're also your own woman too. We're adults, and we understand that."

"I miss him so much," she choked out, squeezing my hand as devastation washed over her. "I might not have birthed him, but he made me a mother. He grew into the most caring, sweetest man."

"I miss him too. I'm sorry for scaring you," I mumbled. "And for breaking your trust. I just loved the rush of danger, and it became a part of me. Has Dad already wrecked the Corvette?"

She sighed, letting my hand go to rake her fingers through her hair. "We're not going to destroy your car." She looked tired, as if I'd made her admit defeat. I wished she'd go home and rest, but every time one of my dads showed up to take her, she shooed them away again.

I sat up straighter despite my muscles screaming at me. "You're not? But I fucked up."

"I think you learned your lesson, don't you?" she chuckled dryly. "And you're Supra's burned to a crisp already. I need you to promise me you won't race again unless it's on the track."

"You'll believe me?" I asked with surprise, her expression hardening.

"This is your second chance. You don't get another one after this, okay?" Her eyes bounced between mine as she waited for an answer. Turbo wouldn't run another race now even if he didn't get thrown in prison, not after almost losing both Reid and I, and I had no intention of racing with anyone else.

"I won't race again. Turbo was finishing up anyway, and I don't want to go through anyone else. I'll just have to convince Beckett not to kill him so he can race me on the track instead."

She studied me, her lips set in a firm line that she rarely threw my way.

"I don't want you associating with him anymore."

"If you forbid our friendship, my agreement will only be a lie," I answered honestly. "He's one of my best friends, and he's had my back a lot. I need your word that he won't get hurt. It wasn't his fault. I know Beckett had plans for him that you most likely approved of."

"Are you caught up in his other business deals?" she asked lightly, her eyes not leaving mine. "I want the truth since I'm pretty sure you've been stringing me along with a lot of lies lately, and I can't promise you shit about his safety. Yes, Beckett and Maddox were doing Psychos' business at the track that night."

It hurt to know she'd gone behind my back like that, but I let it slide. That wasn't what was important right now, making sure she didn't try again was my priority.

If she got to know him, she'd probably like him.

I blew out a breath, keeping my voice low. "You know the night in Crestford? Where the Supra got shot at and Zavier was with me?" She nodded, waiting for me to continue. "Turbo had asked me and Reid to help him move some crystal. Reid refused, but the rush was too tempting for me. I agreed, and Zavier found out and refused to let me go alone. The rest was true, those Crestford brats chased us down because they'd been told to tail anything connected to Turbo, but the burning cars were Turbo's work, not theirs. There's been no other times I've done runs with him though, because if I wanted to do that shit for a living, I'd just join the crews."

"Are the races how you know Blake?"

I winced, knowing she'd give Blake a talking-to. "Yeah. We've been racing together for a few years now. We've all become really good friends lately, except Slick who's always been a problem."

"Is he the guy who Stone and Cruz had to help deal with in Rawson that time at the gas station?" she asked flatly, waiting for me to nod before she let out a sound of annoyance. "I'm so pissed he's dead and I can't tear him apart myself. I can't believe so many people knew about you being involved with the races, but no one said anything. I thought they were loyal to Beckett."

"If they had to choose her or me, they'd choose her," I shrugged, ignoring the jealousy that spiked inside of me. "They just stay out of personal drama. If Stone had been asked directly, he wouldn't have lied. He doesn't like me."

Mom laughed, amusement filling her eyes. "You honestly think that? If Stone didn't like you, he would've ratted you out real fast, and Cruz has been hanging around reception with Logan most of the night too."

"Beckett hates me," I grumbled, but Mom gave me a reassuring smile.

"She's scared for you, that's all, and she'd be feeling overwhelmed with information too. You know she has trust issues, and she probably feels betrayed by her friends right now. Give her some time to calm down, okay?"

"Does Ryder know?" I asked on an exhale, not wanting to fuck up his recovery despite being angry with him.

"No. We're still not allowed to contact him, but we don't want to worry him even if we could tell him. You're okay, so you can tell him about it when he comes home. Unless you don't want to see him," she said seriously. "I know Luna wants to visit when it's allowed."

"I don't understand why she's so persistent about it. He assaulted her."

"Yes, but she knows he wasn't himself and she wants to help him heal by forgiving him," she murmured. "She's a sweet girl. Way too good for our family."

"There's no excuse for Ry's behavior. What if he'd raped her? That's all I can think about," I said softly. "How can I forgive him? I'm so angry about it. Luna might be a gentle soul, but I'm not. I want to beat him bloody for what he did."

"I know, baby," she replied, lying down beside me and carefully pulling me in for a cuddle. "We'll all figure it out together as a family, I promise. Get some rest. We can talk later."

"Don't you have badass crew stuff to do?" I joked, but she just held me tighter and got comfortable. I didn't dare tell her she was hurting me. She already felt bad enough and she needed this, so I pushed the pain away and let her hold me.

"Nothing is more important than you kids. Today, I'm just Mom. I'll be here when you wake up."

It was sweet of her to say, but I knew she was just tired herself.

Especially when she fell asleep minutes later.

"Hey," I smiled as I poked my head into Reid's room later that night since Mom had thankfully agreed to go home at dinnertime when Skeeter and Diesel showed up. I was supposed to stay in bed, but I got bored quickly and figured I'd visit Reid.

It was the early hours of Monday morning, and I was surprised to see him sitting up in bed, wide awake on his phone.

His eyebrows almost hit his hairline when he saw me, and he seemed to run his gaze over me multiple times as he looked for any damage. "Hey. Logan said you totaled the Supra?"

I closed the door as I stepped into the room, making my way to the chair beside the bed to try and get comfortable. My body ached and my head hurt like hell now that my pain meds were wearing off, but I was grateful not to have broken bones like Reid.

"Technically, Slick totaled it," I replied with a huff, giving him the rundown of what had happened.

He was quiet as I explained everything, his brow creased with worry. "Is Luna okay?"

I sighed, shrugging my shoulders. "I think so. She was taken home, and I haven't seen or talked to her."

"Call her."

"It's late as fuck, and as much as my phone's in one piece, the battery's dead. I'll see her when I get out if she even wants to see me. Now she knows I'm alright, she'll probably go back to hating me."

I tried acting like it didn't bother me, but I heard the pain in my voice. I'd become such an emotional wreck.

"There's no way in hell that that's going to happen," he chuckled, wincing and pressing his palm to his chest. "I'm glad you're not feeling like I am right now. This sucks."

"I have no idea how I didn't break any bones," I admitted. "The Supra caught fire not long after the guys helped me out of it. Pretty sure I'm supposed to be dead right now."

"You and me both," he sighed, typing on his phone for a moment before looking back up at me. "Turbo's freaking out."

"You're talking to him right now?" I asked, snatching his phone the moment he nodded, hitting the call button and making Reid snort.

"You're welcome."

I ignored him, growing impatient as it kept ringing until Turbo finally answered, his voice rough. "You're worse than a woman, asshole."

"I am a woman," I said dryly, his attitude changing completely as panic filled his tone.

"Donovan? Shit. Are you okay? No one will tell me anything."

"I'm fine. Only bruises and a few cuts with a concussion," I explained. "How long did the cops hold you for?"

"I only got out a few hours ago. They've done their investigation and can't prove I was involved," he chuckled but it sounded forced. "And I'm glad you're alright. Should you be on the phone if you're concussed?"

"You worried about me?"

"Between you and Reid, I've had enough heart attacks to last me a lifetime," he grumbled, but there was teasing in his voice. "You're never racing again, you know that, right? Blake and I were talking an hour ago, and I'm pulling the races. She's basically the only racer I have left anyway."

"I figured. If I can convince my family to leave you alone, I'm hoping you'll race me on the track sometime. You're actually a challenge," I answered, making Reid laugh.

"He'd better come and race us there, or I'll assume he's a pussy."

"I heard that," Turbo muttered, the sound of him lighting a cigarette reaching me before he replied again. "But of course I'll come kick your asses on the track if me showing up won't end in me dying."

"I'll keep you safe," I grinned, putting my feet up on Reid's bed. "Do you know how Luna got home? I haven't heard from her."

"Cruz and Drake took her," he confirmed.

"How do you know? Have you seen her?" I asked hopefully.

"I'm with Cruz right now."

That surprised me. They weren't exactly friends or anything. "You're hanging out with Cruz? Where?"

"In the hospital parking lot. Are you coming down for a smoke or not?" he asked, and I could hear the smile in his voice. I hung up, getting to my feet and grabbing the wheelchair in the corner.

"What are you doing?" Reid asked slowly as I placed it beside his bed.

"I'm breaking you out of here for a while. Cruz and Turbo are outside," I replied, frowning at him. "Can you even get out of bed, or do you have a catheter in?"

"I made them take that shit out when I informed them Raven was bringing some of my clothes in so I could get out of that fucking gown. Logan's a good buddy and he's always here to help, so the nurses only have to deal with me when he's not here."

"What leg damage do you have?" I questioned as he pulled the blanket back, showing me the full leg cast he had on one leg, and a brace around his other ankle.

"My whole leg and foot's fucked, but my other ankle's just got a bad sprain. I'm not supposed to be on it."

"Can you get in the wheelchair with your fucked-up arm?"

"Yeah. I'll probably need help though," he grunted with embarrassment that I ignored. I knew it hurt his pride to ask for help, so I didn't want to draw attention to it.

I moved beside the bed so he could swing his good arm around my shoulders, and we somehow managed to get him into the wheelchair without causing either of us too much pain. I had no idea how, considering he had a lot more weight on him than I did, and as much as I was a strong bitch, even I knew most men I encountered were way stronger than me.

Hence why I carried a bat everywhere.

I scowled at the thought of my long-lost bat, making Reid frown at me. "What's wrong? Did I hurt you?"

"I just remembered my bat's ruined," I said with a long sigh, his eyebrow quirking as I turned the wheelchair around and started pushing him towards the door.

"I'm surprised you haven't ordered a new one online already."

"I need to hold it and decide if we're meant to be together or not," I deadpanned, opening the door and pushing him out into the hallway. "Maybe we can go shopping together when you're free."

He snorted, glancing over his shoulder at me. "I don't think I'd enjoy shopping for weapons with you. No offense, but take Turbo."

"Pussy," I taunted, pushing him down the hallway and into the elevator. His whole body relaxed the closer we got to reception, and I knew he needed the fresh air as much as I did.

It was a shame I couldn't just bust us out permanently.

"Excuse me?" the woman at reception called out, but I waved a hand at her.

"Don't panic, we're coming back in. It's not like he'd get far anyway."

"But—"

I glared at her, and she instantly shut her mouth and sat down in her chair, pretending to get back to work. I understood her concern, Mom would tear her apart if I took off, but I wasn't going to do that.

"You have no idea how nice this is," Reid murmured as

the cool breeze blew over both of us as we got outside. "I hate being stuck in that fucking room."

"I don't blame you. I'm going crazy myself and I've only been in here a day," I replied, spotting Turbo and Cruz waiting by Turbo's car. They were deep in discussion, but when we got closer, their heads swiveled towards us and Turbo instantly jogged over to take Reid's wheelchair from me.

"Damn, I didn't know you were bringing the banged-up has-been with you," he joked, making Reid flip him off.

"Missed you too, Lavaro."

"When are they letting you out?"

"Soon, hopefully," he huffed, eyeing the cigarette in Turbo's hand. "I'd kill for one of those."

"You can have one if you want, but I'd bet money on you choking to death on it, and you're not supposed to smoke if you're healing from a collapsed lung," he answered, offering his cigarettes to me. "I suppose you're healthy enough to have one."

I took one, not wasting any time as I lit it and drew in a deep lungful. "You're my hero, Lavaro. Are you guys just hanging around the parking lot for the fun of it?"

He smirked, leaning back against his car. "Not likely. Cruz was waiting inside, but they kicked him out when it got late. I found him out here like an abandoned puppy."

I turned to Cruz who didn't show an ounce of shame. "You were waiting for me?"

"Yeah. I told your girl I'd keep an eye on you. She was texting me earlier, freaking out that she hadn't heard from you." Hope sparked in my chest, and it must have shown on my face because he let out a chuckle. "I think you're forgiven. Near-death experiences usually do that to people."

"She could come and visit me if she's that worried. She's

had all day," I muttered, earning an amused glance from Turbo as teasing filled his tone.

"Wow, you really are a girl."

"Fuck off," I scoffed as I flipped him off, dragging on my cigarette before blowing the smoke out as I continued. "Is Archer making her stay away from me?"

"I think you can imagine how worried he is considering she was kidnapped, Donovan," Cruz said dryly. "And they're dealing with Tempest too, so it's a little bit hectic in the Hendricks household at the moment."

"The fuck did her psycho sister do now?"

"She left Luna with Stanley and Slick at the party. They're talking about sending Tempest to some whacky shack facility too. It seems she's on a downhill spiral like your brother, but she's refusing to admit she needs help. Trust me, Luna would prefer to be here with you than be stuck in the middle of that," he replied, patting the roof of his car with a wink. "Want me to be your getaway driver? I can take you to her and you can climb through her bedroom window. I bet she'd feel like a real princess then."

"I hate to admit it, but my body hurts too much to attempt a break-in like that. I'll leave that style to the real king of breaking and entering," I answered as my mouth curved into a smirk, a bark of laughter leaving him.

"You make it sound like it's difficult. Just scope the place out, cut some wires to disable the security, and—"

"Just because I'm not going to be racing on the street anymore, doesn't mean I'm in the market for a new career," I said, cutting him off with a smile. "But I'll be sure to find you if I change my mind."

"I hope so. I'd give you the Night Thieves 101 crash course. I have a huge success rate," he grinned, running his eyes over Reid. "You won't be getting laid for a while. What *didn't* you break?"

"Har har," Reid fake laughed. "My dick's perfectly fine, but thanks for your concern. I'll just make them get on top and ride me."

I rolled my eyes, finishing my cigarette and leaning back on Cruz's car to cross my arms. "Yeah, you're a real chick magnet in that wheelchair. I bet they'll be lining up in no time."

The guys cracked up laughing, but Reid scowled at me. "Bite me, Donovan. You're not exactly a favorite amongst the local women right now."

"Like I give a fuck. There's only one woman I care about, the rest can choke on your dick for all I care," I threw back, his lips kicking up.

"Always knew you were a big teddy bear beneath that hard exterior you insist on showing."

"Bite me," I mocked, motioning to Turbo. "So, why are you here? You're lucky Mom left, or you probably would've been decapitated right here in the parking lot by now."

He shrugged, eyeing me seriously. "I was considering going to your house and speaking to them, but after that warning, I'll wait until you're with me. I take it they're pissed with me?"

I snorted, raising an eyebrow. "You honestly think I can keep you safe? You have way too much faith in my abilities. Yes, they're pissed at you. Maybe I'll let them get you since you didn't take Luna home like I asked the other night."

"If anyone can convince them not to tear me limb from limb and dump me in acid, it's you," he said with a straight face. "And I kept her safe, didn't I? She refused to leave without you. Sue the girl for being in love with you."

Cruz's phone rang, and he cringed as he hit answer. "Uh, hey, Donovan. What's up?"

Everyone shut up, and Beckett was yelling loud enough through the phone that I could hear parts of it.

Apparently, they were watching us on the surveillance cameras.

I turned and looked up at the one closest to us, flipping it off with a taunting smile and making Cruz groan.

"Yes, she can hear you because you're screaming at me like a banshee."

"Tell her to go to fucking sleep and mind her own business," I said sweetly, and he handed the phone to me as he rolled his eyes.

"She wants to talk to you, and I'd prefer it if you would so I don't have to be the middleman."

I took it, pressing it to my ear. "You checking up on me, big sister? Don't panic, I'm not escaping," I chuckled as a huff of annoyance left her.

"Tell that bastard to leave before I come down there and put my knife through his chest."

"He can hardly walk, so that's not very fair," I joked, and I could almost hear her teeth grinding with frustration.

"Not Reid, Ander. I want him gone."

"Yeah, and I want a lot of things that I don't get, but I'll get over it," I replied. "Good night, Beck." I hung up before she could yell at me.

Turbo sighed, giving the camera a small wave. "I'd better go to save the drama. Let me know when you're feeling better. We'll catch up."

"Are you honestly running away from my sister? You're Ander fucking Lavaro. Your business has just as much reach as ours," I said in disbelief, but he shook his head and unlocked his Supra.

"Your sister's psycho and I don't want to deal with her. I'm not stupid enough to think I could take on your family either. I might be a big player, but your family's got a fucking army. Call me, alright? I'm glad to see you in one piece."

I grinned, moving towards him and throwing my arms around him in a hug, my muscles screaming in protest. "Aw, I'm so glad you came to see me too."

"Get off me," he grunted, but he let a smile slip as he turned, dropping his arms gently around me to return the hug. "If you need anything, just let me know. Get a hold of Blake too. She's worried about you."

"Tell her I'll speak with her soon. I'll let my family drama blow over first," I said as I stepped back, and he nodded in return.

"Will do. You call me if you need anything too, Reid."

"You can come and blow me if you're offering," Reid said lightly, and Turbo laughed as he climbed behind the wheel and shut the door, leaving the parking lot as quietly as possible.

Cruz sighed, glancing at his phone to check the time. "I should probably go too, now I know you're good. I have to be up in a few hours for a job."

"What job?"

"Someone's hired us to steal some flashy jewelry that apparently belongs to their family," he shrugged, a frown tugging at my lips.

"How do you know if they're telling the truth?"

He grinned, opening his car door to lean on it. "I don't give a shit about that. If they pay me, I'll take it."

"Don't get arrested," I teased, making him snort as he slid into his seat.

"You too." Then he shut the door, leaving me and Reid to get back to our rooms to try and get some sleep.

Apparently, our late-night stroll had worn me out, because the moment I got Reid back in his bed and I got back to my own, I passed out hard.

80
100
120
140
160
180
200
220
km/h
240
260

Chapter Twenty-Nine

Luna

I kept my head down as I walked through the school halls on Monday afternoon, trying to ignore the whispering around me. Everyone knew I'd been kidnapped and Riley had been in the hospital, so the gossip mill was at full speed.

An arm dropped around my shoulders, and I knew it was Landon without having to look up. He'd been glued to me all day, which I was grateful for. Beckett, Maddox, and Jett hadn't been at school, and with Ryder gone, I had no one else.

"Are you heading straight home? Or did you want to hang out at mine?" he offered as we walked, a sigh leaving me.

"I don't think I'm allowed to go anywhere. Dad's freaked out about Raymond taking me."

"He can't lock you up forever."

"He'll find a way," I grumbled, cringing when I heard someone tell their friend that Riley and Raymond had been racing over me because I'd been sleeping with them both. That was one of many rumors that had been circulating.

"Riley's home now, so you could visit her?" he suggested lightly, my chest aching at the thought. We hadn't spoken since the crash, and I had no idea how to handle the situation. I loved her, but I wasn't sure if I could be with her if she was going to keep risking her life for the thrill.

"She might not want to see me," I finally said as we walked outside towards the parking lot.

"She does."

"How do you know?"

"Because she's right in front of you," he chuckled, giving my shoulder an encouraging squeeze. I jerked my gaze up, finding her leaning against her Corvette with her arms crossed and her hood over her head, a guarded look on her face.

I pulled away from Landon as we got closer, my calm walk turning into a run after a moment as tears burned my eyes. Her expression softened as I reached her, and I couldn't help it as I threw myself at her, probably hurting her from the force of it as my legs circled her waist.

"You're okay? When did they let you out of the hospital?" I choked out, her arms wrapping around me instantly.

"I am now that I know you don't hate me. They let me out this morning," she said quietly in my ear, her arms tightening around me. "I missed you. Did that fucker hurt you? Let me look."

She put me back on my feet, gently taking my face in her hands to tilt my head. She softly ran her finger over the bruise on my temple, anger burning in her eyes. "That prick's lucky he's dead already."

"It wasn't Raymond," I murmured, not wanting to tell her the truth, but refusing to lie to her. "It was Stan."

"I'm going to kill him," she growled, pulling away to get in her car, but I stopped her.

"Please, don't," I begged, her eyes narrowing. "Not because I don't want him hurt, but because I want to spend time with you. Things have been hectic lately, so don't add to it. Please."

She relaxed, teasing my throat with her fingers. "I'm surprised you're talking to me."

"I thought I lost you," I murmured, dropping my hands to her waist. "I'm still mad about the racing, but that doesn't mean I don't love you. If I'd lost you the other night, we never would've had the chance to be something together."

Landon faked a gag, lightening the mood. "You two are gross."

"Aw, you feeling left out?" I grinned, pulling him in for a group hug. He pretended to put up a fight, but he was laughing. It felt good to have all three of us together.

"Ew, cooties!"

"Come with us this afternoon. We can all hang out," I suggested, but Riley gave him the side-eye.

"No offense, but you should probably go home. I'm likely to spend the rest of the day between your cousin's thighs."

"Riley!" I huffed, her eyes flashing with amusement.

"What? It's true. If he thinks a hug's gross, I can't imagine how horrified he'd be to see boobs."

"I'm leaving," he singsonged, ruffling my hair. "Stay out of trouble. Both of you."

"Doubtful," she teased, turning back to me before he'd even walked away. "Come home with me. I have a surprise for you."

"What is it?" I frowned, and she gave me a playful wink.

"You'll see. Jump in."

I slid into the passenger seat, ignoring everyone who

was watching us like we were the local entertainment. I was surprised her car was still in one piece considering her family's usual way of dealing with irresponsible driving was by destroying their wheels.

"They didn't blow up your car?" I asked as she climbed behind the wheel and shut the door.

"They think I've been punished enough. I crashed, wrecked the Supra, and learned my lesson," she said lightly, and I couldn't help the snort that left me.

"Did you though? Won't you miss it in a few weeks and end up right back where you started?"

I didn't bother hiding my annoyance. If she wanted to repair the damage between us, she needed to understand how important her safety was to me.

She started the engine as she shook her head, turning her attention ahead of us so she could leave. "Turbo's not hosting them anymore, and I won't race for anyone else. We'll just have to race on the track if I can convince my family not to kill him."

"Really? No more street racing?" I repeated as relief hit me, wanting to make sure I'd heard her right. "Promise?"

"I promise, baby," she murmured, giving me a small smile before putting the car in gear and easing out of the parking lot, heading towards her house.

We didn't talk much on the short drive, just being content with each other's company, but I let out a low whistle as we pulled into the driveway and I saw a baby blue Supra by the garage. It was similar to the one Riley had just lost, but it looked like a newer model.

"Damn, who got an upgrade?"

She parked, unbuckling her seat belt before opening the door. "You did."

Then she climbed out and shut the door behind her,

leaving me sitting in stunned silence.

After a moment, I snapped out of it and scrambled out of the car, following her towards the shiny, new car.

"What the fuck did you just say?"

She smirked, taking my hand as we got closer. "Knocked your socks off that hard, did I? You're cursing."

"That's not my car," I sputtered, trying to wrap my head around it.

"Sure, it is. I picked it myself," she said proudly, fishing a set of keys from her pocket and dangling them in front of me. "Go on, get in and check it out."

When I didn't move, she took the keys to unlock it, guiding me around to the driver's seat and encouraging me to sit in it. "So, you like?"

"Riley—"

"C'mon, just take it. I gave you my other Supra, and I wrecked it. I can't have my girl taking the bus," she joked, and I looked up at her with wide eyes.

"This would've cost a fortune."

"So? You're worth it," she said seriously, leaning over to kiss my cheek. "It's partially a gift, as well as an apology for being a bitch. I can't return it, so you have to keep it."

"It's beautiful," I murmured, running my hands over the dash. "Thank you."

"Do you want to take it to the track for a spin? It's fast," she said with excitement, but I shook my head.

"Not right now. I want to go inside so we can talk."

Her face fell a fraction, but she tried to cover it up with an eye roll. "The track sounds like more fun."

"Talking's an important part of a relationship. If you want one, you need to meet me in the middle," I answered, getting out and locking the car. "Even if it makes you uncomfortable."

She grumbled but followed me inside, and she surprisingly took me straight to her bedroom and shut the door behind us so we could talk in private. I thought she'd try to get out of it.

"What can I do to fix this?" she asked the moment we were sitting on her bed, devastation flashing across her face. "I know the car won't. I'm not trying to bribe you with it. If you decide you still don't want to fix it, I understand."

"I think we just need some time to heal. I hated that you didn't put my concerns first, but I also know that it wasn't fair of me to make demands and put you on the spot like that," I replied honestly, her shoulders relaxing at my words and making me realize just how tense she really was.

"The reason why I needed to finish the races was because, in most of these street racing clubs, it's practically law. Once you're in, you're in. Part of me saying that was my own selfishness though," she said softly, crossing her legs and pulling her hood over her head. "Turbo would've let me out, I knew that, but I wasn't ready to go."

"And now?" I asked slowly, my chest tightening at the thought of her choosing the adrenaline rush over me.

"It's going to be an adjustment. I've been getting that rush for years, and it'll be weird not having it. I'll just have to find something else," she said with a half shrug, and I crawled towards her, pulling her hood back to see her face properly.

"I hear I'm a good distraction."

Her lips quirked into a smirk, her eyes dropping to my chest to look down the gap in my dress. "Is that so?"

"Uh-huh," I smiled, giving her a light push to encourage her to lie down. "I know of lots of things we could do to give you a rush."

"Unless you're going to push me out of a plane, I doubt

it, no offense," she chuckled, but her eyes were burning with need. "Feel free to test your theory though."

I licked my lips, trying to figure out how to blow her mind without looking like a fumbling mess or hurting her, and I ended up dropping my lips to hers, running my hand up the inside of her hoodie to toy with her nipples.

I'd start small, then work my way up.

She groaned into my mouth the moment I touched her, and when her fingers ran through my hair to control the kiss, I confidently spread my fingers around her throat and gave it a light squeeze.

"I'm in charge, *baby*," I whispered over her lips, moving my hand down to the elastic of her pants to start tugging them down, acting like I knew what I was doing. I wanted to see her completely submit to me, the thought sending heat straight to my core. "All you're allowed to do is lie there and take it."

"I'm officially God's favorite," she choked out, boosting my confidence as I threw her pants across the room as she tugged at her hoodie. She yanked it over her head, watching me intensely as I kissed down her bruised chest and stomach until I reached her pussy, holding her gaze as I swiped my tongue lightly around her clit.

I knew she wouldn't let me back off despite the chance of hurting her, so I didn't bother asking.

I took my time, learning where her sensitive spots were and making her squirm. It tasted so different than going down on a guy. Guys tasted bitter and salty, but Riley had a hint of sweetness mixed with tangy.

I liked it.

She hesitated before reaching down to cup my cheek, her voice rough. "You're fucking gorgeous."

I took her hand in mine, giving it a gentle squeeze as I

started thrusting my tongue in and out of her, switching between that and toying with her clit to drive her wild. She was cursing at me quietly, her eyes locked on mine as she jerked from the sensations.

It wasn't enough, I wanted her to be a trembling mess as she soaked the sheets.

"Do you have a vibrator?" I murmured, confusion in her tone as she replied breathlessly.

"You don't think I like this?"

"I know you do, but I want to give you more," I answered, licking around her navel and placing kisses across her stomach. "I want to make you come so hard you black out, if it won't hurt you too much."

"Bottom drawer," she replied without argument, watching me curiously as I scrambled to find it. She had multiple items in the drawer, so I grabbed a pink vibrating dildo and held it up to her.

"You like this one?"

"You could do anything to me right now and I'd like it," she said seriously, widening her legs to give me more room as I got comfortable again. I must have looked confused about how to turn it on because her fingers ran across my lips as she spoke. "Press the bottom."

I did, a steady buzzing sound filling the room as I gave her a cheeky glance. I leaned forward, hoping I looked attractive somehow as I spat on her pussy, a low groan leaving her.

"Have you been looking at my porn history or something? This is just like a video I watched the other night."

"Did you get yourself off?" I asked lightly, rubbing the silicone through the wetness and teasing her entrance.

"I did. You want to know what made me come? That vibrator with images of you spread out on my fucking hood," she grinned, jerking slightly as I moved the vibrator up to her clit.

"Next time you get yourself off while thinking about me," I whispered, a naughty smile spreading across my lips. "Video it and send it to me. I want to watch."

"Fuck," she growled, starting to crack. "Stop playing with me."

"Who's playing?" I chuckled, pushing the vibrator inside her and wrapping my lips around her clit. She bucked, her fingers ending up in my hair again, but she didn't try to take over.

I was pretty sure she was just holding on to anchor herself.

"Keep doing that," she begged, her thighs clenching as she fought herself to stay in place, her fingers tightening even more in my hair. "Jesus fucking Christ, Lou."

I pushed the vibrator deeper, pulling it in and out slowly as I licked and sucked her clit, building her up until she had my head clamped between her thighs and literally screamed my name.

No wonder she liked me being vocal. It was empowering and insanely hot.

I pulled back, turning the vibrator off before crawling up her body to place a soft kiss on her lips. "Was that a good rush?"

"If I could move, I'd fuck you through this mattress," she replied with a huff. "You've managed to stop my limbs from working."

"You can have your way with me later. I'll stay the night."

Dad would lose his shit, but he knew I was safe here.

"This wasn't what I had in mind when you said we

needed to talk," she joked, wrapping her arms around me to keep me on top of her. "Are we okay?"

I nodded, getting comfortable since it didn't seem like she was going to let me go. "We're okay. I love you, and I want to be your girlfriend."

"You have no idea how long I've been wanting to hear you say that to me," she said quietly, giving me a serious look. "I love you too."

We ended up napping for most of the afternoon, and I shouldn't have been surprised when she ended up between my legs multiple times throughout the night, definitely keeping her parents awake.

For once, I didn't care.

Riley

My body was burning the next morning, but I wasn't going to tell Luna that. I was way too battered and bruised for the things we got up to last night.

We were getting annoyed glances from my parents throughout breakfast, but no one said anything. It was a pretty quiet day, and I even let Luna put one of her terrible movies on and watched the whole thing with her.

Blake came over to spend some time with Kate, and they joined us, which was nice.

It was never peaceful in my house for long though.

"You think you can scope the place out, you stupid cunt?" I heard Maddox bark from the other room, and I tried to ignore it until I heard Turbo's voice.

"I wasn't scoping anything out. I told you, I'm here to see Riley."

I cursed, giving Blake a look. "Keep Kate in here. This

might get messy."

"Is that Ander?" she said with worry, and I didn't have time to ask why she was calling him that.

"Just stay in here," I warned, leaving the room and closing the large doors to try and block some of the noise. I didn't need Luna witnessing this either, so I was glad she'd stayed on the couch.

"Hey!" I whisper-yelled at Maddox as I watched him drag Turbo into the kitchen. "We have too many foster kids here right now for you to pull this shit. What are you doing?"

"This prick," Maddox gritted through his teeth, shoving him ahead. "Was scoping the house out."

"I was walking to the front door to knock," Turbo said dryly, keeping his attention on me. "I was just talking to Reid about the track, so I thought I'd stop by to—"

Maddox punched him in the face, hard, and I managed to get between them before they could end up in a fistfight. Turbo could hold his own, but he wasn't a trained fighter. Maddox would destroy him.

I pressed my back against Turbo's front to make sure he stayed back, keeping my eyes on my brother.

"This fucker isn't coming to the track," Maddox spat, and I wasn't surprised when Beckett and Jett joined us. I knew they were here somewhere if Maddox was.

"Why not?" I asked lightly, crossing my arms against my chest. "He's one of my best friends, and the track is the only place I'm allowed to race."

Beckett snorted, mimicking my pose as she stood beside Maddox. "He's not fucking welcome."

"It's not your track," I reminded her, irritation in my tone. "The whole family owns it. You want me to race safely? Then let my friends come to the track."

"He's not your fucking friend!" she exploded, her eyes flashing with violence. "He doesn't give a shit about you! You were just someone who had the funds to race!"

"Uh, excuse me," Turbo said, joining the conversation and placing his hands on my shoulders to gently move me to the side, his cheek already swelling from the hit he'd just taken. "I do give a shit about Riley. She's family to me."

"She'll never be your family," Beckett threw back, glaring at Blake as she appeared beside us. They'd never get along. Blake didn't put up with alpha bullshit, which was one of the reasons I liked her.

"You can't build a track to keep people safe, then refuse entry to them," Blake scoffed, standing beside Turbo and taking his hand. "You don't think Ander could afford to build a track in the Heights? He'd take half the racers with him. People use your track because it's fancy, free, and safe. You think the Heights kids would come anymore if they had their own? Or the Crestford kids would travel further than needed? Everyone just wants to race, and the only thing that's special about your track is that it's the only one around."

"Babe, I'm handling it," Turbo muttered, my eyes narrowing. I'd never heard him call her that before.

Were they dating? It looked like it from the way he continued to hold her hand.

She glared at him, her voice sharp. "You think I'm going to let her speak to you like that? Stay out of it."

"Yes, boss," he smirked, noticing me staring at them and making him clear his throat as if it would cover up the entire conversation.

They were definitely fucking.

Before they could keep arguing, Mom appeared out of nowhere.

"There's no reason Ander can't go to the track."

Beckett's jaw almost hit the fucking floor. "You're not serious, right? There's a million reasons why he can't go. Did you forget he's the reason Riley and Reid almost died? Or that we're going to make him disappear?"

"We don't have to like him, but Riley and Reid are adults," she grumbled, surprising me as she took my side about it. "If Riley wants to keep racing with her friends, I'd prefer it to be on the track where it's safe. Ander doesn't do dumb shit to win, do you, Lavaro?"

"I want to win from skill, not cheating," he confirmed, eyeing Mom suspiciously. "You'll let me race there without me ending up dead?"

She shrugged, her eyes running over all of us. "If you keep it on the track and can abide by the rules, then sure." Her gaze stopped on Beckett, her voice lowering. "And any plans you had to deal with Ander, you can forget about. Be mad at him, but I'm calling off the job, so don't drag the Psychos into it."

"I shouldn't be fucking surprised that you're bending your own rules for your favorite child," Beckett laughed dryly. "You'll do anything for her, won't you? You wanted him dead, and now you've sure changed your opinion on him fast."

"Fine. Ban them all from the track, but don't bitch at me in a few months when they all start racing on the road again and one of them dies," Mom snapped back, making Beckett shut her mouth. "Keep your enemies close, Beckett. It's better that way. Stand down, that's a fucking order as your boss, not your mother."

Maddox kept glaring at Turbo, but I relaxed. No one would be allowed to hurt him now that Mom had said so.

Turbo surprised me when he spoke directly to Mom, his

voice calm. "I really do care about Riley. She's my best friend, and almost losing her and Reid made me realize I can't go back to being on my own. I have other businesses to run, which you know about, but for the first time ever, I have a way out of a lot of things. I've given up all the car stuff, so I appreciate it if I'm allowed at the track. I'd like to apologize for not being able to do anything more the night Slick took Luna and hurt Riley. I wanted to keep them both safe, but—"

Mom put her hand up to silence him, apparently hearing enough. "I don't fucking like you, Lavaro. This isn't an olive branch to form an ally with us, it's simply me knowing you're not one hundred percent to blame, and that Riley's sneaky and she'll find a way around it if we don't allow it." I tried to hide my smirk before she saw it but failed. She raised an eyebrow, her voice flat. "This doesn't mean I want him in the house."

"To be fair, Maddox dragged him in here," I said lightly. "But I'll see him out."

"Good," she muttered, giving him the side-eye before pointing at Beckett. "You three, in the office."

Kate and Luna wandered out once the drama had died down, and we all headed outside to talk before we got in trouble.

"So," I said slowly, pointing at Turbo and then Blake. "Is this a thing?"

Blake rolled her eyes, but Turbo looked uncomfortable. "Yeah. We wanted to tell you about it once you were feeling better."

"Don't panic, I won't bite your head off," I chuckled, pulling Luna in front of me to wrap my arms around her. "We fixed our problems and got back together."

"Good. She was fucking pathetic without you, Luna," Turbo said playfully, and he was lucky I didn't punch him.

"Asshole," I hissed, but Luna laughed, the sound making me smile.

We all talked for ages until Turbo finally left, and Blake said goodbye to Kate before leaving too. I had a feeling they were going to meet up since her exit was more abrupt than normal.

Kate ran off to do some homework, leaving me and Luna alone.

Lukas and Jensen were cooking dinner when we walked back into the kitchen, and Jett was sitting at the table alone.

"They talking business?" I asked as I sat beside him, knowing it was one of the only reasons why he wouldn't be included. "Or did my brother and sister decide you were ruining their taboo relationship vibe?"

He grinned, leaning back in his chair. "They'd miss me too much. They're beating someone up down there, and I don't want to watch."

"Pussy," I snorted, but Luna shivered.

"I don't blame you."

"How did we end up dating psychos?" Jett asked seriously, and Luna grinned.

"Because there's something wrong with us."

"Hey!" I laughed, swatting at her playfully. "I'm not that bad!"

"No? I've seen you beat someone to a pulp with your bat while being completely silent. That's psychopathic behavior," she answered dryly. "Right, Jett?"

"Right," he confirmed with a nod, glancing over at my dads. "What's for dinner? I'm starving."

Jensen looked up from chopping garlic, narrowing his eyes. "Who said I was feeding you?"

"C'mon, Jense. I date your daughter. I deserve a good feed," he joked, making Jensen smirk.

"We're having a barbeque, so there should be some left for you."

"I appreciate it," he chuckled before checking his phone. "Shit. Logan's at my place looking for me."

"Let me call him," I insisted as I snatched his phone, quickly hitting the call button before Jett could take it away from me.

"My ass is ready for you, baby cakes," Logan drawled. "You want to top me this time?"

"Evening, Donahue," I murmured, a groan leaving him.

"Where's my man? What did you do to him?"

"You know, I'm starting to think you have gay tendencies," I deadpanned, swatting a hand at Jett as he tried to take the phone back. "We're doing a family thing, so you'll have to go home and let Lopez rail you instead."

"That's no fun. I bet fucking him would be like trying to have a conversation with a brick wall," he grumbled. "It's a shame Reid's not home yet. He'd blow me."

"You're terrible," I huffed, changing the subject. "How is he today?"

"Better. They're hoping he'll be discharged tomorrow."

"No shit? Let me know if you need a ride. I'll sort something out for you guys," I offered.

"Aw, you do love us. Shit, Rae is calling me. I'll talk to you later," he said quickly before hanging up.

I handed the phone back to Jett, his eyebrow raised. "Reid getting out?"

"Sounds like it. You'll lend me your car to pick him up, right?" I teased, knowing there was no way in hell he'd give me the keys.

"Like fuck."

"It's alright, you can use the Escalade. It has more room," Jensen offered, putting the steak in a bowl of marinade. Lukas was making burger patties, but he glanced up with a worried look.

"Do they need anything? I know they won't accept help, but it's not like they've got parents around to help them."

"I dealt with the hospital fees and Reid's car stuff. I think they're okay," I shrugged, but Luna frowned.

"Should we make them some meals? Then they don't have to cook for a week or two until he's settled at home again."

Lukas smiled, and I could already see the wheels turning in his head as he started thinking of meals for them. "That's a good idea. I'll make a bunch of stuff tonight so you guys can give it to them tomorrow when you take them home."

Skeeter walked in, annoyance on his face that he wasn't hiding very well. "Make extra food for dinner. Rory opened her big mouth and invited the Hendricks' and the Bates'."

"No Evans'?" I asked lightly as if I was confused, his eyes instantly clashing with mine.

"No."

"Aw, why not? It's a family dinner, so shouldn't my favorite Uncle Rage be coming?" I said and faked a pout, earning the middle finger.

"You kids suck sometimes. Stay out of my sight until dinner."

I grabbed Luna's hand, giving her a wink. "I have an idea. Come upstairs."

"Put pillows over your faces," Skeeter said bluntly, stalking from the room and making me chuckle.

At least we got out of helping.

80
100
120
140
160
180
200
220
km/h
240
260

Chapter Thirty

Riley

As much as Archer and Lexi were glad that I was alright, they weren't impressed with me about the whole racing and break-up issue. So, I wasn't surprised when they asked Luna to go home for the night. As much as it sucked not having her beside me, I had to play my cards right.

I needed them to trust me again, which was understandable.

It was the next day, and I was leaning against the Psychos' Escalade having a cigarette as I waited for Logan to bring Reid out. It was a little after lunchtime, but it looked like it was late in the afternoon with the way the clouds were overcast.

The moment Logan wheeled him out, I grinned. "Hey, Speedy. I hope you've showered since being in this place. Should I keep the windows down?"

"Bite me, Donovan," he scolded, but his smirk gave him away. "Logan was very helpful with assisting me in the shower. Right, buddy?"

Logan scrunched his nose with annoyance, stopping

them in front of the car. "Don't remind me. I've seen way more of you than any friend should."

I snickered, giving Reid a wink. "He'll have to do it for a few more weeks too. Unless you can get Raven to help. She might do it to save him."

Logan looked horrified at the thought, shaking his head. "Nope. I'd never allow her to be traumatized like that. I'll continue to suffer and take one for the team."

"You're such a good boy. It's not like you haven't seen me naked before, we tag team a lot," Reid deadpanned, hissing out a breath as he shifted in his seat. "Can you fuckers help me out of this thing?"

I frowned as a nurse walked towards us with crutches. "Uh, you're bringing the wheelchair, right?" I asked slowly, making Reid snort.

"Fuck no."

I ran my eyes over him, a blank look on my face. "But you have a fucked arm."

"I'll manage." His voice was sharp, and I let out a sigh. With his wrecked arm, he was going to struggle with crutches.

"Reid—"

"Our house isn't made for a fucking wheelchair, Donovan. Butt out of it," he snapped, making the nurse pause beside us with worry.

"Here you go, Mr. Barron."

"Thank you," he grunted, letting Logan take them from her as he managed to get them in the back seat. Between me and Logan, we got Reid into the front passenger seat and made sure he was buckled in before giving the nurse the wheelchair so she could head back into the hospital.

"Sorry, he's really grouchy today," Logan said under his breath, but I shrugged.

"I don't blame him. He's been stuck in here for weeks, and he's probably bored and uncomfortable. The trunk's full of cooked meals for you guys too. Lukas and Jensen cooked a bunch last night so you guys don't have to cook for a week or two."

His face softened, and he rubbed the back of his neck awkwardly. "Uh, thank you. That was nice of them."

"I think they're getting empty nest syndrome or something. We went from a full house to fuck all," I chuckled. "Marla's about to leave it seems, and with me being the only permanent kid there, I think they're just trying to stay busy."

"Tell them we appreciate it." He gave me a smile before opening the back door and climbing in.

Reid barely spoke the whole drive to Hawthorne Heights, and I didn't push him to talk. He was allowed to feel miserable.

I wasn't surprised when Raven walked out to help, giving me a filthy look. "Thanks for bringing him home."

"That hurt to say, didn't it," I drawled, opening the trunk to start unloading the food since Raven and Logan were helping Reid. He shook them off with annoyance, forcing himself to get inside on his own with the crutches, and Logan let out a sigh.

"Don't mind him, Rae. He's a cranky bastard right now."

"Why? He's home," she asked lightly, but I could hear the sadness in her voice. They were a family, and it was obvious how close they all were despite it only being a friendship.

I bit the inside of my cheek to stop myself from answering, knowing she didn't want to speak to me.

I followed Reid inside with my arms full of insulated

bags, doing multiple trips back to the car to unload it all while Raven and Logan talked between themselves.

When I'd placed the last bag in the kitchen, Zavier materialized behind me like a ghost, scaring the shit out of me.

"Fucking asshole!" I snapped as I pressed my palm to my chest, concern lining his brow as he noticed me wince as pain bloomed through my muscles.

"You're still in pain? I didn't mean to scare you."

"Well, I did crash my car," I deadpanned. "But, no. This pain is from days of fucking my girl."

"Stop bragging. Not all of us get laid, you know," he joked, motioning to the bags. "What's all this?"

"Your meals for the next couple of weeks. Lukas and Jensen went a little crazy. They take their *stay-at-home dad* jobs seriously." I opened the freezer to start stacking it, finding it practically empty, and I suddenly realized just how broke they were.

I knew I lived a life of luxury, but I never really noticed just how other people lived.

"Don't look at us like that," Zavier grunted, knowing exactly what I was thinking. "We're fine, and we never go hungry."

I glanced at him, keeping my voice quiet. "What about bills?"

He shrugged, helping me unpack the food to avoid meeting my gaze. "They haven't taken the house. I've been slipping money into the accounts to keep it balanced, and I think Reid did the same with his racing money."

"Do you guys rent or own the house?"

"It was Raven's parents', but there's mortgage repayments on it that we've had to keep up with. Her mom bailed forever ago, and her dad fucked off after that. If one of them came back, they could kick us all out," he admitted, his jaw going tight.

"You should get your own place. If you're paying off the mortgage, you could be using it for rent money. I bet my parents have a house they could rent you," I offered, but he shook his head, conflict on his face. "Rae won't leave, so we stay."

I made sure the others weren't close by before speaking again in a whisper. "Are you still doing runner stuff for that drug dude?"

"No. I got out," he answered, his face serious. "You can't tell anyone I did it, okay? I swear to God, I'll kill you."

I blinked at him in surprise for a second before nodding, knowing he wasn't making a joke. He'd kept my secrets from Beckett, who seemed to be his best friend, so I'd respect his wishes and keep his secrets buried too.

I never thought I'd like him, and I still wasn't sure if I'd count him as a friend, but he'd made his way off my shit list.

"What are you two talking about?" Reid grumbled from behind us, making us jump. For a big dude on bulky crutches, he sure was silent.

"He was just scolding me for racing," I said smoothly, and I could tell by the look Reid threw my way that he didn't believe me.

"Whatever." An engine roared outside two seconds before Logan's voice reached us from the porch.

"Uh, Reid? You might want to come and see this."

"There's no fucking way," Reid murmured under his breath, hobbling outside with us behind him, and my eyebrows shot up as a black Challenger almost identical to his pulled into the driveway.

The only thing different was the matte black paintwork now had a shiny top coat.

Reid turned to me with a question in his eyes, but I put my hands up in front of me and shook my head. "Nope. I have no idea what's happening."

The engine shut off, and Turbo climbed from the driver's seat with a grin on his face. "Hey. I hear you're having car problems."

"You bought me a car?" Reid asked in disbelief as Turbo walked towards us, amusement on his face.

"I bought what was needed to put your baby back together. Bits of the motor was alright, and some of the body was fixable so I used what I could. I gave your audio system an upgrade though since I couldn't save the interior."

Reid stared at it in stunned silence, but Logan spoke up tightly. "What did it cost?"

Turbo shrugged, handing Reid the keys. "You don't need to know that bit."

"How can we pay it back then?" Logan demanded, a frown taking over Turbo's face.

"You're not. I fixed it because I wanted to. Slick was a problem, and I didn't handle it before people got hurt. I know this won't mean I'm forgiven," he said lightly, glancing at Raven who was surprisingly quiet. "But I knew it would be helpful to you guys, and I'm kind of being selfish about it because I need Reid to have a car for when we race on the track."

Logan snorted, crossing his arms. "You honestly think Beckett's going to let you anywhere near that place?"

"Actually," I said slowly, clearing my throat. "Mom told him he's allowed. She'd prefer us being able to race in a safe space instead of me sneaking off to do it on the streets again. Beckett's not happy about it, but I think she'll let it slide. Will she be nice about it? Doubtful. But once she gets to know him properly, she should back off a little."

"No shit?" Reid asked, finally finding his voice as a smirk spread across his face. "We can all still race together?"

"Yep. It seems people have been asking about racing in groups instead of one-on-one, so hopefully, if Mom can figure out the safety stuff, we can all race against each other instead of taking turns," I smiled and suddenly knew why Reid was so grouchy.

Like me, his addiction was the street races, and he thought he'd never get to feel like that again. Now that he had his car back and had hope about racing us all again, his mood had completely shifted.

Raven seemed to notice it too, and as much as I knew she didn't like me, she mouthed a thank you. I didn't feel like I deserved any credit, but I gave her a small nod, turning my attention back to Turbo.

"So, are you buying me a new car to replace the Supra since you're handing them out?" I teased, making him chuckle.

"I heard through the grapevine that you already replaced the Supra."

"My girl looks hot in her new wheels too," I winked, glancing down at my phone as it started ringing, Luna's name flashing on the screen. I answered it, my stomach doing that stupid little flip that it had been doing lately whenever I heard or saw her name. "Hey, baby."

"How long until you leave the Heights?" she whispered, alarm bells ringing in my head. She sounded scared, and I hated that.

"I can leave right fucking now. What's wrong?" Everyone's attention landed on me, but they stayed silent so I could hear her properly.

"I'm at the diner in Ashburn hiding in the bathroom. Stan came in with some friends and he said some nasty stuff, and then he said he was going to let his friends fuck me until I learned my lesson."

"I'm out," I said to the others without hesitation as anger filled me, Turbo's brow creasing.

"What happened?"

"Stan's threatened to let his friends rape Luna. She's locked herself in the bathroom at the diner," I answered quickly, pulling my keys from my pocket and walked towards the Escalade. "Baby? You stay where you are. I'm coming, okay?"

"I don't want him to touch me. I think he's blaming me for Raymond dying," she choked out, and I yanked the driver's door open and climbed behind the wheel.

"I won't fucking let that happen. I'm leaving right now, I promise. Do you want me to stay on the phone?"

"Please."

The passenger door opened as I started the engine, and Turbo slid into the seat with a bat in his hand, Logan and Zavier climbing in the back.

"We're coming too," Turbo said firmly as he held the bat out to me, and I wasn't going to argue. I had no idea how many friends Stanley had with him. "This is for you."

"You got me a bat?" I asked with surprise, but a smile spread across my face as he nodded.

"I had a feeling it would mean more to you than a fancy car. Good timing, right?" he asked with a grin.

"Is that Ander?" Luna asked softly, joining the conversation through the speakers.

"Yeah. Do you know how many friends he has with him?" Turbo asked, and I let the guys talk to her while I started driving towards Ashburn Valley.

I hadn't expected them to jump at helping me, but I had a feeling they were doing it for Luna.

I'd found out Luna had been texting Logan regularly for updates on Reid while he'd been in the hospital, and I was glad Logan had her to lean on a little. Especially since Raven had been giving him the cold shoulder for a while.

I broke all the road rules on my way and didn't realize how anxious I'd been without my bat until Turbo handed me the new one. The moment I parked, my fingers wrapped around it tightly as something settled inside of me. I pulled my hood over my head, telling Luna we were here so she could relax more, then we bailed from the car to start making our way towards the diner door.

My eyes caught on Stanley's piece of shit car, and a smirk slowly crept across my face as I toyed with the bat in my hand. I might as well leave an extra message.

I brought the bat over my shoulder, bringing it down hard against his car windows, the shattering glass fueling my rage until I was pummeling the panels and the hood, leaving no part of the car in one piece.

I was sweating as my muscles ached, but it felt good to finally let some of my anger out.

The side mirrors were now lying on the parking lot ground, his car alarm was screaming around me, and I didn't stop until I heard Stanley's voice.

"What the fuck are you doing?!"

I turned to face him as adrenaline pumped through my veins, Turbo, Logan, and Zavier standing close by to back me up if I needed them to.

"I was just fixing it. Do you love it?" I taunted, his face turning red with anger.

"You'll be paying for that!"

"I think I did you a favor. It was a write-off anyway." His friends joined us, and I couldn't stop the grin on my face. They were scrawny fuckers, and most of them looked drunk. It would be an easy fight if it came down to it. "I heard you're bothering my girlfriend. Did you think I was going to let that slide?" I asked, dropping the bat over my shoulder lazily. "You're stupider than I thought."

"That cunt fucked my life up!" Stanley snarled, clenching his fists by his side. "I was so close to getting that money, but she ruined it!"

Knowing he'd been dating her for years just to inherit some money pissed me off. She was so sweet, and she'd given him her everything when he was lying straight to her face.

When she'd told me, I'd been devastated for her.

Turbo moved beside me, speaking quietly in my ear. "I'll go get her if you're good out here?"

I nodded, waiting for him to leave before I continued. "I don't usually give second chances, Stanley. If I offered you to leave town with your balls still attached to your body, would you take it?"

"You think I'm scared of you? You even brought backup, which tells me you didn't think you could win," he laughed, faltering when Zavier stepped forward and got in his face.

"You think it's fair for five of you to go against one woman? How about you talk shit to me instead, asshole. See what fucking happens."

"This has nothing to do with you," he grunted, and I did well not to jump as Logan cackled with laughter.

"You think you can fuck with Luna and we won't step in? I bet you feel really tough scaring women. Does it make your dick hard?"

"Are you all fucking her now? Is this like Riley's twisted, fucked-up family?" Stanley demanded, and before I could smash his face in, Zavier let out a low chuckle, patting Stanley's chest.

"I'm assuming you've been talking to your granddaddy, right? Is that what's got you so angry at Luna? I bet he wasn't happy to find out about your little plan."

I had no idea what they were talking about, but I didn't have to wait long.

"That bitch somehow got a hold of evidence from my fucking phone and sent it to him! I'm going to destroy her!" Stanley shouted, waving his arms around. "You know what he did with that money? He gave it to her!"

At first, I thought I'd heard him wrong, but when he kept ranting about how she'd ended up with his money, I knew I'd heard him correctly.

That old dude had given Stanley's inheritance to Luna.

She hadn't mentioned it to me, so I was pretty sure she didn't know about it yet.

Zavier laughed. Loudly. "He actually gave it to her? Damn, I bet that hurts. I doubt it was enough to compensate for the past few years of her having to put up with you, but it's a good start. I'll have to send him a thank you card."

"How did she get stuff from my phone?" Stanley kept shouting, giving me a glare when I leaned against his car and my bat hit it. "Watch it!"

"Sorry. I'd hate to dent it," I deadpanned, crossing my arms. "Is this really why you just threatened to let your friends rape my girl? Because your grandfather gave her money? Money really is the root of all evil."

His friends suddenly looked confused, one taking a step to the side. "Uh, what are you talking about? I'm not a fucking rapist."

I sneered, pointing at him with my bat. "You don't think she told me that he walked in here, telling her you were all going to take turns with her?"

His eyes went wide, and he shook his head. "No! We

came here to eat, and he seemed to be arguing with her across the room when she was leaving the bathroom. He said she stole from him and we hung around to back him because her family has connections or something. I swear, I wasn't going to touch her! We only met Stan a couple of weeks ago!"

I glanced at the other guys, all of them looking just as confused by the entire situation, making me realize they didn't know their buddy as much as they thought they did.

"Did he even tell you who her family is?" When they all said no, I smiled. "Her father's the leader of the Reapers of Chaos crew, and her uncles are part of the Bloody Psychos. I'm her girlfriend, Riley Donovan."

They all took a step away from Stanley, not willing to risk their lives for their newfound friend.

"What the fuck, Stan?" one hissed, taking another step back as a precaution. "You're starting wars with the crews? The fuck is wrong with you?"

"They won't do shit," he scoffed before crying out as Turbo moved behind him, confusing me. Luna scrambled to my side to wrap her arms around my middle, and Turbo kept his face blank, pulling back to reveal a bloodied knife in his hand.

He'd fucking stabbed him.

"Crews like to bide their time, waiting for the right moment to strike. I guarantee if they knew every little detail about your behavior towards Luna, you'd be in a hole by now. I'm Ander Lavaro. I'm not a patient man."

Stanley's friends scattered, not wanting to be caught up in the bullshit Stanley had brought upon himself, but I couldn't take my eyes off Turbo. I knew who he was outside of the racing world, but I'd never seen him so cold before.

He'd threatened me, I knew about his businesses, and I'd heard stories about him.

I'd never seen him stab someone before though, he was usually more laid-back.

Stanley clutched the wound with his hand, his face twisting with pain. "You fucking stabbed me!"

"Yes. Would you like another one?" he offered flatly, his eyes lifting to mine. "I'll deal with this. May I borrow your vehicle?"

"Are you going to ruin the interior?" I joked lightly, but the hint of a dark smile tugged at the corners of his lips.

"I'll get it professionally cleaned before returning it."

"You'd better since it's not mine, it's my parents'. What are you going to do?"

"Use your imagination. Just know that it's going to hurt," he chuckled, the sound sending shivers down my spine. "I'll deal with his car too. Get Luna home, and we'll all meet at the track tonight, okay?" I didn't want to leave him with this mess, but I needed to get Luna out of here.

"Call me if you need me," I said seriously as I took Luna's hand and tugged her towards her car, a laugh leaving Turbo.

"I prefer to work alone in this situation." He looked at Zavier, seeming ready to say something, but he stopped when he remembered Logan was there. "I'll drop you guys off on my way to Pine Valley. I want you both at the track later too. I want to see what Logan's got behind the wheel."

Logan's eyes lit up, and I almost felt bad for never noticing how badly he'd wanted to be in the driver's seat. He enjoyed being a passenger for Reid, but since he didn't have a car, it made it difficult for him to be one of the drivers.

"I can't use Reid's car, dude," he said despite the glee on

his face. "It would be a kick in the guts to see his car racing while he sits on the sidelines."

"I'll sort it out. Just show up and be ready to race," Turbo replied, holding his hand out in my direction. "Keys."

I tossed them towards him, and he caught them as he started hauling Stanley towards the trunk. Stanley's bravery was long gone as he thrashed about, fear consuming him as realization hit that he wasn't getting away.

People walked by, but the moment they saw me, they averted their eyes.

No one was going to call the cops if my family was involved.

Turbo let out an annoyed huff, putting Stanley in a headlock and finding the right pressure point to knock him out, impressing me. "Need a hand getting him in the car? Why are you going to Pine Valley?"

"I've got it," Zavier said, cutting Turbo's response off. "You girls go. We'll see you later. There's a guy in Pine Valley that uh, handles these things."

Logan gave him a strange look that probably matched mine. I didn't want to know why Zavier knew a creepy guy that disposed of bodies.

Luna wasn't stupid, she knew her ex was about to be murdered, but the less she saw the better.

"Thanks, guys." I nodded, letting them know I appreciated their help before I took Luna's keys so I could drive her home, trusting the guys to handle the rest.

Luna

"Excuse me?" I choked out once we were sitting on the

couch at my place, and Riley told me what Stanley had said about me getting his money. "That's not possible."

"Why not? Check your bank," she suggested, and I scrambled for my phone, logging in to my bank app to check the balance. My eyes went wide, and I dropped the phone in shock. "What? You're rich as shit now, aren't you?" she grinned, grabbing the phone from the living room floor to turn the screen towards herself. "Holy shit, Lou."

"What the fuck is happening?"

I had millions of dollars.

"You're loaded," she laughed, holding the phone out for me as it started to ring. I took it with shaky hands, but I didn't recognize the number. I hit the answer button before holding it to my ear, my voice full of questions.

"Hello?"

"Luna Hendricks? This is Michael, Stanley's grandfather," a man said, making my eyes go wide.

"Sir, you have to take that money back. Keep it, I don't—"

"Nonsense. I've heard and seen a lot of reasons why you deserve it," he replied sharply, cutting me off. "I'm sorry, I had no idea my grandson was so selfish. I thought the money would give him some incentive to sort his life out, but it seems all I did was cause problems for you."

Riley raised an eyebrow, and I put my finger to my lips, wanting her to stay quiet as I answered him. "It only got bad recently. He—"

"The boy's a fool. It sounds like he had himself a lovely, sweet girl, and he threw it all away. If you don't wish to keep the money, you may donate it to whatever charities you want, but I hope you keep some for yourself. I don't have much time left on earth, and the only family I had left was my grandson. I'll die happy knowing someone will appreciate my wealth and use it for good. Spend it however you like, and I hope you find real love. Don't let his stupidity scare you away from something that can be so beautiful."

"I, um, I have a girlfriend," I mumbled, and as much as Riley rolled her eyes at how awkward I was in saying it, the smile gave her away. She loved that I was happy to tell people about her.

"You're a smart girl. Men are pigs," he chuckled, relaxing me. "I wish you and your girlfriend all the best. Buy yourself something nice, you deserve it." Then he hung up before I could thank him.

"Did he hang up because you're dating a girl?" she asked, sounding irritated, but she smirked when I shook my head.

"No. He told me to keep the money, and that I was smart for dating you because men are pigs."

"That old dude knows what's up," she answered, tugging me onto her lap to face her and tossing my phone aside onto the couch cushions. "What will you do with all that money?"

"I have no idea," I admitted, still not being able to believe I had so much sitting in my bank. "I don't have college fees since your family covered that, I don't have car repayments because you bought it for me, and my family isn't in any nasty debts. Who do you think sent him proof?"

"I have no idea. My money's on one of our hacker friends."

"I want to know so I can give them some of the money," I huffed, but she wrapped her arms around my middle, pulling me down against her chest.

"We'll figure it out later. For now, I think we should nap before heading to the track later. I'm fucking tired."

I heard the front door slam and was surprised when

Tempest stormed in, her attitude going from angry to blank in a matter of seconds when she saw us. Dad had kept her away from me since the night I'd been taken, not that it had been hard. She'd rarely come home.

"Oh. You're home," she muttered, glancing at Riley whose face had turned to stone. "Mom told me what happened. I didn't know they were going to—"

Riley moved me off her lap, getting to her feet and making panic fill me. "Riley, don't."

She ignored me, not caring that Tempest stood taller than her in her heels. "You fucking left her alone with that bastard. She was scared of Stanley and Slick, but you still walked away. You have no excuse."

She stared down at her, seeming to choose her words carefully before replying. "I thought they'd just say a few mean things then send her home crying. I didn't know they were going to hurt or kidnap her."

Riley grabbed her wrist hard over her jacket, making Tempest wince. She didn't fight her off though, knowing Riley wouldn't let go until she wanted to. "You shouldn't have let them scare her in the first place. Were you too fucking high on cock to give a shit? You know Slick's a rapist, right? And an abusive piece of shit? He could've done anything to her, and you didn't give a shit."

"I was mad at her!" she exclaimed, frustration and fear flashing across her eyes as Riley's grip tightened.

"Because my dumbass brother got too fucked up and assaulted her?" she snapped, making me flinch at the violence in her tone. I should've stopped her, but part of me liked that she was trying to protect me. I didn't owe my sister shit. "You're blaming her for him not being here? News flash, Tempest. He did it to himself, and he *wanted* to go to rehab so he didn't do it again. Take a lesson from him.

If you're fucking yourself up on drugs, alcohol, and sex to make yourself feel better, then maybe it's time you took a long hard look at yourself. What's going to happen when he comes home? You think you can continue to party with him and act like he never left? You're everything he needs to avoid to stay clean, and you'll lose him if you don't make changes too."

"We're just friends," she bit out, getting angry. "He won't throw me away like trash. I don't have to stop partying to keep him around."

Riley let go of her wrist before slamming her palms against Tempest's chest, making her stumble backwards. "You're a selfish cunt. If my brother relapses because of you, you'd better be a real fast runner. For his sake, I hope he gets out and realizes just how pathetic you are."

"He'll never push me away," she said more confidently as she jutted her chin out, and I hated to admit that Riley was right. Tempest was selfish if she was going to have temptations around Ryder when he was trying to get clean.

Dad walked in, pausing when he noticed Riley and Tempest chest to chest. "What happened now?"

"Riley's being a psycho!" Tempest whined as she pushed Riley away bravely now that Dad was here, and for once, Dad looked at Riley for her answer and not blaming her. It seemed to surprise all of us because it took a moment for Riley to realize he was waiting for her to speak.

"Oh. She thinks it's going to go back to how things were before when Ry comes home. I'm trying to convince her that if she cared about him at all, she'd sort her own life out and get clean too."

"It's not up to Tempest to keep Ryder on the straight and narrow," Dad said, but before Tempest could smirk too wide, he continued. "But I agree. If she gave a shit about his health and safety, she'd want him to succeed."

"But, Dad!"

"I love you, but I don't like who you're becoming." A muscle in his jaw ticked, his voice firm as he continued. "You're spiraling, but you won't tell me why. I can't help you fix it if you won't speak to me, and you fight me on literally everything. You want to live a lavish lifestyle without lifting a finger to earn it, and you make choices that you know are wrong, but you do it anyway." Angry tears clung to her lashes as Riley moved back to the couch beside me, not wanting to get in the middle of the impending meltdown, but Dad spoke again, his voice softer this time. "No matter what, I will always love you. You made me into a father, and I will always have your back, but I want you to have a successful life, Tempest. That means growing up and taking responsibility for things. I don't think you understand how terrifying it is for me and Lex when you run off for days, not communicating with us. We worry every time that we'll get a call to identify your fucking body or that you've been kidnapped. I don't like that you have a sex life, but I also know you're an adult. I really wish you wouldn't flaunt it so much. Someone might hurt you."

"You're worried I'll get raped?" she laughed bitterly, swiping at her eyes. "They can't rape me if I want it."

He closed his eyes, defeat on his face. "For your sake, I really hope you're never put in a position where you don't want it and they don't care because by the time you come to me, the damage will be done. I can avenge you, kill anyone who touches you, but I can't take away the memories or the pain. Please, remember that."

"Don't worry about me. We all know you only give a shit about Luna," she scoffed, giving me a scathing look before stomping to her room. I didn't realize I was crying until Riley wiped my cheeks.

"Hey, don't let her get to you."

"If she finds out about the money, she's going to buy loads of drugs and probably die," I choked out, making her frown.

"It's not for her, it's yours. She has no right to spend any of it."

"I can't keep it from her," I mumbled, and Dad cleared his throat, raising an eyebrow.

"Uh, what money?"

"You might want to sit down," I replied, waiting for him to sit in the recliner before I explained the entire situation to him, his eyebrows almost hitting his hairline by the time I was finished.

"How much?" he finally asked slowly, and I handed him my phone with the banking app on the screen, not being able to say it out loud. "You've never met him before?" he asked without taking his eyes off the screen.

"Nope. He's dying, so he wanted to make sure someone got his fortune. Since Stanley messed it up, he wanted to compensate me for the trouble," I said as I swallowed the lump in my throat. "I don't know what to do with it."

"The best thing to do is probably speak to Rory," he suggested, finally meeting my gaze. "We have money, but not that kind of money. She'd know the best ways to handle it, and she can probably help you set up some investments to help it grow too."

"Can I get us a nicer house? I want to help you and Mom."

He smiled, tucking my hair behind my ear. "You're sweet, and I'm glad I did something right to make you into such a thoughtful woman, but we're fine. Maybe you and

Riley will want your own place in the future, so save it for that, alright?"

"Do we have any bills? Or—"

He chuckled, leaning down to kiss the top of my head. "We're not poor, Luna. Between the Reaper's businesses and Wet Dreams, we do perfectly fine. We just can't afford multimillion-dollar mansions or million-dollar cars."

I knew how much Tempest hated her shitty car, and that she was angry that I always had a nice one thanks to my friendship with Riley.

"Do you think I could get a nice car for Temp? I have one, so I think I should get her one too," I said slowly, his expression full of warmth.

"Talk to Rory first, then you can discuss that idea later if you really want to do that. I want to make sure you've got that cash insured and safe first, got it?"

"Yes, Dad. Do you mind if I go to the track tonight? A bunch of the others are going," I asked as Dad started walking away, speaking over his shoulder in a teasing voice.

"Sure. As long as Cruz is there to make sure you're okay."

He found way too much joy in that when Riley cursed, his laughter trailing after him as he left the room.

80
100
120
140
160
180
200
220
km/h
240
260

Chapter Thirty-One

Luna

"Hey," Raven smiled as she walked towards me and Landon at the track later that night, her blue hair tied back in a messy ponytail. "Where's Riley?"

I knew they weren't getting along, so the question threw me off a little. "Uh, she's over there." I pointed behind us to where Beckett, Maddox, and a few others were parked, Riley standing beside Ander like a guard dog. I cringed, not keeping my thoughts to myself. "She's making sure no one kills each other."

"Why are you over here then?" she asked, pulling three cigarettes from her pocket and offering two to us. I took one and Landon took the other with a small smile of thanks, and I leaned forward so she could light the end for me before I replied.

"Riley being in the middle of it will probably just make it worse," I joked, blowing out the smoke and watching it swirl into the night sky as Landon lit his. "I can see the track better over here anyway."

"Is the track really safe to race on?" she asked absently

as she stared at the cars that were currently racing, her voice tight.

I couldn't blame her for being worried, especially after almost losing Reid. I hated the thought of Riley racing too, but I knew this place was the safest place for her to do it.

"Accidents can happen, we learned that when Riley's brother's car crashed and burned with him inside," I said quietly, my chest aching at the memory. "But if people respect the rules, we rarely have any problems. Lloyd died because someone wanted him to, not because he was racing."

"That doesn't make me feel better," she grumbled, and Landon gave her a reassuring pat on the shoulder, not seeming to notice how tense she became from his touch.

"This track has so many safety measures in place. This is the safest place on earth for our little speed freak friends to get it out of their systems." Raven crossed her arms tightly, sending out huge *back off* vibes, but Landon was a dumbass and just kept talking. "Rick's the clipboard guy, and he's trained in first aid now, too."

"Landon," I muttered, grabbing his arm and pulling him back, making Raven's muscles loosen a fraction. "Personal space. Can't you read body language?"

He gave me a look as if I was crazy, but he cringed when he noticed Raven's posture. "Oh. Sorry."

"It's fine," she replied, but Landon glanced at his watch, letting out a curse.

"Shit, mine and Jett's race is about to start. I'll be back soon." Then he jogged off to his car, leaving me with Raven.

She glanced over at Reid who was sitting in his Challenger with the door open, talking to Logan and Zavier. "Those boys do the dumbest shit and wonder why I yell at them all the time."

I snickered, drawing her attention. "All guys are like that. They're wired differently, I swear."

"Reid should be at home, but he insisted on being here. Zavier drove us here, but I know Reid would've done it if he could. He's miserable watching everyone except himself be able to drive his car."

"Is Logan racing tonight?" I asked, a sigh leaving her as she studied me, wondering whether to have an in-depth conversation with me or not. Just because we talked sometimes, didn't mean she trusted me.

"Ander's racing him, yeah. I don't like the guy, and I wish the guys would stay the fuck away from him. He's trouble," she finally stated, her face twisting with disgust.

"He's no more trouble than Beckett is. She's in a crew and does dodgy shit," I said carefully, not wanting people to think I was talking shit. "But you like her, right?"

"Beckett hasn't almost gotten my guys killed."

"You can blame Ander if it makes you feel better, but it's not his fault. It was his organized event, but he didn't force Reid to get in the car and race. Give the guy some slack. From what I've heard about it, Ander stayed with him until paramedics arrived. You saw him at the hospital. He was covered in blood. That was from trying to keep Reid alive," I said softly, my eyes moving to Beckett as she argued with Ander about something. "He's tried hard to keep me safe when he's needed to, and he cares about his friends a lot. You don't have to like him, but don't hate him. He's really nice."

"Ander Lavaro can bite me," she said sharply, stalking back to Reid's car without a backwards glance. I winced, knowing I'd pissed her off and probably ruined the chance of a friendship between us, but Raven was a prickly person.

She didn't seem to have friends outside of the guys and Beckett, and she was easy to piss off.

It wasn't up to me to pry into her personal life, but she showed signs of trauma, and I hated that I couldn't help her.

I wandered over to the others, sliding my arms around Riley's waist from behind. "Hey. Are you guys playing nice?"

Maddox snorted, not taking his eyes off Ander who was standing beside us. "It would be easier if Lavaro wasn't here."

"Leave him alone," I grumbled, Maddox's dark blue eyes shifting to mine. "He's nicer than you most days."

Ander laughed, and Beckett was trying hard to keep a smile off her face as Maddox scowled at me. "You're supposed to be on our side, not his."

"I'm on Riley's side," I grinned, motioning to Ander. "Which means I'm on his side by default."

"Thanks," Ander said dryly. "I'm really feeling the love, Hendricks."

I squealed as someone grabbed me from behind and gave me a bear hug, my heart rate calming when Riley turned and scowled. "Cruz! You scared her half to death."

He relaxed his hold slightly, chuckling in my ear. "Sorry. I heard you got a gift today."

The others went back to their conversation about hating Ander, so I turned to speak to Cruz, pushing his arms off me. "Did you have something to do with that?"

"I'm offended. You think because I can hack into things that it was me?" He looked extremely pleased with himself, giving himself away.

"You didn't have to do that, but thank you," I said quietly.

"I didn't do anything," he replied lightly, giving me a wink. "But, you're welcome."

"I want you to have some of it," I said quickly, and he assessed me for a moment before shaking his head.

"I didn't do it to get a payout, Hendricks. I could hack into anything in the world and pull money if I wanted to. You deserve nice stuff, and I only have rich friends, so I had to cheat a little and make you rich too. We're officially besties now, you know?" he joked, ruffling my hair.

"You're weird," I huffed as I swatted his hand away, making him laugh.

"You fuckers wouldn't like me if I wasn't." He gave me another wink before walking towards the others, bumping fists with Riley on his way towards Beckett. I watched them all interacting, and couldn't help but remember when our circle was a lot smaller.

Beckett didn't speak to anyone outside of her family, Riley would either be hanging out with me and Landon or off getting laid, Maddox was always glued to Beckett or some girl, and none of these other people would've dared hang out in our spot.

My heart ached that Ryder wasn't with us, but I knew the moment I could visit him, I would. He might've scared me the last time we hung out, but he was trying to do the right thing now.

I respected him for that.

Riley draped her arms over my shoulders, pressing her front to mine as she placed a quick kiss on my lips. "Hey, you want to be my passenger?"

"You're racing?"

"Blake's almost here. Ander's racing Logan, so I'll race Blake," she explained, frowning when I shook my head. "Why not?"

I smirked, my arms snaking around her so I could grab her butt. "I want to race."

"You haven't raced in ages."

"That's because I usually just come with you," I pointed out. "But I've got a flashy new car that my hot girlfriend gave me, so I want to take it for a spin."

She chuckled, burying her face in my neck. "You race Blake and I'll be your passenger then. I know how she races, so I can give you pointers. Are you sure you can even drive that fast without freaking out? After the way you flipped out at me last time, I'd say you can't handle it anymore."

"That was different and you know it. A track with good lighting, rules, and safety measures in place is nothing like that death race shit you pulled. You were speeding along pitch-black roads and narrowly missing parked cars and the other racers. That wasn't fun at all," I scowled. "And I already know that Blake will beat me, there's no avoiding it."

I didn't care, I wasn't as competitive as the others, I just enjoyed the race itself.

"I'll teach you all my tricks," she offered, pulling back but keeping her arms around me. "Hey, Turbo. Your girl's going to race Luna instead."

Ander looked at us with surprise, his eyes landing on mine. "You race?"

My face heated at the attention, but I nodded. "I do it for fun sometimes on the track, unlike you psychopaths. I want to see what my new car can do."

"If I knew you raced, I would've challenged you instead," he teased, knowing Logan was walking towards us.

"Hey! No one's taking this race from me! Where's my car then, asshole? You and me, right now. You're not getting out of it," Logan exclaimed loudly, and Ander smirked as he pulled a set of keys from his pocket. "Here."

Logan frowned. "Is it a gift or a loan?"

"I'll decide after the race. Maybe if you win, you can keep it," Ander said slyly as he started walking towards a burnt orange Roadrunner that was parked close by. "It's not as fancy as some of the cars here, but I have a feeling you appreciate having wheels, no matter the price tag."

"No takesies backsies!" Logan hollered as he ran towards the car, climbing behind the wheel and shutting himself inside as if Ander would try to stop him. It had two thick, black stripes down the hood, and it had a hardtop, unlike the few convertible ones I'd seen over the years.

"You got him a '69 model?" Riley asked dryly. "Just wait for all the pickup lines he uses to get girls in that."

"It might have been on purpose," Ander admitted with a grin as Logan started the engine, letting it roar to life. "It could do with a little bit of work with the interior, but it's in really good condition and the motor runs perfectly."

"You're a softie," I chuckled, his eyes narrowing on me.

"Don't ruin my street rep or I'll make sure Blake kicks your ass out there."

As if on cue, Blake arrived, parking beside us and climbing out with a cigarette hanging from her lips. "Sorry I'm late, I was with Kate."

"Don't worry about it," Ander said dismissively, surprising me as he tugged her against his chest and kissed the hell out of her. I knew they had something going on, but seeing it was weird.

"Stop distracting her," Riley grumbled. "Blake, you're racing my girl tonight."

Blake turned to us, running her eyes over me with confusion. "For real?"

"She's a good racer, she just usually prefers me giving her a ride here," Riley answered, tugging me towards my car. "Get ready to lose, Mrs. Lavaro."

Ander growled, calling her a cunt, but Blake flipped her off with a laugh. "I'll meet you guys at the finish line!"

Landon and Jett finished their race, and I was surprised when Landon won. No offense to Landon, but Jett was a frequent racer and usually took on Maddox and Beckett.

Ander and Logan's race was called, and we watched as Logan kept up the entire time, only losing by a second. If he'd driven the car more, he probably would've won.

I was pretty sure Ander was full of shit too. The Roadrunner had more power under the hood than a standard engine.

"I won't go easy on you," Blake teased as she parked her car beside mine on the track once the guys had moved, and I gave her a wink.

"I'd be mad if you did."

Riley was practically bouncing in the passenger seat, not used to not being the one behind the wheel. It was making me nervous, but excitement was washing through me at the same time.

Blake was a good racer, and I knew I probably had no hope against her, but I was glad she wasn't acting like she was more skilled than me. Some people that raced turned their nose up at others, and I hated that.

"We'll get the security footage later so you can watch it," Riley beamed, her window down and the cool breeze making her hair twirl around her face. She had her hood off, and I couldn't help but admire her. She had a natural beauty to her that I'd always been jealous of, and I was so lucky to be able to wake up next to her most mornings.

Dad agreed to let her start staying over at my place, as long as he didn't hear anything he shouldn't.

Riley heard that as a challenge to keep me quiet, much to my horror, and I wasn't looking forward to her testing it out in case it failed and my parents heard me.

The new fancy lights at the starting line flashed green, and I slammed the car into gear, lifting my foot off the clutch and pressing my other foot down hard on the gas, the tires squealing as I took off like a bullet. Riley whooped from beside me, the sound like music to my ears as it mixed with the engine roaring.

Blake was right beside us, her Pontiac keeping enough distance from my Supra to make me relax.

I didn't want to risk an accident, or Dad would definitely ban me from the track.

My heart hammered as I shifted through the gears until we were flying along the straight, and Riley shouted advice the whole way like I knew she would. I didn't mind, she was a better racer than me, and I'd never say no to free tips.

I wasn't as skilled on the corners as Blake, so it was no surprise when she overtook me and surged ahead, laughter leaving me as we gave chase.

I couldn't remember the last time I'd raced, but I wouldn't leave it this long again. I'd forgotten how much fun it could be.

Riley was screaming at me to go faster, our laughter filling the car as we barreled across the finish line just behind Blake, my cheeks hurting from smiling so much.

We idled beside Blake's car, and she gave me a wide grin. "Not bad. I shouldn't have expected anything less from Donovan's girl though."

"We should do that again another time," I blurted out in my excitement, her face softening.

"I'd like that. Meet you back with the others?"

"Sounds good," I nodded and watched her drive across the field before I slowly made my way after her, Riley watching me silently with a stupid smile on her face. "What?"

"You're so fucking hot. Ugh, I almost can't take it."

"You can take it like a good girl," I cooed, trying to avoid my face from heating but failing.

"I think you should keep driving and find somewhere dark and quiet so I can fuck you on the hood and break her in the right way," she groaned, her hand resting on my thigh. "And definitely keep saying naughty stuff. It's extra hot coming from you."

"As much as it's tempting, we can't bail on Ander, remember? He might get killed by your sister," I joked, making her shrug.

"Hey, I said I'd *try* to keep him safe. I can't promise anything though. Accidents happen."

"Stop thinking with your pussy."

"How about you come and put yours on my face?" she threw back, sliding her hand higher. I almost stalled the car as my foot slipped off the gas, making her grin. "The moment I get you alone, I'm going to lay you out and make you forget your own name, baby."

She was going to be the death of me.

Riley

Logan was showing off his new car to Luna, and as much as I was annoyed that he'd stolen her away from me, I couldn't stay mad at the fucker. He was grinning so wide that I was surprised his face didn't crack, and Luna was so fucking happy for him.

"That was a nice thing you did," I said to Turbo as he moved to stand beside me, watching Logan and Luna.

"Why is everyone so shocked when I'm nice?" he grunted, butting out his cigarette before handing me a bottle of vodka. "You like this one, right?"

"You remembered," I grinned, taking a mouthful before passing it back. "We should all meet up for lunch and a few games of pool at the bar sometime."

He ran an awkward hand through his hair, blowing out a breath. "You know, I appreciate what you're doing."

"What's that?"

"I wouldn't have any of you fuckers outside of my races if it wasn't for you, you know? Blake never spent time with me, Logan and Reid didn't want to risk people finding out about the street races, and even you didn't see me unless we had a race on. The moment you started changing shit up, everyone jumped on board. So, thank you."

I looked at him, tilting my head. "Since we're besties, are you going to tell me what happened with Stanley?"

"What can I say? He pissed his pants, ugly cried for an hour or two, and ended up bleeding out when I got bored and slit his stomach open. You should've seen the look on his face when he realized his intestines were on the floor," he smiled manically, making me cringe.

"You're more psycho than I gave you credit for. If you ever get bored doing your own thing, hit my parents up. They'd love someone like you on jobs."

"Sorry, but I heard crew members have to play nice together. I doubt Beckett or Maddox would allow that," he said dryly. "Besides, how many people does your family kill? They don't need more help."

"If you want to tell them where those Crestford brats live, that would be appreciated," I said seriously. Skeeter had been trying to hunt them down, but it was as if they didn't exist. Nothing pissed my family off more than people fucking with us and then walking around without punishment.

"What brats?"

"You know, those rich pricks who shot at us that night." I frowned, recognition hitting his face.

"Oh, the wannabe gangsters? You won't find them."

I huffed, giving him a dirty look. "We don't let people get away with shit, asshole. My parents have been trying to track them down, but it's like they've vanished."

He smirked, his voice low. "Like I said, they won't find them."

He had that dark look in his eyes that I'd seen earlier when he'd stabbed Stanley, surprising me slightly. "You killed them?"

He dropped an arm around my shoulders, tugging me closer as Beckett watched us with confusion. She'd definitely heard me.

"Shut your mouth. We're in public," he murmured. "But trust me, no one fucks with me or my friends and gets away with it either."

"Your girlfriend's going to get jealous if you don't get off me," I said sweetly through my teeth, making him snort.

"My girl knows she's got nothing to worry about. She's not insecure like most of you women. Besides, she does that thing with her tongue that I like. I'm not going to stray anywhere."

I laughed, shoving him back. "I didn't need to know that."

"Payback for me witnessing your late-night rendezvous

with Luna when you spread her out on the hood of your car," he joked, making Cruz gasp at me from close by.

"Excuse me, don't be such an animal. She's too sweet for that kind of behavior."

I knew we were being loud by the way Luna tensed.

"You think you know her, but that good girl over there? She does some really fucking bad things when we're alone," I replied with a smirk, making Luna spin around and glare at me with pink cheeks.

"Riley!"

"What? Don't be ashamed of those skills, baby. You've earned bragging rights," I teased, laughing as she ran at me, shoving a hand over my mouth.

"You're the worst," she hissed in my ear, but she melted against me as I ran my hands over her ass, giving it a squeeze.

"You're not even mad," I scoffed, nipping her earlobe as I spoke softly. "Wait until we get home. I've been envisioning you on your back for me with my vibrator on your clit."

She shuddered, earning me a filthy look from Maddox. He could hate hearing about my sex life all he wanted, but we'd had to put up with hearing his until he'd started dating Beckett and moved out with her.

I missed them, but that had been a blissful day.

Luna pried herself away from me, stalking off with embarrassment as Cruz chased her, and Beckett raised an eyebrow at me.

"Are you really going to leave him alone with her? He's a whore."

"He's in the friend zone. Luna would shut him down so fast," I said confidently. "Where'd Jett go?"

"Where else? He's with his boyfriend," she deadpanned,

motioning to Logan's car. "They haven't seen each other much lately, so they've probably been going through withdrawals."

"Let them have their playdate tonight. Claim him back later," I suggested, giving her a sly glance. "If you have to, play dirty. Use your pussy to get what you want."

"You'd be surprised how much power their bromance has," she sighed, and Maddox tucked her against his side, kissing the top of her head.

"Let him miss out, babe. I benefit from it."

"I know," she smiled, not seeming as annoyed about the whole thing as she had the last time we'd spoken about it. I hoped that meant they were okay again.

"Speaking of the power of pussy," I drawled, pulling my hood over my head. "I'm going to drag my girl home so I can have a midnight snack. I'll see you tomorrow."

"You're bailing already?" Beckett asked with surprise, giving Ander the side-eye. "Hear that? She's leaving you here unguarded."

Turbo smirked, fishing his keys from his pocket. "Nice try. I also have an appointment with pussy. I'll see you next time, Beckett."

She glowered, and I just rolled my eyes and waved goodbye to them all, wandering off to find Luna. It wasn't hard, she was leaning against Cruz's car, talking to Drake who'd appeared out of nowhere. I'd almost bet money on him sneaking out so Stone didn't know.

That man seemed to run a tight ship.

"Hey, Lou? Get your sweet cheeks in the car. We're leaving," I called out, making her frown.

"But it's early?"

"Never too early for pussy, baby. We'll pick my car up tomorrow," I winked, making Drake groan.

"You two are bailing to fuck? Does your house have inside security? Never mind, I'll find out for myself. If I find anything, I'll be adding it to the spank bank."

I punched his arm before snagging Luna's hand to pull her away from him. "You're gross and I'm telling your boss that you're here."

"That's a cheap shot," he grumbled, glancing at Cruz. "Wanna get laid?"

"With you? No thanks. Knox would have my balls," Cruz said dryly, turning to us. "We'll stop by the house later in the week for a beer, if you're up for it?"

"Sounds good. We'll be in touch," I agreed, saying goodbye and leading Luna to her car, taking the keys so I could drive.

We waved to Reid and Raven who were still sitting in his car, and I was glad to see a smile on Reid's face. It would take some time for his body to heal, but he'd be back on the track in no time.

I couldn't fucking wait.

"I can drive, you know?" Luna complained, and I gave her a cheeky grin as we shut ourselves in the car.

"I know, but I want to watch you fuck yourself while I drive."

"What?" she sputtered, her cheeks turning pink as she stared at me.

I leaned over, teasing her lips with mine. "I want you to get yourself off on the way home, and then I want to clean your fingers with my tongue. That way you'll be warmed up for me when we arrive."

"Can we detour? I want to fuck you against the car this time," she said boldly, and I lightly grabbed her throat to keep her still, licking her lower lip.

"Start fucking yourself then. If you can come really fast, I'll make a stop on the way."

The moment I eased back and started the car, she made sure the windows were up so no one could see in, and she snaked her hand down the front of her pants, instantly doing as I asked.

She was wearing jeans, so after a second, she let out a frustrated sigh and unbuttoned them, giving herself more room.

"I hope this proves how much I love you," she grumbled, and I couldn't help but reach out to tweak her nipple through her shirt, making her squeal.

"I love you too, baby."

The moment she sucked in a sharp breath as she started fucking herself for me, I almost ran off the fucking road.

I always knew there was a bad girl hiding under that good girl mask.

80
100
120
140
160
180
200
220
km/h
240
260

Printed in Dunstable, United Kingdom

64085163R00347